Nancy Hanks Lincoln

Born: February 07, 1784
Died: October 05, 1818
Age 34

My Name Is Nancy

The Journals
of
Nancy Hanks Lincoln

Mother of the sixteenth President
of the United States of America

By

Deborah Keller

Author's Note

This is a work of historical fiction.

While some of the characters and incidents can be verified they have been altered and rearranged to suit the purpose of this manuscript. These characters and their actions, despite their resemblance to actual known persons and events are the product of the author's work. Accordingly this book should be read solely as a work of fiction, not as a version or interpretation of history.

I would like to thank The Bostic Lincoln Center for keeping the story alive and Isothermal Community College for the use of the Tryon Room Historical Resource Center.

There are excellent reference books available with biographical information on many of these characters, but as has been stated previously this is a work of fiction.

I wish to thank and acknowledge the many people who assisted and provided aid and encouragement on this project. *Ludy Wilkie* for his research and information on the history of Abraham Lincoln and who introduced me to Nancy Hanks through his play, *Lydia Clontz* of The Bostic Lincoln Center who steadfastly keeps the legend alive, my editor *Gayle Clayton* who pushed me to continue my writing, my children *Kim Haynes* and *George Griffin* who believe I can move mountains and convinced me of it also, last but absolutely not least, my beloved husband *Clyde* who fed me, made me coffee, went with me to research, listened and lived with these characters for months on end, edited nonstop and who never ever one time complained. Thank you for believing in me. This is for you.

- Deborah

In memory of
Brian Stacy Griffin
"never forgotten"

Contents

*"All that I am, or ever hope to be,
I owe to my angel mother."*
- Abraham Lincoln

October 2, 1818

To My Dearest Son Abraham,

I am penning these words with great sadness as I fear I will be leaving this world soon. I am not afraid of death, I know it is where true happiness lies for us all. I do hate that I am leaving you at such a young age to deal with the trials of this world without me by your side. There are things that I wish you to know and remember.

First and foremost is that I will never truly leave you. We are bound by more than mere flesh and I will be with you for all of your life. You will feel me near when you need me. I will walk silently beside you until such time as you are ready to come home with me. You know your legacy, I have seen to that. It will come to pass and you will be ready.

Remember your place in this world and continue to strive until you reach it. Staying here with Tom will be difficult for you but you owe it to him. He took us in and gave us a name and some respectability and for that you must stay with him until you are of proper age to leave. I hope I did not do you a disservice when I changed your age and made you three years younger. I know it has been difficult for you but it has enabled you to go to school longer and your education is critical for your future. It will mean staying here with Tom longer but I ask that you do that to honor me please.

Remember my son that Tom is not a bad man. He is uneducated and coarse at times but he stood by us and we made the best that we could of our situation. He has paid for his transgressions. It was difficult on us both when Tom, Jr. died but it hardened Tom. He so wanted his own son. He is not hard on you on purpose, he is just bitter being reminded of what he has lost.

Take care of your sister, she is but a baby. I am sure Tom will do right by her. He will surely remarry as he has two children to care for. Please help your new mother to adjust and always be respectful.

Remember who you are. You are a Tanner and an Enloe. You come from a long line of educated gentleman and you are a Changeling. Stay on course and continue to learn. It is something you will do forever. There is always something new to learn. Listen and watch people, learn who they are and what they think and then you will know how to proceed.

I am giving you my journals. I have always planned on giving them to you when you were older and would understand but it seems that fate has determined that you are to have them now. I ask you not to judge me or the other people in my life. I was but a young girl trying to find my way. I want you to understand that we are all human and mistakes are made. Never deny who you are and your feelings to yourself. Remember our experiences make us who we are. I have lived, loved and lost. I have felt passion and hope as well as sadness and grief. You will experience all these things in your life.

My journals are all that I have to leave you. I want you to read them and know me for the person that I am. My son you have been the bright star in my sky. I have never one moment regretted your birth. You have brought me such incredible joy and pride.

Take these journals and keep them hidden as I have done. They are for you to take out and read when you need to feel me close. My soul resides between the covers of these books. I am giving them to you for safekeeping my son. It will be difficult when I am gone, you will face a terrible grief but know I am and will always be in your heart. Look in the water and see my eyes looking back at you. Keep them with you for all your life, they are for you only.

Always know how much you are loved by me. There is no love greater than of a mother for her child. You will do great things my son. I have been shown that. Greatness resides within you. You have the gift of understanding. Use this gift in your life's pursuits. There will be those who will try to influence you and who will use rumor and gossip to destroy you. Stand strong, say little, and listen. The answers will come to you.

I am placing this letter in the front of the journals for you to read after I am gone. I am going to give them to you tonight to hide in our special place. When you are ready read them, and read them often. Much love to you my son and courage. Life can be short but it is truly precious. Make of it what you can while you can. Remember if you need me go to a place where you are alone, close your eyes and call for me. I will come to you. I will always be with you. I will come for you when it is your time and we shall walk together hand in hand in sunlit fields of gold.

Eternally yours,
Mother

Journal 1
(Nancy Hanks)

In the year of our Lord 1798 .....

My name is Nancy. I am fourteen years old. It's the first thing I learned to write, my name that is, Nancy Hanks. Mr. Enloe made me learn to read and write. He even makes the slaves learn to read the bible. I knew how to read a bit when I came here but I could not write my letters. It has been two years now and Mr. Enloe says I have gotten quite good at it. I have been studying figures too. I am struggling with multiplying numbers right now but I know I'll get it. Even Mrs. Sarah thinks it's good how quick I picked it up. She has had me helping teach the slaves bible reading in the evenings.

Mr. Enloe brought me home this book he called a journal. I was a bit disappointed cause it had no words in it but then he explained it was for my words. I laughed and told him nobody wanted to read my words. He said they are for you to remember things by when you get old. He told me I was to write down things I saw and things I thought every night before I went to sleep. He told me this journal was for me to read and write in and I was to show it to no others. I held it close as I had never had anything that was just for me. I always had to share everything.

I will try to write down things that happen during my day and maybe some thoughts just for fun. I already wrote about the gift of the journal. Today was like any other here on the farm. I helped cook breakfast, washed clothes and looked after the little ones for Mrs. Sarah, after feeding them lunch I put them down for a nap and worked on my figures for a bit. I had to clean the house and help get dinner ready.

Bessie does the cooking but I help fetch things she needs. She teaches me how to cook, says every woman gotta know how to cook, slave or free. After I help clean up after dinner I go down to the slave cabins and help them read their bible verses. We do our reading for a bit and then we all sing by the fire. I love to sing their songs, they are always about feelings, and working hard, and missing home. I know kinda how they feel. I mean I am not a black slave, but I am a white bonded girl and I don't know where my family is either or even who my Daddy really is and I never had no home till here so I sing the songs kinda sad too.

--- Feels funny writing to myself, but Mr. Enloe said "It was important" so I will try to do it. He ain't a man you want to cross but still a lot sweeter than Mrs. Sarah. I think I will keep this under my mattress so nobody else will see it like Mr. Enloe said.

--- Hello, Journal. I'm just going to say that so it feels like I am writing to somebody other than just me. I still feel a little silly writing down words for nobody. I ain't got nobody to write real letters to so I will just pretend you are my friend. It has been a while since I wrote anything, we been so busy I just plumb fell asleep when I got to my room.

Mr. Felix and some other men have been here for a few days, huntin' and talking, and eating and drinking and making some more messes. I been cleaning nonstop. Bessie likes it when Mr. Felix comes round. He always puts Mrs. Sarah in a good mood. She giggles and laughs like a young girl when he is around. Bessie says they were sweet on each other as children but Mrs. Sarah up and married her a real rich man when she got Mr. Abraham. It's nice to hear Mrs. Sarah laugh some so I don't mind the extra cleaning.

Mr. Felix brought the children some rock candy from town and he gave me a piece. I broke it in half and shared with Bessie. It sure was good. I hadn't had rock candy in a long time. Bessie liked it so much she gave me some extra bread and butter to keep in my room. I wish my Mama had been more like Miss. Bessie, all fat and singing and cooking in the kitchen. My Mama weren't never that way. She was a real pretty woman and was always getting' fixed up for some man. I don't remember her cooking much. She must have cause I didn't start cooking much till I was bigger. We ate a lot of soup and taters. Didn't get no bread much, I really like bread.

--- I am so happy I have a nice big house to live in and plenty of food and friends at church. I give thanks to God every night for bringing me to the Enloe house. It's the first home I ever had with regular meals, clothes, my own room to sleep in and I even got shoes. I had a little trouble with shoes at first but I got used to 'em. Now they ain't so bad. I'm so grateful that I would just die for the Enloe's. I ain't never had anybody be so good to me. I must be the luckiest girl in North Carolina. The good Lord sent Mr. Felix to bring me here. Praise to the Lord. I gots to go to sleep now, got to get up early to help get Mr. Felix and the men off. Bessie wants to pack them all a meal for their trip and I gotta help.

--- It's seems so quiet with all the company gone. Been washing linens all day from where they all was sleeping on 'em. Mrs. Sarah ain't gonna have no dirty sheets in her house. I had to wash some twice today. The youngin's were running and playing and knocked down two of Mrs. Sarah best sheets. I hurried up and washed them again so they didn't get no whupping. Bessie said they deserved one but I didn't want it to be on account of me.

Bessie wants me to write a letter for her but we can't tell nobody cause it's against the law for slaves to write letters. She said she got a sister that lives up North and can read and write and she wants to send a letter by the preacher next time he goes North. He don't cotton much to slavery but he preaches in the South so he ain't got no choice. He likes Bessie cause she always makes him an extra pie to take home when he comes to Sunday dinner. I like Miss. Bessie too, even though sometimes she hits me upside the head if I don't do something right in her kitchen. She just shakes her wood spoon at me and says "Hard heads makes soft behinds." I try to get it right the first time.

I went to get the sheets in this evening and the sun was setting so pretty in the sky. The clouds looked like red fire up against the mountains and the sky was so blue it looked like my Mama's eyes. I just looked and looked till it was almost dark. I felt like I was standing in a paintin' by God. I had to rush to get the sheets folded for ironing in the morning. Watching that sky was worth getting a scolding by Mrs. Sarah for taking so long. I got to go to sleep now my candle's getting low. I hope I don't think too much about my Mama or my sister Mandy tonight. It always makes me sad, but I know how lucky I am so I won't complain. Good night Journal.

--- Well, it sure was busy today. Mrs. Sarah's got a bee in her bonnet about something. I just tried to stay out of her way. She can get in her moods sometimes. Miss Bessie says she is the strongest white woman she ever knowed. She said she gets in one of her moods every time Mr. Felix leaves. Bessie thinks she shoulda married Mr. Felix instead of Mr. Abraham but she always says it in a whisper. Some things are just better not being heard. Mrs. Sarah was running around yelling for all of us to do stuff all day long. I don't think she ever sat down and took a breath. Nothing I did was right today. I swept out the parlor three times and Mrs. Sarah took the broom out of my hands and started sweeping herself. She told me to go help Bessie in the kitchen. Whew, what a day. I never worked so hard in all my 15 years. Goodnight Journal.

--- I got up early this morning and went down to help Bessie. The babies were still asleep and I didn't hear Mrs. Sarah stirring. She let me stir the grits while she kneaded the bread. She talked to me about my first days here at the house. She said I sure was a sight when Mr. Felix brought me in, dirty, smoky, smelling, and barefoot. If anybody but Mr. Felix had brought me to the house Mrs. Sarah would turned 'em right back around. She said Mrs. Sarah came and told her that I would be no good to the house and Bessie told her that I had goodness in my eyes. She told Mrs. Sarah not to worry that she would teach me how to behave. I smiled and told her thank you cause she had taught me a lot and was kind to me.

She then got all worried looking and told me she had a dream that I would live a life of great sorrow. I patted her back and told her I would be ok and not to worry. She frowned and told me I lived in a dangerous world. I was not a slave but I weren't no family member either. She said I had to be careful around the men in the house that they knew I wasn't one of theirs and that they would take advantage of that. I laughed and told her they didn't take no notice of me. She said "Not yet they don't but they will, you is growing really fast these days and soon you will be a full blown woman." I told her not for a long time, I liked being a girl. The babies started crying so I had to go help Mrs. Sarah and I didn't get to talk to Bessie no more today.

Mrs. Sarah seemed a bit better today and even told me I did a good job with the babies. She let me go sit and read outside for a bit today. That's my favorite thing to do. I love to sit under the big tree out on the edge of the house and read. I can't thank Mr. Abraham enough for letting me learn to read. When I read I pretend that I am a daughter of the house just waiting on company to come to dinner. I have pretty dresses and my Daddy rides a big white horse and always smells like cigars.

It made me start to wonder about my real Daddy. I remember a big man in a hat with a loud laugh that used to pick me up and swing me around when I was a little bit of a girl but after Mandy was born we had to move and I never saw him again. Mama never much talked about him. I asked her one time and she said you and Mandy come from gentry in Virginia but not to ever expect them to do nothing for you. They didn't cotton to our kind. I asked her his name but she said he weren't man enough to give it to us so I didn't need to know it. I think iffen he had stayed our lives would've been different. Mama got hard after Mandy was born. I think she missed him as much as she was mad at him.

Oh, Mama I loved you so. Your pretty hair and your sky blue eyes. I used to watch you sleep at night. It was the only time you looked peaceful. Why did you leave us? Was we so much trouble you just couldn't stay? Maybe you just got tired of it all. I could see that, it was hard but I would never leave my babies, no matter what.

--- Bessie called me to come in to help set the table today and told me the preacher was coming by. I sat the table and went back in the kitchen and the strangest thing happened. Mrs. Sarah came in the kitchen and told me to set another place at the table. I went in and the family was seated along with the preacher. I sat down a new plate and started to leave when Mrs. Sarah told me to sit down. She said it was time I started eating with the family. The preacher smiled and patted her arm and I sat down in shock.

I had never got to eat with the family before. I don't even remember what we ate I was so scared. Afterwards when I got up to clean the table Mrs. Sarah told me to let the slaves get it and to go watch the children as they played outside. It was like a dream. I ran in the kitchen to tell Bessie goodnight and she just shook her head sayin' "No good will come of this, I just know it." I am almost too excited to sleep journal but I got to get up early so I'll be saying goodnight now.

--- Just a quick note, a busy and strange day. I'll tell you about it later. Goodnight.

--- I am sorry I have not written in a bit. Everything seems so strange. Mrs. Sarah got me some good hand me down dresses from a neighbor and told me she wanted me to start dressing better around the house. It seems that the preacher done told her it was her Christian duty to treat me sorta like a family member. He said it warn't right that I be spending so much time with the slaves me being a white girl and all. He said I had to learn to behave like decent folk so I could have a decent family someday. Mrs. Sarah puts high stock in what the preacher says so she started changing the ways I done things. She told me I got to help watch the children and learn to sew and not spend so much time with Bessie. I was really sad about not spending as much time with Bessie cause she was the closest thing to a friend I had.

Sunday I went to church and sat with the family for the first time. The lady sitting behind us heard me sing and told Mrs. Sarah I needed to be in the choir. Mrs. Sarah said I was too young but the lady told her that was nonsense that voice knew no age. She was older than Mrs. Sarah with a big black hat. Mrs. Sarah told her she would think about it.

Mr. Abraham will be home soon and I wonder what he will think about all these changes. I met some girls at church today, Polly Price and Nancy Leake. They was real nice and said they would see me next Sunday. I been living here two years and ain't met nobody but company to the house and the slaves. It's exciting to meet new people.

I waited till Mrs. Sarah laid down for her nap and I hurried in to tell Bessie about church. She just shook her head and said "No good will come from this, I just feel it." I laughed at here and twirled around in my new dress and told her everything would be fine. I ran back upstairs with the children before Mrs. Sarah got up. Gotta go now. Goodnight journal.

--- Mr. Abraham got home late last night. I heard him laughing and calling for Mrs. Sarah. She got up and had the slaves get him something to eat. After a while I heard her laughing with him. It felt good to lie in my bed and hear them both laugh. I felt happy. The children were a handful this morning. They knew their Daddy was home and he brought presents. Mrs. Sarah told them he needed some rest and they could see him after lunch. They were a handful all morning.

Finally it was lunchtime. Mr. Abraham told everybody they had to eat first and then he would give them their presents. He gathered everybody around and asked very solemnly if they had been good while he was away. Everyone shook their head yes and he looked at Mrs. Sarah. She tried to be stern but she smiled and said they have all indeed been good children.

He gave everybody their presents and then he looked at me and said "I have not forgotten you Nancy." He then gave me a beautiful shawl. It was the softest shawl I had ever felt. He laughed and said Mrs. Sarah told him I was going to church with the family so I needed a good shawl. Mrs. Sarah shook her head and said it was a bit much but Mr. Abraham just laughed and said they couldn't have me going to church looking like a ragamuffin. He hugged Mrs. Sarah who shooed him away laughing the whole while. I asked him if I could go put my shawl away and he waved me on. I put it safely away and went back to caring for the children. When I retired to my room I took it out and put it on. I never felt so pretty in my whole life.

Mr. Abraham was the best man ever and I was the luckiest girl in the whole world. I am going to go to sleep and dream about my wonderful shawl. Goodnight journal.

--- I have been so busy with Mr. Abraham back that I have not been writing. He asked me today if I had been writing in my journal. I hung my head and told him not in a while. He put his fingers under my chin, lifted my face and told me that it was important. He said I needed to write down my thoughts so that later in life I could understand why I made the decisions I did. He told me he wrote in his journal everyday and that I should do the same. I felt like I had let him down so I promised to write more often.

--- I am writing but boy am I tired. It was a long day and the children were full of themselves. One of the boys talked his brothers into putting wood ash from a fire on their faces and clothes and they ran around screeching like Indians. They got soot all over everything. Mrs. Sarah tanned their hides good. I will be cleaning soot off this house for the rest of my life…little devils. They sure had a good time playing through. I asked them if it was worth it while I was scrubbing the soot off them in a tub out back. They grinned and said "Yep, sure was Nancy." I just sighed and kept scrubbing. Boys are just boys sometimes I guess.

Mrs. Sarah was mad all day after that. Someday when I have boys I may just cover us all with soot and run around and play with them. If I'm gonna have to clean it up I want to have some fun with it first. Goodnight journal I'm going to sleep now.

--- A wagon rolled in early this morning. Mrs. Sarah had a friend having some troubles so she was going to her house for a couple days. She got the house up and after breakfast told me to keep a close eye on the children and she would be back soon. If I had any questions to just ask Mr. Enloe but not to bother him unless it was important. She told Bessie to keep a close eye on me and make sure I was cleaning the house proper. Bessie had packed her a basket of food and told her she would handle things and for Mrs. Sarah to not worry we would all be here when she got back. We all watched her wagon until it was out of sight. The children started running around and yelling "Holiday, holiday." It took all me and Bessie could do to get them to calm down. They all looked miserable when I told them they still had to do their chores and schoolwork. Bessie swatted a few of them on the rear to get them going. It was a fun day.

I got my housework done and had the children doing their reading when Bessie smiled at me real big and said "Come into the kitchen I got a treat for us." She had made a small cake and we sat down and ate every bite of it washed down with fresh milk. We laughed and talked and she told me about her family.

She said she had five brothers and sisters that she knew about. They had all lived on a big plantation when she was small. Her Mama was the family cook and they got to live in a small house right off the kitchen. Her Papa worked in the fields as the foreman's best man. Her Mama had taught all of them how to cook. She wanted them all to be house slaves and not to have to work in the fields. Her younger sister was real good at doing hair and by the time she was ten she was doing all the fine ladies hair in the house.

Everything was good until the lady of the house died. After that the Master got mean and he just didn't care. The house started falling apart and he started selling slaves. They were lucky she said it took a while before he got to them. Her Papa was sold first. It was a sad day, her Mama cried and cried and didn't sing anymore. Then they started selling her brothers and sisters. Her Mama told the master she needed the children to help her in the house with the cooking. He told her she could keep two, a boy to help with the outside and food gathering and one to help with the cooking. She said "It broke Mama's heart to have to choose" Mama was consoled that one of her children was going to the same family that Papa had been sold to. The mistress of the house had four daughters and needed someone who could do hair. We would not see her again but at least she would be near Papa.

One day I was in the kitchen cooking when Mama came in and just looked stricken. A friend of the Master's had stopped by and was moving to North Carolina and needed a cook. The Master had agreed to sell him me. My Mama told me to go pack my things that I was leaving after dinner. As the horses rode off I watched my Mama until she was out of sight. I never saw her again."

I reached out to touch Bessie's hand and she just brushed it off saying "Don't go be feelin' sad that's just the way it is for us slaves." "We don't get to be free." She brushed me out of the kitchen reminding me that I had to go to get the children. I was feeling bad for Bessie. At least her mother did not leave her on purpose like mine did me. I thought a lot about Bessie for the rest of the day. How sad that people and families could just be bought and sold like cattle. I was indentured and had to stay but the Enloe's couldn't sell me to anybody. Well journal it's been a long day and I am very tired. I think I will go to bed now. Goodnight.

--- My what a day. I am so excited I can hardly write. It was just a normal day today until after dinner. I had put the children to bed and was tidying up when Mr. Abraham asked me to come in his study and keep him company for a while. I took my mending in with me and sat down in the study. I am not very good at mending anyway so I could listen to him. He was smoking a cigar and drinking some kind of spirits.

It so nice to sit and pretend I was one of the family. He talked about his father and how he was a schoolteacher. He talked about why it was so important for people to know how to read and write. He asked me if I was still writing in my journal. I shook my head yes. I was afraid to speak out loud because I didn't want to ruin the moment. He told me how proud he was of how I was turning out. He said he knew I was a smart girl when he saw me with Mr. Felix that day. He asked me if I was happy. I again just shook my head yes. I was so happy right then I couldn't breathe. He laughed and said "I'm glad, I want you to be happy Nancy, you deserve it. God knows you have had very little of that in your life." I just kept sewing.

He talked about his friends and Mrs. Sarah. He told me that she was a sometime hard but very good woman. He said she was a true pioneer that nothing or nobody could stop that woman when she made up her mind to something then he laughed and said "Except Felix. Good old Felix can get around her like nobody's business." I just smiled. He stopped talking and we just sat there quietly for a while. He then asked me to come sit by the stool at his feet and sing a song for him. He said my singing always made him feel good.

I sat and sang one of the slow songs that the slaves sang about having a better life and he began to stroke my hair. About that time Bessie came rushing in and said "Oh, I thought I heard Miss Nancy singing and wanted to make sure everything was all right." He told her everything was fine but she stood in that doorway with her arms across her chest and said to me "Don't you think you need to get on to bed as you got to get the children up and going in the morning." Mr. Abraham looked at me and said "Bessie's right child you need to get on to bed."

I got up and took my mending to put it in the cabinet when Bessie whispered behind me "No good will come of this child. You don't need to be sitting with the Master after dark." I laughed and gave her a hug and ran up the stairs. I was so happy and she wasn't going to make me feel bad. Oh journal what a night! Is this what it feels like to be the lady of the house? I so want to be that someday. Someday I am going to get married to a fine gentleman and we will sit by the fire after the children have gone to bed and I will sing for him. I am going to dream about this all night. Goodnight journal.

--- Everything seems the same but I feel different today. I don't know why. I asked Bessie and she said I was just becoming a woman and we have days like that. It's was just in our nature. Then she told me not be taking on airs about myself because of last night. When I asked her what she meant she said "Gentleman sometimes can suffer from a moment of weakness when they are alone and drinking and I didn't need to make last night a habit. If Mr. Abraham asked me to sit with him again I was to tell him I was busy."

I laughed and told her last night was the best night of my life. She looked very, very sad and said "Child no good can come from it, no good at all. I will pray that the good Lord Jesus will look after you. You gonna need it." I just brushed her off and told her she worried too much that someday I was going to marry a gentleman and have my own house. She grabbed me by the shoulders and said "Child wake up, girls like you don't marry no nice gentleman like Mr. Abraham. They might want you around but not for no marriage." When I asked her what she meant she said "You need to get on with your chores. We will talk later."

Later that evening after I put the children to bed I was standing near the stairs hoping Mr. Abraham would call me back into the study. He called my name and before I could take a step Bessie was in his study asking him if I could help her in the kitchen for a bit. As I stomped off to the kitchen Bessie swatted me on the rear and told me to hush up she was just trying to protect me and Mr. Abraham. As I sat and peeled potatoes for her in the kitchen she told me about how men were about young girls living in their house. I got all puffed up and told her that Mr. Abraham did not look at me like that. She snorted and said "Mr. Abraham is a man and all men are like that."

She talked and talked while we peeled potatoes. I really didn't listen much and daydreamed of when I had my own house. After we finished she walked me up to my room and made sure I was in for the night. I don't know why she's acting so strange. Why Mr. Abraham would never hurt me. He was the best man in the whole world. Goodnight journal I am going to sleep now.

--- It has been so busy since Mrs. Sarah got home. She decided to clean the house from top to bottom. Mr. Abraham left on one of his many trips. Bessie had told me to keep quiet about my night in the study. She said Mrs. Sarah would pitch a fit. She didn't have to worry, it was my special time and I didn't want to share it with anybody. I think Bessie worries too much some times. She is keeping me as busy as Mrs. Sarah lately. I am plumb wore out so I will say goodnight journal.

--- It has been a busy time and Christmas was on us before we knew it. This was my first year singing in the choir. I sang a song all by myself up there. I was scared but Rev. Joe told me to just sing to God so that's what I did. I raised my head up and I sang to God. How funny it felt to be sitting with the families at church in the choir just like I belonged. Jesus sure had blessed me by bringing me to the Enloe house. I just know good things will be in store for me in this life. I just know it. Merry Christmas journal. Goodnight.

In the year of our Lord 1799 .....

April – It has been a busy time lately. Mr. Abraham left on another trip somewhere. The days are getting longer and Nancy Leake had been stopping by in the evenings to see me. She is my age and we are in the choir together at church. We laugh about being the two Nancy's. We sit out back near the creek and practice our hymns for Sunday service. Mrs. Sarah don't seem to mind this too much. She even said it was nice to hear some church music during the week.

I really like Nancy Leake. We laugh and giggle and talk. Sometimes she brings Polly Price with her and we all three sing and play and talk about the boys at church. They tease me about Adam Springs and tell me that he has eyes for me. I laughed and told them it was ok cause I had eyes for him right back. He would walk down by the river and set traps in the evenings when I would be outside. He always waved at me. Adam was a gentleman who had just got back from a college. They say a college is place where people go to gets lots of learning. Adam had just bought a farm.

Nancy Leake and I talked about how we were going to get married and live near each other and that our children were going to play together. We giggled and laughed until after dark. Bessie got one of the slaves to walk Nancy Leake home. I love Nancy Leake she is my best friend. Oh how lucky I am to have a friend. Goodnight journal.

--- It's been a while since I wrote anything. I am not as good at this as Mr. Abraham says to be. It's just sometimes the days are just the same and I don't see the importance of writing it down. Today however is different. Adam Springs came over for dinner tonight and was talking about trying to get his house in order. Mrs. Sarah said he needed a couple of slaves and Adam said he just wasn't ready for the responsibility of slave ownership yet. Mr. Abraham then asked him if he wanted to hire me and Widow Byrd from town to get his house straightened out. Mrs. Sarah huffed and puffed about it but Mr. Abraham said that Adam could just pay them for my time. I sat there with my fingers crossed and Mrs. Sarah finally said that if I was going with the Widow Byrd she would allow it. I had to cover my face with a napkin cause I was smiling so big. Adam said he thought that would be a fine arrangement. I am going to go live at Adam Springs' house. I will get to see him every day. Yay, I am the luckiest girl in the world!!! He said he would come for me after he made arrangements with the Widow. I am so excited I don't know if I can sleep. I have to try. Good night journal.

September- I have not written in this for a long time. I moved into Adam's house with the Widow Byrd and we began to work. It has been a long and hard chore. Adam had been so nice. We finally got to where Adam, the widow and I would sit down at the end of the day in his study. I would sew and the Widow Byrd would nap.

Adam and I have gotten very close over the past two months. I sit with him in church and he has even held my hand a few times. I think I might be in love with him. The house looks so fine. I can imagine living here and raising my children here. I can tell by the way he looks at me that he loves me too. I can't rush him though, it's not ladylike. The widow knows how I feel. She is a quiet woman and doesn't say much.

I miss Bessie. I wish she was here to talk to sometimes. She always knows what to say about these things. Adam told me tonight that it was nice just sitting in the study of his own house. He looked at me and said "You have made things so nice here Nancy." After we had all gone to bed I remembered that I had left my sewing in the study and I rushed down to put it up so I wouldn't forget in the morning. As I picked it up I saw a shadow and almost screamed. It was only Adam however.

I tried to hide behind the chair as all I had on was my nightgown. Adam took me by the arm and pulled me out from behind the chair and took me in his arms and kissed me. I have never felt like this before. I had never kissed a boy before in my clothes much less in my nightgown. He had his arms around me and I felt like I was on fire. He was kissing my neck, my face and his hands were all over me. The next thing I knew we were lying down on the couch and he was on top of me.

As he was pulling up my nightgown over my legs we heard a noise outside and he jumped up and ran to the window. It was only a cat but the moment was broken. He helped me off the couch and apologized and told me I needed to go straight to bed. I didn't say a word but went straight to my room. I am writing this now because I cannot sleep. I know I should not have let him pull up my gown but I wanted him to. I liked how it felt.

Is this why my mother left us I wonder? She liked how this felt so much that she left her children for it. I don't think I could ever leave my children but this sure was a powerful feeling. I don't know what's going to happen but I think something will. I better try to sleep a little bit. Good night journal.

--- Adam would not look at me today at all. We went about our chores and he told us he was going hunting for a few days. I was disappointed in one way but relieved in another. I really wished Bessie was here. I needed to talk to her. Nancy Leake was visiting family near us so she came by for dinner and we had a fine time. I told her Adam kissed me but left out the part about the nightgown. I didn't want her to think badly of me. She was all excited and talked about me and Adam getting married and we could all live close and be friends forever. It was a great night. I'm going to marry Adam Springs and live in this house forever. Goodnight journal

--- Adam came back today. He brought some game with him and fresh fish from the river. We had a wonderful meal tonight. After the Widow and I cleaned up we all went into the study. Adam kept looking at me and I kept looking at him. The Widow finally stood up and said she was retiring for the evening. We both told her goodnight. We sat in silence for a while. Adam finally cleared his throat and said "About the other night....I am sorry if I behaved rashly but you just looked so beautiful standing in the moonlight and I lost my head." I looked up at him and said it was alright I enjoyed it and smiled at him.

He stood up and pulled me from my chair took me in his arms and held me tight against him. He looked deeply in my eyes and I told him I thought I loved him. He kissed me long and hard and whispered "I think I love you too." We moved over to the couch and began to kiss harder and harder. He touched me all through my clothes and I touched him back. He wanted me and I wanted him. He struggled with my clothes and managed to unbutton my bodice and pulled up my skirt. All of a sudden it became an urgent need for both of us. It hurt a bit and I cried some but I didn't care. I wanted him as much as he did me and if he loved me it was all right.

Afterwards he dried my tears with his handkerchief and just held me close by the fire. It was magical. I am truly a woman in love now. I came up to bed and cleaned up and began to write this down. I know I should wait until marriage but it can't be wrong when you love each other and it feels so wonderful. Oh I have never been so happy. I am going to be Mrs. Adam Springs and live happily ever after. Oh Mama, I forgive you for leaving us. This feels wonderful. Goodnight journal.

October - It has been several weeks now since that night by the fire. Adam and I make love every chance we get. It is wonderful. I feel sure soon he will ask me to marry him. I look at the house differently now, it's going to be mine soon. He told me not to tell anyone about us as he doesn't want to hurt my reputation. He is truly the most thoughtful man. I am so happy. I can't wait to tell Bessie she was wrong. I am going to have my gentleman after all. Nancy Leake knows something has changed with me but she thinks it is just because Adam told me he loved me. He says it all the time now when we are together. I am so happy. I am going to have strong happy children with him. I have to go to sleep now. Adam's parents are coming over for dinner tomorrow with Felix Walker and I have to everything just right for them. Goodnight journal.

--- The dinner went well tonight but Adam's mother kept looking at me funny. It was almost like she knew. Adam and I did not say anything and we never touched each other but she made me nervous. Mr. Felix kept joking and laughing at dinner but it felt strange. Maybe I am just being too nervous about it. I hope they will accept me into the family. Adam's family comes from old money and they seem to be a bit formal like. They are staying the night so I can't see Adam tonight. I miss him. I am glad they have come to see how nice the house is but I can't wait for them to go home tomorrow. Good night journal.

--- Adam's family left today but Mr. Felix stayed. He and Adam decided to go hunting for a few days. Adam came in to get some food to take with them before they left. He held me close and whispered "Soon", then he kissed me hard on the mouth. I looked out the door and saw Mr. Felix walking around the corner. I don't know if he saw us or not but I don't care. We are going to get married soon I know. I heard Adam's mother say that it was about time for him to settle down and get a wife. I am sure that he will ask me soon. I am so happy I could just hug myself. Goodnight journal.

November - It's been a while since I have written in you, journal. Adam has been quiet since Felix left. We still make love but he doesn't talk to me as much. I am trying not to press him about getting married but it's hard. He has been riding over to his parents a lot lately and having dinner there. He says his father just wants to talk. I don't know. I feel like I have done something wrong but I don't know what it could be. I haven't changed one bit. I love him more every day and tell him so. He doesn't say it back to me as much these days. I guess men just don't say it like women do.

I wish Bessie was closer. I miss her. I wish my Mama was around so I could talk to her. I feel like she might understand. Oh well it will be better tomorrow. Goodnight journal.

--- Oh journal I don't know what to think. Today was terrible. Nothing I did was right. Adam yelled at me for being clingy when I asked him where he was going and I cried. The Widow thought we had both gone crazy. Adam stormed out saying he couldn't get any peace in his own house anymore. Mr. Felix showed up after dark to spend the night and he and Adam had an argument in the study. I don't know what it was about but Adam kept saying he was his own man and Mr. Felix kept telling him he had responsibilities he had to live up to. I snuck up to Adam's room after everybody went to bed but Adam just sent me away telling me he was tired and had a lot on his mind. I know something is wrong but I don't know how to get him to tell me. I can't really talk to him with Mr. Felix in the house. I pray that tomorrow is a better day. Goodnight journal.

--- My heart is broken, totally broken. Adam's parents came over and stayed for a few days and this morning after breakfast in front of everybody Adam told me I had to go back to the Enloes. His mother said since Adam was getting married it didn't look right for me to keep living here.

Married? He's getting married to somebody else? I felt the color go out of my face and Mr. Felix slid a chair under me so I didn't fall down. He got me some water and Adam's mother got me a wet cloth. She fussed a bit around me and told me how nice I had gotten the place and how grateful they all were to me. I had done a good job and would be back home before Christmas.

Home, what did she know about home? This was my home, mine and Adam's. I had cooked and cleaned and loved with him and now I was being sent away. I could not believe it. I told them all I was sorry but I had not been feeling well for a few days and I would be alright. Adam just stood there and didn't say anything. Mr. Felix offered to help me to my room to lie down a bit. Mrs. Springs looked relieved that I was leaving the room.

When I got to my room Mr. Felix looked at me and very kindly said "I know this is a shock to you Nancy but it is for the best." I just shook my head and sat down on my bed. He then said "I am going to take you back to the Enloes tomorrow. Rest a bit and then pack your things, the Widow can take care of the house today."

He left and I just sat there. I was too sad to even cry. I quickly packed my belongings and just stared out the window. I came down for dinner assuring Mrs. Springs that I was better. I helped the widow clean up after dinner and we both cried a little when we hugged each other goodnight. I had grown very fond of the Widow Byrd. The family was in the study so I just went to my room.

I think I just want to curl up and die. Maybe my broken heart will just stop beating tonight and I can die in my house and my bed before I have to leave in the morning. If I die in my sleep journal you know it will be from a broken heart. Goodnight journal it may be my last one.

December - I have been back at the Enloes for a month now. I was too unhappy to write for a while. It's almost Christmas and people have been visiting a lot and the children are excited. Mr. Abraham has noticed how quiet I have been and he keeps asking me if Mr. Springs treated me alright. I just tell him I am fine. Mr.

Abraham asked me to sing some Christmas songs for the guests after dinner tonight. It was the first time I have sung since I got back. It did make me feel a little bit better. I guess Mr. Abraham is pretty smart that way. He knows singing always makes me feel better.

I haven't said anything to anybody except Bessie. She fixed me some hot tea and patted my back a lot and just shook her head. She sat down and took my hand and told me that "Fine gentlemen like Mr. Abraham and Mr. Adam just don't marry servant girls. It just ain't right". She told me even if Mr. Adam did love me he had to marry somebody his family approved of. I told her about Adam coming to my room late that night and telling me how sorry he was but it was something he had to do. He wanted to make love to me that night and I told him no. He just hung his head and looked so sad but he turned around and left. I almost called him back but I still had a little bit of pride left. Bessie told me that there would be other men in my life and that I just had to let it go.

I just threw my arms around her waist and hugged her and to my surprise she hugged me back. She told me I was too trusting a child and she worried for me. Today was a better day. Singing the Christmas songs helped. I really was back home. I get to see my sister Mandy on Sunday's at church and the routine was the same at the Enloes. Nancy Leake told me how sorry she was that Adam was marrying somebody else but that I would find someone else.

I guess it's time to forget Adam Springs and move on. I promised Bessie I would write another letter for her to send to her sister with the Rev. Joe. He is coming over for dinner after church on Sunday and she can give it to him then. I will try to write more often. It's just that I have been too sad. Goodnight journal.

--- The Enloes went to spend the day with some friends in town so Bessie and I had some time to write her letter. I asked Bessie which sister this was and she told me it was the sister who did hair so well. I asked Bessie how she got to Pennsylvania when she had been sold to a man in South Carolina.

Bessie told me that when her sister's Master died his wife remarried an abolitionist and they freed all their slaves. The new Master had family in Pennsylvania that told them that they would give jobs to any of the slaves that wanted to move. Bessie's Papa and sister packed their bags and left. Her sister went to school and learned how to read and write and she got paid to fix ladies hair now. Bessie sounded real proud. She said her sister had her own business. I asked Bessie how she knew about all this and Bessie said that her sister wrote letters to her old Mistress in South Carolina and asked her if she would find out what had happened to her mother and siblings. When her sister found out who Bessie had been sold to she started to ask questions to see who might know her or her Master.

Rev. Joe knew Bessie's sister's old Mistress and when he realized Bessie had been sold to Mr. Abraham he decided to contact her. Rev. Joe started writing letters to her sister and helped her locate all of them. Bessie found out her Mama had died and two of her brothers had run away and joined her sister up North.

I asked Bessie if she was going to run away. Bessie just laughed and said she had no reason to run away. Mr. Abraham was good to her. She had a nice life. I said "But don't you want to go live with your sister?" She just laughed and said "I would like to visit her but slaves don't get to do that."

She then told me "Hush and write her letter so it would be done before the Enloes got back from town." She told her sister about her days and the children, she told her how good Mr. Enloe was to her and she told her about me. She told her she was happy and hoped all was well with the family. She wished them all a Merry Christmas.

I finished the letter and put it in the envelope for Rev. Joe to mail after his visit Sunday. Bessie thanked me for writing her letter for her and gave me a piece of cake for writing it for her. I love cake and Bessie knows it. I was feeling better about life all way around. It was a good day. Goodnight journal.

--- Today was Christmas. We all poured into the wagon and went to church. I sang beautiful Christmas songs and felt so much better. We had a light snow starting on the way home and the children were all excited. We had Christmas dinner and then opened presents. I had made a handkerchief for Bessie and some dolls and things for the children. We were all excited on the ride home. Dinner was wonderful and afterwards Mr. Abraham and Mrs. Sarah sat down with everyone to open presents. It was a wonderful time. I gave Bessie her handkerchief and she gave me a nightgown she had made me. Mrs. Sarah called me in and she and Mr. Abraham gave me a new dress to wear to church on Sundays. The dress was a hand me down but it was new to me. It was a special day. I hardly thought about Adam at all and to top it all off Bessie had left me a piece of cake in my room. I think I feel happy again. Goodnight journal and Merry Christmas.

In the year of our Lord 1800 …..

February - It has been cold here. We have been cooped up in the house for a while now. Even Mr. Abraham's temper is getting short. We had had snow for a week now and the children are running out of games to play. Bessie is threatening to thrash all of them if they don't stay out of her kitchen. Mr. Abraham asked me if I had been writing in my journal and I felt guilty because I have not written in quite some time. He again told me it was important that I write down an accounting of my days but sometimes I think it is just silly. My days are just one like another so why waste paper writing about them.

Today was different however. The magistrate was looking for somebody and he stopped to spend the night, while he was there he pulled Mr. Abraham aside and talked to him. Later he and Mr. Abraham called me into the study and asked me to sit down. I was frightfully scared. I thought somebody had died. The magistrate told me he was sorry to tell me that my mother had been found with the man she had run off with and to keep from going to jail they had to get married. I looked at him and said "Is that all?" He said it was a mighty powerful crime to run off with a man and abandon your children. I asked him if she was coming back and he just looked at me kindly and said no she is going to stay where she is. She said her girls were being looked after better than she could do.

I was a little sad but not surprised. I was glad she weren't dead. Mr. Abraham said I could go to my room after that. I heard Mrs. Sarah muttering about white trash and being worse than a wild cat but I didn't want to listen. I knew she was talking about my Mama. She didn't have to tell me. I was the one she left.

I thought a lot about how I felt about Adam. Would I have run off with him without getting married? I don't know. Was I just like my Mama after all. I did lie with him without being married but he told me he loved me. He told me if you love somebody it's alright. I decided that I might give up everything for a man but not my children. When I have children I will love them and teach them and take good care of them. They will grow up strong and smart and make something of themselves. They would always know how much I loved them even after I was dead and gone. I would always put their needs first. I wasn't like my Mama and I wasn't gonna be. I was different, my Daddy was a gentleman and even though I didn't know his name I know I come from good stock all the same.

Hearing about Mama makes me sad however. I remember how pretty she was and when she was happy, listening to her sing. Her eyes were like the blue, blue sky. I got my eyes from my Daddy she would say. They were light gray with a dark ring around them. Adam said they were beautiful eyes. I don't know I think Mama's blue eyes were prettier, even Mrs. Sarah's brown eyes were prettier than mine. Oh well it's a sin to be vain the preacher says. I'm just going to go on to bed and dream of warm summer days to come. I just need to put Mama out of my head and go to sleep. Good night journal.

March - I am so excited I don't know if I can go to sleep. I got to do something today I have never done. I got to go with Mr. Abraham by myself to go pick up some venison from the neighbor. We took the cart so he could pick up some other things and Mrs. Sarah told me to go so I could help pack the meat properly to bring back. I think she wanted me to go so Mr. Abraham would come back home quickly. He liked to stay at the neighbors' house for days at a time when he went. She always fussed about them drinking homemade mash and being drunken fools when he went there.

I was so happy that I started singing as soon as we were out of sight of the house. Mr. Abraham joined in with me. We laughed and talked all the way to the neighbor's house. When we got there I helped the neighbor's wife with getting the meat together and packing things in the wagon. Mr. Abraham and the neighbor had gone off down to the creek. We waited and waited. Finally it was getting dark and they came back up the path arm in arm laughing. The neighbor's wife told Mr. Abraham he needed to spend the night as it was too cold to ride all the way back to his house. He just laughed and said he had enough mash in him to stay warm. He grabbed a few bottles of mash and put them into the cart then before I could say anything he grabbed me up and swung me in the cart.

The neighbor's wife gave me some skins and a rug and told me to wrap up tight and try to stay warm on the trip. She gave me a lantern and told me to hold it tight so we had enough light to get home by. We left out as the sun was going down. It was cold but Mr.

Abraham did not seem to feel it. He laughed and joked and kept asking me if I was warm enough. Then he grabbed me and pulled me close and told me to sit close to him to stay warm. He smelled my hair and told me I smelled like sunshine. I laughed. He asked me why I didn't laugh as much as I used to before I went to Adam Springs' house. I told him I was just a grown woman now and I shouldn't be laughing like a child. He got quiet for a minute and then pulled the rug open that I had wrapped around me. He looked me over up and down and said "By George you are right, you are a full grown woman now and a right nice looking one at that."

I pulled the rug back around me tight as it was cold. He laughed and said "Scoot closer girl I won't bite you at least not so as it would hurt." I laughed at him and drew closer. He put his arm around me and started to sing. I asked him if he was drunk and he laughed and said "No girl I'm just keeping warm." I tried not to fall asleep but it was hard, I had gotten warm in the rug and laid my head on Mr. Abraham's shoulder.

I woke up feeling his hands on me under the rug. He was breathing hard and had stopped the horse. When he saw I was awake he told me to not be scared he wouldn't hurt me. He ran his hands over me and said huskily "You are a grown woman ain't you child." He slid his hand up my skirt and it made me feel as hot as fire. He touched my private parts and kinda moaned. I just stayed still. I knew I should say something but I just couldn't. Mr. Abraham was the nicest man I had ever knowed and if he wanted to touch me then he could go ahead.

The outside air was cold on my thighs and I shivered. It seemed to bring him back to his senses. He pulled my skirt back down and pulled the rug around me. He took a long drink of the mash and started the horse back towards home. I didn't say anything and neither did he for a long while. When we got closer to the house he said "Girl, I am sorry I acted badly back there. I am just a man that had a little too much to drink and was acting a fool. Don't say nothing to anyone about this please. I will make it up to you I promise." I told him it was ok that all I wanted to do was make him happy. He laughed and said "Girl, you do that just by being around every day."

When we pulled up to the house Mrs. Sarah was standing by the door with all the lanterns on in the house. She was sure enough mad. She told Mr. Abraham that she thought we were lying dead on the road somewhere and how dare him scare her like that. He laughed and jumped off the cart and ran up the steps and grabbed Mrs. Sarah and swung her around and kissed her hard on the mouth and said "So you missed me old girl." She yelled at him and told him how dare he come home drinking and smelling like mash. He yelled at Bessie and the house slaves to unload the cart and told me to get to inside and get warm.

He picked up Mrs. Sarah with her fussing and all and carried her up the stairs. Bessie was just a laughing and said "The Master's in high spirits tonight. We'll have another Enloe running around here afore too long." I went in and washed up and came up here. I had to write all this down. I could hear Mrs. Sarah fussing and laughing all at the same time. I knew what they were doing but I didn't care. I loved them both and just wanted them to be happy. If touching me helped him bed Mrs. Sarah then it was ok with me. Oh journal it does make my body remember Adam. I do so like the way it feels when a man touches me. I must have more of my Mama in me than I thought. Oh well, what a day, what a day, Good night journal.

--- It's been a few weeks since my trip to get the meat. Mr. Abraham did not say anything about our trip but he bought me a pretty blanket for my bed. Bessie raised her eyebrows about it but she didn't say anything. He told Mrs. Sarah that the Widow Byrd had sent it to me. I was helping Bessie in the kitchen when Mrs. Sarah came in saying she had gotten a letter and that we were going to have company from South Carolina in a few days. One of Mr. Abraham's friends was building a tavern and was coming by to talk to him about it. She was excited because Mr. Felix was coming too. Bessie told me it meant we had to do all the sheets and get the guest rooms ready.

I was excited because Mr. Felix always put Mrs. Sarah in a festive mood. Mr. Abraham came in the kitchen while I was bending over getting the wood. I felt him watching me and I stood up and looked at him. I got all red in the face at the way he was looking at me. Bessie cleared her throat loudly and asked him if there was anything she could do for him. He just told her he had come in for a glass of water. She poured him one and he went back into the house. Bessie walked over to me and whispered "Child, be careful, they'll be trouble in this house afore this is finished. I see dark clouds on the horizon. You stay away from Mr. Abraham you hear. I seen that look on a man's face before. It a hunger and it just gnaws at 'em. You can awaken some powerful demons with that kind of hunger. Pray child and I will pray with you that this house be delivered from evil. You are a good girl and you just don't understand the ways of men. Oh, I pray for you child."

I finished helping her in the kitchen but when I got to my room I looked at my hands and I ran them over my body. Did I cause a terrible hunger in a man? Is that what happened to Adam? I got on my knees and prayed that I did not cause any trouble. How could something that felt so good be so wrong? I wasn't hurting anybody. I just wanted people I loved to be happy. Why if Mrs. Sarah asked me to walk through town plumb naked I would with my head held high. I loved the Enloes, all of them. They were the only family I had ever really known. I will try to be more careful around Mr. Abraham so I don't cause no trouble. I was a grown woman of 16 now and didn't need to act like no child. Oh journal I love living here. Goodnight.

April - Well today was the big day. Mr. Felix arrived with the rest of the company. Mr. and Mrs. Orr seemed like nice folks. They had built the tavern in South Carolina and I think Mr. Abraham is going to put some money into it. Mr. Felix pulled me aside after dinner and told me he was glad to see that I was doing ok. He said he was worried about me after the last time he saw me. I assured him that I was fine. I asked him how Adam and his new wife was doing and he told me just fine. I said I was glad to hear it and I really meant it. He patted me on the back and said "Atta girl. I knew you'd be fine."

I helped Bessie clean up and gathered all the children together and finally got them all to sleep. They always get excited when company comes to visit. I went down to the kitchen and heard them all in the study. Mrs. Sarah was laughing and had high color in her cheeks and Mr. Abraham looked happy. That's all I ever really wanted was for people to be happy. I guess because my Mama had times where she was just so unhappy it was important to me to make people happy. Happy people didn't leave you. I remember her saying my Daddy used to have what they called melancholy. He just would sit around and mope for days and then he would be alright. Mama said she just stayed out of his way when he was like that. I hope I never have that. Whew, I am tired tonight. Goodnight journal.

May - Mrs. Sarah is with increase! The whole house is excited. A new baby is always fun. She is feeling well. Bessie says she carries babies better than any workhorse she ever saw. The whole house is supposed to go to South Carolina to visit the Orr's. Mr. Abraham says we are going to take our time so we don't rush Mrs. Sarah. She just laughed and said she could get there before him.

We got everything packed and ready today. We are going to head out in the morning. We have three wagons full of stuff. The Enloes have a place down there and we are going to stay a while. It will be fun. I ain't never been to South Carolina. I told Bessie that maybe we would see some of her family. She laughed and said "I wouldn't know 'em if they walked up to me it has been so long." Bessie asked me if Mr. Abraham had looked at me that way again. I told her "No, I hadn't seen him do it." She looked relieved and said "Well maybe he done got that hunger outta his system." I am so excited about our trip tomorrow. I don't know if I can sleep a wink tonight. Goodnight journal.

--- I haven't had a chance to write. It was a long trip and then we had to get the house in order when we got here. Mr. Abraham has been gone most of the time and Mrs. Sarah keeps going but she does get tired. You can see it in her eyes in the evenings.

I've had my hands full with the younger ones. They want to go swimming every single day. Mr. Abraham had one of the older boys teach me how to swim so I could watch the children. I love being in the water with them. It is so much fun. My swimming clothes are so heavy when they are wet. I wish I could swim naked like the boys talk about doing. I bet it would feel wonderful.

Mr. Abraham came down to the river today and stripped down to his underclothing and jumped in the water with the children. I was watching from the bank. They were laughing and playing and he was dunking the younger ones. It was wonderful. He yelled for me to come get in the water and join them. I ran into the water and soon we were all playing. The boys would try to swim underwater through his legs while the girls were just hanging on his arms. He would play a game where he put the children on his knees and went deep in the water and then threw them up in the air where they splashed down. It looked like so much fun. The children started telling him to throw me up in the water. I shook my head no and told them I was too big. He laughed and grabbed my arms and pulled me over to him. He put his hands around my waist and took me under water. The next thing I knew I was flying out of the water in the air and splashed down. It was so much fun.

We all took turns flying off his knees. It was getting about time to go in and he said "Nancy come on over here and do it one last time." He put his hands around my waist and I felt him slide them over my bosom. He just squeezed them lightly and brushed his hands over my hardened nipples. I felt his hardness up against my hips as he pulled me down on it in the water. He pushed up hard against me and then threw me up out of the water. My head went under and I swallowed too much water. He came over and got me by the arm and asked if I was all right. The children were all laughing. He held me very close to his body and ran his hands up and down me under the water. I could barely breathe. He then squeezed my bottom and told me it was time to go.

I got out of the water and helped dry off the children. Mr. Abraham said he was going to stay in for a while. I went back to the house wondering if he was going to pleasure Mrs. Sarah tonight like he did before. I didn't think she would let him, being with child and all. He wasn't drinking this time I didn't think, so I didn't know.

After dinner I avoided Bessie and went to my room. I had enjoyed today in the water and I didn't want her to make me feel bad about it. I like how Mr. Abraham feels. His manhood feels like it is big as a log. Adam's was not that big I was sure. I wonder how it would feel to lie with a man who was that big. It might hurt but I don't think so. I think it would just feel good. If Mr. Abraham ever asked me to lie with him I think I would. I've never loved anybody like Mr. Abraham. He has been the nicest man in the world to me. I think I would do just about anything for him or Mrs. Sarah but I think I better not tell Bessie about the river. There is no need to worry her. Goodnight journal.

June - We are going to be leaving soon. I will miss this place. Mr. Abraham has not come down to the water again since that last time. I kinda keep hoping he will.

I did something truly wicked today and I can't tell anybody but you journal. I snuck down to the river and stripped off all my clothes and swam naked just like the boys do. It was the greatest thing ever. I loved the way I felt in the water without any clothes on. I pretended I was just a big old naked fish floating along. I floated on my back and felt the sun on my chest. It was the first time I had been naked outside that I could remember.

I stood on the bank after and let the sun dry my body before I put my clothes back on. I know it was brazen but the sun felt so good on my skin. I think I must have some savage in me as I liked being naked outside. Is this the curse of the flesh that I like how my skin feels without clothes? Maybe this is something I got from my Mama. Who knows but I have to be careful. Mrs. Sarah would tan the skin off my hide if she knew I was outside naked. I think Bessie might even take a switch to me. It felt so good but I am a little red in tender places tonight. I hope I don't have the sunburn that the boys talk about. I am going to go to sleep feeling good about myself. This was an adventure. Sometimes I wish I had been born a boy. They have so much fun. Goodnight journal.

--- Since we were leaving in two days I decided I had better try to get another swim in before we left. It was really hot today and most everybody including the children had settled down to rest and just fan themselves. I told Bessie I was going down to the river for a bit but that I would be back soon. She told me to be careful and not talk to no strangers.

I got to the river in the late afternoon. I took off all my clothes and carefully laid them on a bush. It felt so wonderful to stand naked and let the breeze from the river blow my hair. I stood there for a bit with my hands over my head and just twirled like a little girl. I had never felt so free. I thought I heard something but I looked around and did not see anything so I thought it must have been a squirrel. I lowered myself in the water and swan in slow circles then I floated on my back. I watched the clouds float by and was almost half asleep when I heard a noise. I quickly went under the water and when I poked my head up I saw Mr. Abraham sitting on a rock near my clothes. He laughed and asked me if I did this often. I shook my head no. I told him to turn his back so I could get out and get my clothes. He laughed and said "Why are you ashamed of what God gave you? I've been watching you since you first got here and there is nothing I ain't seen girl."

When I realized he had seen me twirling and playing with myself in the water I held my head up and said "No, I ain't ashamed. I like how it feels to be naked." He laughed out loud and said he agreed with me. He said he liked being outside naked too. I stood there a minute not knowing if he was going to take off his clothes or not. I secretly was hoping that he did. I was curious to see what the big man looked like naked. He looked like he was thinking about it but he said you better come out and get dried off before people start looking for you.

I walked out of the water with my head held high. I could see the sweat on his upper lip. I didn't know if that was from me or from the heat outside. I walked over to get a towel and found he was holding it. He said "Let me dry you off Nancy." He started drying me off with the towel taking great care with my breasts and between my legs. He ran his hands up my thighs without the towel and felt my wetness. It had nothing to do with the river.

He stroked me and made little grunting sounds. I started to moan as it felt so good. He sat me facing away from him on his lap. I could feel his maleness straining in his breeches as he bent me over and rubbed my back and started moving me over him. He was squeezing my nipples so hard that they hurt but I liked it. Then he said softly in my ear, "You would let me wouldn't you Nancy, you would let me take you right here on the riverbank." I said "I would do anything you wanted Mr. Abraham." He pushed harder against me and said "I think you like this as much as I do. Do you Nancy? Do you like it when I touch you?" "Yes" I whispered, "Yes I like it. It feels so good."

He stroked my maidenhood until I was moaning with pleasure and then he was suckling my breast. I thought this is it. It is going to happen. Suddenly he threw me away from him and ripped himself out of his breeches and jerked at himself until it was over. I was confused. The bible said it was a sin to spill a man's seed on the ground and yet that was what he had done. He just looked at me and said hoarsely "Nancy put your clothes on and get back to the house. Do not speak of this to anyone. I will talk to you of it later."

I started to cry as I thought I had done something wrong. I told him I was sorry that he could have put his seed in me instead of spilling it on the ground. I didn't mean to make him sin. He shook his head and laughed harshly and said Nancy you are still such a girl. This was not the sin I was worried about. Get dressed and get back to the house.

I hurriedly got dressed and when I got back to the house Bessie met me with a worried look and asked me if I had been crying. I told her no, I had just been swimming and had water in my eyes. She then wanted to know if Mr. Abraham had found me. He had come looking for me right after I left and before she could think about it she told him I was going to the river. I told her I hadn't seen him. She looked relieved.

I knew she would be angry about today. I was just walking around like Jezebel in the bible enticing poor Mr. Abraham. No wonder he acted like that, a naked woman just all over him. I enjoyed it and wished he had not stopped. I had never felt like that not even with Adam. I felt bad that he couldn't bed Mrs. Sarah since she was with child. Maybe that was why he spilled it on the ground. I didn't know that men did it like that. I had read it in the bible but I didn't know what it really meant till now.

We did not get a chance to talk that night. He went to bed early with Mrs. Sarah when the children did. I guess I have too much of my Mama in me to fight this. I laid on the bed and touched myself like he did. It wasn't as nice but it felt good. I wonder if that was what he was doing to hisself while I was swimming.

I don't care though if he wants me to do this with him I will, he is the nicest man in the world and the only family I have. I love him and he loves me so that makes it all alright as long as you love each other. Adam had taught me that. Love conquered all. I did not love him like I did Adam but it was still love and if it made him happy and he made Mrs. Sarah smile then it was alright with me.

Goodnight journal I'm going to miss swimming naked when we

go back home.

--- The Orrs came over for our last dinner here. Bessie caught Mr. Abraham brushing up against my bottom in the kitchen. I though her eyes were going to pop out of her head. When he walked out she said "Girl that didn't look good. Has the Master been pestering you that a way long." I kept my head down and said "No." She shook her head and put her arms across her bosom and said "Something gotta be done. This house can't take that kinda trouble. Mrs. Sarah was not a tolerable woman and her with child gonna make it worse." I told Bessie everything was fine but she just frowned and said "Girl I done lived a long time with men and I know better. There is a storm brewing in this house as sure as I standing here."

During dinner the Orrs were talking about needing some help at the tavern. They needed someone who could cook but could clean and wait tables too. Bessie heard them talking and spoke up saying "Why can't Miss Nancy stay and help 'em at the tavern she knows how to cook and wait on people." Mrs. Sarah spoke up and said "Why Bessie that's a wonderful idea. Nancy can stay and help you at the tavern." Mr. Abraham said "But Sarah don't you think with the baby coming you will need her at the house." Sarah just hushed him and said "I had babies before Nancy came I guess I can have one without her. Is there any other reason for her to not stay?" Abraham said no, he guessed not and if the Orr's wanted her she could stay.

The Orr's were delighted. I liked them well enough and if I stayed I could still swim for a while. I would miss the Enloes and Bessie but this might be fun. It was all agreed and I would go to the Orr's in the morning. I was excited, I had never been in a tavern before. Ok journal here we are on another adventure. I am a hard worker and know I will do well. My Mama did tell me one time that when you worked for somebody you had to give them your best and then some so that they would ask you to come back again. It was good advice. I guess she taught me some good things too.

Oh Mama I wonder where you are and if you are happy. I wonder if you ever miss me and Mandy. I wonder if Mandy ever thinks much about me. She looked happy with her family when I seen her at church. Last I heard they had adopted her. Good for Mandy she would get a family. Well journal, Mr. Abraham did not come and talk to me tonight so I guess everything is all right. Goodnight journal.

December - I am working so hard here but I love it. I wouldn't mind staying here forever. It will be different not singing in the church this year at Christmas but I get to sing for the Orr's.

Christmas - It was a wonderful day. I was singing Christmas songs and we had special food and friends of the Orr's came by. I was a little sad thinking about the Enloes but I love my life here. It's a busy one but I am suited to it. Goodnight journal.

In the year of our Lord 1801 …..

August - Well it has been a long while since I wrote hasn't it. I love, love, love working for the Orr's. They treat me so good and let me keep my tips. For the first time ever I have some of my own money. The people that come into the tavern are all so nice and we get a lot of travelers. I like to listen to them tell their stories about where they have been. They talk about the different states and territories. One of them even showed me a map of the United States. I ain't never seen a map before. Our country is so big.

The Orr's have books and they let me read what ever I want. I have been reading about our history and what happened with England and the war. I am so proud to be an American. In this country we can be what ever we want to. I may be an indentured servant but I was making some money and someday I would marry a gentleman and have a nice house and my children would go to school and maybe be great doctors or lawyers.

There is a nice young man named John Calhoun who comes around a lot. He does something with the government in Washington but his family lives near here. I think he likes me, he always leaves me a nice tip and he smiles at me a lot. When he found out I could read he promised to bring me a book all the way from Washington.

Tonight after I had finished in the tavern I was out back hanging out the wash and singing one of the old slave songs I remembered. I turned around and Mrs. Orr and John Calhoun was standing there. I stopped embarrassed and they said "No, don't stop go on it is beautiful." Mrs. Orr asked me if I would sing in the tavern some. She said I could keep all the money I got from singing. John Calhoun just looked at me and got on one knee and said "I am a slave to your voice beautiful lady." I giggled and told him to get up that I didn't have enough money to have slaves. He said "It don't matter you own my heart now."

It was so exciting. I was working, making some money and was going to get to sing. I was reading about history and I helped Mr. Orr with the bookkeeping. Not to mention that I got to meet lots of different people and now a rich young gentleman was sweet on me. Life is good and I am happy. I feel guilty that I feel so happy here after all the Enloes did for me. They will always be family to me but I loved my independence working here and best of all I get to sneak off and go swimming naked all the time. I am brown all over from the sun and I love it. I am just real careful that no one sees me. Goodnight journal I just wanted to tell you how happy I am tonight.

September - John Calhoun and I have taken to walking along the river bank in the evenings. Mrs. Orr said it was ok that it was good for young people to see each other. He comes by a lot especially on the nights I sing. He always gives me good tips for singing and tonight he brought me a treat, Chocolates from Charleston. I had never had chocolates before. They tasted like a little bit of heaven melting in your mouth.

I confessed to John that I swam naked in the river. I asked him if that made him think any less of me. He said no he liked my sense of adventure. He asked me if I was ever afraid I would get caught. I told him I was always very careful. He said he would like to see that sometime. I laughed and said maybe someday I will tell you when I am going. He put his arms around me and kissed me. It was nice and I felt warm all over. He let me go and stepped back and got on one knee and apologized for being so forward and asked for my forgiveness. I pulled him up by the arms and laughingly told him there was nothing to forgive and I had wondered what had taken him so long. Then I kissed him back.

I think the summer moon went to my head. We kissed and kissed but he did not try to touch me anywhere else. After a while he said that it was past time to return and we did not want to worry Mrs. Orr. He was a true gentleman. Oh journal I really like him. He might be the one I have been waiting on. Goodnight journal. I will dream of John tonight I think.

November - Tonight John and I were walking by the river and he gave me a ring. He said it had belonged to his grandmother and he wanted me to have it. It was beautiful and it fit perfect on my little finger. I had never had a ring before. I looked up and him and asked what it meant. He smiled and said it is a promise ring. "Will you promise to just love me and no other?" I threw myself in his arms and said "Yes, yes, yes."

Tonight we went a little farther than just kissing. He opened my bodice and suckled me and I felt his manhood through his trousers. I thought he was going to pull up my skirt but he stopped and said it would not be proper. I told him I did not care about proper I loved him but he told me we needed to wait. I fixed my bodice and we walked back to the tavern. I don't know if I can sleep tonight I am aching for him so bad. Goodnight journal I'm going to try.

--- John came by today and said he was going to be gone for a bit. He had to travel with his family to see some friends. He made me promise to wait for him to come back and not fall in love with anybody else. He brought me a fine silver chain to wear his ring on so I could wear it when I was working. I promised I would wear it every day to remember him. That night on our walk he asked me to sing to him. I did. He sat on a rock and just listened and watched my face. When I finished he said "I wished it was warm so we could go swimming naked in the moonlight." I laughed and told him it was too cold and we would freeze. He said "I would love to see you naked you are so beautiful."

We sat and kissed but it was so cold we had to walk back. As we stood at the door to the tavern he whispered "Can I come to your room tonight? I promise not to touch you I just want to see you before I go so I can have the picture of you in my mind." I told him to wait until after midnight when everyone was asleep and I would light a candle and meet him at the back door. At midnight I went to the door and let him in and we crept up to my room. It was chilly but the moon was shining brightly through my window. John sat on the bed and we kissed for a bit and then he asked if he could see me in the naked in the moonlight.

I pulled my nightgown over my head and stood by the window so he could see me. It was chilly standing there and I was excited. He stood up and came to me saying "You are as beautiful as a marble statue." He began to run his hands over me as if I were a statue. He started at my neck and caressed my entire body. I had never had a man touch me like that. I kept having tiny cold chills and shivered. He asked if I was cold and I told him no. My skin felt like it was on fire. He kissed me then long and hard with his hands going up and down my back.

He moved me back to my bed and he laid me down. He stood over me and just looked and looked. I asked him if he was alright. He asked me to turn over and lie on my stomach. He had taken off all his clothes and he laid on top of my back. I could feel his hardness against me but he made no moves. He said "I just wanted to feel you."

He got up and put on his clothes and helped me with my night gown. I was shivering with nerves or cold I did not know. He held me close and kissed me softly and said "Goodbye I will come back for you as soon as I can." I let him back out, closed the door and came back upstairs and wrote it all down for you.

I truly think he is the one. I am wearing his promise ring and when he comes back I am sure he will ask me to marry him. Oh I feel like a princess in one of the tales I read. My Prince is going to come and save me from this life and we will live happily ever after. Oh journal I am so in love and so happy. This is how life is supposed to be. Goodnight journal.

December - I got a letter today. I ain't ever got a letter before so I was real excited. It was from Nancy Leake. She told me she asked Mrs. Sarah if she could write me and she said yes. She said Mrs. Enloe done had the baby and it was a girl and everybody was fine. She said Bessie told her to tell me she missed me and hoped I was being good. She told me about the church and that they missed me in the choir. Rev. Joe said the Christmas carols always sounded sweeter when I sang them. She told me about all the Enloe children and how they was growing. She said she hoped I got to come back soon.

I read her letter ten times today every chance I got. It felt so special. Me, Nancy Hanks, getting a letter with my name on it. It made me feel important. People that get letters all the time just don't know how special it is to get a letter from somebody. When I get married and have my own house I will write letters to people I know so they know I think they are important. I think writing to people is one of the best things a body can do. I'm so glad Mr. Abraham made me learn to write and read good and do my figures. Now, that I got some of my own money it is more important than ever.

John's been gone a couple of weeks. I don't expect him back

until January sometime. I sure miss him and our walks. He talks prettier than any man I ever heard. He says stuff that almost sounds like a song. He reads me poetry a lot. I like it myself but it does sound better when he reads it. Well, it's almost Christmas and this will be another Christmas without the Enloes. I will miss all the children opening their presents and squealing with delight and I really miss Bessie's bread and cake. I love her cake. I am going to go read my letter one more time before I go to sleep. This is a special day. Goodnight journal.

--- We closed early today for Christmas. The Orr's and I had a special dinner and then I sang Christmas carols for them. After dinner we exchanged presents. I had taken some of my money and bought them something but I was surprised at what they got me.

Mrs. Orr made me a new warm shawl and bonnet and hand muff. Mr. Orr gave me a new thick blanket for my bed. Then they handed me a special box and said the Enloes had sent it for me to open on Christmas. I was so overcome that they had thought of me that tears filled my eyes. There was a card in it that all the children had signed and it even had Bessie's mark on it, one of the children had even wrote Bessie by it. It had drawings on it and said Merry Christmas Nancy.

I think it is the sweetest thing I ever had. They had also sent me two work dresses and an apron. I just felt like the luckiest girl in the world. Christmas just couldn't get any better. Mrs. Orr cleared her throat and said that nice Mr. Calhoun left a package for you too. It was the fanciest box I had ever seen tied with a beautiful ribbon. I just held it and kept looking at it when Mrs. Orr said "Go on and open it I have been dying to see what it was since he gave it to me to keep."

I carefully untied the ribbon and opened the box and a beautiful silk scarf was folded with a note from John. It said *"I thought of you when I saw this in Charleston so I got for you for Christmas. It is a silk head scarf from France. I hope you like it. Until we meet again, John"*. Mrs. Orr carefully lifted it out of the box and held it up to the light. It had beautiful colors and you could see through it. We were both amazed at how beautiful and soft and satiny it felt. I had never felt silk before. Mrs. Orr told me to put it up and only wear it on special occasions. She smiled and said I think that young master John is powerful sweet on you. Mr. Orr put his hand on my shoulder and kindly said "Nancy, you need to be careful with young men of means. They get all kinds of ideas in their heads and I like you too much to want to see you hurt." I just giggled. John would never hurt me, why I had his promise ring up in my room.

We sat down by the fire and all had some hot rum with spices before we went to bed. This had to be my best Christmas ever, ever, ever. I looked at my card again and I saw Mr. Abraham's name but not Mrs. Sarah's. That was ok, cause I have everybody elses, somebody had even wrote Baby Elizabeth on it. I just hugged it close seeing all their faces in my mind. I took John's scarf out and rubbed it up against my face. It was so soft and changed colors when you looked at it through the lamp. I folded it carefully up and put it back in the box and tied the ribbon. I put my card on the table. I felt a little guilty for as much as I missed the Enloes I was really happy here. I'm sure they will understand when I marry John and become a great lady. Goodnight journal. I'm going to say my prayers and go to bed.

In the year of our Lord 1802 .....

January - It's almost the end of January and I have not heard from John. I was a little disappointed cause I thought he might write me a letter. Mr. Felix stopped by today. He is traveling up to see the Enloes and said he wanted to stop by and see how I was doing. I told him I was doing just fine. He smiled and said he was glad to hear it. Mrs. Orr stopped by his table and he asked her if I had been working hard for her. She smiled and patted me on the back and said she is a joy to have around, all the customers really like her and Mr. John Calhoun has been sweet on her since he heard her sing. Mr. Felix raised his eyebrows and said "John Calhoun?" I blushed and said he just liked to hear me sing. Mrs. Orr said "Oh it's more than that, he got her a scarf from France for Christmas." Mr. Felix looked at me real long and then said "Well, I'm sure that was a real nice present for you Nancy." I just smiled and said that John was a fine young man. Mr. Felix looked up and said "I agree, I totally agree, he is a fine young man."

When he said that I got a chill that ran down my spine. I don't know why but it did. Mr. Felix is staying tonight and headed out to North Carolina in the morning. I told him to tell everyone I said hello and to please specially tell Bessie that I missed her too. He asked me if I was happy. I told him I was the happiest I had ever been. He just laughed and said "Happiness changes my girl, it changes all the time." I came on up to bed and said my prayers first. I love it here and I want to stay. Goodnight journal.

February - Guess who came back today! You're right! It was John. He came in the tavern and bought a drink for the whole room and asked me for a song. Afterwards he gave me a gold piece for a tip. A real gold piece. I ran up and put it in my room for safe keeping. My heart was pounding. He asked if we could meet near the river tonight. I told him I would be there.

I paced around all day waiting to see him. Finally I was able to sneak away to meet him. He ran up to me and picked me up and swung me around and then kissed me real deep and hard. He told me how much he missed me and now that he was with me again he could breathe. I laughed at him. He always says the funniest things. He told me he had a surprise. We walked a little further in the woods and came upon a small cabin lit with a fire and a lamp. He opened the door and inside was a table, two chairs and a big bed. He laughed and said "I fixed this up for us so we could be alone and not freeze to death." I twirled around and told him I loved it and it was beautiful.

He started taking my clothes off slowly and then got faster and faster saying "I just want to see you, I have ached to see you for months now." I stood by the fire totally naked trembling with excitement. He just sat down in the chair and said I just want to drink you in with my eyes. He had me turn around and hold up my arms over my head. He then asked to face away from him and bend over. I did what he asked but I felt silly bent over like that. Next thing I knew he was rubbing my back and my bottom and just holding me close to his body.

I stood up and he cupped my breast in his hands and whispered in my ear "I just love to look at you, I love to touch you and if you are ready I want to love you." I turned to face him and said yes, I was ready. He carried me to the bed and I watched him undress. He slid down beside me and it was blissful. He was slow and gentle and did things that Adam had never done. I just rode this feeling it went up and down and I just went with it. John kept telling me he loved me and promised that we would be together forever.

We finally had to get up so I could get back. He put out the fire and the lamp and told me he had bought this little cabin just for us. We had a place to be together. He was so gentle and sweet with me and just kept asking me if I was alright. I laughed and told him of course. He said "I do not want to offend you with being too forward in these matters." I told him he was being silly. We loved each other and nothing was wrong when you love each other.

I was so excited, he said we were going to be together forever. Before too long he would ask me to marry him. I got to my room without anyone seeing me. I took out my promise ring and put it on my hand so I could sleep with it. I had to write all this down so I could remember how special this night was. Oh journal, I love John so much.

March - John and I go to the cabin every chance we get. He teaches me to do new things that he has read. I told him I would do whatever he wanted. It has been an adventure. We have a magical love. He told me today that he was Sir. Lancelot and I was Lady Guinevere. When I asked him who they were he told me he would bring me the books so I could read the story. He said today that he had to go away for a few weeks with his parents but that he would be back. I held him tightly before telling him goodnight. He kept saying how much he loved me and he wanted us to be together forever and always. Oh I am so happy. Goodnight journal.

April - John has been back for a few weeks now but he seems different. When we go to the cabin he holds me so hard I can't breathe. He tells me over and over again that he can't live without me. His lovemaking has gotten harder and harder like he is driving himself. He sits and doesn't talk for long periods and just looks at me lying on the bed naked. Sometimes he just has me sit in his lap and he strokes my hair. I keep asking him what is wrong or if I had done something and he tells me no.

Tonight when I asked he said that I am perfect. I laugh and tell him if anybody's perfect it's him. He got real agitated and started pacing the room and saying he wasn't perfect, he was in fact a cad and a cheat. I got real scared and asked him why he would say that. He just grabbed me and said "You love me don't you Nancy, you'd love me no matter what?" I said "Of course I would silly! A woman always loves her husband." He jumped away from me like I burned him. "Why would you say this?" he asked. I said "Well we love each other and you gave me a promise ring so I thought we were going to get married."

I started to cry and he held me so tenderly and said "I love you more than life itself and I do want to be with you forever, please don't cry I would never hurt you." I felt better after that but I can't shake this feeling that something is wrong. Please God don't let it be like Adam again. I just don't think my heart could take it. I belong with John. I love him and he loves me. Oh journal, please let this be alright.

May - Mr. Felix showed up today. I just can't shake the bad feeling that I have. Every time something changes in my life Mr.

Felix is there. He was friendly and just asked how I was doing. I told him fine. He smiled and asked if I was still happy and I said "Yes" and he said "Well I hope you can stay that way."

I don't feel good about seeing him today. It feels like a dark cloud coming before a storm. I met John tonight but he could not stay long as he said Mr. Felix was visiting with his family. He told me he was going to have to go away for a while with his family soon but when he got back we would see about getting our own house. As we were leaving the cabin I thought I heard something in the woods but John told me it was my imagination. I was so excited I didn't think anymore about it.

Mrs. Orr came up to my room tonight and just sat and talked. She talked about how much of a help I had been and how much she and Mr. Orr thought of me and then she gave me a necklace that had been in her family. She said she didn't have any daughters and she wanted me to have it. I thought this was a little strange but I thanked her for it. She hugged me real tight and told me to get some rest as it was going to be a hard day tomorrow for everybody. Her voice cracked as she said goodnight. I don't know what she means about a hard day. I love working here and I don't ever think it's a hard day. Oh journal I will be so happy when John and I get married and move into our own house. I'm gonna be Mrs. John Calhoun. I wrote it down so now it's real. Goodnight journal.

--- Oh journal I can hardly bear to write this. This has been the worse day of my life. My world has been burnt down to the ground and I feel like I am nothing but ashes. Mr. Felix and John came into the tavern for lunch today. I knew something was wrong cause Mrs. Orr put her apron up to her face and ran upstairs.

After I had served them lunch Mr. Felix asked me to sit down with them. I looked at Mr. Orr and he shook his head yes. Mr. Felix said "Nancy I think John has something to tell you." I looked at John and he just hung his head and would not look at me. Felix said sternly to John "Buck up boy and be a man and tell her." John looked at me and tears welled up in his eyes and he said "I can't, I just can't I love her too much." Mr. Felix said "If you care anything about her at all you should be the one to tell her about this." John jumped up out of the chair and said "I can't, I can't do it" and ran out the door.

I just sat there like a stone and looked at Mr. Felix and waited for him to speak. He reached out and took my cold hand in his and said "Nancy, I know you have developed a fondness for young John and it seems that he has for you too but you need to understand how things work for young wealthy gentlemen." I just shook my head afraid to speak. This sounded like something I have heard before. Mr. Felix said "I know this will come as a shock to you but young John is getting married next week."

I don't remember crying but I must have been as all of a sudden Mrs. Orr was there with a handkerchief. Mr. Felix explained that the marriage had been planned for quite some time and it would make John a large landowner. It had been planned by his family for some years now. He told me that if I truly cared for John I would let him go so he could marry this girl. I just kept shaking my head. Mr. Felix said "Now Nancy be sensible a girl of your station cannot marry a man of young John's station. It just isn't done here in the South." He then told me I needed to pack my bags as he had made arrangements for me to return to the Enloe's house as he felt it would not be good for young John to have me so close to his new wife.

When he said that, I jumped up and ran out of the tavern all the way to our cabin in the woods. When I got there I found John waiting with his head in his hands. I just kept asking him why over and over. He finally looked at me and said "I had to Nancy, it's what is expected of me. I tried to talk them out of it. I told them I was in love with you and they said if I stayed with you and did not marry their choice that they would disinherit me and I would have nothing. I can't be poor Nancy, I don't know how. I have to marry her but Nancy, I can still buy us a house where we can raise our children and I can come and see you. We can still be together."

I just stood there with my blood turned to ice. He grabbed me around the waist and said "You said you would always love me and forgive me anything, please Nancy, please forgive me this." I pulled his arms from around my waist and I looked at him and said "I was a bastard child John. I didn't know who my Daddy was and still don't. He left us when his family decided they didn't want us anymore. No matter how much I love you I would never do that to a child of mine. I will not live with you and you married to another woman and bear your bastard children so your family can just send us all away without nothing." I ripped the chain off around my neck and threw it and the ring at him. "There!" I said, "No more promises. I am leaving in the morning to go back to the Enloes and you just need to go live your life."

I walked out of the cabin and he ran behind me screaming my name. Suddenly Mr. Felix was there and got him by the arms and slapped him across the face hard and told him to quit sniveling like a baby and get some backbone. He yelled at him that at least he could let me leave with some dignity. I just kept walking and would not look at either of them. I walked up to my room, packed my few belongings and sat on my bed. I was too numb to even cry.

My life was over again. No husband, no house, and now no more working with the Orr's. I had to go back to the Enloes whom I loved but it would just not be the same. I had lived some life, some free life and I wanted more. Now it was all over. At seventeen my whole life was over. I will leave with Mr. Felix in the morning and I will not cry. I will not let them see me cry. I just may never cry again. I am writing this down because I need to remember how cold I feel today. I am even leaving my gold coin and scarf for Mrs. Orr. I don't want nothing of John's.

How alone I really am in this world. Men lie and they cheat you. The only man that has never lied to me has been Mr. Abraham. At least I will get to see him again. Goodnight journal, I don't know if I can write in you anymore. I just feel broken inside.

July - It's been a long time journal. So much has happened that I just hadn't felt like writing. Tonight, however something happened that got me to thinking so maybe if I write it now I can deal with it more clearly.

We were two days into our journey when the Enloe's oldest boy met us on horseback and told Mr. Felix that he needed to bring me to Adam Springs' house. It seemed that his wife had took ill and he needed some help with her and Mrs. Sarah promised him me. Mr. Felix didn't look any happier about it than I did but neither one of us could say no to Mrs. Sarah. When we got to Adam's house he didn't look none to happy to see me either. He said he was sorry, that he didn't know that Mrs. Sarah was gonna send me he thought I was still in South Carolina. I told him not to worry none I was here to take care of Mrs. Springs. He told me it was just until her sister could get her affairs in order and move down here. No more than a month he hoped. I just shook my head and went into the house.

Mr. Felix stayed the night and then headed out back to the Enloes. He patted me on the shoulder and told me I was a good woman to stay and care for Mrs. Springs. I smiled at him and told him it weren't her fault. I settled in to taking care of Mrs. Springs. She wasn't much older than me. Seems she had come down with pneumonia in January and it had affected her lungs. The doctor had her staying in bed so she wouldn't get too tired. I cooked and cleaned and looked after her. I didn't see Adam much. He stayed away most times until I had gone to bed.

I guess it should feel hard to be in the house that I thought was going to be mine someday but after everything that had happened with John I just didn't care. One day had run into the next and I just was marking time until Mrs. Springs sister got here. Tonight however I was mending by the fire when I looked up and Adam was standing in the doorway holding his hat in his hands. I asked him if he needed anything and he said "What I need is to talk to you Nancy." I just looked at him and said "Have a seat it's your house." He sat down on the couch across from me.

He told me how sorry he was for everything that had happened and how grateful he was for everything I had done for him and his wife. I just kept sewing and didn't say anything. He told me that she had been sick for such a long time now and he was worried about her. I finally said she looked good as long as she stayed still and that I was sure she would get better with time. He agreed and we just sat there while the fire died down.

I finished my sewing and stood up to go to my room when he jumped up and put his arms around me and said "Nancy, it's been so long since I've been with a woman. I need you." He had started unbuttoning my dress and moving towards the couch. I stomped his foot hard and he let me go. "How dare you!" I said, "Your wife upstairs sick in your marriage bed and you down here trying to pleasure yourself with me. What's wrong with you? Why would you think I would do such a thing?" He got on one knee and begged me, said he needed to be with me and I was even more beautiful now than I was before. He asked me to just let him, just this one time.

I was sickened by the sight of him. I don't know why I ever thought I loved him in the past. I told him to get up off the floor and quit acting like a fool, that he needed to be a grown man and act like one. He had responsibilities and if he couldn't understand that I sure did. As I walked out of the room I turned and told him that if he felt like getting on his knees it better be to pray for his soul and not to pester me. He just stood there as I walked out.

When I got in my room I put the chair under my door just in case. What is wrong with me? Why do men act like this around me? Is it true that all men are just animals? Bessie used to warn me about men or is it just something I inherited from my Mama. Did she do this to men? Even Mr. Abraham had acted plumb crazy with me at the river that day but now I have to take some of the blame for that one. I was parading around naked and I can't expect a man to not act natural around a naked woman.

I did like it, I liked it with Adam, I liked it with John, and I liked what happened with Mr. Abraham. Maybe that's why I'm being punished with all this unhappiness. Is it unnatural to like how it feels? Somehow I don't think so. If it was such a sin why did the good Lord make it feel so good? Why men in the bible were laying with women all the time? Wasn't Samson beguiled by Delilah? Didn't King David throw away his soul for a woman? I will say I have not been with a man I didn't love and even though I was being foolish I did think I was going to marry them. I'm just a girl with thoughts and feelings just like everybody else and I deserve to be happy just like everybody else.

I hope Adam stays away from me I just don't have the energy or the heart to fight him. I will find love again someday and it will be somebody that loves just me. I hope Mrs. Springs' sister comes soon. I'm ready to go home to the Enloes. Goodnight journal, I hope I got nothing to write for a while.

--- Glory be, Mrs. Springs' sister arrived today. She seemed like a sweet woman. After she visited some with her sister, I showed her around the house and showed her the notes I had left her about the household. She seemed shocked that I could read and write. I held my head up and told her not all indentured servants were ignorant.

She apologized and said she didn't mean to hurt my feelings she was just happy that I had left her such good notes. I packed my belongings and prepared to leave the next morning. I was going by wagon with a couple of Adam Springs' slaves back to the Enloes. I can't wait to leave here. It is just a place of bad memories and best forgotten things. Goodnight journal.

August - Mr. Abraham admonished me for not keeping up with my journal so I will try to do better about writing now that I am back home. Dinner was embarrassing tonight. One of the older boys whispered something about me to the other and they both got the giggles and Mrs. Sarah put her foot down and demanded to know what they were talking about. When they got all red faced and told her they were talking about how pretty I was she was livid and made them leave the table without dinner. She told me to leave too but Mr. Abraham intervened and told her it was not my fault that boys would just be boys. We were to all finish our dinner and then I think he winked at me. It was hard to tell.

I told Bessie about it later when we were collecting the laundry. She just laughed out loud and said "My them boys are growing up." I told her Mrs. Sarah sure got mad. She told me to watch out that Mama Hen would be coming after me about her chicks. I said what ever for them boys are just youngin's what would I see in them? I wanted a man not some young wet behind the ears little boy. "Oh" she said "You want a man? I thought you done sworn off men." "Oh Bessie" I said "You know what I mean." She swatted me on the rear and we both laughed.

All in all it was a good day. It is good to back home. The children all running around getting into everything and the new baby Elizabeth is a delight. She had took to me and me to her. I guess I am just getting older, when I hold her I think about having my own children someday. Nobody will ever love a child like I will mine someday. Goodnight journal

--- Well Bessie was right it didn't take her long. This morning right after breakfast Mrs. Sarah told me she wanted to speak to me in private. We went into her study and she started talking about how she had always tried to be good to me and that they had taken me in as a young girl and taught me how to read and write and dress and act proper. She then told me that my servitude was almost up and I would be making the choice to go or to stay on as a paid servant. She said she had hoped that I would stay as I was a big help with the children and they cared about me "However" she said, "You are not to get ideas in your head about any of my boys. They will not marry you, it will never ever happen and I want to make sure you understand me on that."

I laughed before I could catch myself. She looked at me and said "Is this funny or is there something I should know?" Her face looked like a raging thunderstorm getting ready to burst at any minute. "No, no, no" I quickly said, "There is nothing going on, them boys are children and I am not interested in children at all, as a matter of fact I am kinda sweet on Richard Martin and I think he likes me." She stopped in mid sentence and said "Hummm Richard Martin, he would be a good catch for you if you could get him. He ain't wealthy but he has some money and land. Why Nancy, I think that might just be a capital idea. I will talk to the ladies of the church about it and see how they feel." I said "Mrs. Sarah shouldn't it be about how me and Richard feel." "Oh balderdash, young people just mess these things up when they do it themselves" she said.

Poor Richard I thought, we had better talk soon so he knows what I done got him into. Later when I told Bessie she told me that Richard seemed to be a nice young man and I could do worse. We laughed cause we both knew I had. She told me not to mess this one up by bedding with him first. She said "You get that ring in front of the preacher afore you ever do that again." "I promise" I told her and that I had seen the error of my ways. She gave me a big old hug and said "Miss Nancy you don't know how sweet and trusting you is. I swear I don't know a soul that don't like you, even Mrs. Sarah and she don't like anybody exceptin' Mr. Felix."

We finished the laundry for the day. I sat outside for a bit before bed tonight and looked at the stars. Widow Byrd had told me my Mama had stopped by to see me and Mandy when I was in South Carolina. She said Mandy's new Mama would not let her see Mandy. It would have been nice to see her but it would have caused problems. Mrs. Sarah didn't have no use for my Mama at all.

I wonder what made Mama act like she did. I think she might

have loved my Daddy whoever he was cause she never said much bad about him, it was always his family that she was mad at. All she would say was that daddy was a weak man. I don't know. I wish I could remember him more. I remember a big man with a big hat that used to swing me around and let me ride a horse with him. I wish she would have told me who he was. I like to pretend that he was a fine rich gentleman with lots of learning and I was just like him and his family.

The stars sure were shining bright tonight. I caught a glimpse of Mr. Abraham out walking on the property smoking his pipe. He looked at me sitting on the porch and walked over. "Beautiful night out here tonight ain't it Nancy?" I said "Yes sir it sure is." "Are you happy again Nancy?" "Yes sir" I replied. "Good" he said, "I was worried about you after you got back from South Carolina. Mr. Felix told me all about what had happened. I am sorry Nancy you deserve better than that."

I got tears in my eyes cause Mr. Abraham truly did care about me. He saw my tears and wiped them with his handkerchief. "Don't cry child. You know how much we all love you around here don't you? You are like family. I have watched you grow up from a little girl to a beautiful and spirited woman. You will be a prize for any man you choose Nancy." I jumped up and gave him a big hug and he hugged me back and said "You know your hair still smells like sunshine. Time for you to be getting' in, it's late" and as I ran up the stairs he swatted my bottom and I laughed.

Oh journal it's so nice to home where I belong. I love Mr. Abraham and all the others. There is never anything I won't do to make them happy as long as I live. Goodnight journal.

--- I managed to speak to Richard at church today after choir practice. I told him what happened with Mrs. Sarah and said I was sorry but that she had put me on the spot. He got all red in the face and started to stammer. I told him that it was alright and if he didn't feel that way about me I would explain it to Mrs. Sarah. He said "No, no, I do like you, I like you a lot. Do you like me really?" I smiled at him and said "Yes Richard Martin I like you a lot."

He rode with me back to the house after practice. When I got home he waved bye and rode off. Bessie came out of the kitchen just a smiling saying "Why Miss Nancy I think you done gone and got yourself a fella." We walked back into the house and she smiled and said "I got you a piece of cake saved. Why don't you take it back to your room." I took it up and ate it. It was wonderful. I love Bessie's cake. What a wonderful day. Thank you Lord, you are truly good. Goodnight journal.

September - Richard came by and asked Mr. Abraham and Mrs. Sarah if he could call on me. Mrs. Sarah had talked to the ladies of the church about it and they all agreed it was a good match so they agreed to let him come by. Nancy Enloe thinks it is so romantic. She is fourteen and all she wants to talk about is love and John Thompson. I told her she has got plenty of time for love and that her parents did not like John Thompson so she had better hush talking about him. I might as well tell a bird not to sing.

Richard stayed after he got permission and we sat out on the big porch and watched the stars. We talked for a while until Mr. Abraham came out and told Richard it was time to go. Richard shook my hand and told me and Mr. Abraham goodbye. Mr. Abraham told me to sit down with him and talk a bit while he smoked his pipe. He talked to me about paying me wages when my service ended if I wanted to stay.

I told him of course I wanted to stay. He put his hand on my thigh and said "Nancy you know we want you to stay, especially me. Just seeing your face everyday makes me happy." He began to rub my thigh through my dress and said "I have missed you Nancy. I have often thought of that day by the river. Did you swim naked for John?" I shook my head no. "Mr. Felix told me about your cabin in the woods. Is that where you would lie with John?" He hand rubbed harder up my leg. "Yes sir" I said "but I did think we was going to get married." "I understand" he said "But tell me Nancy did you like it, did you like it when he touched you? Did you like being naked in front of him?" He had placed his hand between my legs at this point. I was breathing hard and so was he. "Yes" I said," I like being naked, I know I shouldn't but I do. I guess it's just my Mama in me."

He was stroking me with his hand and said "Do you like this Nancy?" I did not answer and he stroked harder and said "Do you like this?" I looked up at him and said "Yes, I like it Mr. Abraham, I like it." He stopped and took a long drag off his pipe. He took my hand and placed it on his manhood. "Do you feel that Nancy?" he said. "Do you feel how hard I am for you." He felt huge. "Did John feel this big Nancy, was he this big inside you?" "No," I said "John was not this big." He moved my hand and said that that was good because it meant that I was still tight. He said "Tight is good Nancy." I didn't know what he meant so I just shook my head.

I asked him what he wanted and he smiled and brushed his hand against my breast and said nothing for a minute and then said "Nancy, I just want you to be happy. It is good that you like how it feels to be touched by a man. It will help make you a good wife. A good wife needs to know how to please her man so he won't go to other women." I asked him if he had gone to other women. He just looked off and said "Mrs. Sarah is a fine woman but she does not seem to enjoy being touched by a man much and she has been with child a lot of our marriage. A man has needs Nancy and those needs must be taken care of. You need to remember that to be a good wife. I want you to be a good wife, Nancy, don't you want to be a good wife?" I said "Yes sir", and he said "Well since you don't have a Mama to teach you I will teach you about it." "Oh Mr. Abraham" I said, "Thank you. No one has ever cared about me like you." "I do care about you Nancy" he said, "I care about you a great deal. You are in my blood. Now off to bed with you, it's late."

I left and ran up to my bedroom. I was trembling with desire and excitement. Mr. Abraham was going to teach me how to be a good wife. What did that mean? I really did not know a lot about men. My experiences with Adam and John were just like children playing. I had a feeling that Mr. Abraham had something different in mind. Oh well, journal it has to be alright if Mr. Abraham says it is. He loves me and just wants the best for me. Goodnight journal.

--- I got a new dress today for the Harvest dance. I am so excited, it is blue with ruffles and lace and just floats when I twirl. It is beautiful. Ok, it's not really a new, new dress but it's new to me. One of the ladies in the choir gave it to me because her daughter outgrew it. I can't wait to wear it. Richard is just going to love it. I feel beautiful in this dress. I put it on and looked in Mrs. Sarah's mirror and I just didn't even recognize myself.

She yelled at me for taking so long in putting it on but I didn't care. Nancy Enloe came in and just squealed about how pretty it was. She said "Richard will ask you to marry him for sure when he sees you in that dress." I laughed and said "It ain't the dress that a man asks to marry." She said "Yeah but it sure can help sometimes." After she left I thought she might be right. It sure does help. Sometimes a pretty package makes the gift inside just seem that much more special.

I remember the silk scarf all wrapped up with that pretty ribbon. Mrs. Orr cried when I gave it to her the morning I left but I didn't want anything that John gave me. Oh well, that's enough about John, I will not let him ruin my happiness today. I don't think Richard is ready to ask me to marry him yet. He is a cautious man and takes his time but that's ok I am willing to wait. Maybe he will like the dress enough to kiss me at the dance. Just a kiss though I am not going to mess this one up.

Mr. Abraham had been hunting. I hope he gets back in time for the dance. I can't wait for him to see how pretty I look in the blue dress. Mrs. Sarah's been all excited too. Mr. Felix is supposed to be there and Miss Nancy is about to drive us all crazy about the dance. It's her first dance and she whispered to me that John Thompson was coming.

She sure is crazy about that John Thompson. He has been hanging around the house a lot lately with the Enloe boys. He seems nice enough but Mrs. Sarah don't like him cause he's just the son of a poor sharecropper. She's funny about stuff like that. I am so happy I could just hug myself. My life is good, maybe it is finally turning a corner. By this time next year maybe I'll be married and have my own house. I want to be the best wife and mother ever. I'll know how to keep my husband happy and we will take our children to church on Sundays and let them play in the creek and then just sit on the porch and hold hands while the sun sets. It will be perfect. I just know it will. Goodnight journal I going go to bed and dream of dancing all night.

--- Oh journal I think I may have made a terrible mistake. Tonight was the dance and it was wonderful just like I dreamed. I danced and danced. Mr. Abraham had gotten back and I even danced with him. He told me I looked fine in my new dress and the ribbons in my hair were right pretty. Richard and I held hands and he rode back to the house with me afterwards. Right before he left he kissed me real quick on the cheek and ran off to his horse. I waved bye feeling happier than I had felt in a long time.

When I got to my room Miss Nancy was waiting for me. She was all excited and so bright eyed she looked feverish. She told me that her and John Thompson were going to run off and get married. He had made arrangements. She just had one problem she needed me to help her by going with her to meet him so I could bring back the horse. She said she knew her Daddy would be mad that she ran off but he would never forgive her if she took a horse.

I tried to talk her out of going but she said that her Mama would never allow her to marry John and she loved him. She kept saying it was the only way. When I told her no, that I could not help she said ok then she would just have to let the horse run free. I knew how much Mr. Abraham loved his horses and I just couldn't do that. She promised she would not tell anybody that I helped her. She said I could be back with the horse before anybody knew she was gone.

Mr. Abraham had gone to a tavern with some friends after the dance and Mrs. Sarah had retired to bed. I told Miss. Nancy that there would be hell to pay when Mrs. Sarah found out. She said she would be way off in the mountains by then. John Thompson had some family in Kentucky that was gonna give him some land and a cabin when they got there. I told her to let me change clothes and she grabbed my arms and said there wasn't time. They had to leave right then if I was to get the horse back by morning.

I grabbed a heavy shawl and off we headed to the barn. She had the horse ready and we both jumped on it and rode off into the night. We finally met up with John Thompson and after many tears and hugs they were off and I was bringing the horse back home. I had a feeling of dread all the way back. I just knew I was gonna be caught. I made it back to the barn and everything was still quiet. I hurriedly got the saddle off the horse and put it up and ran like the wind to my room. I threw off my dress and tried to lie down but I was so restless I decided to just write in you for a bit. Oh journal I just don't feel good about this at all, not at all. Goodnight journal I pray that everything will be alright.

--- Well, the kettle boiled over this morning when Mrs. Sarah found out that Miss Nancy was gone. Miss Nancy had left her a letter telling her that she was getting married to John Thompson and there were going to Kentucky. Mrs. Sarah was fit to be tied. She sent one of the boys to go find Mr. Abraham and fetch him home. She kept asking me if I knew about this. I just shook my head no and didn't say anything. She told me if she ever found out that I had a hand in this she would never forgive me.

By late afternoon Mr. Abraham still wasn't back and Mrs. Sarah was ringing her hands and walking the floors crying. Bessie finally made her a tonic and took her upstairs. Late that night Mr. Abraham got home and Mrs. Sarah roused the whole house yelling at him to go find Miss Nancy. Mr. Abraham told Mrs. Sarah that he would get some men and go out first thing in the morning after her.

Mrs. Sarah was mad that he didn't leave right then and he told her that it was senseless to strike out in the dark. She told Mr. Abraham that he could just go sleep in the barn till daylight then so he would be ready first thing. Bessie just looked at me from the kitchen door and rolled her eyes. Mrs. Sarah turned back to the hallway and yelled for all of us to go to bed the show was over and she went in her room and slammed the door. I saw Mr. Abraham go into the kitchen with Bessie.

I am worried journal. If Mrs. Sarah found out I helped Miss Nancy she might just turn me out and Mr. Abraham might just let her. He can't say nothing when she is in one of her moods. Oh journal I am so scared. Please dear Lord let them never find out the part I played in this. Goodnight journal.

--- Mr. Abraham headed out first thing this morning to get some men and go after them. Mrs. Sarah stayed in bed today. Bessie said the tonic she gave her will help her rest. The children were all quiet today almost like there had been a death in the house. It was one of those days where you spoke in whispers.

After we fed the children lunch and Bessie took some more tonic up to Mrs. Sarah we sat at the table talking. She looked at me and said "Miss Nancy please tell me you didn't help them children run off." A tear ran down my cheek and I told her that I had to because of Mr. Abraham's horse. She grabbed her apron and said "Lordy, Lordy, evil has down come to pass over our house. Oh Miss Nancy you know iffen Mrs. Sarah finds out about this she will never ever forgive you. You know that little Miss Nancy was the apple of her eye. I don't even think Mr. Abraham can save you from this one." I begged Bessie not to tell. "They will never know" I said, "I was back in the house before anybody woke up." Bessie said she was gonna pray that nobody ever found out and told me I need to pray hard too. I told her I was.

Mr. Abraham and the men came back near dark. Mrs. Sarah came running downstairs in her nightgown screaming "Did you find her?" Mr. Abraham took her by the arms and walked her back into their bedroom. Bessie had me come help her get food ready for all the men. While I was getting the plates out I heard Mrs. Sarah wailing and saying "No, no no. You have to go and get her and bring her back." I went back into the dining room and heard no more.

After a while Mr. Abraham came down to eat a bite and asked Bessie if she could go check on Mrs. Sarah. He thanked the men for helping him and told them they could stay the night. Most of them decided to go ahead and leave. They told him he was right to quit looking that the couple had too big a head start and anyways they were already married now. They wished him luck with Mrs. Sarah. He just shook his head and said it's going to be hard on her. They left and he went back in his study.

I ain't never seen him look so tired. Bessie came back down and told me Mrs. Sarah was sleeping. She said that Mr. Abraham and the men had rode up to the stage stop and the man there told them the preacher down the way had married Miss Nancy and Mr. John early yesterday and that they had lit out for Kentucky. After talking to the preacher who told Mr. Abraham that even if he went after her she was Mr. Thompson's wife now legally and he couldn't make her come home if she didn't want to and besides they had such a head start it would be hard to catch them anyway. Mr. Abraham talked to the men and they decided the preacher was right and it was best just to come home and give Mrs. Sarah the bad news. Bessie looked at me and said "They can't never find out what part you played in this never, ever, ever."

I went to my room feeling like the world was pressing on my

shoulders. Bessie was right Mrs. Sarah would never forgive me. Oh journal I hope they never find out. If God will let my part in this stay secret I will never ever do another bad thing ever. My heart is breaking for Mrs. Sarah's pain. I can hear her crying even in my room. It's a sad, sad day for everybody. Goodnight journal, I sure hope tomorrow is better.

October - Mrs. Sarah is still moping around the house. She gets teary eyed if somebody mentions Miss Nancy. She is shore mad at Mr. Abraham. She barely speaks to him and he looks like he's aged a year. So far ain't nobody found out my part in all this. I guess my prayers are working.

Richard has not been over for a while. We are kinda like a house in mourning around here. Bessie says it will be better before too much longer. She said it just takes Mrs. Sarah some time.

I have been teaching the younger children how to write their letters. Mr. Abraham said it was a shame that I couldn't be a school teacher. He thought I might be real good at it. I was beaming. He smiled at me and said "You know my Daddy was a school teacher. He always said everybody ought to know how to read and write. He would be real proud of you Nancy. You are a smart, smart girl." I smiled and told him I must a got that from my Daddy. Mama always said he was smart. Mr. Abraham asked me if I knew his name and I said no just that he was a gentleman from a good family. Mr. Abraham patted me on the shoulder and said "Well he did good having you. You are a fine girl Nancy." My heart sang. There ain't nothing as wonderful as Mr. Abraham saying something nice about me. I hope he is getting over Miss Nancy running off. Goodnight journal.

--- Mr. Felix got here today thank goodness. If anybody can cheer up Mrs. Sarah it will be Mr. Felix. I think she went all day without crying one time. She even fixed her hair up for dinner. Maybe things are getting better. He told me congratulations on my young fellow Richard. He said "I hear he's a good boy and you should do fine." I thanked him and he leaned over and said "Now don't be telling him about Adam and John. There is just some things a woman needs to keep to herself." I told him not to worry I had done put them out of my mind and didn't ever want to talk about them again to anybody. He said "That's a good girl." I have put them out of my mind mostly but sometimes I dream about being with John in the cabin. I never had done anything that had felt so good. I hope it is that way with Richard, if not then I just will have to make it that way. I will have to ask Mr. Abraham about how to do that for a man. He will tell me I know, but not right now. This house is just starting to get over everything. I'm saying my prayers and hoping they are working journal. Goodnight.

--- Oh journal my life is over. One of the children was playing in the barn and he found my hair ribbon. He had tied it around his arm. Bessie saw it first and yelled at him to come in the house but he laughed and ran off. Mr. Abraham saw him and grabbed him up and brought him to Bessie. When Bessie went to take the ribbon off his arm Mr. Abraham said "That looks like one of the girl's hair ribbons." He took it from Bessie and said "I better give this to your Mama, she will have a fit if she knows you have been snitching your sisters' hair ribbons." Rubin got mad and said "I didn't snitch no ribbon it was in the barn by Rebel's stall."

I felt myself go white as a sheet. It was my hair ribbon from the dance. It must have fell off when I brought the horse back for Miss Nancy. Bessie saw my face and shooed me out of the kitchen before Mr. Abraham could see me. I ran up here to look for my ribbons and sure enough one is missing. Oh journal I don't know what I'm going to do. What if they find out it's mine? I am almost afraid to go back downstairs. Please Lord don't let them find out it is mine.

--- What a terrible day. Last night I was so scared and nobody said nothing about the ribbon but this morning after breakfast Mrs. Sarah called all the girls into her study and pulled out the hair ribbon and asked who it belonged to. Nobody said anything. She went on and on about how she tried to have nice things for the girls and if they didn't care anymore about them than to lose them in the barn then why did she bother. When nobody said anything she said she was going to check everybody's ribbon drawer and whose ever it was, was going to be punished. That hair ribbons were for special occasions and not for running around playing in the barn. She went through every girl's room and didn't find the missing ribbon. For some reason she didn't go through mine. I guess she forgot I had a set of ribbons.

I thought I was safe until at dinner Mr. Abraham asked if she found who lost the ribbon. Mrs. Sarah told him how she checked every girls ribbon drawer and they were all there. He then said "Well maybe it was our Nancy's ribbon that she wore to the dance. I guess she could have dropped it when she ran off." Mrs. Sarah hung her head and looked so sad and said "I guess it could be." Mr. Felix told her not to worry her pretty head about a ribbon there was no harm done.

I was holding my breath cause I remember that Miss Nancy had on yellow ribbons in her hair that night and the ribbon that Mrs. Sarah had was white. I hope she don't remember that. If she does she is gonna know it is mine and throw me out of the house for sure. I told Bessie my fears and she told me to just pray about it, that that was all we could do. I sure am praying hard journal. I am praying real hard. Goodnight journal.

--- I am writing this with tears in my eyes. It occurred to Mrs. Sarah sometime today that Miss Nancy was wearing yellow ribbons the night of the dance and she remembered that I was wearing white ones. She came storming up to my room and opened my ribbon drawer but it was empty. She came downstairs like a whirlwind yelling my name. Bessie and I ran into the hallway at the same time. She wanted to know where my white ribbons from the dance were. Before I could say anything Bessie said "I took 'em from her after the dance Mrs. Sarah to starch 'em so they would be ready again if anybody needed 'em. I didn't know that they was just Miss. Nancy's. I thought they were for all the girls." Mrs. Sarah looked at Bessie and at me and asked Bessie where they were. Bessie said "I put 'em in the ribbon drawer off the closet Mrs. Sarah where you keep all the extra ribbons." Mrs. Sarah went into the room and got all the ribbons.

Sure enough my white ribbons was in there but there was only one. Mrs. Sarah asked Bessie where the other one was she said she didn't know maybe one of the boys or the slaves got it and that's how it got into the barn. Mrs. Sarah looked at me and at Bessie and said "Neither of you better be lying to me. If I ever find out that this is your ribbon Nancy Hanks you are as good as gone and Bessie you better not be covering for Miss Nancy cause if you are you ain't too old to get horsewhipped for lying." She stomped off back upstairs.

I looked at Bessie and her forehead was sweating but she was smiling. "I got the idea last night Miss Nancy. I knew Mrs. Sarah would remember Miss Nancy's ribbons was yellow and yourins was white so I went to your room and got your ribbon and starched it and put it with the others. She will think it's yours but she can't be sure. As long as she ain't sure Mr. Abraham won't let her kick you out of the house." I hugged Bessie with all my might. She had saved me but I didn't want to be the cause of her getting horsewhipped. I told her that and she said "As long as you don't go telling nobody then nobody's gonna know."

Bessie is the best friend I ever have had in the world. If I was able to free her right now I would. We finished out the days chores but Mrs. Sarah keeps looking at me mean. She knows it's my ribbon. I am afraid she is going to make life hard around here for me. I have to keep my mouth shut because I don't want Bessie to get no whipping. I guess sometimes you got to tell a lie to protect people. God can't fault you for telling a lie if it is helps others.

I am going to have to watch out for Mrs. Sarah, with Mr. Felix leaving tomorrow she's going to be in a bad mood anyways. Oh journal I just can't believe that Bessie helped me like that. It just makes me cry that she cares about me so much. I'm glad I help her write letters to her sister up North. She is wonderful. I wish I had had a Mama like Bessie but if I did I wouldn't be me then would I? Goodnight journal.

November - Things have been going well. Mrs. Sarah keeps watching me out of the corner of her eye but she has not said anything else about the ribbon. Richard has been coming back over. He is so sweet. We hold hands and talk about the future. He wants to own a big farm someday and have lots of children. He always squeezes my hand and blushes when he talks about having children. Tonight he kissed me on the lips. It was sweet and not like the hard passionate kisses that I got from John but I liked it.

I talked with Polly Price and Nancy Leake at church and they said that I am the first girl he has ever been sweet on. I think I may have to teach Richard a few things when we get married.

It has started getting really cold in the evenings so we have to keep more wood on the porch for the fire. I was getting some wood tonight for Bessie when Mr. Abraham came up the steps. He asked how Richard and I were getting along. I told him just fine. He said "Has he kissed you yet? I blushed and said yes but just one time. He laughed and said "I can't believe you are blushing over a kiss. It's not like it's your first one girl." I smiled and said "It was my first one like this." He stopped laughing and came closer to me and said "Show me." I asked "Show you what?" He said "How he kissed you." I leaned over and lightly kissed him on the lips the way Richard had kissed me.

He grabbed my head and pushed me against the wall and he kissed me deep pushing his tongue deep in my mouth, biting my lips and squeezing my breast hard. When he moved his face back I could barely breathe. He was still squeezing my breast hard and he said "Now that's the way a man kisses a woman. Did you like it? Nancy, tell me did you like it?" I could still taste the tingle of blood on my bottom lip and my breast was throbbing from his grasp. My loins were on fire. Did I like it? Oh yes I liked it. I just shook my head yes.

He let go of me and said "Good. That's lesson one. The kiss. We will work on it so you will know what a man likes. You want to make Richard happy don't you Nancy?" I said "Yes sir I do." "Well," he said "Then it will make me happy if you let me teach you how to make him happy. I want you to learn how to be a real woman Nancy." I was starting to breathe again and I said "I do want to learn how to be a real woman Mr. Abraham. Thank you for offering to teach me. I will try to learn good." He smiled and said "I'm sure you will Nancy. You are a smart girl. Now we can't say anything about this as Mrs. Sarah would not let me teach you anything and you want to surprise Richard on your wedding night right?" I said "Right."

I was trembling all over when I brought the wood in. Bessie noticed that Mr. Abraham came in the house behind me. She pulled me to the side and asked me if everything was alright. I told her everything was fine. She said "Mr. Abraham ain't trying to pester you none is he?" I thought about the lie about the ribbon and decided it was ok to tell Bessie a little lie about Mr. Abraham. "No," I said "I was just cold." Her eyes got narrow and she said "Girl you need to be careful about Mr. Abraham. He got the eye for you." I laughed and said "Bessie Mr. Abraham ain't like that." She just said "he's a man ain't he and all men are like that even Mr. Abraham." I told her not to worry he weren't pestering me.

He's just teaching me I thought, that's different. He just wants to help me be a better wife to Richard. Thank goodness I got Mr. Abraham to help get me ready for this life and he's right Mrs. Sarah wouldn't allow it at all. I been sitting here in my room thinking about Mr. Abraham and excited about learning how to be a real woman. I am ready to learn. Goodnight journal.

December - Mr. Abraham was teaching me how to kiss better today in the barn when Mr. Felix came walking in. He pushed me aside like I was poison. Mr. Felix didn't say anything about it. He just looked at me and said "I think Bessie is looking for you in the kitchen." Mr. Abraham started to say something and Mr. Felix just held up his hand and said "I think Nancy ought to go now Abraham before Bessie sends someone else to find her don't you?"

I tidied up and ran to the kitchen to see Bessie and see what she needed. Bessie looked surprised when I asked her and said "I ain't seen Mr. Felix, didn't even know he was here." Then she pulled some straw from my hair and asked me what I was doing in the barn? I said I had chased the cat in there trying to get a biddie back that he snatched. She just raised her eyebrows and said "Don't let Mrs. Sarah see straw in your hair she be thinking the worst."

I didn't see Mr. Abraham or Mr. Felix until dinner. After dinner when I was getting the children ready for bed I heard Mr. Felix and Mrs. Sarah just a laughing downstairs. He always makes her happy. I don't think he will tell her what he saw today but I don't know. Am I sinning cause I'm letting Mr. Abraham teach me these things? I just don't know anymore. The bible tells me one thing but Mr. Abraham tells me something else. I asked him if this was a sin and he told me no that we weren't sinning cause we weren't hurting nobody. He said a sin is when you hurt somebody and as long as I don't tell ain't nobody getting hurt. I know he must be right being a magistrate and all. Mr. Abraham is a smart man and he knows his bible better than I do. I got to get some sleep cause we start cooking tomorrow for the big meeting this week. Everybody in town is coming over it seems like, even Richard. I'm looking forward to seeing Richard. Maybe he'll kiss me too. Goodnight journal.

--- It was a big day journal, people started coming early and they came all day long. Richard got here but he was talking with the men. We had tables set up all around the house. I'm glad it wasn't real cold outside. After everybody ate Mr. Abraham stood up and told them all he wanted to go to Oconoluftee and start up a town there. He said he had some land and he could get some land for the others real cheap if they wanted to go. He said it would be a good opportunity.

Everybody was talking about it. He told them to think about it and he was planning to leave in the late spring to go up there and whoever wanted to go was welcome to go with him. Everybody was talking so Richard and I went out on the porch. He was so glad to see me he hugged me tight and kissed me quick on the lips. He told me he wanted to go with Mr. Abraham and that he could start a farm and build us a house up there. I was so excited that I threw my arms around his neck about that time Mr. Felix came out on the porch. Richard pulled away from me and Mr. Felix said "Well I heard you and Nancy was courting' I guess it's true." Richard blushed and said "Yes it was true he was callin' on me now." Mr. Felix said "Congratulations she is a nice girl." He kinda looked right through me and I was blushing all way down my neck.

I told Richard I had to go help Bessie and I would see him at church on Sunday. I left them there talking on the porch. Mr. Felix knows everything about me, but when he comes around things always seem to go bad with the men in my life. I sure hope nothing happens with Richard. I just couldn't bear it. Well, I got a lot of cleaning to do tomorrow so I'm going to say my prayers and go to sleep. Goodnight journal.

--- Today was Christmas. Mrs. Sarah gave me a heavy winter dress. It wasn't new but I didn't care I love it. Richard rode over and gave me a shawl, he said it had belonged to his mother. It is so special. He said he is making arrangements for the trip this coming spring. I am so excited. We are going to start a new life in Oconoluftee. It will be a wonderful place to raise our children.

Bessie has sure kept me busy since the big meeting. I don't have a minute to myself anymore. She had a hundred things for me to do in the house every day. I asked her if she was mad at me and she just put her arms across her bosom and said "I ain't mad child I just love you like my own and somebody needs to look out for you." When I asked her why I needed looking out for she just huffed and said "Idle hands are the devil's workshop, go get busy." It was alright cause she had made pound cakes for Christmas and I got a special piece just for myself. I am so happy. I love Christmas and today I especially love Bessie. I hope I can make cakes like her someday for my children. Goodnight journal, Merry Christmas!

In the year of our Lord 1803 …..

January - It's a new year and my service with the Enloes will be up this summer. Maybe by then Richard will have our house built and we can get married and then I can work for the Enloes for some extra money. Mrs. Sarah has been making lists of things she will need for the trip. She has been in a better mood since she got the letter from Miss Nancy. It seems she and John Thompson have a house and some land in Kentucky and are doing well. She is not going to be too far away from the land in Oconoluftee I think, so maybe we can go see her I hope. She told Mrs. Sarah to tell me hello in the letter. Mrs. Sarah looked at me awful hard when she told me but Mr. Abraham told her to leave it be, that Nancy had liked me and that was all it was. I hope she never ever finds out about my part in that. She would never forgive me even now.

Mr. Abraham sure has been quiet since Mr. Felix left he don't hardly look at me anymore but I been too busy to ask him if anything is wrong. We sure got a lot to do between now and this spring. It's going to be so much fun. Bessie said she heard there was Indians up there. I ain't never seen an Indian before. I wonder if they wear clothes or just run around naked like the preacher says. He calls them savages but Bessie says these are friendly ones. We'll see I guess. Goodnight journal.

March - It has been way too busy to write. Mrs. Sarah has got the house upside down getting things packed and put up. Bessie says Mr. Abraham is going to rent the house out. I sure will miss Puzzle Creek. It's been my first real home.

Richard has started talking about marriage lately. I told him he needed to ask me first. He got all embarrassed and said he had to ask Mr. Abraham for permission. I told him that was silly cause Mr. Abraham already knew. He said that he had to ask him anyway cause it was the right thing to do. He is going to talk to him Sunday after church.

Bessie asked me to write a letter for her to her sister since she is headed out to the wilderness. She wanted to make sure she knew where she was. I told her I would next chance I got. I got a minute to talk to Mr. Abraham alone today. I asked him if I had done anything to make him mad at me. He said no but he had thought a lot about my "lessons" and decided that maybe I knew enough about being a good wife and he needed to just trust me on my own. I don't know why but I felt disappointed. I thanked him for what he had taught me and he got all red in the face and told me not to thank him. He didn't even want me to think about it ever again. He just wanted me to concentrate on my cooking and sewing skills. That those were things I would need.

Bessie came running out back where we were and said she needed me in the kitchen right away. She sure gave Mr. Abraham a hard look before she came back in. She asked me what he was talking to me about. I told her he was telling me I needed to work on my cooking and sewing skills for when I had my own house someday. She looked relieved and when I asked her what she needed she said she forgot and for me to go check on the baby. Bessie sure acts strange sometimes. Goodnight journal.

April - It's happening, we started packing the wagons today. Mrs. Sarah says it will take a week to get everything ready. Everybody that is going is all going together. The children were a handful today constantly getting in the way. Mrs. Sarah finally had me take the smaller ones down to the orchard to play and away from the wagons.

It was so nice and warm today. We were running and playing hide and seek. I had unbuttoned my blouse some and pulled up my skirts and tucked them in my waistband so I could chase the children. I was running through the orchard when I ran headlong into Mr. Abraham. I hit him so hard we both went down. As I tried to get up I realized I was straddling him with my bare legs showing. He took both hands and ran them up my legs under my skirt. I could barely breathe. He was breathing hard and I could feel him stirring underneath me. He was rubbing me hard with his hands and said "You like this don't you Nancy?" I said "Yes Mr. Abraham I do." He started moving my hips over him and said "God help me I like it too."

About that time one of the children started yelling and he let me go. I jumped up and quickly pulled my skirt back down. He jumped up and looked around for the children. I told him they were hiding for hide and seek. He put his hand out and touched my breast lightly. "You would tempt a saint, girl" he said, "and God knows I ain't no saint." He dropped his hand from me. "I said I'm sorry Mr. Abraham I didn't mean to tempt you." He said "Don't be sorry girl the fault's not yours." He looked so sad it about broke my heart.

He left and I gathered the children up. When I got to my room tonight I got to wondering. Did I tempt him? Did I tempt Adam and John? Was it me that caused these things to happen? I had read about temptresses in the bible. I didn't think I was one of those but maybe I need to ask Bessie. She would know. I don't want to be the cause of men doing bad things? I'll talk to Bessie when I help her with her letter. She will set me straight. Goodnight journal.

--- Mrs. Sarah had to go to town today so I sat down to write a letter for Bessie. She told her sister all about us moving and where we were going. She talked about the family and Richard asking Mr. Abraham for permission to marry me when he gets a house ready in Oconoluftee. She told her sister to pray for me and her that we would make the trip alright and that the savages would be friendly. It was a nice letter.

When we finished she got us both a piece of warm bread with fresh butter. I can bake but no where near as good as Bessie. I asked her if she thought I was a temptress? She laughed and said "Child why would you ask such a thing?" I told her I was wondering if the bad things that happened with Adam and John was my fault because I was a temptress.

She thought on it for a minute and said "Child I guess all women are temptresses. It's just the way God made us. It ain't that it's a bad thing unless you use it for bad things. Men are just tempted by woman. It says so in the bible all over the place. Look how Eve tempted Adam. Men got to learn how to leave women alone. It's hard for them cause it ain't in their nature. That's why they go to church and get married and still some of 'em can't get over it. Some women know this and they just use a man's weakness against him and then again some men are just weaker than others. Who done called you a temptress missy?" I just told her I heard some of the men talking about it and got to wondering. Bessie said "Men are just men and you can't expect them to be any different. You just gotta learn how to live with 'em." I told her I didn't think Rev. Joe was like that and she laughed and said "No he done give that part of hisself to God not like Mr. Abraham." I said "Oh Mr. Abraham ain't like that." She said "Child, when Mr. Abraham gets to drinking he really likes the women. I done heard stories from town about him. Now don't get me wrong Mr. Abraham is a fine man and some of them girls said he is real fine" and she laughed, "But even a fine man can get randy with the devil's juice in him and Mr. Abraham likes his spirits." Then she said "I know you done seen how he looks at you sometimes, it's been all I could do to keep you busy and away from him. Mr. Felix done told me I needed to keep you busy in the house and watch Mr. Abraham around you."

I blushed down to my toes and said "I don't mean to tempt Mr. Abraham." She said "Child don't take it so hard, it's best that you know especially since you gonna be a married woman before years end. Mr. Abraham is a good man and he keeps a good house but he is a man after all. It ain't your fault you done growed up so pretty and goodness knows you done been with two men and that kinda shows on a girl. It's just a natural kinda thing that men sense. I think that Mr. Richard will be good for you. He don't seem to see things as strong as some other men do." I asked her if Mr. Felix said anything else to her about me. She said Mr. Felix was my friend and he felt responsible for me since he was the one that brought me to this house. She said he had my best interests at heart. I was glad he didn't tell her about me and Mr. Abraham in the barn that day.

Mrs. Sarah got back and everything got hopping as usual. I am sitting here journal wondering about what Bessie said today. About women and men and how there natures are. I just need to figure out where I fit in. Surely people can overcome those feelings and just have them for their husbands and wives and about strong drink, my poor Uncle Dickie drank so much that it killed him when the house caught on fire. Drink just ain't good for men and my Mama was a temptress. That much I do know. My brain is tired thinking about all this. Goodnight journal.

--- This is my last night at Puzzle Creek. I am going to miss this place. It was my first real home. I may not get to write much on the trip. I saw Richard for just a bit today, everything is so busy we ain't had no time to talk much. I wonder if my Mama will ever come back this way looking for me. I did go say goodbye to Mandy this morning. I gave her one of my shawls to remember me by. She seems so happy with her new Mama and Papa. They love her a lot. I know she will have a good life.

Rev. Joe decided to go with us so Bessie is happy that she can still get letters to her sister. She was worried about that. Polly Price, Widow Byrd, and Nancy Leake are coming to say bye in the morning. I will miss them. I am starting on a new life tomorrow headed to a new place. I'm going to get married and live in a house in the mountains and raise happy children that all read and write and I'm going to learn to bake a pound cake just like Bessie so I can make one for Christmas and birthdays. Nobody ever cared about my birthday but I will about all my children. Their birthdays will be the most special day of all. To hold a little body that belongs to me and loves me completely will be the most special thing of all. Goodnight journal tomorrow will come early.

May - We have been here for a week now. The house is nice it looks a lot like the one in Puzzle Creek. Mrs. Sarah said they been building on it for a year now for Mr. Abraham. It looks almost finished to me. Mrs. Sarah and Mr. Abraham have gone with Mr. Felix to visit some new homesteads so I got a chance to write. So much has happened I just don't know where to start. I am hoping that writing it down will make it make more sense to me. I guess I'll just start from when we left.

There was ten families in all going to Oconoluftee along with Mr. Felix and Rev. Joe. We rode for a couple of weeks up through the gorge. It was beautiful riding along the river. Some Indian guides met us near the big rock chimney to guide us onto Oconoluftee. They told us tales at night around the camp fires of the little people who lived in the mountains and the wood spirits who took the form of women to seduce men so they could have Changeling children. The Indians said these children were powerful spirits who could do magic. They said any man who was brave enough to lie with a wood spirit would gain wisdom and riches. Bessie laughed and said even Indian men made up stories about women.

It was a good time. We all worked together and helped look after each other and the children. At night I would sing around the campfire. The Indians said I sang like the wind spirits. They sometimes would sing me the wind songs. When we were about a week away from here we were met by some other Indians. They had just caught a deer and offered to share it with us. It was really hot that day so Mr. Abraham made camp early so they could skin and cook the deer. We helped cut the meat and put it on the pot to boil. The Indians dug some ground up and put hot coals from the fire in there and then wrapped some of the deer in leaves and buried it to cook. We had potatoes boiling and deer meat in the stew. It got so hot that the children were sitting under the wagons to play. The men once the deer was in the ground went down to the river. Bessie said she saw Mr. Abraham take a couple of jugs of whiskey with them.

We cooked in the heat and finally we went to sit in the shade by the wagons. Later that evening the men came back up to the camp laughing and singing. Mrs. Sarah and some of the wives were fit to be tied because the men had been drinking whiskey. We fixed food for everybody. Bessie said that would quiet the men down. It seemed to for a bit and then the Indians pulled out some jugs of their own and they all started drinking again. They were sitting by the fire drinking and singing and telling stories. We had cleaned up and I asked Bessie when the meat from the pit would be ready. She said we would dig it up tomorrow before we left out. Everybody was tired from the heat and the food. Bessie went over to talk to the other slaves and I told her I was going down to the river to wash out my hair. I was hot and nasty and my hair was full of smoke. She gave me a bit of Mrs. Sarah's rose soap and told me to be careful.

It was a full moon so the path to the river was well lit. I got down by the river and put my hands in it. It felt so cool and wonderful after the heat of the day. The rocks had formed a semi-circle so that there was a pool near the bank. I undid my hair and stuck my head in the cool water. It reminded me of the river down in South Carolina. I sat bank on the bank to soap up my hair. The moon was shining on the water turning it to silver in the night. It was so beautiful. I could hear the sounds from the camp far off. It sounded like they were still laughing and singing. I decided to just take a quick swim and bathe in the pond. I had not had a proper bath for three weeks. I quickly took off my clothes and plunged into the water. It was much colder than I expected but still felt wonderful after so long without a bath. I soaped up good with the rose soap and washed my hair then I just sat and felt the cool water around me.

After a bit I stood up in the pond with my back to the bank and raised my hands towards the moon and stretched. I felt like as much a part of nature as one of the trees. I heard a gasp behind me on the riverbank. I spun around and there stood Mr. Abraham. He said "Glory be I done found myself a wood spirit." Before I could move he had rushed into the pond and picked me up. He smelled like strong whiskey and tobacco. He said "Wood spirit, I know what you want and I'm the man to give it to you" then he kissed me hard and deep. I pulled my head away and said "Mr. Abraham I'm not a wood spirit I'm Nancy, Nancy Hanks."

He looked deep in my eyes and then held me away from him and said "Stand in the moonlight and let me look at you." I just stood there trembling and said "See Mr. Abraham I am Nancy." He walked all way around me looking me all over and then he ran his hands up and down my body and said "You know me, Spirit, you know what shape I desire." Again, I told him "I am not a spirit I am Nancy." He just grabbed me and held me tighter and said "You're not going to trick me into letting you go. I know what you want and I'm going to give it to you."

He started kissing me and touching me all over. I was burning with desire but again I said "I am not a spirit I am Nancy." He laughed and said "Well Nancy then you done let a Spirit possess you. You smell like roses and sunshine, don't no woman smell like that that I've ever been with."

I felt so strange with him all over me and being naked in the moonlight and I wondered was he right? Had I been possessed by a wood spirit? Is that why I took off all my clothes and was raising my hands to the moon in the water when Mr. Abraham saw me? He was touching me and getting more and more urgent. He kept saying "I'm going to give you want you seek Spirit."

He stripped off his clothes and laid me down on the mossy river bank. He looked deep into my eyes and said "Do you like this" as he touched me inside. I nodded my head yes. I was embarrassed but I did like it. He laughed and said "You do like it don't you spirit?" I nodded yes. He then said "Do you want me to take you Spirit?" I just looked at him and he said "Answer me Spirit" as he probed harder and harder with his hands. "Do you want me?" he said, "Say it, say it out loud." I moaned and decided to let the Spirit take me over and said "Yes, I want you, I want you now."

He threw my legs wide apart and thrust himself deep into me. I cried out in pain and he put his hand over my mouth. "Hush, spirit" he said "I am not sharing you with any of the others tonight." He kept thrusting saying "Are you going to be quiet spirit?" I shook my head yes. He moved his hand from my mouth and kept pounding harder and harder. I saw the sweat pop out on his face.

He said "Move with me Witch. I need you to move with me." I began to move my hips with him, moaning with passion. He said "Oh yeah that's more like it." He got faster and faster until I was moaning loudly. He softly yelled and spent himself and collapsed on top of me. I was lying still and trying to breathe as he was a big man. He raised up on one arm and looked at me. Still keeping himself in me he began to touch me and suckle my breast. His teeth biting my nipples softly then getting harder and harder. He laughed and said "You are a witch" when I felt him stirring in me again. He said "I going to give it to you again spirit. You will get your money's worth out of me tonight" and he took me again.

This time it was slower and he took more time. It did not hurt and I was meeting him stroke for stroke. I felt the wood spirit in me strong. I pulled his hair, bit his lip, scratched his back. He laughed and said "Now that's how it's done." He finished and pulled out of me. He rested for a bit beside me with his arm thrown over me. I stirred some and he said "Oh no, I'm not letting you go yet spirit. I been hungering for Nancy for a long time and I'm gonna get my fill tonight with you." I remember telling him to do what he would with me. He said "Don't worry Spirit, I plan to."

He teased me and touched me and stroked me until I moaned with desire wanted him to take me again. He said "You are in fact a witch for only a witch could do this to me." He placed my hand on him and he was hard and strong again. He grabbed me by the waist and rolled me over on top of him and placed me over him. As he slid me down onto him it took my breath. I felt like I was being split in two. He started moving me up and down and said "Now you do it, do it until it quits hurting. It will you know, the more you move. You take me this time spirit. You want my seed then you work for it."

I began to move, I had never felt like this before. He held my breasts tightly as I moved over him. I felt the moon and the trees in me as I came crashing over him. He was bucking me like a horse until we were both spent. He rolled me off of him and whispered "I have never felt like this before." I said "Me neither." He sleepily said "Well you should get your Changeling out of this night."

He closed his eyes and after a few minutes I realized he was asleep. I slid out from under his arm and went down to the river and washed myself off. I looked at my body in the moonlight and did not recognize myself. I must truly be possessed. I heard Mr. Abraham snoring so I quickly put my clothes back on and hurried back up the path to camp.

Everyone was sleeping in the wagons. Bessie and a few of the other slaves were still talking quietly by the fire pit. I walked up to Bessie and was trembling like a leaf. I was coming back into myself and was terrified. Bessie saw me and said girl what done took you so long. Then she saw how I was shaking all over and said "Lordy, Lordy girl did you see a spirit down by the river." I shook my head yes. She got me a blanket and told me to lie down beside her. She put her arms around me and said "Don't be scared child, it's all right ain't nothing gonna bother you with ole Bessie here beside you." I buried my face in her chest like a little child and feel asleep listening to her heart beat.

She woke me up the next morning to help fix breakfast and asked if I was feeling better. I told her yes. I was feeling better and wondered if last night was a dream except I was sore when I tried to walk and ached like I had been beat. I bent over to pick up some wood for the cook fire and my breast just ached. After I got the fire going I stopped and went behind the wagon and unbuttoned my dress. I had dark bruises on my breasts and even some light bite marks. I buttoned my dress up quickly so nobody would see. It must have been real. It wasn't a dream.

I went back out to the fire and the men were staring to stir. Several went down to the river to relieve themselves. A while went by when they come walking back up the path with Mr. Abraham between them. His head was soaking wet and they were laughing at him for passing out buck naked on the river bank. They said he starting telling them some wild story about being seduced by a wood spirit coming out of the water naked. They figured he was still drunk from last night and threw him in the river. He was wet and laughing with them when Mrs. Sarah went and took him by the arm and said she didn't not want to hear any more foolishness from him or any of the other men. For them to just get it out of their system and go eat some breakfast. She was just a fussing talking about whiskey making men plumb crazy in the head.

Bessie was laughing and said men was just little boys in big bodies, said Mr. Abraham done let them Indian tales go to his head. She said he'll feel foolish when he sobers up some more. We stayed busy digging up the deer and wrapping it to eat later, we packed up and started off. By late afternoon Mr. Abraham and some of the other men were looking right green in the face. Mrs. Sarah said it served them right drinking and acting like fools. I stayed in the wagon away from Mr. Abraham. I didn't see him until the next day. He walked past me and I was too scared to speak. He stopped and said "Are you alright girl? You look like you done seen a ghost." I said I was fine and he walked on. He didn't seem to remember any of it especially my part. If it hadn't been for the bruises I might have thought it was a dream. Maybe I was possessed by a spirit.

We traveled onto to the house and Mr. Abraham never said anything and he did not treat me any different than he did before. Richard tried to talk to me but I didn't want to talk to any man. Bessie was laughing when she told him I got scared by a river spirit and he laughed with her. I stayed close to Bessie for the whole trip after that. We got here and got unpacked.

I been sitting up here in my room wondering what really happened that night down by the river. Was I possessed by a spirit that seduced Mr. Abraham? I kept telling him I was Nancy but it was like he couldn't hear me and now he don't remember any of it. I just don't know what to think. Did I sin if I was possessed? The bible talked about people who got possessed by the devil. Is that what it was like. I am just going to have to try to put this out of my mind or it will drive me crazy. I wish I could talk to Bessie about it but I don't think I better say anything to anybody. I don't want them thinking I am a witch or something. I'm just going to try to work harder and read my bible and pray and try to be nicer to Richard, poor boy he didn't do anything wrong and he's working hard to build us a house. I hope years from now when I read this it will make more sense to me. Right now I'm just all jumbled up inside about it. I am going to go downstairs and see if Bessie needs me. I feel better just being near her. Oh journal, if you were a person I'd ask you to pray for me.

June - Things are starting to settle down. Richard is coming along with the cabin and we are holding church in the schoolhouse that Mr. Abraham built. I only have a few more weeks till my service is up with the Enloes. I have decided to put the past behind me. Rev. Joe says we are all in a new place and it's a new start. Richard and I talked to him about marrying us as soon as he finishes the cabin. He thinks it will be a wonderful start to our life together. Rev. Joe told me that I needed to put my past behind me and concentrate on my future. He said my future is whatever I make it to be.

I sang two solos at church today and I felt like God was right there in the building with us. Mr. Felix told me he was proud of me today, that I had grown up to be a fine woman. I keep dreaming of having my own house with children playing in the yard the only bad thing is I always dream there's a storm a comin' on the horizon. Good night journal.

July - Well today was the day. My servitude is up. Mr. Felix stood up at dinner and talked about how he brought me to the Enloes. It seems like a hundred years ago now. He talked about how well Mrs. Sarah taught me and her Christian charity in taking me in. He talked about me being a hard worker and having earned my place in the community. He said he was proud that I was going to marry Richard and be a neighbor. Mrs. Sarah even smiled. Mr. Abraham then said I could stay on and help with the children but that I would be paid a wage from now on and Mrs. Sarah said if I liked I could come and help her with the children.

It was a joyous day. Bessie even made my favorite pound cake. I am so happy I could just burst. I think I ate too much pound cake because I sure have a stomach ache tonight. Stomach ache or not it's still the best night of my life. Goodnight journal.

--- I have had a stomach ache for several days now and this morning when Bessie was frying ham I had to go outside. I have never had food turn my stomach before. I couldn't eat breakfast. I told Mrs. Sarah I wasn't feeling well she looked at me and said "You don't have good color" and sent me to my room. Bessie came up and brought me some broth. I ate all of it and was feeling much better by lunchtime.

Richard came by after supper. He said the cabin should be finished in a couple of weeks and we can plan our wedding. I just laughed and said I been planning all my life. We been getting closer and closer. Tonight he kissed me hard and I kissed back. He was breathing hard when he pulled back and kinda laughed and said "I have to control myself with you Nancy, it won't be long through." I laughed and said "No it won't" and I kissed him again. Mr. Abraham came out on the porch and Richard said he would be going.

After Richard left Mr. Abraham sat down on the porch steps and asked me if I was happy. I told him I was the happiest I had ever been. He smiled and said "I'm glad. You know that's all I ever really wanted was for you to be happy. You deserve happiness Nancy more than anybody I know." I thanked him and was about to go in when he said "You do know I care for you don't you Nancy?" I turned around and said "Why Mr. Abraham I love you and Mrs. Sarah too." He smiled and said that was good but for me to always feel like I could come to him if I ever had a problem. He said "I will always try to be here for you Nancy." He stood up and I ran over and hugged him tight and then ran in the house before he could say anything.

My stomach had butterflies in it I was so happy. I decided I was hungry and went in to ask Bessie if she had any ham left from dinner. She fixed me a slice on some fresh bread and a cold glass of milk. It tasted like heaven. She said shore glad to see you got your appetite back girl. I hugged her and said the world was just wonderful. It is journal, the world is just wonderful. Goodnight journal.

August - I have not been able to eat breakfast for a couple of weeks now and I feel the butterflies in my stomach all the time and my dress is getting tighter around the waist and my bosom. I just don't understand it. I am hungry all the time after lunchtime. Bessie told me just today that I was eating dinner like a farmhand. She laughed and said now that I was getting married in a couple of weeks I was getting fat.

It just turned August here and the afternoons are hot. Bessie says it's called Dog Days. She's right, even the dogs just lie around in the evening. Richard and I were walking a bit in the orchard when the butterflies in my belly got real strong and I had to sit down. He asked me if I was feeling ok and I told him I was just eating too much since we moved here.

We spooned for a while and he put his arms around me to kiss me and said "You are putting on a little bit of weight but it feels good to me" and he laughed. I pressed up close against him and said "You feel good to me too." He kissed me again and said "I don't know if I can wait much longer Nancy. I want you powerful bad." I said "I want you too Richard." He went to kiss me again and started to rub my breast when I yelped. He jumped back like I shot him and said "I didn't mean to hurt you I am so sorry." I looked at him surprised and rubbed my breasts myself. They did hurt and felt all full and funny. I leaned up against him and said "It's just a woman thing, they'll feel better tomorrow." He smiled and said as long they feel better by our wedding night. I told him not to worry it would be a night to remember.

We walked back to the house so he could leave. I went inside and asked Bessie if I could have some bread and butter as I was powerful hungry. She fixed me some and told me to sit down with her for a bit. She started asking me if I was still sick in the morning but better by noon. I said yes, she said "You been putting on a little weight too ain't you." I said "Yes." She said "Anything else funny or strange going on?" I told her about the butterflies and about my bosom feeling sore when I touched it.

She looked at me real hard and said "Now Miss Nancy, have you and young Mr. Richard been lying together like man and wife after what all I told you." I told her no, I been waiting like she told me to even though it sure has been hard. She shook her head and said "When was your last pass of the moon child?" I thought a minute and said "I think it was when we just started on the trail. Maybe that's what's wrong, it's just been building up cause of all the excitement of moving here." Bessie with a very worried look on her face told me to go on up to bed and let her study on it tonight. We could talk tomorrow. I bet that's what it is, just all that stuff needing to come out of me, no wonder I been feeling so strange. Maybe she had a medicine that could bring it on. Goodnight journal.

--- Journal, oh journal it just can't be true, it just can't. This morning I was sick again, even Mrs. Sarah noticed it and was looking at me funny. She asked me if my dress was getting too tight cause it was pulling across my chest and gaping this morning. I told her I was just eating too much and she looked at me and said "Well it ain't been breakfast." Her face looked like a black cloud all day.

Bessie pulled me aside after lunch and said we needed to go see her friend that lived down at the river. She was an old slave midwife and might can help me. We went down to her friend's cabin and she told me she needed to check me out. She had me unbutton my dress and she felt my bosom and asked me if they were fuller and felt heavy and sore to touch. I told her yes, she then told me it was going to be embarrassing but she needed to look at my privates. I asked her why and she said she needed to see what color they was.

I pulled my skirt up and let her look. She just said uh huh and told me to lie down on the table. She then pulled my skirt up over my belly and put her hand on it. She stood up and called Bessie into the house and told Bessie to put her hand on my belly. I was having awful bad butterflies. Bessie laid her hand on my belly and jerked her head up wide-eyed. She looked at her friend and said "How far?" Her friend said "I'd say a couple of months or more."

I stood up and pulled my skirt down and said "A couple of months what?" Bessie sat me down by the table and told me that I was with child. I just shook my head and said "I can't be. Richard and I have never laid together that way." She said it must have happened on the trip out here. I started to cry and Bessie asked me what happened. I told her about being possessed by the wood spirit and Mr. Abraham. I told her everything. She and her friend just sat there. When I finished she said "It's all my fault. I promised Mr. Felix I would watch you and protect you from Mr. Abraham and I let you go to the river. Oh Lordy, Lordy it done be's my fault." I told her it weren't Mr. Abraham's fault, he thought I was a wood spirit. She shook her head and said when a man's drinking he'll say anything to justify what his base nature wanted. I told her I wanted it too so it had to be the wood spirit. She said it didn't make no never mind the wood spirit wasn't here now and I was.

I looked at her and asked what am I gonna do? She talked to her friend that said she could make a drink that could cause me to lose the child but I was pretty far along and it might not work. I jumped up and grabbed my stomach yelling ain't nobody gonna hurt my baby, nobody. Bessie got me calmed down and said well if you want to keep it then we got other problems. First you got to tell Mr. Abraham so he can figure out what to do. He is a good man and this is his responsibility. Mr. Abraham ain't one to shirk responsibility.

I just hung my head and said I just don't know how to tell him. Bessie said "Well you better figure it out quick cause you gonna be showing in a couple weeks." Then I thought of Richard and I started to cry. "What will I tell Richard I said? We are supposed to get married in a couple of weeks." Bessie's friend said "Just marry him and then tell him, he can think it's his. We can always say it come early. Why women do that all the time."

I held my head up and said "I can't do that to Richard, he is a fine man and deserving of an honest wife." Bessie's friend looked at her and said "Ain't gonna be no easy way out of this one. You just better tell the father quick so you can make some arrangements cause everybody's gonna know soon."

Bessie walked me back to the house crying all the way. She kept saying "I knew bad things were coming by the way he used to look at you but for the life of me I though he was over it. Oh Lord help us all!" I was quiet at dinner and just asked to be excused to go to my room. Mrs. Sarah was still looking at me funny.

What to do? What to do? How am I going to tell Richard and Mr. Abraham and what am I going to do when Mrs. Sarah finds out? Richard ain't gonna want me and Mrs. Sarah won't let me stay here. I got no place to go. Oh little baby of mine what am I gonna do. I have cried till my eyes swelled shut. Oh little baby in me, I will take care of us somehow. I wonder if I was really possessed by a wood spirit will you be a Changeling like the Indians said. Will you be born with magic and wisdom like they said? I am so scared but little baby I love you so much and I will never ever leave you no matter what. Goodnight journal, I'm praying but I don't know if God can hear me.

--- I got up this morning and told Bessie I was headed down to see Richard after lunch. I was gonna tell him I couldn't marry him. I cried last night until I couldn't cry anymore. I am grieving for the life I have lost but I will not grieve for you little baby of mine. You are a precious gift from God and the wind spirit of the mountains. I carry you in my belly with pride.

I got to Richards house and it looked so pretty with the sun shining down on it. Richard had been working on the house and he took a break to stop and talk to me. We walked down to the old oak in the yard where Richard had put a bench for us to sit on. Richard sat down but I told him I needed to stand. He knew looking at my face that something was wrong. He was quiet for a minute and then he asked me what was wrong. I told him that I loved him with all my heart and I wanted him to believe that. He said "And I love you too Nancy. What's wrong, there ain't nothing so bad that we can't work it out together." I then just blurted out that I couldn't marry him in two weeks or ever.

He jumped up and grabbed my arms and said "No, you can't mean that. Our house is almost finished. Who put this idea in your head?" I said "You don't understand Richard, I just can't marry you because I'm with child." He looked so confused and said "That's impossible, we hadn't, I mean it hadn't, you know what I mean, I ain't never touched you that way Nancy. It just ain't possible." I said "It's possible Richard I am with child by another man and I can't marry you."

He just sat back down hard on the bench and put his face in his hands and just shook his head. "I'm awful sorry" I said. He looked up and said "Sorry, you're sorry? Nancy you would not do that sort of thing I know you wouldn't. Who forced themselves on you? Tell me who it was and I'll horsewhip him within an inch of his life." "Oh Richard you can't do that" I said. He looked at me and said "I can and I will. Don't know how a decent man can take advantage of a girl, especially one who is betrothed to another. Go ahead and marry me Nancy and we'll just tell people it's my child. They won't know no better. I'll raise it as my own. I love you Nancy."

I said "Richard it wouldn't be right." He yelled "What's right about any of this, you calling off our wedding with just two weeks notice, you carrying some man's bastard seed in your belly, and somebody evil forced you into this situation. Tell me what's right about any of that. I promised to marry you Nancy and I will. I will stand by you and raise this babe as my own. It's the least I can do to protect you since you been forced against your will into this." I looked at him and said "Richard listen to me I was not forced, no one took me against my will. I let him do it. I don't know why but I let him. It was not an evil or bad man, he was just drinking way too much. It was Mr. Abraham and he don't even remember it."

Richard got really mad and said "Don't be defending that old randy bastard. He made you do it, I know he did." I said "Richard I think I was possessed by a wood spirit that night. He came to me and I just let him have his way. He even asked me if he could and I said yes. He thought I was a wood spirit too." Richard walked around and around the bench and said "Let me get this straight, you think you were possessed by a wood spirit and Mr. Abraham was drunk and told you that you were possessed and then had his way with you and now you are carrying his seed in your belly and he don't know about it." I softly said "Yes."

He grabbed me by the arms. "Nancy, that's crazy, can't you see that's crazy. He made you believe that story so you would agree. Did you yell, did he ever cover your mouth to keep you quiet?" he said. I said "He covered my mouth one time when I yelled cause it hurt, but then he moved his hand away. I was the spirit Richard, I could feel her in me. Mr. Abraham kept calling me spirit. I was willing Richard. That's why I can't marry you. It ain't right to ask you to bear my burden." He just yelled that he was going over to see Mr. Abraham about this right now. I begged him to wait and let me tell him first as he didn't know about the baby. "I come to you first Richard" I said.

He said he would wait till tomorrow but he was coming over after lunch and gonna give Mr. Abraham the horsewhipping he deserved. He said he would talk to me tomorrow. I left and cried all way back to the Enloe's house. I had broken Richard's heart. I could see it in his eyes. I was just gonna have to tell Mr. Abraham soon. I got back to the house and Bessie had me wash my face with cold water. She looked as bad as I did. She just hugged me and said

"Child I would take this misery from you if I could." I told her I needed to go write in my journal. I had to get some of this misery out of me before I talked to Mr. Abraham.

Oh my sweet little baby, you ain't done no harm to nobody. Don't you worry what ever happens I will always be there for you. I've got to go down to supper now. Whatever happens it gonna happen tonight I'm afraid.

--- I'm at Mr. Felix's right now journal. Mr. Abraham is downstairs talking with him. We are leaving for Puzzle Creek as soon as day breaks. I tried to get Mr. Abraham alone so I could tell him but every time I started to talk to him Mrs. Sarah was right there at his elbow. She seemed to know something was up. I wrote him a note to meet me in the barn and slipped it to him at dinner. I saw him read it and crumple it up and throw it towards the fire in the kitchen.

After dinner I slipped out to the barn and waited for him. He came walking in and said "What's wrong Nancy? I can tell you've not been yourself for a few days now. Is it Richard, has he got cold feet?" "No sir" I said, "It's me. I told Richard today I couldn't marry him." He said "Why Nancy, has he been cruel to you, have you met someone else?" "No" I said "It's nothing like that Mr. Abraham." "Well, Nancy, then tell me what it is. I told you that you could always come to me. You know how I feel about you Nancy" he said. "Oh Mr. Abraham" I cried, "do you remember the night by the river when you was drinking so bad and you said you saw a wood spirit come up out of the river." He said "Yes, but that was a dream, it weren't real."

"Yes it was Mr. Abraham" I said with my voice cracking, "It was real sure enough. It was me coming up out of the water. I tried and tried to tell you but you kept calling me a spirit and telling me you wasn't gonna let me get away and after a while I thought I had been possessed by a spirit." He took me in his arms and said "Child why didn't you come to me with this before now. Oh Nancy I am so sorry, I would not have used you like that. It must have been the drink. I love you Nancy. I would never hurt you." "Oh Mr. Abraham I cried "It is too late I am with increase" and I put my hands on my belly. "That's why I can't marry Richard, it weren't be right."

He pulled me in his arms and starting stroking my hair trying to get me to stop crying. About that time Mrs. Sarah came bursting out from behind a stall screaming like a madwoman. Mr. Abraham pushed me behind him. Mrs. Sarah was crying and yelling and hitting Mr. Abraham's chest holding the note I had written him. She was screaming "I knew when I brought that white trash daughter of a harlot into my house there would be trouble. She's just like her no good Mama sniffing around a man till she runs him plumb crazy with desire. I've seen her looking at you Abraham and I've seen you looking back. I am no fool."

Bessie ran outside to see what the screaming was about and when she heard Mrs. Sarah she sent one of the houseboys off to fetch Mr. Felix. Mrs. Sarah told Mr. Abraham that he had sinned against her, their children and even worse God. She called him an animal, a rutting pig, said he was like a dog chasing a bitch in heat. She told him God would never forgive him for what he done to her. She then caught sight of me behind him and said "Don't think you are going to get off easy you harlot. You temptress, you knew he was drunk that night by the river and you seduced him by making him think you was an Indian spirit, humph as if those even exist. You used your body to get him to take you ,you Jezebel. You wanted to have his child so he would keep you up didn't you. Well don't think you are going to get a penny of Enloe money for that bastard in your belly."

She then looked at Mr. Abraham and told him he was going straight to hell. I ran up to her and said "Mrs. Sarah it's not his fault he was drinking and thought I was a wood spirit. He's a good man Mrs. Sarah he didn't mean to do no harm. I love you both Mrs. Sarah I wouldn't do nothing to hurt you." She slapped me hard across the face and said "You don't know the first thing about love you white trash liar. Don't ever say that to me again, as a matter of fact don't ever speak to me again." Mr. Abraham got between me and her and tried to calm her down. She just screamed at him to quit protecting his concubine. She yelled at Bessie to get out there. She told Bessie "You take this no good piece of white sickening trash up to her room and pack every single thing she has and then I want you to throw everything she touched out in this yard. Do you hear me Bessie? You take her and do it now."

She turned back to Mr. Abraham and told him to take his clothes he wore on that trip and pile them up on that slut's mattress and burn it all and pray that his soul didn't burn in hell the same way. She yelled at him "Get her and her bastard belly out of my house, out of my sight and I don't ever what to see even a trace of her ever again." She ran in the house and got the chair I had sat in at dinner and threw it out in the yard and said "Burn this damnable chair too. I don't want nothing in this house that she even touched. I want her wiped from my life."

She was walking around in the yard beating at her chest and pulling her hair. Bessie grabbed me and we ran upstairs. Bessie helped me throw all my belongings in a sack. We heard Mr. Felix hollering for Bessie. She yelled back to him that she was in Miss Nancy's room. He took the stairs two at a time. Bessie met him at the top. He said "What in God's name is going on here?" She said "Oh Mr. Felix only the good Lord and you can help us now. Evil done befell this house." He said "What? Bessie, what?" and he saw me standing behind her white as a sheet, my face still red with Mrs. Sarah's handprint on it. Bessie said in a rush "Mr. Abraham got drunk and thought he laid with a spirit but it weren't no spirit it was Miss Nancy possessed of a spirit and now she is with child. Mrs. Sarah done found out and she plumb lost her mind. She be cursing Mr. Abraham and wanting us to burn everything Nancy done touched. That'd be the whole house Mr. Felix. You gots to help us, she be pulling her hair and crying and screaming like a crazy woman." Mr. Felix looked at me and at Bessie and said "Oh My God" and ran downstairs yelling Sarah's name.

We went to the window and watched him get Mrs. Sarah by the arms, she was screaming and crying and beating on his chest. He just pulled her tighter and tighter in his arms until she finally laid his head on his chest and just shook with sobs. My heart was broke, I never ever meant to hurt anybody this bad. Bessie hurried me down the stairs and out the back door. She told me to go down to the slave cabin and wait, that somebody would come and get me soon.

I ran all way down there. No one asked me any questions, they just tried to get me to drink some water and rest. After a bit Mr. Abraham came down with a sack of clothes and two horses. He told me we was going to Mr. Felix's for the night and leave for Puzzle Creek as soon as day broke. We rode over to Mr. Felix's house. He sent me upstairs to sleep but I am too upset so I wanted to write this down. I probably won't get a chance to write on the trip. Poor Richard, I don't know what Mrs. Sarah will say to him when he comes over tomorrow. I did not mean to bring this evil down on our head but I can't feel that you are evil baby. The Indians say you are a Changeling and that means you will be good and wise and have powers. I think maybe the good Lord let the wood spirit enter me so you could come into this world. Rev. Joe says God does everything for a reason. I think you are going to be a mighty powerful reason. We are going to be alright little baby. I just know it. Goodnight journal I don't know when I'll next write.

September - I've been back at Puzzle Creek now for a couple weeks. The renters have been very nice to me. Mr. Abraham explained the situation to them. He took full blame for everything. Polly Price and Nancy Leake came over to see me as soon as they heard I was back. They didn't say too much about the baby and I was just not ready to talk about it much. Mr. Abraham stayed for a few days and made sure I had the things I might need. He gave me some money and told me not to worry he would compensate the Turner's for letting me stay. I was sad to see him go.

I watched his horse from the window until it was out of sight. He told me he would work it all out and I believe him. The trip down here was not bad, it was cool at night but we made do. A couple of his Indian friends met us on the third day to travel with us. It was actually a very peaceful trip. After about a week one of the older Indians would sit with me in the evening and talk while the other men hunted. Somehow he knew the whole story about the baby. I guess word spreads fast with the Indians. He told me stories of the wood spirit taking over young Indian maidens and the children they conceived were very special. They were said to have powers and to be born wise beyond their years. A gift given to them for being Changelings.

He told me I was honored to be chosen for such a great treasure for no common woman could bare a Changeling child. I only half believed him but it was nice to talk to someone about the baby. Mr. Abraham didn't mention it much except to ask if I felt alright every now and again. The old Indian was really wise, when I was still feeling sick in the mornings he fixed me some ground root that he put in water and my sickness went away. He said being sick was a sign of the child's strong spirit. This must be a strong one I laughed. He smiled back. He told me to laugh more it lifted my spirit and made the child happy.

During the coolest nights I slept curled up with Mr. Abraham in his bedroll. He said it was to keep me warm. He never one time tried to touch me on the trip. Near the last day before the Indians left us I had been left alone with the old Indian again. We sat cross legged and held hands while he chanted. Then he smoked a pipe for a while with a sweet smelling tobacco that made me kind of sleepy. He started to tell me of my baby. He told me I would bear a strong and healthy boy, that he would be tall of stature with dark hair and penetrating eyes who could see men's true souls. He said he would grow up to be a great leader of men but at great cost. He warned me to teach him not to get lost in his misery. He put his hands on my belly and sang an Indian song. When he finished I asked him what it was about. He told me he was asking the Great Spirit to watch over and protect this child and to entwine mine and my baby's souls forever through time.

I held my hands over my baby and silently told him that the Indian was right. I would never leave him, not in this life or the next. He then got on his knees and looked directly in my eyes and said "I see great pain in your life, you must work through it. You must be strong for the child. You carry a great chieftain, teach him your strength he will need it." He then stood up and the spirit of the encounter was over. He emptied his pipe and cleaned up around the camp. He fixed me a soup that he said would give me strength for the days to come. I held his hand and thanked him. I meant it, he had been so kind to me.

The others came back and we ate the fresh meat they caught. The next morning the Indians made their leave and as they were leaving the older Indian gave me a small necklace of beads for the baby. Mr. Abraham told me that was a great honor. I thanked him and they rode away. The next night was our last before getting to Puzzle Creek. Mr. Abraham sat by the fire smoking his pipe. I was just sitting and watching the fire. He cleared his throat and said "Nancy, the child agrees with you, you look beautiful sitting there. You are shining like an angel by that fire." I smiled and thanked him.

He said "Please don't be ashamed of this child. It coming into this world is no fault of yours. You never did anything but try to make all of us happy. That's all you ever wanted was happiness and I knew that. I will gladly take the brunt of this sin. I did lust for you in my heart and that's why I was so ready to believe that you were a spirit that night. The sin of this lies at my feet."

I told him to stop, there was no sin. He was not in his right mind and I was overcome with the wood spirit. God meant for this baby to be inside of me and God does not suffer sin so this baby is not a sin. He said "I hope others can see it that way, I truly do but Nancy most people have closed minds and have to put blame on someone." I said "Then they will just have to blame someone else." He smiled and said "You are such a precious jewel child."

He asked me if there was anything he could do for me. I told him to please be kind to Richard for I was afraid I had broken his heart and I know how bad that feels. He asked me if my heart was broken over not marrying Richard. I just told him it was not meant to be and that was that. That night we wrapped up in the bedroll together and he put his arms around me. He said "This is our last time alone together Nancy and I just want to tell you that I do love you." "Oh Mr. Abraham" I said, "I love you too and Mrs. Sarah and Bessie and all the children. You are the only family I have ever known. Please promise me you will go home and make this up to Mrs. Sarah. I can't bear for her to carry such sorrow."

He buried his face in my chest and said "Nancy you are so good, none of us deserved you, none of us." I snuggled up closer to him and told him to get some sleep as we had to get going early. When I woke up he was already getting us some breakfast and packed up camp. We rode in silence all the rest of the way in. I am here now and feeling at a loss. I am not a servant so I have no chores but I can't just sit here. I asked Mrs. Turner if I could help with the house or help teach the children their lessons. She seemed relieved that I wanted to do something. I think it might be ok staying here for a while. Goodnight journal, goodnight baby.

October - The days are getting cooler. Mrs. Turner had helped me alter some of my clothes so I can wear them once the baby gets bigger. I am getting better at sewing these days. I have a much rounder belly that sticks out a little. I guess I am about five months along. Bessie told me before I left that the baby should come sometime in February. I need to make some blankets to help keep him warm. I keep thinking of him as a him since the old Indian told me it was a boy. I need to think about a name soon I guess or maybe I'll wait till I see him first and name him then. Goodnight journal, goodnight baby.

--- We were having a normal day today when we heard a horse come riding up hard. To all our surprise it was Mr. Abraham. He was rushed and out of breath and looked like he had been riding a long time without sleep. After he ate a bite and rested a bit he told me I had to come back with him to Oconoluftee soon as possible. I said "I can't go back there Mr. Abraham, Mrs. Sarah hates me." He told me "Bessie said that after we left Richard came to the house the next day and asked to see you. Mrs. Sarah started screaming at him to go away and he started yelling he wasn't going nowhere till he saw you. Mrs. Sarah then told him that he would never see you again." He asked her what she meant and she said "Mr. Abraham has done took her away out of my sight. I told him not to come back until he got rid of her and you should count yourself lucky that she's gone too." He started yelling at Mrs. Sarah that she nor Mr. Abraham better hurt a hair on my head or he would see to it that they both paid. She yelled back "That white trash done got herself in this mess, not me." Richard told her that Mr. Abraham forced himself on you and everybody knew it. He said "Nancy didn't do anything but love all of you and you treat her like this." She ran him off with a broom screaming and beating in the air.

Richard got upset and told all the settlers what had happened. They all care a great deal for you Nancy and rumors started. Felix tried to tell them I had just taken you back to Puzzle Creek but Richard told them he was afraid that Mrs. Sarah made me kill you and I took you away to do it. The talk got louder and louder. Right before I got back they were rounding up a party to go look for me. I came back home without you and it got worse. There was nothing Felix could say to convince them that I had not done you harm. Then one night Felix came riding up to the house and told me they were putting together a lynching party and I had to go and bring you back as fast as possible. Sarah said no that you could not come back but Felix asked her if she would rather I hang instead? You know Sarah, she didn't answer right away and Felix had to yell at her that they would be there in the hour. She finally said "She can come back but she can't live in my house. I will not have it." Felix said you could stay at his house till he worked something else out.

Bessie packed me a bag and I lit out on a horse riding hard away from there. I could see the faint light of the torches when I left. Felix stayed to talk to the crowd but Nancy you see why you have to come back. If I don't come back with you I am afraid they will not only hang me but burn down my house leaving Sarah and the children homeless and without a father." I told him we could leave as soon as he was rested. He told me to put some things together and we would leave at day break. Well little baby here we go again on a long trip. At least I don't get sick in the mornings anymore. Good night journal, good night baby. We got some busy times ahead.

--- We made it back here in record time. We would ride and then sleep a couple hours and ride again. It was really cool at night so we had some furs to sleep with. The Indians met us again and rode with us through the mountains. Mr. Abraham said he didn't want to push me but I am young and felt strong. The old Indian made me the strength soup and I drank it every day.

We got back late at night and went to Mr. Felix's house. It felt nice to sleep in a bed again. The next morning we got up and Mr. Felix made Mr. Abraham ride home and he took me around in a buggy. We rode around to everyone's house to let them see me and that I was alright. The first question out of everybody's mouth was did Mr. Abraham hurt me. I assured all of them that I was alright. The only house we missed was Richard's and I was just not ready to face him yet. Later that evening Richard showed up at Mr. Felix's house to see me for himself. I told him I was all right and everything was fine. All he said was "Good, I'm glad" and he turned and left.

Poor Richard I do so hope he gets over this. I don't know how long I will stay here. Bessie came over and said that Mrs. Sarah don't allow nobody to even say my name in the house but Bessie says she says it all the time when she is yelling at Mr. Abraham. I just hugged Bessie so hard. She is who I missed most. Well journal I am here at Mr. Felix's house and I am just sewing some baby blankets waiting to see what is next. Goodnight journal, goodnight my bouncy baby.

November - I been here two weeks and even Mr. Felix knows it ain't gonna work. Mrs. Sarah is just getting crazy with me being here and Richard has just gotten mean to all his neighbors. Mr. Felix said people are still whispering things about Mr. Abraham and he feels now that they know I'm alive he needs to get me out of there for the best of the community.

It has gotten colder and I am worried about me and the baby traveling back down the mountain in the winter time. Mr. Felix has talked to several trappers who say if we leave now we got time to get down before the weather gets too bad. He has fixed me up a wagon this time with lots of furs to stay warm. He decided to take me himself along with the Indian guides. He don't think Mr. Abraham should leave with me again. Again, I have packed up all my things. Bessie made me a pound cake. She said she heard pound cake would help keep me warm. We both laughed at that. I hugged her real hard and said maybe I'll see you again. She just told me to take care of that little Changeling I was carrying. I watched her till she was out of sight. I hope I get to see her again sometime. I guess I'm headed back down the mountain again. I'll write when I can. Goodnight journal, get ready to ride again little baby.

December - I have been recuperating since the trip back. Widow Byrd has been taking such good care of me. I had a terrible cold and fever by the time we got back to Puzzle Creek so Mr. Felix brought me to Widow Byrd's so I could be closer to the doctor. It's almost Christmas time.

We left Oconoluftee and met the Indians on the second day out. It was the same two as before. The older Indian had words with Mr. Felix about me traveling so far but Mr. Felix told him I was young and strong and would be fine. I stayed in the wagon a lot as it was fiercely cold. We ran into snow several times. Mr. Felix and Mr. Abraham had fixed up the wagon for me with blankets and furs so I would be warm. The trip actually was kind of fuzzy. The old Indian fixed me strength drink like the time before. It did make me feel better. I would get out and walk around some when we stopped and I think that's how I got my cold. I was out too long and got chilled to the bone. Even the furs could not help get me warm. The old Indian came into the wagon with me and shook his head sadly. He felt my head and then began to chant. He then gave me something really bitter to drink. He said it would help me rest. Well it sure did, I think I slept almost all the way back.

I remember being hot and trying to throw off the furs but the old Indian would just cover me back up and chant. Widow Byrd was plum worried when we got to her house. I think the Indian scared her. He came in all the way with me and stayed for a couple of days to give me strength drink. She was scared but she let him stay. The day he left he told me that I would be alright but just feel weak for a while. He put his hands on my swollen belly and blessed the child within then put his hands on my shoulders and blessed me. He smiled sadly and said I shall not see you again but my spirit will be with you and the child always. I hugged him and he looked embarrassed and left quickly.

It is nice here. I sit by the fire with Widow Byrd. She is knitting something for the baby. I just sip on hot tea that Mr. Felix left with honey. I am weak but getting stronger by the day. The baby is rambunctious. He kicks all the time and that comforts me and makes me laugh a little at his strength. He will be a strong one for sure. Widow Byrd says it's good for him to kick so strong, it means he's healthy.

I think now is the time for me to cherish this child and just be content to carry him. It will only be for a few more months and then I'll get to see him. I hope to be well enough to sing at church by Christmas. It would mean so much to me if I could. Widow Byrd says we will ask the doctor. Oh well if I can't sing there I will just sing here. I'm tired now so I am going to sleep for a while. Goodnight journal, I hope the baby will sleep a little bit too…he is such a kicker.

--- Good news the doctor let me go to church today to sing the Christmas hymns. It was wonderful. I stood up to sing and the sun broke through the clouds and shone through the window right down on me. I could feel the warmth from it on my face. It felt so good I raised my face to it and sang my song straight to God. I even raised my arms at the end towards the sun. Everyone in the congregation was quiet and then I noticed some of the ladies crying. I spoke before I thought and said "Don't cry, this is a beautiful time for all. We are celebrating the birth of Christ" and I put my hands on my belly and smiled at them and said "I could understand Mary's joy. A child being born is always a special time for us all. Praise God from who all blessings flow."

The preacher stood up as I sat down and said that I had just about said it all. He spoke just a bit and wished us all a Merry Christmas. He came over to Widow Byrd's after the service and told me that he had thought to himself that Mary must have looked like me when she was carrying Jesus. He said the sun shining on me when I sang took his breath away. I blushed and said it just felt so good to feel the sun. He patted me on the shoulder and said "The whole church loves you Nancy, don't ever forget that. We will remember this day for a long time." It was so sweet of him to say such nice things. I love the church members too.

Widow Byrd and I shared a nice Christmas dinner and exchanged small gifts. She pushed me off to bed saying I needed to rest but journal I feel rested. I feel at peace. I have never felt such peace as I did lying here listening to the fire crackle and feeling my baby kick. I got up to write about today but it is chilly so I am crawling back under the blankets after I put out my candle. Goodnight journal, goodnight sweet baby.

In the year of our Lord 1804 …..

January - It snowed again today. It is beautiful to look at but cold to go out walking in. Of course Polly Price says I don't walk anymore I waddle like a duck. She is so funny. She and Nancy Leake are so excited about this baby. You would think it was theirs too. I am trying to learn how to knit but I just am not patient enough. Nancy Leake has already made two blankets and a little gown. Widow Byrd and I have been cutting and getting my tie diapers ready. The ladies from the church have come over and brought some things for the baby. It is so wonderful how nice they all are. They never say anything to me about Mr. Abraham even thought I know they all know.

I hope I can stay at Widow Byrd's house for a while. I like living with her. Mr. Felix gave her money for taking care of me and the baby. She says she is grateful to have the extra money but likes the company even more. I sat in the rocker today by the fire and the baby just kicked up a storm making my dress bounce up and down. Even Widow Byrd laughed at how active he is. I can't wait to see him and actually hold him in my arms. I haven't told Widow Byrd but I know he is a Changeling child. He is special and will be special all his life. I have to make him aware of this so he will be prepared. I think maybe though it should just be between me and him as others would not understand. Oh journal I am so happy and at a place of such peace. I never thought there was such a place as this. Goodnight journal, goodnight baby.

February - My back has really been hurting this week. Widow Byrd says it's because the baby has dropped. He is sitting much lower in my belly than he has been. He better come soon or I might just burst. She seems to think it won't be long. All I want to do here lately is clean. I have cleaned the cabin from top to bottom and fixed the cradle and folded all the blankets. I sit here tired but thinking about what else I can clean. I wish I could clean the outside but it is too cold to be out much. I don't know why I want to clean so much. Widow Byrd says it's normal for women to get like that before they have their babies. She is getting as excited as I am for the baby to be here. She asked me what I was going to name the baby but I told her I would decide when I saw him. I'm going to try to get some sleep. Widow Byrd keeps saying I'd better rest now because they will be little sleep when the baby comes. Goodnight journal, goodnight baby.

--- I had a very strange dream last night. The old Indian man came to me and told me to go to the river and collect water to wash the baby with after he is born. He said children of the wood spirit must be cleansed with blessed water from the river. He showed me the spot to collect the water and then he stood and chanted over the river. I woke up suddenly and knew I had to go do this. I gathered up a bucket and got dressed to go as it was quite a walk from the Widow's house. She tried to talk me out of walking so far as a light snow had started to fall and she was worried about the baby. I bundled up and told her I would be fine that the Indian spirit was watching over me. She harrumphed and said it was foolish to believe in those Indians. I laughed and told her it would be fine and would probably help work out the pain in my back from sleeping.

I was about half way there when the pains got worse. I stopped to rest for a bit and they got better, by the time I got to the river they were gone completely. I found the spot that I had dreamed about easily and filled my bucket with water. As I left to return home the snow began to lightly fall again. It was beautiful. I continued to walk carrying the water marveling at the beauty around me. I was surprised that I was not cold or tired. I felt better than I had in days, almost like a young girl. The pains started right as the house came into view. I almost doubled over from the first one as it took my breath but it was over almost as soon as it began. I felt like I must have just gotten tired.

The Widow met me on the porch with a very worried look. She had seen me stop in pain. I assured her I was ok and we went into the house. I was beginning to feel a bit chilly for the first time. She wanted me to sit by the fire and eat a bite but I was not hungry. I did sip some hot tea and honey. While sitting there the pains came back, not as strong as the first ones but definitely there. I had several more over the evening and Widow Byrd told me I overdid it with the walk and I needed to go to bed. I did not disagree with her but I wanted to write down about the trip to the river. The candle is getting low so I need to finish. I do feel a bit strange tonight and the baby seems to be very still tonight. I guess he doesn't like the pains either. Goodnight journal, goodnight baby.

--- Oh my goodness, what a week it has been since I last wrote. I woke up in the middle of the night with the worst back pains I have ever had and then my bed was wet all over. I cried out in pain and Widow Byrd came running in and told me the baby was coming. She threw on her shawl and ran to get the doctor. We sure are lucky to live near the doctor. It seemed like it took forever. I have never hurt so bad in my life. I felt like I was being ripped apart. Widow Byrd bless her soul held my hand and bathed my head in water the whole time. I think I was in and out of it. Widow Byrd says I was talking to the old Indian a few times. I really don't remember that. All I know is that it was all worth it. I have the most beautiful baby boy ever born to a woman. Even Widow Byrd says he is a beautiful baby.

I have never felt like I do right now. When the doctor wrapped him in a blanket and handed him to me I looked at his beautiful eyes and called him Abraham. The doctor asked me if I was sure I wanted to call him that. I looked up at him and said I got nothing to be ashamed of in this baby and he shall be called after his father. I never knew my father's name. I never want him to feel that way. Widow Byrd cleared her throat and told the doctor it's her right to name him what she wants. He said ok and he wrote down Abraham Hanks, born of Nancy Hanks and Abraham Enloe, February 12, 1804 in the bible.

Widow Byrd took Abraham to wash him up and I told her she had to use the river water I had gotten the day before. She sputtered and fussed but heated it up and cleaned him with it. I look at him every day and know I am blessed. He is a Changeling baby, I can see it in his eyes. They are wise already and him just born. I want to hold him all the time but Widow Byrd says I have to put him down some. I will just a bit when he is sleeping but when he is awake I hold him. He is down right now so I can write. He is perfect in every way.

There is no sin on his head nor mine. We are where we are supposed to be he and I. He is special, I know it and I will make sure he knows it all his life. I am still quite tired so I am going to try to sleep a bit. Goodnight journal, goodnight my special, special son.

March - Widow Byrd told me I needed to stay in with the baby for a month but I am so restless and ready to take him outside that I can't stand it. Nancy Leake and Polly Price came over to see the baby. They agreed with me he is the most beautiful baby ever. I think Widow Byrd loves Abraham almost as much as I do. She was rocking and singing to him the other day. He is such a good baby, he hardly ever cries unless he is hungry. Widow Byrd says I am fortunate because I have so much milk. I am glad because he is hungry all the time and I want him to be strong and healthy.

I have started reading the bible to him every night. I want him to get used to the sounds of the words so when he starts to read he will know them. He just lays there and quietly watches me when I read. I think he likes the sound of my voice. I sing to him when I am putting him to sleep. He snuggles up close to me when I sing and goes to sleep. It is the most wonderful time.

I finally have something all my own to love and someone who will always love me. I will never ever leave him. He is part of me and I will always be part of him. I will teach him all I know and help him go to school to learn. He will be the smartest boy ever, can't help but be with his grandfather a Virginian gentleman and his father a learned magistrate. He comes from proud blood and I am proud of him. Goodnight journal, goodnight sweet Abraham.

April - I took Abraham to church today and had him baptized. They preached sprinkled water on his head and said a few words. He never even cried when they put the water on his head. I sang a solo with him in my arms today. Widow Byrd said it made her cry it was so beautiful. I hope Abraham can sing, it is a great comfort in trying times. It has been amazing how the community has accepted me and Abraham. There are a few whispers but not many. I hold my head up as I am very proud of my beautiful baby. I keep him with me always. I just do not feel that I can hold or love him ever enough. He will be walking on his own soon enough so until then I will hold him close. I hear him stirring so it must be time to nurse. Goodnight journal and hello my little hungry boy.

May - I got a letter today from Mr. Abraham and some money for Widow Byrd. He said he was glad to hear that the baby and I were doing fine. He was proud it was a boy. He said he sent money for the baby as well as Widow Byrd but I gave it all to her. He said he would be coming down this way soon to check on some property and would like to see me and the child. He closed saying that he thought of me often with great affection.

It was nice to get a letter. I wish I could write him back but I do not dare. I am making a little money now with my sewing. I am really glad that I kept practicing my sewing. I like to do it right. I read the letter to the baby today. I try to read as much as possible to him. He will just sit and listen to the sound of my voice. He is a watcher. He watches everything with those dark eyes of his. I know it means he is learning just like the old Indian said he would. It will be interesting to see Mr. Abraham's reaction to the baby. Little Abraham looks just exactly like his father. Widow Byrd says he looks more like him than any of his other children. I think I may have to agree with her on that one. Well, the baby is starting to stir so off I go. I will write later.

June - It has been a busy time. Abraham is sitting up. He tries to turn the pages of the bible when I read it to him. I have to move his little hands because he would tear the pages but I swear he is trying to help read. I always show him the first page where the doctor wrote his name down and tell him that is your name Abraham. I tell him the stories of the old Indian and how he is a Changeling child. He doesn't understand yet but he will.

A rider came in today and said Mr. Abraham and Mr. Felix would be here tomorrow. I am anxious for Abraham to meet his father. I am a little nervous about Mr. Felix coming. Seems like he always has trouble for me following him. I am feeling a bit vain but glad I have my figure back after having the baby. My waist is not as small as it was but it went back down considerable. I will dress Abraham in his best. It will be nice to present Mr. Abraham with his son. I know he will be as proud of him as I am. Goodnight journal, tomorrow will be a big day. Sleep well my son for tomorrow you will meet your father for the first time.

--- He came today. He was riding his big black horse and looked like a tall big tree sitting on his horse. Mr. Felix was with him. I was on the porch with Abraham in my arms. Mr. Abraham came up to me and politely inquired after my health. I told him I was well. Mr. Felix said he would go inside and speak to Widow Byrd. Mr. Abraham took the baby gently from my arms and unwrapped his blanket. He looked him over from head to toe. Abraham never uttered a sound he just fixed his dark eyes on his father's face. Mr. Abraham held him up and a big smile lit his face. "Why he looks just like me" he said. "Is it true you named him Abraham?" "Yes," I said "I always want him to know and be proud of who his father is. You are the best man I have ever known Mr. Abraham." He looked deep in the baby's eyes and said to me "it is as if he is looking through to my very soul." I told him "Yes he was, the baby had the powers of the wood spirit."

He wrapped the blanket around Abraham's little legs and sat him down on his lap while he sat in a chair beside me on the porch. He asked me if I was happy at Widow Byrd's. I assured him that I was. He told me he would keep sending me and the baby money. He did not ever intend to leave us destitute. I thanked him but told him I was making a little money sewing but he said "I need you to take this money Nancy. It is the least I can do for the both of you." I told him I would take it if that is what made him happy. "All I ever wanted was for you to be happy Mr. Abraham" I said. He looked at the baby and said "I sure wish I could bring you back home with me boy."

I snatched Abraham off his lap and said angrily "You will not take my baby from me." He apologized and told me he didn't mean just the baby. He said "I wish I could bring you both back to Oconoluftee so you would be closer then I could come over and check on you more often." I asked him if that was possible and he sadly shook his head and said "No, Sarah would never allow it." "True" I said, "she shore does hate me now." He said "Nancy, you are like a poison in her soul but one that I placed there not you. None of this is your fault."

I asked about the children and about Bessie. He said they were doing fine but Bessie sure did miss me. He handed me a package that Bessie had sent me. I opened it up and it was a baby blanket and a piece of paper with Bessie's mark on it. I smiled and told him to tell

Bessie I would treasure it. He then gave me a bigger box from him. It had diapers and baby clothes in it. He said Bessie had gone through some of the children's clothes and packed them for the baby. There were even a few toys and a hand carved rattle. Abraham reached for the rattle and I gave it to him. He just shook and shook it and then laughed at the noise. Mr. Abraham just laughed and said "I made that for you son. Glad you like it so much."

We visited for a while and Widow Byrd called us in to have a bite. It was a pleasant meal. Mr. Felix held the baby and proclaimed he was a very fine specimen indeed. Mr. Abraham laughed and said "Did you expect any less from a son of mine?" I think Widow Byrd was a bit scandalized but she didn't say anything. I went into the other room to feed the baby and looked up and saw Mr. Abraham standing in the doorway. He said "There is no more beautiful site than a mother suckling her babe." He walked over and rubbed the top of the baby's head while he ate. "Looks like he has a good appetite" he said. I told him I had plenty of milk and Abraham ate well and often. He lightly touched my breast and said "I am glad for the both of you." He put his arms back down by his side and said "I am sad for myself. Such a fine son born in such a state." I told him that our son would be a great and learned man, that I would see to it. He was not to worry. He just looked sad and said "I am afraid it is my lot in life to worry about you both now."

I moved the baby and adjusted my bodice. He got down on one knee and put his arms around the both of us laying his face against my breast. Abraham grabbed a handful of his hair. He said "Oh Nancy I do so care about you and this child. I just want you to be happy. Are you happy Nancy, really happy?" I for the first time did not feel like the girl I had once been I was now a woman. I put an arm around him and lightly kissed the top of his head and said "I will always love you Mr. Abraham and be eternally grateful that you gave me this child." Mr. Felix walked into the room and cleared his throat and said "Abraham we have to go now." Mr. Abraham got to his feet with moist eyes and said "I do not deserve your affection Nancy." I smiled and said "It did not matter you will always have it and it will live forever in the form of our son."

He tried to give me even more money but I declined. It was enough to just see him and have him acknowledge his son. Mr. Felix patted my shoulders and told me he was proud of the fine way in which I had handled this situation. I thanked him but still had a cold chill when he touched me. There is no good for me around Mr. Felix. I held the baby and we watched them ride off.

Widow Byrd came out on the porch and we sat there in silence watching the sun go down. At dinner she told me that Mr. Felix had given her money for us staying here and told her to let him know if it ever became a problem. Widow Byrd said she told him she felt like I was her own daughter and we were not a bother. I hugged Widow Byrd and told her that I loved her too. It was an eventful day for sure but slightly unnerving. I was ready to go back to our normal routine. The candle is almost out. Goodnight journal, good night baby Abraham and safe travels Mr. Abraham.

August - Everything has been going well. Abraham is growing, he sits up and genuinely laughs at things now. He loves having his belly tickled. I still read to him every night. Widow Byrd thinks it's foolish but she doesn't realize who he is. Nothing about learning for him is foolish.

I got a letter today from Mr. Abraham. He will be at Puzzle Creek soon for a week and he wants to see me and the baby. It will be good to see him again but I am concerned at the tone of his letter. He says Mrs. Sarah has still not forgiven him and she still nightly raves about the situation. I had hoped Mrs. Sarah would understand that it was not Mr. Abraham's fault. I do not want her to hate me. I still love her and am deeply sorry that this has hurt her so much. He did say that Bessie sent her best to me and the baby.

Ah, Bessie, I do so miss her. Little Abraham would love Bessie. I hope Mr. Felix is not coming with him. I worry when that man comes around me. I have been singing at church with the choir on Sunday's. It makes me feel close to God when I sing. I feel his presence strong in the church. Widow Byrd says my sewing is getting to be the best she has ever seen. I am glad because it helps me earn a little money to put back. I wish I could cook bread like Bessie though. I try but it is just not the same.

Widow Byrd fusses at me to eat more, she says I'm getting too skinny since the baby was born. I laughed and told her if I could cook like Bessie we would all be fat. She is right however I have had to take up both my dresses. I eat but I just keep getting smaller. I guess it's just being so busy after having the baby. I try to keep him outside as much as possible. The air is good for him. He loves when I take him down to the river. I see him developing his powers more every day. The way he looks at people when they talk to him, the way he picks up things and studies them. He is very, very smart. Everything a Changeling baby would be. I am so proud of him. The candle is low so goodnight journal. I will kiss my sweet boy's head and we will dream together.

--- It was a day of foolishness all way around. Today was one of those hot steamy dog days of August. The air was so humid you could almost feel it on your skin. Abraham was fussy and hot too. I decided to take him down by the river to see if we could find a cool breeze. It was afternoon and most everybody was staying still trying not to get too hot. When I got down to the river it didn't feel any cooler. I got a cloth wet and sponged Abraham off. It was so hot I stripped him down and just dipped him in the water. He laughed and splashed water and kicked his feet. The water felt so cool on my skin I decided to just strip down and get in the water with him. It was glorious in the water. I held onto Abraham and we played in the water kicking and splashing, floating and staying in the cool water.

After a bit I knew it would be time to go in. I cradled him tight and walked in the water back to the riverbank. As I neared the bank I looked up and saw Mr. Abraham standing near my clothes. I ducked back down in the water to cover myself. He said "Nancy, you do not have to be shy it is not if I have not seen you like this before." I told him to turn his back and he said "Nonsense I will hold the baby while you get out of the water." He came to the edge of the water and held out his arms for Abraham. I handed him my laughing wet baby and I walked out of the water.

He watched me hungrily as I dressed his eyes never leaving me. After I buttoned up my bodice I reached for Abraham. He handed him to me but then put his arms around me and pulled us close. He whispered in my ear "You still smell like sunshine you know and your body is slimmer than before you had the baby. I think you still have that wood spirit in you Nancy." I looked up at him and he kissed me hard on the lips. Abraham started to cry as he was being squashed between us. I pulled away from him and soothed Abraham. He said "Nancy, I want you so badly, I can't stop thinking about you and that night by the river. You have possessed a part of my soul and captured it in our son. I want you to be with me." I looked at him and felt such sorrow. "Mr. Abraham I love you" I said "truly I do but I also love Mrs. Sarah and we can never be together. What happened that night by the river was something beyond both of our control. It had to be for Abraham to be born, but that was what it was for. I would not be a kept woman for John Calhoun and I will not be for you. I am a mother now and have responsibilities to my child."

He looked at me and said "Let me Nancy, you know how much you liked it, you would like it now. Remember how it felt when I touched you" and then he touched my breast. It took my breath for a moment for I did remember how much I liked how it felt and it had been a long, long time but then Abraham let out a cry. He was hungry and it was time to nurse. I felt my milk give way and soak my bodice. Mr. Abraham touched the wetness of my breast and moaned slightly saying "Nancy I need you it has been so long you don't understand Sarah has not let me touch her since you left. I am a man, I have needs" he touched himself and asked "Do you want me to sin again?" I was trying to soothe Abraham and I dared not expose my breast to feed him. I was afraid Mr. Abraham would lose control. I told Mr. Abraham that I was not responsible for his sin and I had to take the baby home. He finally saw in my eyes it was not going to happen.

I told him good day and I ran home with Abraham. I did not feed him until I was safely inside. I cleaned up and changed my bodice. I was churning inside. I did not know Mr. Abraham was at Puzzle Creek yet and why in the world was I foolish enough to bathe naked in the river with the baby? Every time in my life I have done that it has caused trouble. Foolish, foolish, foolish girl I though to myself all evening. I was acting like a temptress and that I was not going to be. There had been enough grief caused by what had happened between me and Mr. Abraham for a lifetime. He was such a good man and I did not want to be the cause of any more trouble for him and Mrs. Sarah.

Maybe he was right, maybe I still have some of the wood spirit in me. Could it be that once inside me it would never leave? I did desire him but it had to have been the wood spirit. I would not act like that. I would have to make it a point to be very modest around Mr. Abraham and make sure Widow Byrd was always around. He is a good, good man but as he himself said he is a man.

I held my sweet boy tonight long after he fell asleep and just watched his little body dream in my arms. He is truly a magical being and his conception was meant to be. It was pure and it was good. I would not sully it with a sin now. I just won't do it. He is going to be a great man someday and he needs to be proud of his Mama. I kissed his cheek and put him down. I needed to write this down today so I can remember it and be strong next time I see Mr. Abraham. If he cannot be strong then I must be for both of us. He doesn't understand how special his son is but I do and I will never forget it. Goodnight journal, I do so hope I can sleep tonight. The wood spirit feels very strong.

September - Mr. Abraham has been here for several weeks now. I did not see him again until Sunday at church. He sat in the back but from where I was in the choir I could see him looking right at me. Several people looked at him sternly during the service. It really is amazing how much Abraham looks like him. I heard several people whispering about it after the service. The preacher came up to me after the service and stayed right by my arm. He even offered to walk me and Widow Byrd home.

A few days after church Mr. Abraham stopped by the house. He came in and played with the baby a bit and then asked if he could talk with me outside. Widow Byrd saw the worried look on my face and said "Nancy I will leave the door open in case the baby needs you."

We went out on the porch and sat down. He placed a hand on my knee and said he was sorry for his display down by the river. He said "I heard you laughing and came down just to talk to you but when I saw you naked playing in the water with the baby I guess the devil just came over me. I have never seen anything more beautiful except you in the moonlight." I looked at him and told him "I was sorry for tempting him the way I did." I guess he was right that I did have a bit of the wood spirit left in me but that I was stronger and I would not let her take control of me again. He moved his hand off my knee and let out a deep sigh and said "I thought you might say that Nancy, but we are joined by Abraham and we will always have a connection. I will try to honor your wishes and not pester you about this but I cannot deny that you set my blood on fire when I touch you."

I looked at him and said "Then Mr. Abraham you must not touch me for I do not want to be the cause of any more of your pain." He got a faraway look on his face and said "You really are pure of spirit Nancy and I fear I will burn in hell someday for my lustful ways just as Sarah says." I grabbed his arm and said "You must never say that Mr. Abraham! God knows you are a good man and no one has ever been better to me than you." "Oh Nancy" he said and lightly kissed the top of my head as he stood up to leave. He said "I really want to do something for you and Widow Byrd for taking such good care of little Abraham." He handed me an envelope for Widow Byrd and said his goodbyes.

Widow Byrd brought the baby out to me as soon as he left and noticed that I had a tear in my eye. She asked if I was alright. I told her yes that Mr. Abraham just could be so sad sometimes it broke my heart. She shook her head and put her arms around me and said "Nancy save your heart for little Abraham do not let it break for the likes of him." She kissed me on the head. I think Widow Byrd really does love me. I gave her the envelope and just sat on the porch and rocked Abraham. I don't know why I feel so sad for Mr. Abraham journal. He is a magistrate, a learned man, and a wealthy landowner but yet he has a sadness in him. I am sorry that he can not be around to watch Abraham grow up but that is the price he has to pay just as I have to deal with little Abraham being born a bastard to an unmarried mother whatever the reason.

I will make it up to him. I promise. He will never feel the pain that I did. I will do something someday to make it right for him. People born with a name do not understand how lonely it can be for people who was born without one. Even if I never had my father's name I would have liked to have known what it was. I know he was a Virginia gentleman and I guess that will have to be enough. This day has wearied me. There are days I feel so much older than my years, this is one of them. I forgot to ask Widow Byrd what the letter was but I guess I can do that later. Goodnight journal.

--- Mr. Abraham had been gone for about a week when Widow Byrd sat me down after dinner and said she needed to talk to me about his letter. I got Abraham settled while she cleaned the dishes. We went out to sit on the porch and watched the stars. She said "Nancy I am going to tell you what Mr. Abraham said in his letter. He told me to wait until he was gone to tell you about it but I am going to say right off that if you don't like it we won't do it. It will be your decision." I could not imagine what she wanted to tell me so I said "Well go ahead and tell me what was in it. What do you think I won't like?" "Well Nancy" she said, "Mr. Abraham's renters are moving soon and he wants us to move to Puzzle Creek. He said he wants little Abraham to grow up in the house his father built. He worries that we do not have much room here and he says it is the least he can do for his son. He said the two slaves he had left would stay there and we could hire someone to help with the cooking and cleaning. He has several farmers leasing the fields so we would not have to work them. What do you think Nancy? Do you think you could go back and live in that house?"

I thought about it a while before I answered. "Do you think it would make me look like a kept woman?" I asked her. She said "Oh my goodness no Nancy, everybody knows you are not like that and besides I will be there with you so nobody would talk." She looked at me and said "He didn't ask you to be that did he?" I told her "No and that it didn't matter if he did I would not do that to little Abraham. Why, if I was a kept woman I said I couldn't go back to church much less sing in the choir and I love singing in the choir." I told her I thought it would be a good idea and a good place for little Abraham to live. She jumped up and said it would be wonderful to live in such a nice big house and we could start packing soon. She was so happy she twirled.

I sat outside for a while thinking about moving back into Puzzle Creek. Some of my happiest memories were in that house. I want little Abraham to have happy memories of it too. The only dark cloud on the horizon was worry about how Mrs. Sarah would take it. This was not going to make her any less angry at Mr. Abraham when she found out I was living in her house. Oh well she was far away in Oconoluftee and I was here in Rutherford County so we should all be alright. Here I am going back to Puzzle Creek but this time I have my Abraham with me. What a glorious life we will have he and I and the best part is Mr. Abraham's library. I can read to my heart's content there. Journal, we are going back home, you, me and Abraham. Goodnight to you.

October - We are all moved in. Abraham and I share the large bedroom that used to belong to Mr. Abraham and Mrs. Sarah, Widow Byrd has the room down the hall. It feels so quiet here without all the Enloe children running around but I am sure Abraham will be running before too long. He is pulling up to things now, his little legs are getting so strong. He can crawl faster than I can run I think and he is so curious. He gets into everything. Yesterday he crawled into the fireplace ashes and before I could get him he had crawled all over the sitting room. We cleaned ashes all day. Little imp. He says Mama now and a few other words. He is so much smarter than other babies even Widow Byrd says so.

I am teaching him to be careful when we turn the pages of the bible. I let him touch the pages when we turn them but I hold his hand so he doesn't accidentally tear them. He touches his name at the front to the book now and points to himself. I have been doing that since he was born. We touch his name and point to him and say Abraham and he giggles. He just points to the name and then giggles. It always makes me laugh when he does this. He is so smart.

There is a slight chill in the evening air now as fall moves in. It won't be long before the big yearly barn dance. Has it really just been two years ago? So much has happened since that dance. Widow Byrd asked me if I was going to go. I told her I haven't decided yet. I just don't know how it would feel. Polly and Nancy Leake are going and they so much want me to go. They both have beau's now so I would be the only one without anybody. There have been a couple of young men at church that smile at me but their Mama's jerk them up quick when they notice. Everyone treats me so well but little Abraham cannot be ignored and who wants an unmarried woman with a married man's bastard to care for? I realize it would be asking for the world to get a man willing to take another man's child and call it his own. I dream that someday I would meet someone who would not care and would love us for ourselves but I'm afraid it won't be anybody from Puzzle Creek.

I got a letter today from Nancy Enloe, I mean Thompson now. She is living in Kentucky with John and is so happy. John has done well and is doing some farming and a little land speculating. She wanted to write and tell me she heard about the baby and how she knew her mother won't like it but she was glad that we were related now since little Abraham was her half brother. I hadn't really thought about that. Abraham had a slew of half brothers and sisters. She said they had not been blessed with a child yet but they tell her it takes time with some women. She hoped she would see me again someday and that she and John would be forever in my debt for helping them elope. She said she was glad I was still living at Puzzle Creek, it was a good place for a baby. She apologized for her parents behavior to me. She said I know none of this was your fault and even John knew about Father's womanizing. She said she loved me very much and wished me and the baby the best. It was a very sweet letter and I was glad to hear from her.

So much has happened since those days of my greatest worry being getting my hair ribbon tied correctly. Abraham is waking up from his nap so I better go get him. He will be into everything as usual. I do so love that child. He is the most amazing creature ever born on earth. He has a head full of dark hair and dark soulful eyes. I tell him the story of the old Indian and how he is prophesied to be a great and wise man. It is important that he knows this. He must be prepared to become a great leader of men. I do hope he never loses his laugh. It is like music to me. I will write later journal. The master will wait no more.

November - I went to the dance and took Abraham and helped with the food. I did dance one time with the preacher and one time with the doctor. It was so fun. Abraham was spoiled by everyone there. Poor boys that came with Polly and Nancy had to share them with little Abraham. He was the hit of the dance with everyone. He laughed and giggled and tried to say words. Every time he saw me go past he would yell Mama, Mama, Mama and just laugh. It was a wonderful evening. When we got home I was tuckered out. No lost hair ribbons, no secret lovers running away, just a tired Mama and a sleepy baby. It has been nice here lately but I was troubled today when Mr. Felix showed up. He said Mr. Abraham will be stopping by for a few days and they would be staying here. They had been doing some land trading and decided to stop for a few days and do some hunting and see some people. I didn't mind, after all this is Mr. Abraham's house. It just felt strange getting the house ready for him.

Mr. Felix played with the baby some and proclaimed him to be the smartest baby he has ever seen. I smiled and just said why of course he is. He held him up and said "He sure looks likes like his daddy, more so than any of the others I think. It's good you named him Abraham, cause he is the spitting image of the man." After dinner I put Abraham to bed and was sitting by the fire doing a bit of sewing while Mr. Felix smoked. He asked me if I was happy. I told him yes I was. I asked him about Mrs. Sarah and he said she was doing better. I asked him if she had forgiven Mr. Abraham and he said "That one will be a long time coming. Mrs. Sarah don't forget easy." He then said "I hope she don't find out about you living here cause I'm afraid it will start her up all over again." I told him I hoped she didn't either.

We sat in silence for a while and then he asked me what I wanted out of life. When I said I just want to be happy and raise my baby. He asked me if I didn't want to have a husband and my own house someday. I laughed and told him that would be nice but it would take a special man to accept Abraham as his own. We were too well known around here for anybody to be interested. He said it was true everybody around here did know the story but he said "They don't hold it against you Nancy, mostly they blame Abraham." "Oh" I said "I wish they wouldn't. It was not his fault, he was overcome by the drink and the wood spirit." He said "You really don't blame Abraham for your situation?" I said "No sir I do not. It was meant to happen the way it did so as to bring little Abraham into the world. The old Indian told me so on my last trip back from Onconoluftee. He explained about the wood spirits and the way these things happen so that a Changeling child would be born. Abraham is a Changeling child."

Mr. Felix laughed out loud and said "If that is what you believe Nancy who am I to dispute it." I didn't say anything else, he just didn't understand how very special Abraham was. I gathered up my sewing and bade him goodnight. He is not a bad man journal but he sees things differently from other people. Mr. Felix is a man that tries to keep everything balanced in life. He wants everybody to like him and he wants to be the one that solves their problems. It just seems like I am always somebody's problem when Mr. Felix is around. I can't say I won't be glad when he is gone but I do look forward to having Mr. Abraham see how much the baby has grown. Goodnight journal, it has been a long day.

--- It had been two days since Mr. Felix arrived when Mr. Abraham showed up at lunch time. He was dirty and dusty from the trip and after he ate went to clean up and rest a bit. He came down later to play with the baby. He was astonished at how much he had grown and how smart he was. He looked over the house and said everything looked well cared for. He asked if I liked living here. I told him I loved it, some of my happiest times were in this house. He said he noticed that I had taken his old bedroom. I told him that it worked well for me and Abraham. He said there were enough rooms for Abraham to have his own room but I told him I liked having him close and it worked out better when he woke up at night to nurse. He asked how much he nursed at night. I told him he did often as he was growing and always seemed to be hungry to nurse even after eating table food. He just let out a big laugh and said "He is my boy ain't he." I just didn't say anything. He apologized for laughing and said "Oh it's just a man joke Nancy. Don't take it so hard."

I asked him how long he planned to stay and he said "Just a few days. Felix and I have to get back before the snows set in. We are going to do a little hunting and catch up with a few old friends. Are you trying to run me out already girl?" I shook my head no and said I just wanted to make sure we had enough food for them at meal time. He patted me on the back and said it would be fine. Mr. Felix came into the room and they started discussing who they wanted to see and where they were going. I left them to it.

After dinner I excused myself and took Abraham up to our room and stayed with him. I asked Widow Byrd to entertain the men so I could stay up stairs. I'm just a bit uncomfortable staying under the same roof with Mr. Abraham. I keep hearing Bessie say "Ain't no good gonna come of this child, no good at all." So journal I am going to make sure that nothing happens if I have to stay in this room for their whole visit. I sure hope I don't have to however, I like hearing them talk and seeing Mr. Abraham play with the baby. He loves him, I can see it in his eyes. Well, it is time for me to stop writing and get to sleep. Goodnight journal.

--- They left this morning to go back to Oconoluftee. We had breakfast and saw them off. Mr. Felix had his fur coat on and Mr. Abraham had his over the saddle. It will be cold going over the mountains. It seems odd that it has been a year since I made the trip back here with Mr. Felix. I still do not remember a lot about it except the old Indian talking with me and fixing me special tea. It is good that they are gone.

Last night Mr. Abraham and Mr. Felix had been to the Red Tavern drinking with friends. They came in late and loud. It woke up the house. As they came upstairs to bed I heard Mr. Felix tell Mr. Abraham not to come into my room that it was not his room anymore. Mr. Abraham laughed and said everything under this roof is his. Mr. Felix laughed and told Mr. Abraham to go to bed and get some sleep. I laid there awake for a while but everything had seemed to settle down. I had just drifted off when I felt a hand on my thigh under my gown moving up my leg. I gasped and a hand was placed over my mouth. Mr. Abraham said "Hush girl, don't wake the baby, it's just me." I was frozen in fear.

He moved his hands gently all over my body. He cupped my breast and whispered "So full and firm." He began to stroke my private place and I began to struggle. I did not want to do this and the baby was beside me in the bed. I moved his hand off my mouth and whispered "Stop Mr. Abraham, please stop. I do not want to do this." He laughed and said "But Nancy I do so want to do this." I started to cry and again asked him to stop. He was drunk and got angry. He raised his voice and said "This is my house and you are mine so I will take you when I will" and he began to struggle with his breeches to loosen them. I slid out of bed and ran out into the hallway. He chased me and knocked over a table.

The baby began to cry and he caught me near the window. I was pushing against him and telling him no and he was pushing my nightgown up and saying it was his right. About that time Mr. Felix had heard us and come out into the hall. He didn't grab Mr. Abraham but said to him "I think the girl is not so inclined Abraham." Abraham told him to shut up and go back to bed. Mr. Felix laughed and said "I can't do that Abe old boy." Mr. Abraham turned around to Mr. Felix and said "Do I have to fight you Felix?" Felix laughed and said "No, Sarah's the one you fight with not me." At the mention of Mrs. Sarah's name all the passion and anger went out of him.

Little Abraham was crying quite loudly at this point and Widow Byrd came out of her room and asked if everything was alright. Mr. Felix just looked at me and said I needed to go check on the baby and told Widow Byrd that everything was fine but that I had had a nightmare and would she sleep with me for the rest of the night after we I got the baby calmed down. She came and put her arm around me saying "Poor child, you done been through so much, of course I'll stay with you tonight." Let's get that baby settled down first. Mr. Felix took Mr. Abraham by the arm and led him back to his room.

I did not tell Widow Byrd what had happened. I just nursed Abraham back to sleep and we crawled into bed to get some rest. This morning Mr. Abraham had quite a headache on him from last night. Mr. Flex was pouring strong hot black coffee for both of them. We fixed them some breakfast and packed them some food for the trip. Mr. Abraham came into the kitchen while I was cleaning up and apologized to me for his behavior last night. He said he didn't remember a lot of it but that Felix told him he had acted like an ass to me. He asked me to please forgive him and that it would never happen again. I didn't tell him he was darned right about that. I would put a chair under my door the next time he stayed under my roof drinking. I just told him to put it out of his mind and get to feeling better that no harm was done.

He kissed Abraham on the head right before they left and looked at me with such sad and longing eyes. Even Mr. Felix could see his pain. They got on their horses and rode off. I spent the day cleaning and keeping busy. I did not want to think about what would have happened if Mr. Felix had not come out into the hallway. Drink did funny things to a man. I remember Bessie saying it could turn them into wild animals. I guess she was right. That's what it felt like, like I was cornered by a wild animal. It didn't even seem like it was Mr. Abraham doing those things. I am going to put it out of my head and not think of it anymore. It will serve no purpose. I will try to teach Abraham about the evil that befalls a man when he drinks strong spirits. It is nice to have the house back to normal. I hope it stays that way for a while. Little Abraham is sleeping like an angel tonight and I think I will go join him. Time for a peaceful night's sleep. Goodnight journal.

December - It is a week before Christmas and we had a beautiful snow. I bundled Abraham up and let him play in it. We both laughed and played till we were almost frozen and came inside. Widow Byrd had mixed some sugar and cream together with the snow and we ate it. It was wonderful I never tasted anything like it. Widow Byrd says it is so nice to have a house with such rich stores in the kitchen. Sugar is a wonderful thing to have and we are very sparing with it. We decided to make a potato soup and bread. We took bowls of the steaming soup and fresh bread and sat near the window to watch the moonlight rise over the snow as we ate.

It was a special night for us all. I am so happy here. I am singing two special songs for Christmas service at church and the preacher is coming over to the house for dinner afterwards. Life can be so wonderful sometimes. I hope the Enloes are as happy in Oconoluftee as we are here. Goodnight journal.

---Christmas was a lovely time. Singing songs at church and coming home with Abraham and the Widow Byrd to Puzzle Creek was so special. I feel very blessed. Goodnight journal.

In the year of our Lord 1805 .....

February - Abraham's birthday was today. We celebrated all day long. Widow Byrd and I sang songs and she made a special little honey cake for him. We laughed as he got it all over himself trying to eat it. He is standing up and walking while holding on to things. Soon he will take off on those little legs and it will be a chase all day. Oh just the thought makes me smile. I am the happiest I have even been. As I was reading the bible to him tonight he reached out and turned the page before I could grab him. He took the edge ever so lightly and turned it to the front and pointed at his name and then looked at me until I said "Abraham." He said something that sounded like Bubbabam. I think he is trying to say his name. Oh he is the smartest baby ever. He was tired and went to sleep without a fuss. I love him with all my heart. Goodnight journal.

March - He is walking alone! I was doing some mending and he pulled up to the chair and just turned and walked to the other side of the room. I squealed and jumped up and he immediately sat down on the floor. Widow Byrd came running and we spent the better part of the day having him walk back and forth to us. What a special, special day. He is wearing me out these days. Goodnight journal, I'm tired.

April - I got a letter today with some money from Mr. Abraham. I guess I should feel bad about his sending money but I don't. It is for his son after all. Abraham is walking everywhere. He has learned how to go up the stairs and then slide down them. I have to watch him so he doesn't get hurt. Mr. Abraham asked about him. He said he missed seeing him and hopes he is doing well. I was afraid he was coming to visit but he didn't mention it. He said if I needed anything to please write to Mr. Felix and he would get it to him.

My sewing is doing so well these days. I helped make a wedding dress for one of the girls at church. It was so much fun to do but made me yearn to have a wedding dress of my own someday. I still dream of being married someday and having a family. I know I just have to have faith and that God will send me a husband when it is time. I just hope that he will love little Abraham like his own when that time comes.

Spring is in the air around here. The birds are singing and trees are starting to bud. Abraham will enjoy getting outside more as it gets warmer. Widow Byrd is watching him right now as I had taken a moment to lie down. Sometimes I get so tired, she says it is because I am so skinny and that I need to eat more. Maybe she is right but I just don't have much appetite. Oh well, writing during the day is a luxury I rarely get. Time to go get my ball of fire downstairs from Widow Byrd. I know she will be tired by now.

June - It has been a wonderful year so far. Everything is running smoothly on the farm. Widow Byrd is thrilled that I have finally gained a little weight. I think it's all the fruit I eat. Abraham loves the strawberries and he gets covered with watermelon when he eats that. He just jabbers away all day now. I understand some of it but it is still mostly baby talk. He makes it known what he wants however. He can be a demanding little fellow when he wants something. I like for him to be strong and he needs to know his own mind and speak out when he gets older. I catch him watching us a lot. He studies everyone he sees. I can hear the voice of the old Indian telling me about his powers. He is growing them even now as young as he is. Oh I have to go he just bit into an onion like an apple and is making the most horrible face. It is so funny. Bye journal.

August - What a hot summer! I take Abraham down to the river and let him wade in it. He loves stripping off his clothes and getting in the water as much as I do. I don't make that mistake anymore. If I get in the water with him I have my clothes on now. He is growing so big. I am teaching him his letters. Widow Byrd says it is way too early but I don't think so. I draw them in the dirt with a stick and he tries to copy me. So far he just makes circles in the dirt but he will get it.

He knows his colors. I will put different colored things on the ground and tell him to bring me the red one or the blue thing or the green thing. He always gets it right. He is such a good boy. He never tries to get down when I am reading to him at night. He loves the books almost as much as I do. I laughed last night at him. He had had a very busy day and he went and got the bible and brought it to me. He was ready to go to sleep and knew we had to read first.

What a smart, smart little boy I have. It is a wonderful life we have. Someday I will have a family to share it with and children running around everywhere. Abraham will be a good big brother and help look after them and teach them what they should know. Good night journal. I am going to go to sleep and dream of all my future children.

October - Our days pass so peacefully here at Puzzle Creek. Polly Price got married and Nancy Leake is engaged. It is nice to see them spoken for. There has been a nice young man at church that has walked us home a few times. He is from the eastern part of the state. He says his family raises tobacco. He is visiting the preacher here. His name is Joshua Pittman. Abraham seems to like him. He swings him up on his shoulders when we walk. I don't know how much longer he is going to stay. He has never asked me about Abraham's father but I guess somebody done told him. It's not a secret here. He seems like a fine man. I hope he stays awhile longer. Goodnight journal.

--- We had the dance last night. It was wonderful. Rev. Joe and Mr. Felix had come down to visit and came to it. Joshua danced with me almost all night. He even picked up Abraham and danced with us both. I felt like a young girl again. Widow Byrd helped with the refreshments and even danced with Joshua herself.

I did get to speak to Rev. Joe and ask about Bessie. He said she was doing well and he was writing letters to her sister for her. When my eyes got wide he said things are not as strict in Oconoluftee about that as down here. I smiled and said I was glad. I asked about the Enloes. He told me Mrs. Sarah was expecting. I looked surprised and he laughingly said "No matter how much cats fight, there always seem to be plenty of kittens."

I was so happy I hugged him. "So everything is alright with them now?" I said. He looked a little sad and said "Nancy, I don't know if everything will ever be alright for Sarah but it is getting a little better between them." "Well, that's ok" I said, "Another baby is just what Mrs. Sarah needs now." Mr. Felix asked me for a dance but I think he just wanted to talk. He asked me how everything was going, talked about how big Abraham was getting and said he had a package for me and Widow Byrd from Mr. Abraham that he would bring by tomorrow. I told him thank you and as the dance ended he asked me about Joshua. He wanted to know how long I had known him, where he was from and was he planning to stay. I told him he would have to ask Joshua himself. He had only been here a month and I didn't know a whole lot about him.

I left him and went back to check on Abraham who was trying his best to dance to the music over by the refreshment table and eat an apple at the same time. He is a silly little boy sometimes. I just love him so much. Joshua walked me and Widow Byrd home after the dance. He even carried a sleeping Abraham for me. Widow Byrd took Abraham to put him to bed so I could say goodbye to Joshua. I told Joshua what a fine time I had had tonight. He smiled and said dancing with me was what made it fine for him.

He took my hands in his and said "I would really like to kiss you if it is alright." I smiled and said I would like that. He lightly kissed my lips, it had been so long for me that I guess I kissed him back a little harder than I intended to. Before I knew it he had his arms around me and was kissing me deeply. I must say that I liked it a bit too much. I felt that lightheadedness that comes over me when the wood spirit is getting strong and I pushed away. I did not want to complicate my life right now acting like that with Joshua. He said he was sorry as soon as I pulled away. I told him it was ok that we were just giddy from all the cider we drank at the dance. He laughed and said that must be it.

I told him I needed to go in and see to the baby. He looked at me deeply and asked if I ever saw the baby's father. I told him I had seen him a few times since Abraham was born but not often. He lived far away and traveled. He then asked me the strangest thing. He said. "Do you love him?" I said of course I loved him. He dropped his head and looked at the ground. "But not like a husband" I said, "he was good to me, he took me in when nobody else would have me. His family cared for me, he taught me to read and write. I will always love him and his whole family." He looked back at me and said "You are an unusual girl." I laughed and said "I am unusually tired tonight so I must go in to bed." I leaned forward and kissed him on the cheek and said "Thanks for a lovely night." I went in and he left. He is a handsome man and I did like how it felt to be in his arms and have him kissing me. I will have to be careful, the wood spirit likes him too and she can be trouble. I hope I see him again. In the meantime it will be a good day tomorrow. Mr. Felix is coming over with a package. We may have to make some pumpkin bread for him. Goodnight journal, it has been an exciting day.

--- Mr. Felix came by today and brought us the package from Mr. Abraham. It has some toys he had made for Abraham, a shawl for Widow Byrd and a book of stories for me. He had sent some money and said he hoped it would be enough to do us through winter. He said he hoped little Abraham had a nice birthday and was doing well. There were a few Indian toys also and Mr. Felix said the old Indian had sent those for the boy. Ah, he had not forgotten my Changeling.

Abraham is getting bigger and stronger every day. He is saying more words and is becoming easier to understand. He loves the horses and an old dog has taken up residence here and he plays with him every day. I fed Mr. Felix a bite and gave him some pumpkin bread to take with him. He told me that Mr. Abraham was staying close to Oconoluftee as Mrs. Sarah was not as robust with this child as she had been with the others. I asked him when the baby's time was and he said he thought in March sometime. I told him I hoped she did well and I would pray for her. He said that would be nice and she needed someone to pray for her. Her hard heart was not helping matters with the baby he was afraid. He kind of laughed and said you know how she is.

He left and rode away. I wish I could write her and tell her how sorry I was for her pain. I will pray for her to not only have a healthy baby but to find happiness. Mr. Abraham does love her, he just forgets it when he's drinking. Thoughts of them have run through my head all day. It makes me weary. Abraham is asleep and the candle is low and so am I. Goodnight journal.

November - It is almost the end of the month. Joshua has come by quite frequently. I think we are growing very fond of each other. He plays with Abraham and Widow Byrd likes him a lot. He told me tonight he has to return East to his family. I asked him if he was ever planning to come back. He told me he had to go home and take care of some things but that he would love to come back if I would have him. I asked him what he meant by that and he said "I love you Nancy Hanks and I love little Abraham. I would like to come back and court you next year if you would allow me to."

I threw my arms around his neck and said "Yes, yes, I would allow you to." This time I kissed him hard. When he kissed me back I felt the wood spirit rise up in me and I just let her go for a bit. When we pulled apart we were both gasping for breath. I said "I will wait until I see you again Joshua Pittman." "And I until I see you Nancy Hanks" he said. He rode off into the night. I had a bad cold chill come over me but I shrugged it off and went into the house. I told Widow Byrd about it and she was as thrilled as I. It will be sweet dreaming tonight journal. The wood spirit and I have a lot to dream about. Goodnight.

December – It has been such a fine Christmas here at Puzzle Creek. I am missing Joshua but I am filled with such hope and anticipation at his return. I have been thinking about him a lot since he left. There is something different here with my feelings. It feels like I have known him forever and could tell him anything. I can't quite explain it but I am sure he is who I have been searching for to love me and Abraham. I can just see our life now, sitting by the fire reading a book , discussing our day, and then going up to bed hand in hand with each other. Oh, the going up to bed sounds wonderful but I mustn't get ahead of myself. I am going to do this proper like. I miss him so much. I am so thankful the Lord has seen it in his mercy to send me Joshua. Even Abraham blessed him in his prayers tonight. I think our life has turned a corner onto a good path now. Who knows what wonders next year will bring to us both. Goodnight, Joshua my love, goodnight journal.

In the year of our Lord 1806 .....

January - We have started another year. Abraham will be two years old next month. How times fly. He is running around everywhere. He is curious about everything. He is trying hard to write letters. I see improvement even though Widow Byrd laughs at his efforts. Widow Byrd wants me to start to call him Abe, she says it will be easier for him to say and write. I forbade it. His name is Abraham and that is what he shall be called. If it takes him longer to write it then it just does. Abraham is the name of strength, it is God's chosen name for his leader in the bible. It is my chosen name for my Changeling. He will lead men, he will lead himself to greatness. He will prosper and he will be a learned man. So it has been prophesized, so it will become truth. He knows even at this young age that he is special. He carries the blood of the gentry of Virginia in his veins and the magic of the wood spirit in his heart. He will do many and wondrous things in his life.

I have asked the preacher if he has heard from Joshua but he has had no letters. I say a prayer for him every night and I try to put away the cold chill I had the last time I saw him. I do so hope he is safe and comes back to us soon. It has become chilly in the room tonight so I think I will put out the candle and crawl under the blankets with Abraham. Goodnight journal.

February - Another birthday, two years old. He has stopped chattering so much and now wants to know how everything works. I have to watch him closely or he will take everything in the house apart. He is talking very well for a two year old. I won't let Widow Byrd talk baby chatter to him. He must learn to talk correctly. I am working more with him on letters. I plan for him to recognize letters by this time next year. He will read early for he is smart. My boy will be a great man someday. It is foretold. I hope I hear from Joshua soon. To bed early tonight. Goodnight journal.

March - A letter, I got a letter from Joshua today. He told me he has been putting his affairs in order and selling some property so he can come back here. He told me of how he thinks of me daily and dreams of me at night. He asked about Abraham and hoped he was doing fine. He said he would be back in a few weeks and to let the preacher know he would be staying with him again. He said he had a present for me and he ended with *all my love, Joshua*. Oh I am so excited. I don't need a present. I just want him to come back. He will be my future. I will have my family and a home and a husband who loves me. He knows about everything and loves me regardless. I am truly the luckiest girl in the whole world.

I will have to eat a bit more before he comes back as I have fallen off some again. I guess I am just going to be thin in the winter time. Good night journal, it truly is a good night. I shall dream sweet dreams tonight.

April - Joshua came back today. The birds were singing and the sun was shining as he rode up. I ran to his horse and he dropped down and took me in his arms and kissed me deeply. I have so missed him. Abraham came running out and he swung him up in the air and placed him on his horse. He led him around the property front several times before putting him down. He gave Abraham a whistle he had made and then he gave me a locket on a chain. He said it had been his grandmother's and he wanted me to have it as a pledge of his affection. I love it, it is the most beautiful thing I have ever had. He stayed for a meal and after a bit of spooning on the porch he rode off to the preacher's house for the night. Oh my life is finally starting. I am so happy. Goodnight journal.

--- I was cleaning and singing around the house this morning when the sound of horses caught my ear. It was Mr. Felix and Mr. Abraham. They said they had been traveling and decided to stop by and check on things here. I felt a cold chill set deep in my breast at the sight of Mr. Felix. I don't know why but it unnerved me. I called Widow Byrd and we fixed their rooms for them. Mr. Abraham went to find little Abraham and play with him a bit. He was astonished at how much he had grown.

Mr. Felix noticed the locket right away and asked me if Joshua had given it to me. I told him yes and that we were courting. He patted my shoulder and said that was a good thing and that Joshua seemed like a nice young man. I asked him about Mrs. Sarah. He said the baby was born small but it was all right but Mrs. Sarah had to get a wet nurse as she just couldn't seem to nurse this baby. I asked him if she was sick and he just shook his head and said "Sick in spirit. She has not gotten over you Nancy and I fear she never will. It has hardened her heart." He said he and Mr. Abraham had left after the baby was born to give her some time. It made me sad inside. I so hoped she had forgiven us both by this time.

Joshua came over and met Mr. Abraham. It was uncomfortable and he was not happy that they were staying at Puzzle Creek. I explained to him that it was Mr. Abraham's house and he had to stay here. He told me that he would try to have a house for us before the years end and we could be married. As we kissed that night I almost gave in to the wood spirit but he was the strong one that night and held back. He soothed my fevered brow with light kisses and said there will be plenty of time for that later on.

He left and I walked back into the house. Mr. Abraham was standing in the front room and he had been watching us the whole time. He looked at me and said "He seems to be a nice man." I said he was and he would be good to Abraham. He said "That is all I could ask for" and he kissed me on the forehead and told me goodnight. I came on up to bed but I cannot shake this feeling of foreboding that I have. I have everything to look forward to and I just do not know where this is coming from. Hopefully things will be better in the morning. Goodnight journal.

May - I am beyond saddened. We buried Joshua a few weeks ago. He was cutting down a tree when they say it broke wrong and fell on him. It crushed the life out of my Joshua. They said he asked for me right before he died. I came home from the funeral feeling so numb. Even Abraham could not rouse me from the depths of my sadness.

Mr. Felix notified Joshua's family and Mr. Abraham tried to take care of me. He was so kind, I did not want to eat or drink but he convinced me that I must for Abraham's sake. He cared for me like a baby. One night he heard me crying in my bed and he came in and just lay with me, holding me and letting me cry. I actually even let him take me one night to try to ease the pain. I thought it might make me feel again, but it didn't. He wants me to go back to Oconoluftee so he can look after Abraham and me. Mr. Felix says it would never work. Mr. Abraham is convinced that it is what he must do as I have no one. They had a huge argument about it with Mr. Felix accusing him of being obsessed with me and saying it would kill Sarah or she would kill him. I just didn't care. My future was over and there would never be a man or a family for me ever again. All I wanted was to give Abraham a legitimate name and a family with a man that loved us both. I let Mr. Abraham take me at night but I am not here. I am off with Joshua, walking hand in hand with the sunshine on our heads.

--- Today I came out of my stupor. A man showed up at Puzzle Creek saying he was Michael Tanner and looking for the girl Nancy Hanks, daughter of Lucy Hanks. I was holding Abraham and told him I was that girl. He looked me over good and said "You have the Tanner looks girl." I said "Excuse me?" and he said "I am your father Michael Tanner. I finally ran into your mother a year or so ago and she told me you might be here."

All of a sudden the sun was shining again. This man was my father of whom I had often dreamed and he had come looking for me. I had lost Joshua but I had found my father. We talked for hours about my life. I left nothing out. He asked about Abraham and I told him of the circumstances of his birth. He said he was sorry he had not come earlier for me but he did not know where to look. I told him I did not care all that mattered was that I had met him now. I am a Tanner, with Tanner blood running through my veins. Abraham is a Tanner.

Glory be my prayers were finally answered. I put him up at the house and finally went to bed. Thank you sweet Lord for this. I feel I have awakened from a long sleep. Goodnight journal, Mr. Abraham will not share my bed tonight.

--- A letter came for Mr. Felix today from Mrs. Sarah. She had found out from a trader that they were at Puzzle Creek and I was living there and she was furious. She demanded that I be turned out immediately and that Mr. Abraham return to Oconoluftee. Mr. Abraham got mad and said she would not tell him what to do with his property. Mr. Felix reminded him that I was not his property anymore. He said he would find me a house. Mr. Felix said Mrs. Sarah would not be happy unless he found me a husband and got me out of the state. Mr. Abraham said where in the world would they find me a husband in my situation with a child? Mr. Felix said let him think on it.

A few hours later he came back and told Mr. Abraham they needed to go down to the Red Tavern, there a man there that owned him some money and he needed to talk to him. I scarcely paid this any attention. My father was playing with Abraham and was marveling at how smart he was. He told me that if me or Mandy had been a boy his family might have seen reason but being girls they sent my Mother packing. He just said there was nothing he could do.

The men all left and went to the Red Tavern. I fixed dinner for the three of us and then went to bed. I remembered to put the chair under the door this time. Goodnight journal who knows what tomorrow will bring.

--- Well let me tell you what today brought. I am still slightly in shock. The men came home late last night singing and laughing. I did hear the door rattle a bit but then it was quiet. During breakfast Mr. Felix began to talk of the night's adventure. He said there was a man they wanted me to meet. His name was Tom Lincoln, a carpenter and a good man who had agreed to marry me and take me and Abraham to Kentucky. I was shocked. "He has never even seen me" I said. Mr. Felix said "It does not matter we told him you were pleasant on the eyes."

I looked at Mr. Abraham and he looked down and said "He is not a gentleman like you are used to Nancy, he is just common folk but I am sure he will be good to you and the boy." I looked at my father and he said that he agreed that this would be the best solution. He even agreed to take us to Kentucky as he was planning on traveling there anyway. Mr. Abraham told me he was going to give us some money to start a life and had a cabin for us to move into near Nancy Thompson so I would not feel so alone.

This was a lot to take in and I asked if I could at least meet him first before I agreed. They said they thought I would say that so he was coming over after lunch. He came over and we met on the porch. I wanted to talk to him alone. He was short with dark hair and very common features. He told me he knew that I had no husband and a small boy but that he could accept that. I asked him what he did and he told me he built things. I finally just asked him why he agreed to marry me. He said "I ain't got nothing but a few tools, no house, no place, no money. All's I do got is my name and Mr. Enloe was willing to pay me good money and get me started if I gave that name to you and the little boy. My name is all I do have and if giving it away is what I have to do to get a start in life then so be it. Besides he is going to forgive the money I owe him from some gambling debts."

I asked him if he could read or write and he said no but he didn't hold it against people who could. He just didn't like learning and wasn't interested in it. I told him I had to have my books and writing tools and he said he didn't care as long as I didn't try to make him do it. I thought about it for a good while realizing that I was never going to get another chance to get a name for myself and Abraham. I could be a good wife and we could at least have a home. I finally looked at him and held out my hand to shake his. He took my hand in his rough short calloused one and we shook on it as I said "I will marry you Mr. Lincoln."

All three men came out of the house where they had been listening and shook Tom's hand. He told Mr. Abraham that they needed to discuss the money and supplies for him taking me and the baby to Kentucky. I went back into the house and saw Widow Byrd standing there with tears in her eyes. She threw her arms around me and said "I will miss you so much child." I had cried so much over Joshua that I just didn't have any tears left. I just hugged her and told her I would miss her too. She said "We need to pack as they want you to leave tomorrow." I stopped and looked at her and said that was not enough time. She agreed but said Mr. Felix said the sooner we leave the better for everyone involved. Sometimes I really dislike Mr. Felix.

I packed our things along with Widow Byrd and I promised her I would write. Mr. Abraham came up to my room and told me this would be for the best. He put his arms around me and gently held me against him. Mr. Felix walked by and said "Abraham you need to let the girl pack." He left and then Mr. Felix came back in my room. He said he knew this was hard on me and very fast but that it would make Abraham legitimate and give me a name. He also said "This will go a long way in healing Mrs. Sarah's broken heart. Mr. Abraham will go back to her and stop yearning after you now that you will be married and you will be far, far away and life can go back to normal." He patted me on the back and said "I know this is not ideal but it is the best thing for all involved and I know you want the Enloes to be happy don't you?" I did not trust myself to speak so I just shook my head yes. "That's a good girl" he said.

When he left I just sat there for a bit. I picked up Abraham, squared my shoulders and said ok, this is for the best and I will make it work. It is after all what I said I wanted, a husband, a name for Abraham and a chance to have a family. In Kentucky there will be no whispers and we will just be the Lincoln's, Tom, Nancy, and Abraham. I don't know when I will get the chance to write again journal. My life is changing and going in another direction. I pray it is the right one. Goodbye Puzzle Creek. Good bye Widow Byrd, goodbye Nancy Hanks. I will leave you all behind here and wish the best for us all. My life will be about Abraham now, plain and simple. I will make him the man he needs to be. Goodnight journal and goodbye.

Journal 2
(Nancy Hanks Lincoln)

In the year of our Lord 1806 …..

July - We are here in Kentucky. Living in a small cabin. It has taken me a while to get it presentable. It has loose boards over dirt and only has one room off the kitchen. It is not much and reminds me of some of the places I stayed with my Mama. Tom was not happy when he saw it. Said Mr. Abraham lied about giving us a decent cabin. My father said it sure wasn't much but he felt that with a little work and with Tom being good with his hands we could make a decent place out of it. He gave us some money before he left to help us work on the house. Tom is getting some boards and he says he can build another room for Abraham later before winter sets in.

He is out working on a neighbor's fence today so I finally had a chance to write. Let's see now, the morning we left Puzzle Creek Mr. Abraham came to me and said he wanted to talk. I told him that everything had already been said. I knew what I had to do and I was prepared to do it. He told me that I did not have to marry Tom, that he would work something out. I held up my head high and said I agreed to marry Mr. Lincoln and we shook hands on it so it seemed we had a contract and I would not the one to break it, beside I told him that he needed to go back and make things right with Mrs. Sarah.

Mr. Felix is right, if I am gone and married to somebody else she will calm down and maybe forgive us both. He went to hug me but I stepped back. "You once told me that to touch me sets you on fire" I said, "So don't do it." He looked so sad that I almost gave in but I would not. That part of my life is over. He belongs to Mrs. Sarah and so be it. I have Abraham and that is all that matters. He told me he had a small gift for me and he would be pleased if I would accept it. He then handed me a new journal. He said it was for me to record my new life in Kentucky.

I thanked him and went downstairs to say goodbye to Widow Byrd. I gave her the locket that Joshua had given me and asked her to please get the preacher to return it to Joshua's family since it had belonged to his grandmother. I am sure they would like to have it back. She promised and I gathered up Abraham and joined Tom in the wagon. We set off for Kentucky. I turned and watched the house until it was completely out of sight. I knew in my heart that I would never see it again.

My father was riding his horse and we had Tom's horse tied to the wagon. We stopped at the stage station and the manager there married us just as he had done Nancy Enloe and John Thompson long ago. My father was our witness. We only stayed long enough to eat a bite and we were on our way. When we made camp that first night Tom told me he understood that even though we were married that we did not know each other so he was ok with waiting to be together until we got to Kentucky. I silently breathing a sigh of relief and tucked Abraham into his bedroll in the wagon and I laid down beside him spending my first night as a married woman alone in a wagon with my child.

It was an uneventful trip. When we got here and saw the cabin Tom was so upset that my father decided to stay a few days and help make it livable. My father went into town to get some materials and came back and said we needed to get our marriage filed at the courthouse to make it legal. We went down to do that and the Washington County clerk said that he did not recognize the station manager's marriage of us and that we needed to do it again.

So for the second time Tom Lincoln and I were married. He never even asked about Abraham, just wrote his name down as Abraham Lincoln. We left there officially as the Lincoln family of Kentucky. My father left promising to come back by and visit some day. I had made Abraham a bed near the kitchen table and had fixed up a room for Tom and I in the back. I was nervous that first night and when he put his arms around me I trembled and burst into tears. He got mad and said he had given me enough time to get used to the idea and it weren't like it was my first time. I just told him I wasn't ready. He stomped out and told me to let him know when I was ready but he weren't gonna wait forever. He married me and he was entitled to share my bed.

I know I cannot hold off him forever but I am just not ready for another man yet. Abraham plays and sings, he misses Widow Byrd but as with all three year olds he is happy exploring his new home. I really don't know how I feel about everything it has happened so fast. I do know that I have a husband, a home and a child to care for so I am going to have to shake off this feeling and just get down to the business of living. So, here I go, hello journal, My name is

Nancy Lincoln, my husband's name is Tom and our son's name is Abraham. Welcome to Kentucky.

--- It has been about a week since I last wrote. I finally told Tom I was ready to be his wife in every way. He just patted my backside and said it was about time. I think he would have took me right there in the kitchen but Abraham was watching him. I just told him to wait until nightfall and Abraham would be asleep. He is not a gentle lover and thank goodness he just does his business and then goes to sleep. It sounds terrible but it actually is a good thing. I am not in love with him but I do appreciate what he has done for us. He did tell me he thought I was a right pretty woman and he could've done worse.

I asked him today if he was going to start on that room for Abraham, he got mad and said he would get to it when he got to it for me not to turn into no nagging woman. He couldn't abide a nagging woman. He left and I cleaned the cabin and got a stew started for supper. Abraham and I went down and played in the orchard near the house. We rolled apples to each other and practiced his letters. He is truly the smartest little boy around. He can even pick out a few words in the bible when I read it to him. He will be reading in the next year I just know it. It will all work out, I going to make sure of it. I am sure I can grow to love Tom with time. He will be coming home for supper soon so I better put you up.

September - Well, we have settled into a routine here. After breakfast Tom goes out and works a bit and I clean the cabin. Abraham and I work on his letters and do a bit of reading. I fix our midday meal. Sometimes Tom comes in and sits down for it and sometimes he just gathers it up and leaves. We have started getting to know some of the neighbors. There is a little boy up the road a piece that Abraham likes to play with. The church is small but nice. Tom said I could go and take Abraham but he didn't cotton much to church folks.

I had to take my dress up again today. I just can't seem to keep any weight on. I feel like I am rambling today journal. I did sit down and write a letter to Nancy Thompson and told her I would like to come visit her someday. I think it would do me good to see someone I know. Abraham and I walked down to the creek today and sat on the bank and watched the clouds. I am trying to teach him to see shapes in them. He did good today he said he saw a dog. It took me a bit but I finally saw the tail. He is such a good boy. He has gotten very quiet however when Tom is around at night. I hope Tom gets the room built before it gets cold. I try not to say anything about it because it makes him angry but we do need a little more space. I would write more but I just can't seem to get my thoughts together today. Hopefully I will hear from Nancy Thompson soon. I need to go start supper. I will write again later when I am a bit more clearheaded.

October - I am so excited, Nancy Thompson is coming tomorrow to visit. She and John are going to visit some of his relatives and they are stopping by here for a visit on the way. I have been cleaning and cooking for them. Tom is even excited but I think it's cause I told him Mr. Abraham is sending us some money with Nancy. I've got clean clothes for Abraham since it's the first time he will meet Nancy. I really hadn't thought much about it but she is his half-sister.

I hope Tom doesn't drink too much tonight. He gets a bit rough when he is drinking. He has met some friends that he likes to go drink with in the evenings some. I haven't met them but he seems to like them a great deal. I am not too fond of drinking spirits but I guess it is just what some men do.

Abraham has learned a new song and Lord love him he sings it all day long. I love to hear him sing. I want him to be a happy child. Tom gets a little upset at his chatter with me in the evenings. He says a man ought to expect quiet when he comes home. He usually quiets down when we read the bible. Tom scoffs at me reading so much but I reminded him that he knew I was a reader when he agreed to marry me. He just says don't expect me to take up with that nonsense.

I am so glad that Widow Byrd gave me her family bible when we left. She said it was all she had to give me as a wedding gift and since it had Abraham's birth in it she wanted me to have it. I read it to Abraham every night. He knows some of the words and I get excited when he says them before I do. He will grow up to be a learned man for sure. He just soaks up everything you tell him. I know he still just a baby but he is smart as a whip. Oh I just can't wait for Nancy Thompson to see him and I can't wait to see her. I don't know if I can sleep a wink tonight. Time to finish up here journal and put you back in your hidey-hole. I will write about the visit later.

--- Nancy and John Thompson came today. I think she was bit upset at the condition of the cabin. It is very small and there are big gaps in the floor but it is clean and as nice as I can make it. She was a bit concerned that Tom hasn't fixed the floors or the spaces in some of the walls but I assured her that he would especially since we would have a bit of extra money from Mr. Abraham. She could not get over how much Abraham looked like her father. She told me he looked more like him than any of her brothers. I asked her not to say anything in front of Tom, I try not to remind him of it. She told me she would not say anything.

She and John played with Abraham and marveled at how smart he was. I had him show her what letters were and colors and then he went and got the bible out and showed her the words he knew. She told me he was the smartest child she had ever seen. I was beaming with pride. She said her and John had been hoping for a baby but nothing yet. I patted her back and told her she had plenty of time. It was sweet to see them together. John was so kind to her and she looked at him with such devotion. It made me think about Joshua and what our life would have been like. I brushed that out of my head. It was not meant to be so no since in worrying myself over it.

Tom came home to meet them. He was nice and polite. I was proud of him. We ate a bite and then they had to be on their way. I walked them out to the wagon to say goodbye and Tom yelled from the doorway for me not to forget to get the money. I got really red faced but Nancy just yelled back "Don't worry we got it here to give to Nancy. Nice to meet you Tom." He waved and went back into the cabin. She handed me the money and said "Nancy, if you are not happy please tell me. I can't bear to think of you living here like this and being unhappy." I assured her that Abraham and I were happy and that Tom might look a little coarse but he was not a bad man. I was very grateful that he helped me out of my situation. She hugged me tight and said she would stop back by on her way home in a few days.

I went back inside and gave the money to Tom. He was very pleased with it. As he was getting ready for bed he grabbed me by the bottom and said "I made a good deal after all." He was nice to me tonight and not as rough as usual. I laid awake long after he fell asleep and finally decided to get up and write a bit. The candle is low and Abraham is sleeping by the hearth. He looks so peaceful sleeping there. I had a cold chill watching him sleep. I remembered what the old Indian told me about him and hoped he could get enough peace in his childhood as I am afraid he will not have it as a man. Goodnight journal, I'd better try to sleep a bit before morning.

December - It is cold here. I have some rags in the gaps in the walls but the cold seeps up through the floor boards. I have Abraham wrapped up as much as I can so he doesn't feel it as much. I am glad that his bed is near the hearth. It does stay warmer at night. It is freezing in my room. I do have some quilts thank goodness. I have asked Tom to do something about the cabin but he gets mad and says that Mr. Abraham shouldn't have put us in this run down shack. I reminded him that Mr. Abraham gave him money to fix it up and he got so mad he almost hit me. He told me it weren't near enough money for him settling down and having to stay in one place not to mention raising another man's child.

I just looked and him and said "You knew all along what the situation was." He just spit tobacco on the floor and said "Yeah, I knew all right. Sold him the only thing I had, my name." I told him if he felt that way I could leave. He said he was sorry and that I didn't have to go. He left to go have a drink with his friends. I can't say I was sorry. Abraham doesn't like it when Tom and I argue. He goes over to his cot and curls up in a ball.

It took me a bit to get him to come out tonight. We read a bit and I tickled him and got him to laughing. He was in better spirits by the time it was his bedtime. I put him to sleep and sat down to write. I don't know what time Tom will come home. I am just going to put you up journal and go crawl under the quilts with my clothes on. Hopefully it will get warm. Tom can be angry and hard to get along with but he is warm at night under the covers. Goodnight journal.

--- Christmas came and went without much fanfare here. I sang at the church service. I asked Tom to come but he didn't. Abraham enjoyed it. He likes it when I sing at church. The ladies of the church gave me some food and clothes and another quilt. I felt bad about taking it but they said it was for Abraham. They whisper a bit about Tom's drinking. They think I don't hear them but I have long experience dealing with whispers. I just held my head high and thanked them.

I did get a letter from Nancy and she sent a small gift for Abraham. I hope we can go see her after the first of the year. She says she has a nice house and plenty of room for us to stay when we visit. John Thompson is doing quite well in farming and is now doing some land speculating. I mentioned it to Tom and he said if he had money he could speculate too. It seems to always be about money with Tom. He says we don't ever have any but he works and does odd jobs for people. I don't know what he does with it. He told me today I needed to write Mr. Abraham and ask for some more money. I told him I could not do that, Mrs. Sarah would know about it and she would be mad as a wet hen. He shook his head and said I need to write to Mr. Felix then or maybe even the preacher at Oconoluftee. I told him that I would write Mr. Felix but not to expect much. Mr. Felix traveled a lot and might not get the letter for some time. He said just send it. We need some more money and he owes me.

I hate when Tom gets like that. I asked him what we needed so much money for and he laughed, an ugly laugh. He said it takes money to keep you and that kid up and since he can't do it he can pay me to do it. I knew enough about Tom to just hush about it. He got mad tonight at me and Abraham reading too loudly and just went to bed. I was glad. It was a peaceful night. I rocked Abraham in my lap like I used to when he was a baby and sang him to sleep. I put him down and checked on Tom. He was snoring loudly so I decided to write a bit.

I miss Puzzle Creek and Widow. Byrd. I miss Bessie, I even miss Mrs. Sarah and all the children. That part of my life seems like a thousand years ago. It makes me sad right down to my bones but I can't let it be seen. I agreed to this life. I shook Tom's hand and said I would marry him. For better or worse I said the words. I have learned a lot in my life and one thing is to keep my word. It is the most important lesson I can teach Abraham and if I don't do it then how can I expect him to. I have so much to teach him and there is so much for him to learn. I tell him about school and how he will go there someday and learn all about the world. I want him to understand that school is the most important place he will ever go. A learned man can do anything and he will be a learned man.

I will not let myself be sad. I am of Tanner blood and I will hold up my head and make my lot in life. Life is what you make it. I will not let Abraham sit and watch me cry and be sad over things I cannot have or have lost. He must learn to be strong in this world. He is Abraham Lincoln, he has a name and a heritage to be proud of. My candle is low and we do not have many so it is time to put it out. Good night journal. Things will look better in the morning, they always do.

In the year of our Lord 1807 .....

February - We celebrated Abraham's third birthday today. We played and sang songs and danced in the cabin. There is snow on the ground so we did not go outside, but it was a merry day inside. Tom came home and was in a good mood. He has starting bringing some spirits home with him to drink in the evenings. As long as he doesn't drink much it generally puts him in a good mood. Last night when we went to bed he made me take off my clothes, said he wanted to feel a woman's body against him. I did as he asked even though it was powerful cold in there. He laughed and said he would get me warm soon enough. He usually is very quick about his business but last night he took his time. I actually started to enjoy it and he was right I did warm up quickly. He had me panting hard and when he was finished he seemed surprised that I had enjoyed it too.

I snuggled up close to him enjoying the warmth of our bodies under the quilts. He was stroking my back almost asleep when he said "You sure have fell off this winter, you not getting sick are you." I just giggled and said I didn't think he wanted a fat wife. He grabbed my bottom and said "Don't seem to be no danger of that" and he roused up again. I thoroughly enjoyed it the second time. I had not felt that way with him before. He even said "It is good to see you finally warming up I had begun to wonder what the old man saw in you." I was sleepy and just let that remark slide. I didn't care. I was warm in the bed with my husband and excited about Abraham turning three. Tom must have drank a little much tonight because he went to bed early and didn't say anything about me joining him. I heard him snoring in the other room so I thought I would write a bit before I joined him.

I think things might be looking up. We don't have much money and the cabin is not much to look at but if we can get along like we did last night and today everything will work out. I might even grow to love Tom Lincoln someday. At least last night I sure did like him. He's not all coarse. There is a heart in there he just tries to keep it hidden. Goodnight journal.

April - My sewing sure has come in handy. Word has got out that I can sew most anything and I am making a little money doing some mending for the ladies that just don't seem to have a knack for it. Sometimes I trade for it but it has helped us a lot. Tom is happy that I am making some money for us. I hope someday to have enough for a rug for the floor so it won't be so cold.

Spring is coming and things are starting to bloom. I feel the season in my blood. Abraham is reading some now on his own. I knew he would be reading early. He is the smartest boy ever. I tell him the story of the old Indian's prophecy and how he was born a Changeling child with a special purpose in this world. I do not talk of Mr. Abraham much but we do talk about his grandfather Tanner. I remind him that he comes from gentry blood and no matter what his station in life is he will return to it someday. It is all about learning. Learning is the key that will open the world for him.

I have asked Tom if Abraham and I could go visit Nancy and John Thompson soon. We have been getting along so well he said we could go soon for a few days. I think spring is affecting him too. He is not as grumpy in the evenings and even plays with Abraham some. Life is getting better. Maybe before too long I can give Abraham a brother or sister to play with. It would be nice to have another baby but the cabin will have to fixed for sure if we have a baby. I think that might be the way to get Tom to work on it. He fixes everybody else's house so he says he is too tired to work on ours. Well, it is getting warmer and it won't matter as much. Hopefully we will go visit Nancy and John soon. I need to go get supper on, Tom will be home soon.

May - The visit to Nancy and John's was wonderful. I had forgotten how nice is was to live in a bigger house. Our cabin is ours but I do wish we had a bit more space at times. Abraham slept in the same room with me while we were there. We had a nice big feather bed. He thought the bed was wonderful. He would run and jump onto in and just roll around and giggle.

It was so nice to sit on the porch in the evenings and watch Abraham play. Nancy was amazed at how he could read words in the bible. I actually sat on the porch in the evening and sang with the slaves that Nancy and John had. They were so surprised that I knew the songs. We stayed for two wonderful weeks.

We got home and no one was here. The house did not look like Tom had been there for several days. I cleaned it up and made supper for me and Abraham but still no Tom. He came home the next day all unkept and smelling of strong drink. I asked him where he had been and he said he stayed with friends. He asked me how much money I brought home. When I told him none he was furious. "That's what you went for was to get some of the old man's money" he said. I just said Mr. Abraham had not sent me any money. He demanded that I sit down and write a letter to Mr. Abraham right then. I told him I couldn't do that because of Mrs. Sarah. "Mrs. Sarah be damned" he said, the old man needs to send some money for you and the boy."

I cried that I could not ask Mr. Abraham for money, besides he had married me and taken Abraham for his own after Mr. Abraham gave him money for us to get started. He started throwing things in the cabin yelling that the old man had made a fool out of him with promises of a cabin. "This place is a shack" he said, "Not worth nothing and he didn't give me near enough money to make me have to stay in one place. Write the damned letter" he screamed. I looked at Abraham cowed in a corner trying not to be seen. He started towards Abraham with an upraised hand and I yelled that I would write the letter if he would just calm down. He pulled up a chair and said "I will just sit here while you write it then."

I wrote the letter to Mr. Felix and asked him to talk to Mr. Abraham. I just told him we had reached some difficulties and needed some money to tide us over. When I finished it, I addressed it to Mr. Felix and gave it to Tom. He took the letter and said he would get it sent out in the morning. I quietly got Abraham ready for bed so as to not rile Tom again. I went into the bedroom to get ready for bed myself and Tom followed me into the room.

As I was undressing Tom roughly grabbed me and said "You done been gone two weeks and came back with no money so at I am at least gonna get something outta this arrangement." He took me hard with my clothes half on. It was brutal. He hurt me and I tried not to cry out as I did not want Abraham to hear me. When he finished he shoved me to the floor and walked out of the cabin.

I got myself cleaned up and put on my nightclothes. I laid in the bed shivering until I finally fell asleep in the wee hours of the morning. When I awoke Tom had still not returned. I started breakfast for Abraham and as we were eating Tom came back. Abraham jumped up and ran to his cot in the corner. Tom just said "Come on back and eat boy, I ain't gonna hurt you." Abraham did not come back until I told him it was all right. Tom pulled up a chair and said "I'm sorry I acted like such a fool last night. I was just all likkered up and in a foul mood. I didn't mean to upset the whole house. You ain't gonna hold it against me are you Nancy?" He looked sorry so I just said it was all right, everybody makes mistakes now and then. He looked relieved and started to eat.

After he finished he said he was going to work on getting some wood to build a room for the boy. As he left he said I got your letter sent off today so hopefully that will help us out. He left and I cleaned up the cabin. I was still sore from the night before. I sent Abraham out to play and I sat down to write. I hope that Tom doesn't do that to me again, in all my life I had never been used like an animal. I let myself shed a few tears and then dried my eyes.

I guess all marriages have their problems. Tom just seemed to have a problem when he drinks too much. It makes him mean. Mr. Abraham when he drank was never mean but I guess he did things he weren't supposed to do either. Drink can be an evil thing for men. I guess I just need to be nicer to Tom. He did take us in and the cabin was a sore disappointment to him. I will add being nicer to Tom in my prayers. Hopefully the Lord will look down upon us even if Tom doesn't go to church. I am going to go outside and put this behind me. There are some things it is just better to forget.

Abraham and I may walk down to the creek and look at clouds. That should soothe my spirit. Time to put you up journal.

July - Glory be! Nancy and John Thompson came by today with some money from Mr. Abraham. Tom was really good for a while but he had been getting real antsy for the last few weeks. He had gathered the wood to start building the extra room but it is still sitting on the side of the house. He has been a little nicer to me and hasn't come home drunk since last time. I lay with him at night but I can't get the memory out of my head of the night he hurt me so. I just can't seem to feel close to him like I did before we went to the Thompson's.

He came home after seeing Nancy and John's wagon go by

where he was working. He was in a good mood and actually quite charming to Nancy during their visit. Nancy gave me the money right off this time. Tom took it and said he would put it away for good keeping. I was so happy to see Nancy and I knew the money would put Tom in a good mood.

We visited for a while and as I walked her out to the wagon she handed me a letter from Mr. Abraham addressed to me. She said she didn't want to give it to me in front of Tom. I thanked her and tucked it in my skirt. She hugged me and said "Nancy, I am worried about you. You are thinner and you have dark circles under your eyes. Do you feel well? Are you happy? Is Tom mistreating you or Abraham?" I laughed and told her we were all fine. I just get tired and running around after Abraham has made me thinner. She looked at me deep and hard and said "You always know that you and Abraham are welcome at our house, no questions asked. If you need to come you are welcome for however long you need to stay." I hugged her back so she could not see the tears in my eyes.

Abraham had run out and hugged John and asked if he could go home with him. I scooped up Abraham and said "You have to stay here with me my little man." He looked at John and said "I like your house." John ruffled his hair and said he could come visit anytime. Tom came out about that time so they both got in the wagon and rode off. I sent Abraham off to play. Tom told me he was going to take some of the money and pay some debts he had and he would pick up a few supplies we needed. I watched him walk off whistling feeling a little guilty that I was glad to see him go for a bit.

I came in to write some before he gets back. I have put the unopened letter in here so I can read it at my leisure. I am just not ready to read Mr. Abraham's words today. I do so hope Tom doesn't come home drunk. Hopefully if he is drinking that much he will stay where he is for the night. I hear Abraham calling me that he has found a rabbit so I better go see what he is up to. Until next time journal.

September - The weather is turning cool. The lumber for the cabin still lies beside the cabin. I have mentioned it a few times to Tom and he just says he will get around to it. Life has been somewhat routine here. Tom has been in a much better mood since he got the money. He said he paid off some debts and he bought a few supplies for the house. I have been doing some sewing and putting back some money and trading for staples.

I have read and reread the letter from Mr. Abraham. He told me he was worried that I might be writing under duress and wanted to know if Tom was treating me right. He said there had been some rumors that had reached his ears about Tom's drinking and gambling. He told me if Tom was to mistreat me or Abraham I was to go to Nancy and John's. He said he had told them to look after us. He said if he needed to he would come up here. He said he has not come because he wanted to give me and Tom a chance to start a new life unencumbered by his presence.

He told me they were all doing well and that Mrs. Sarah was expecting again. He said she seems to be a bit better but she does carry on still about you now and then. He asked about Abraham and said he hoped he was doing well. He then said you know I love you and the boy. If life was different I would have you closer but it is best for all that we have this distance. It would not be good for me to see you often. He closed saying I think of you both almost every day and keep you in my prayers.

I am so happy that Mrs. Sarah has seemed to forgive him. Another baby will keep her busy. It has made me wonder why I haven't conceived. Tom takes me almost every night but no baby so far. I think maybe a baby of his own would soften Tom some.

I did meet a most amazing person yesterday. Abraham and I were walking near the orchard when we saw a very thin young man gathering some apples. Abraham ran up to help him. We began to talk and he told me he was a school teacher. He was from down East in Virginia and come up here to teach school.

I was so excited I could barely speak. I told him that I had already taught Abraham his letters and he could read several words in the bible without help. He started to quiz Abraham and was amazed at his knowledge. I asked him if he thought Abraham could come to school. He was concerned that he was only three but I told him he listened real good and could sit still. I told him if he would let Abraham attend school I would trade out mending and some cooking for it. He agreed as long as Abraham could sit still and not disrupt class. He suggested that I just bring him for half a day to see how he did. I am so excited I can hardly breathe. A schoolteacher that is willing to teach Abraham. The old Indian's prophecy is coming true. Opportunities for Abraham are falling into place. As he was leaving I realized I had not asked him his name. I yelled "Excuse me Mr. Schoolteacher what is your name?" He laughed and said "Mr. Jameston but you can call Matthew." I waved and said "Goodbye Mr. Jameston."

Abraham chattered all the way home. School, even the word excites me. I came home and took special pains with supper. I wanted Tom in a good mood when I asked him if Abraham could start school. He came in and noticed that I was in a good mood. He had had a bit to drink but not so much that it made him surly. We laughed over supper and he even playfully slapped at my bottom when I was cleaning up. I put Abraham to bed and we retired for the night. I slipped off my nightgown and snuggled up next to Tom. He rolled over and said "Humm what's this? My wife coming to me. That's a change I like."

Afterwards he was relaxing so I said I met the new schoolteacher today. He said yes he had seen him, a skinny sickly looking fellow walking around. I told him he agreed to let Abraham go to school for half day if it was all right with him. He pondered on it a moment and said "Well the boy ain't big enough to be much help to me yet and you fill his head with reading and numbers every day. I don't guess they'd be much harm in it as long as it don't cost me no money." I rolled over and hugged him hard planting kisses on his face saying "Thank you, thank you." He laughed and said "If I knew it would make you this frisky I would sent the boy to school myself." He took me again and I was so grateful that I actually enjoyed it too.

The next morning after breakfast I told Abraham the good news. He was going to school. I cleaned up the cabin and put some stew on for supper and set about getting Abraham some school clothes together. I heard him playing outside telling the dog that he was going to school and that the dog was not to get lonely it was only for half a day and then he would come home and play with him. It made me laugh out loud. I thought I had better write in you today journal as I will be getting Abraham ready for school tomorrow and will be busy for a while. School, I just had to write it down one more time. My son is going to school. Oh happy day journal, happy day.

Abraham has been in school for almost three weeks now. I take him in the mornings and go pick him up at midday break. He loves it. Mr. Jameston says he is amazed at how well behaved he is at school. We have talked a bit during the break. I have been bringing him some food in return for Abraham's schooling. He told me how he came from a very wealthy family when he was younger but after his father died his mother remarried and his stepfather gambled away their fortune then killed himself. His sister had married well so his mother went to live with her.

He had been educated and wanted to see a bit of the world so he decided to become a schoolteacher. He said he eventually wanted to go out West. I told him that was very adventurous. He said he had read some books about Indians and the West and it fascinated him. I told him I loved to read but only had my bible but that I never tired of it. Abraham and I read it every night. He said he had a few books with him that he brought from home that I was welcome to read. I told him thank you. I really did not know what to say.

Books to read was just more than I could ever hope for. I gathered up Abraham for our walk home and shook his hand and said "Thank you again. You don't have any idea what this means to me Mr. Jameston." He covered my hand with both his and said "call me Matthew." I looked at him blushing and shyly said "Ok Matthew." He let go of my hands and laughed, "Now there" he said, "We are friends." I smiled back and said a friend is a good thing to have.

He went to gather the children for some more studies and Abraham and I walked home. He seems like such a good man journal. I think he is younger than I am but not by much. A friend, it has been so long since I have made a new friend. I caught myself singing around the cabin today as I prepared our supper. I had better put you up journal. Tom will be home soon and I am not ready to share you with him. He can't read this but I do not want to take the chance that your existence would make him angry. "La la la la".....I'm still singing inside.

October - The leaves are falling and the nights are cool. Tom has patched a few of the holes in the front of the cabin but there are still many more. I am afraid I will not get my extra space built this winter. I have mentioned it but just get a shrug and a wave from Tom. He is drinking a little more these days. He hasn't come home mean but he does come home some nights eat a bite and falls asleep in the chair.

Abraham is writing his letters. Matthew says he is a fast learner. He says he reads better than some of the older children. He is starting on basic numbers. He loves school. He comes home glowing afterwards. It is always nice to see Matthew at midday break. I so enjoy our talks. He is so smart. We talk about religion and politics. He discusses the Revolutionary War and how it happened. I am learning more than Abraham I think. He told me the story of George Washington and how he became president. He told me of how our country started and the bravery of the men who stood against England. It makes me so proud to be an American.

I talk to Abraham about these things and tell him that someday he will be like President Washington and be a great leader of men. He must learn all he can so he can be a great leader. I have been reading a book of plays by a man named William Shakespeare from England. I have a little trouble with the phrases he uses sometimes but he writes about people and feelings and life. It is amazing. It is one of Matthew's books. We discuss it during his break when I pick up Abraham. He gets excited that I like it so well. When I finish this one he says he has another book he wants me to read. He thinks I will like it. I like any book.

I have put up the potatoes for winter and have a sack of flour. We have a cow now that I got from sewing a gown for the cattle farmer down the road. She loved her gown and it was beautiful material to sew. When she asked me what she owned me I asked if I could use it as payment on a calf. Her husband liked her dress so much he just gave me the cow. It is so nice to have milk. Tom was happy when I told him the cow was ours. If he would just patch the holes in the cabin so the wind did not blow so hard it would be so much nicer inside for the winter. I will remind him again.

Someday I will have money enough to get a rug for the floor so it will not be so cold. Tom has gotten us quite a pile of wood chopped and stacked beside the house and I am very grateful for that. I tried to split wood but I just do not have the strength for it. I have to be careful as I do get tired and out of breath easily. Abraham is growing and I need to get him a pair of shoes from the cobbler for school. I think I can trade out some sewing for them I hope. Tom says money is very tight so I have to be very careful. I hope Tom comes home in a good mood tonight. I feel like snuggling next to him. That is one of the nice things about being married. Sleeping with someone. Better put you up journal.

November - We had our first snow. Abraham and I walked to the schoolhouse in it. Only a few of the children showed up. I stayed at the schoolhouse for the half day lesson so I did not have to walk home and back in the snow. It was a lovely day. I listened to the children read and do their lessons and Matthew talking to them about history. I wondered if I had had a different life if I would have been a schoolteacher. I think maybe I would have.

Matthew decided to let school out at the midday break as it was snowing heavier by then. He decided to walk me and Abraham home. It was a fine walk home in the snow. Abraham did not even seem to notice the cold as he skipped along. I found that I had a light cough when I got to breathing hard. Abraham said something about my singing and Matthew said "I didn't know you were a singer Nancy." I blushed and said "I sing at church and I used to sing with the slaves a long time ago." He stopped to rest a minute and said sing me a slave song. I sang a song about being a motherless child, it was a sad one but I always knew how it felt to be motherless. I found myself caught up in the song as I sang it. Feeling every emotion and letting them show in my voice. When I finished it took me a second to realize I was standing under a tree in the snow.

I looked at Matthew's face and he has tears running down his cheeks. I grew alarmed and said I did not mean to upset you. He laughed and said,"No, no you misunderstand. That was the most beautiful song I have every heard. You have one of the most incredible voices. Why, you could sing in opera houses." I laughed and said "I sing in my house and the house of God, that is surely enough."

We hurried on our way, my singing had agitated my cough somewhat. When we arrived home all red faced and laughing Tom was there. He did not look happy to see Matthew. He asked him what he was doing there. Matthew told him he just walked us home since it was snowing. Tom said that we could walk home by ourselves and didn't need no schoolteacher to see us there. He was clearly upset and had been drinking already. Matthew said his goodbyes and left.

Tom was angry and muttering under his breath "What will people think you walking home with the schoolteacher." He grabbed me by the arm and pulled me close. I could smell the liquor on his breath. "That fancy pants teacher got any other reason for walking you home wife?" he asked. "No," I said "he was just being nice because of the weather." He squeezed my arm tighter saying "Well how nice have you been to him?" I told him he was hurting me and he laughed and just squeezed harder. "You like it rough don't you woman?" he said. Again I said "Tom you are hurting me." He leaned into my face and said "You letting that fancy boy plow my fields woman?" I said "No and Tom don't say such things." He said "Maybe I ought to check under that skirt and see for myself if anybody has been there besides me."

He went to grab my skirt tail with his other hand and I said "Tom, not with the boy standing right here. Not even you are that crude." He slapped my face and said "Don't you call me crude, strumpet. I don't have nobody sniffing around me." I started to cry and he said "You think I'm crude? I'll show you crude." He pushed me into the other room and shut the door. I was in pain as it felt like he was breaking my arm. I begged him to let go of my arm that he was breaking it. He flung me across the bed and said "There I let go of it but don't think you are getting off that easy. I know you liked to spread it around with the old man but I'll be damned if you'll do it here and rub it in my face." I swore to him that I had not done anything. He grabbed his belt and said "I'll make damned sure if he looks at you again he will know you're mine."

He then threw me over on my face, pulled up my skirt and preceded to whip me with his belt across my bare buttocks. He beat me until I thought I was going to pass out then he stopped and started rubbing my fiery hot buttocks. His hands hurt almost as much as the belt at this point. He laughed and said "This is the most tender arse I will ever have a part of" and before I could say anything he took me face down on the bed. I could barely breathe as he pushed my head down into the bed. When he finished he rolled me over to face him and said "Nobody takes what's mine. This time it was a whipping, next time I'll brand you like a piece of cattle. You better not be messing with no damned fancy pants schoolteacher." I just shook my head and said ok. I was afraid to say anything else. He told me to get up and fix him something to eat. "All this discipline" he laughed "has made me powerful hungry." He pulled his pants up and laid down on the bed. "Call me when it's ready" he said.

I limped back into the other room and saw Abraham in the corner with his hands over his ears. I kissed the top of his head and told him I was all right. That Tom had just been drinking too much and it made him say harsh things. He hugged me hard and whispered "Did it hurt terrible bad?" I whispered back that it wasn't terrible bad and I would be ok. He touched my face where a bruise was starting from the slap and kissed it saying "This will make it better Mama." I almost cried but did not want Tom to see me. I told him I was better already and I fixed dinner.

During dinner Tom told me I ought to put some snow on that bruise on my face to decrease the swelling. He had sobered up a bit after eating and said he didn't mean to be so rough but a married man can only take so much when his wife shows up at his door with another man. I went and got some snow and put it in a rag on my face like he said. I wished I could just go and sit in the snow in my bare bottom cause that's what hurt so bad. I had a feeling my face didn't look anywhere near as bad as my bottom. Tom went on to bed not long after he ate saying he was plumb tuckered out.

I got Abraham settled down and sang him a little song and he went to sleep. I pulled my bodice down and looked at my arm. I could see the blue black of every single finger of Tom's around it. My chest felt tight but I think it was from shame. How could Tom think I would be a temptress to the schoolteacher? I would not even think of such a thing and my relationship with Mr. Abraham was not like that. I was not a strumpet and never have been.

What have I done to make Tom treat me so? Have I not been a good wife? Have I not tried to keep the cabin clean and food cooked? I even earned some money from my sewing so as to help pay for some of my keep. I must be failing him somehow or he wouldn't treat me this way drink or not. Maybe I am paying for laying with Mr. Abraham whilst he was married to Mrs. Sarah. Tom would not understand about the wood spirit but he should understand about strong drink. Maybe I should tell him the truth about what happened at the river that night with Mr. Abraham? I really don't know if he would believe me or not. Maybe it would be best to let sleeping dogs lie. I guess it is natural of him to think this way of me since he knew Abraham was born out of wedlock. Maybe I am judging him too harshly. The bible says to not judge.

Tom is not a bad man, I think it has just been a lot for him to come to terms with concerning me and little Abraham. I wish I could have a baby, it would ease his mind I think. I am going to stop writing journal and try to get some sleep. I think this will be the night I burn Mr. Abraham's letter. It would be for the best I think. I will try not to anger Tom and be a better wife. I must accept my shortcomings and try to overcome them. I do want to be a good wife and mother and I will just try harder and maybe Tom will not feel like he needs to punish me anymore. I am tired and my chest is tight. I think maybe it is my heart feeling tight except I do have this cough. Goodnight journal, it has been a hard day.

--- This cough has been getting worse for the past several days. I did not take Abraham to school because it hurts to walk and the bruise on my face looks horrible. I don't want anyone to see it. Tom has been very contrite about the whole thing. He again blamed it on the drink. I can barely use my arm so Tom has been fixing meals. I am trying to steam some water and breathe it over the pot with a towel over my face to help the coughing. I feel so weak even little Abraham asked me if I was going to die. I told him no, I just had a bad cough from being in the snow.

I looked at Tom and he actually looked scared and said "You don't think you are that sick do you?" I said no I would be better in a few days. I ate some broth and went back to bed and covered up. I am so cold but my skin feels so hot. I know I have a fever and I am praying to God that it is not pneumonia. Tom actually went to the doctor to get some chest liniment for me. I couldn't lay still so I thought I would write bit before he got back. Abraham read me some bible verses and I asked him to pray for me. I am praying Lord, please let me get better. Abraham needs me. Let me get well, I will be a better wife, I will not do things that will make Tom want to beat me. I will never see Matthew again if that's what it takes. Just let me get better. I am hot right now and would like to go outside to breathe but I know that will make me worse. I am going back to bed journal. Goodnight.

December - Today was Christmas. This was the first day I have really been up all day since I got so sick. The Doctor said it was pneumonia and I was lucky to have survived it. Tom took such good care of me. He would get cool water and bathe me down to try to keep the fever down. I remember him spoon feeding me soup like a baby. Abraham would come and lie down with me when I shivered so much to try to keep me warm. He would say prayers out loud for me to get well. I remember being very cold one minute and hot the next. I could not get my breath for coughing and it felt like it was breaking every bone in my body.

I never knew Tom could be so nice. Ladies from the church came by and brought food and helped look after Abraham. I am so thankful for them all, even Nancy and John came down. Nancy offered to take me to her house but Tom was afraid to move me with it being so cold. He had put rags and boards up on the walls to cover the drafts in the house. I heard him and the Doctor fussing about it the first time he came but I don't remember much after that.

Tom says I was very ill for a long time. It has been several weeks since I first got sick. When the doctor first came he was concerned about the bruises on my arm and bottom. I was really too sick to talk to him about it but I think he guessed where they came from. He doesn't seem to think much of Tom. He always has a short answer for him but he is always gentle and kind to me. He says I have to eat a lot. I have become a sack of bones over this. My dress is hanging on me today. I have my apron tied as tight as it will go.

I asked Abraham if he had been reading the bible at night. By the way he hung his head I can see that it is no. That must be remedied right away. It is more important than ever for him to be reading. I explained that to him and that he needed to do it for me. He promised if I ever got sick again he would read every night. I told him he needed to read every night no matter what happens to me.

Some nice ladies from the church brought us supper for tonight.

It is simmering on the fire and smells wonderful. Tom had to run out but said he would be back soon. I don't think he has been drinking spirits since I got sick. I hope it stays that way. He has a gentle heart in him deep down.

I apologized to Abraham for not having him a Christmas present and the sweet boy hugged me hard and said me being better was the best Christmas present ever. He is so sweet and I love him so much. I can't bear the thought that something would have happened to me and he would be alone. I wanted to try to get supper ready for Tom but I just do not have the strength for it.

Abraham brought me my journal from its hiding place so I could write for a bit. I just really wanted to let you know I was back journal. I am still here thank God. I pray that my strength comes back soon. We still have the coldest part of winter to get through and I want Abraham to go back to school. He is too young to walk there alone and I can't ask Tom to take him and bring him home.

I dreamed of my mother while I was sick. She was hanging clothes to dry in the sunshine somewhere. She looked happy. I hope she is. Having people you love be happy is the greatest gift of all. I look at Abraham to see if he has any of my Mama in him but I don't see it. He looks so much like Mr. Abraham it is hard to see anything else. He does have Tanner blood however. He worries over things and I fear that is the Tanner in him. That, I am afraid, he gets from me. I hope the worried look goes off his little face soon. He is too young to carry such worry. I need to get back on my feet and care for him. Tom should be back soon and I think I will have to retire after I eat a bite. Eating wears me out. Good night journal. It is so nice to be in the world again.

In the year of our Lord 1808 .....

January - I am getting stronger. I can do some cleaning in the house and fix meals. I still get a bit lightheaded when I do too much but I can usually sit for a bit and it gets better. The doctor says it will take some time before I get my full strength back. It is only a few weeks away from Abraham's birthday and I would like to be well by then or at least much better. Tom thinks I may have put just a hair of weight back on but I can't tell. I still look like all bones to me. Abraham says I look like a tall bird. That child is so silly. He will be four soon.

Four years and it seems like yesterday. He needs some new shoes, I can see where his growing toes are starting to put holes in his shoes. I will have to talk to Tom about it soon. I have not been taking in any sewing so there is no pocket money for me to use. Tom seems to be drinking some again but nowhere near as much as he was. He still has been so nice to me. He has not raised his voice to me or Abraham since I got sick.

He told me the other night he was sorely afeared that I was going to die. He said the nicest thing to me. He said "I would miss you girl if you died." I snuggled up next to him and when he asked me if I was strong enough for him to share our marital bed I said "Yes." He was gentle and did not hurt me. He almost acted like he was afraid I would break. It was as if that ugly time before I got sick never happened.

I wonder if God made me sick to straighten things out between me and Tom. It's possible I suppose, the Lord does move in mysterious way. If me getting sick made our marriage better then it was all worth it. He has even been playing with Abraham more. He made him some toys out of some wood scraps he had out back. Abraham talks around him a little more freely these days. It is good to feel like a family. Maybe this spring we will make a baby and Tom will feel complete.

I wish I could make a pound cake like Bessie used to do. Oh they were so good, my mouth about waters just thinking about it. I don't possibly have enough ingredients but I hope someday he can enjoy the sweet taste of pound cake that I did. I am going to go get supper on for Tom and Abraham. I will write in you soon I am sure. Good night journal.

February - We had a lovely birthday for Abraham. He is back in school. Tom has been taking him in the mornings and I pick him up at midday. The walking is helping make me stronger I think. Matthew had the whole class sing to Abraham for his birthday. He told me as I was leaving that he knew it had not been long since my birthday. He remembered me telling him it was before Abraham's. He gave me one of his books to read. I blushed and thanked him. He has not said anything about the last time he walked us home and I will not bring it up. I do not want Tom thinking I am disrespecting him in any way.

Abraham and I walked home slowly as I was not up to a fast walk yet. It was cold but beautiful and the sun was high in the sky. Abraham was showing me how he could blow smoke out his mouth when he talked. He pretended he was smoking a stick like a pipe. He had me laughing so much I had to stop and rest. It feels good to laugh out loud again.

Tom is drinking a bit more, he says there ain't as much work for him these days and it weighs on his mind so he drinks. I haven't said anything about it to him. I don't want to start an argument. The boards are still sitting beside the house for Abraham's room. I guess hopefully Tom will start on it this spring. I told him I felt like I could start sewing again some and would let the church ladies know so we could get a few things we needed. He mentioned writing a letter to Mr. Abraham letting him know how sick I had been but I told him I was just not up to writing to him just yet. He got that heavy browed look on his face but he let it drop.

I sense an uneasiness in Tom. I hope it is the weather. He has been so good and I just don't want anything to spoil it. If he will stay away from the heavy spirits I think we might just get through the winter. Abraham is helping me with supper tonight so I could have a minute to write. Even at his young age he understands how important this journal is to me. It is our secret. I must go now journal and help Abraham.

March - I am worried journal. Tom is drinking more heavily. I really don't know where he gets it as he says we have no money. He is pressuring me to write Mr. Abraham for more money. I do not want to do that. Mr. Abraham has given us enough. I am trading my sewing for food and supplies so we have enough to eat but I never see anything Tom makes. He says that money is his worry and not mine but I am the one who worries.

I am not gaining much weight back and Tom seems to think it is my fault. He accuses me of not wanting to put on weight. I told him that is silly, of course I wanted to put on some weight. I know I am too boney. The other night he was none to gentle in our marriage bed and he complained that my hip bones were digging into him. He rolled me over on top because he said I was going to poke a hole in him with my bones. His dissatisfaction is spilling over on us all.

Abraham has taken to being quiet again when Tom is home and Tom just doesn't like anything. He was fussing about the cabin being unlivable and when I said we had been living in it just fine he blew up and yelled at me. I had gotten a little bit of my spirit back and I told him if he would fix it up it wouldn't seem so bad. His face got all red and he said through his teeth, "Don't be nagging on me woman. I told you I will not hold with no nagging woman." He had a smoldering fire in his eyes.

I quickly changed the subject and asked him about how his feet were feeling. He had been complaining about them hurting lately. He calmed down and said they were still stinging some. I got some warm wet cloths and took off his shoes and rubbed his feet with them. He seemed much calmer and in better spirits after that. He has brought some whiskey home as I have seen him taking a drink out back of the house. I am not sure what to make of that. I hope he realizes how too much drink affects him.

He went to bed early tonight so I decided to write some. I am uneasy journal, Tom worries me. I cannot talk to him about this, it angers him too much. I just pray that I can be a good and gentle wife and that he will come to his senses. Hopefully we will have a baby in our future. I am sure he will stop drinking so much if we had a child together. If you were a person journal I would ask you to pray for me. I have Abraham say a prayer for Tom every night so hopefully God is listening to us. It is past time for me to retire journal. Good night.

April - Things took a bad turn today. Tom got plumb ugly about our money situation. He yelled at me to write for more money. Abraham took off outside. Tom's face looked like a thunderstorm waiting to crash down on us. I told him I didn't feel it was right. He yelled at me that I was a fine one to talk about what was right. He got some paper down for me and pushed me down in the chair and whispered in my ear "You are going to write that letter and you are going to do it now." It was a venomous whisper and it frightened me deeply. I told him I would write the letter.

As I sat down to write I was so upset that some tears fell on the paper. This enraged Tom. He started yelling, "You shed tears for that bastard" and he threw his chair into the wall. He grabbed me by the arms and jerked me up out of the chair I was sitting in. He shook me hard. "Don't you dare shed a tear over that old man in my house. He soiled you and then expected me to clean up his mess. He owes me and hell he owes you. He sold you to me just like a damned slave for me to get his bastard out of the way. I may not be educated but I ain't no fool. The whole town knew what was going on back there."

I said quietly "I ain't nobody's slave and I never will be." He laughed an ugly laugh and said "Well what do you call this life your livin' girl?" I said "I am your wife, not a slave." He said "I'll show you wife, how close you are to slave" and he bent me over the table and took me hard right then and there. "I take you when I want, where I want. Is that slave or it that wife? You tell me woman."

When he was finished he pulled my skirt down and shoved me back in the chair and said "Now can you write the damned letter without tears." I managed to write the letter and he took it from me and said he would get it sent out today. He was reeking of whiskey and tobacco. He told me to get cleaned up and get some supper on. It was after all he laughed my wifely duties.

He left and once I made sure he was gone I cleaned up and went into the other room and had a good cry. I swore he would never see me cry in front of him again no matter what. I washed my face and yelled for Abraham to come home. I fixed supper but Tom did not come home tonight. I don't know where he is staying and right now I do not care. I would bring Abraham into my bed but if Tom comes home I would be afraid of a scene. I hope he stays away long enough to sober up. I am trying to be a good wife but I am not a slave. I pray to the Lord that the blackness in his soul would be lifted. I know he took me and Abraham and gave us his name for money paid to him but I am sure given enough time he can learn to see that I am a good wife and Abraham is a good son.

Abraham asked me if Tom hurt me again and it almost broke my heart. I tried to explain to him that Tom had demons in him when he drank too much and that they tormented him and it made him act out. I told him we needed to pray for him to be released from his torment and we needed to be extra good to Tom. He looked at me oddly but he did pray for Tom that night.

Journal I don't know how to help Tom, I wish I did. He is a good man but he gets taken over by strong drink. I pray for us all three. I will try to be a better wife and mother and show Tom the goodness that is in this house. Goodnight journal, may the Lord watch over Tom tonight where ever he is and bring him home safe on the morrow.

July - So much has happened. I don't know where to start. Abraham, sweet, sweet Abraham had enough sense to grab my journal and bring it with us without anybody seeing him. He is a joy, a gift sent to me by both my God and the Indian ones. He is so much older than his years and has so much wisdom for one whose time has been so short on this earth. This is the first time I have been able to sit down and write. Abraham saw me sitting today in the sunshine and asked me if I felt strong enough to write in my journal. He seemed so relieved when I told him yes. He ran and got my journal and handed it to me like a precious gift. He said I know you are getting better Mama when you write.

He sits right with me barely leaving my side when I am awake. I think he has decided he is my protector even though I have no need of one where we are now. He has been reading the bible out loud to me while I have been bedridden. It has been such a comfort to hear his words. They flow through me like a summer breeze lightening the darkness that has surrounded my heart. I am surrounded by love and light and happiness here. I hope that it will help me fight the darkness that my mind wants to descend to at times.

I am not able to walk yet but I do feel some strength returning.

John has called for Abraham to come outside and help him with the horses. Abraham's eyes brightened up but then he said "I can stay here with you Mama." I smiled and told him to "Go on outside with John, I would be alright with my journal." He jumped up and gave me a very careful light hug and kissed my cheek and said "I love you Mama." I smiled and said "I love you too now go out and have some fun. I will be fine." He still had that worried look on his face when he looked at me but he said "I guess it's ok since you are writing."

Nancy came in with a glass of tea for me and noticed the journal. She said "Are you still writing in that thing?" I said "Yes, when I get a chance." She laughed and said she never could get in the habit of doing it even though she knew she should. She patted my back and said "Drink your tea and I will leave you to your musing. If you need me just yell, I will be working in the other room today." I smiled and thanked her.

She and John are my angels. They swooped in and took in Abraham and I and nursed me back to health. I am alive today because of them. It is a debt I will never be able to repay. I do not know if I have the strength to write of this today. The sun is shining through the window and I feel warm. I can hear Abraham's laughter as he plays with the horses. This will be a dark and violent tale and I am just not ready to face it yet I fear. I am sorry journal I am not as ready to write as I thought yet. I must muster some more strength to face this with courage. I think I will just nap for a while. Until later journal, until later.

--- John carried me into the study so I could sit by the window today. I was watching Matthew playing with Abraham. I feel so blessed that Matthew is spending the summer here working with John. He is continuing his lessons with Abraham and working with John to make money for his eventual trip out West. He talks to me some when I am up in the evenings. He loves to talk about George Washington and the Revolution. One of his favorite people is Thomas Jefferson. He and John talk at length about his philosophies and thoughts on government.

I sit with Abraham by my feet and listen as well as I can. Sometimes the haze comes over me and I drift off. No one mentions my injuries and no one talks about Tom where I can hear them. They whisper. If I had more strength I would ask them not to but I just am not up to it yet. The doctor has a draught that he has me drink for pain. It makes me sleepy but it does decrease the pain. The broken bones are mending, but they say it will take time. The scars not so much, they are still red and angry. Nancy says my face does not look bad but I can feel the damage with my hand. I am not brave enough to look in a mirror yet. I still have a slight cough but I try hard to suppress it as it just hurts too much.

Nancy takes such good care of me. I am so glad she is here. I am as helpless as a baby. I have to be carried and washed and dressed like an infant. She just smiles and says I will regain my strength soon. I hope so. Just writing in this journal exhausts me.

Nancy says Mr. Abraham will be here soon. He is coming to see me and Abraham. I don't know how I feel about that. I do so hate for him to see me this way. I really need to try to understand what has happened to me so I can explain it to him.

He will be so proud of Abraham, he reads to me every night from the bible. I wish he did not have that worried frown on his face so much. He has seen so much in his young life. I had hoped to protect him from some of the harsher things in life but it is not be. At least I am alive. I have beat death twice now so I must be on my guard. There is so much I must teach Abraham and there is so little time. I must help him prepare for the burdens that life will place on him. I must face the facts of what has happened to me so I can move on and so I can help Abraham move on. I must face them but not today. Today I am going to enjoy the sunshine on my face and the joy of listening to Abraham play childish games. There is time for dealing with the past later.

--- Today I was sitting in the study and one of the slaves dropped a metal bucket. It made quite a racket. Abraham came running in the house toward me screaming "Mama, Mama are you all right?" He ran up to me wild eyed and then dropped to his knees, buried his head in my lap and sobbed. "I thought you had died" he said through mumbled tears. "I was scared you died and fell out of the chair." I stroked his head and tried to comfort him but the tears just shook his little body. I felt tears stinging my eyes at his pain.

Nancy came running in wanting to know what all the

commotion was about. I waved her away. I rubbed Abraham's head until I could see the emotion quieting in his little body. Finally he was just laying his head on my lap. I began to sing a lullaby that I had learned from the slaves long ago. He looked up at me very seriously and said "I love you Mama." I told him I loved him too. He said "I could not bear it if you died. I do not want to live if you die."

"Oh my sweet Abraham" I told him, "You are flesh of my flesh, my blood runs through your veins, as long as you breathe I live. I will never die as long as you live. My body may die someday but my spirit will always be within you. Just close your eyes and you will always feel my presence in your heart." He gently put his arms around my waist and said "But I want to feel you with my arms Mama." I wiped his tears off his cheeks and told him I would try harder to get better so we could walk and play together again. He asked "You are getting better aren't you Mama?" "Yes," I told him "I am getting better." "Good" he said and he hugged me a bit harder.

I ruffled his hair and told to stop worrying so much and go out and play. He got up and walked to the door and turned and said "I will go play Mama but I will never stop worrying." After he left I thought to myself is this the part the old Indian told me about. The hard part, to teach him how to live with the constant worry. I must get better for we have much to do and talk about. I see Nancy has prepared me a wonderful bowl of stew so I think I will eat some to gain some strength. Maybe tomorrow will be the day I can face this. I know I must in order to put it behind me. Tomorrow journal, maybe tomorrow.

--- Abraham had a bad dream last night. I heard him cry out and I told him to crawl up in bed with me. He scooted under the covers. I asked him what the dream was about and he said "I was in a dark place all alone and there were so many dead outside. It was all my fault Mama. I didn't kill them but it was my fault they were dead. I was so sad and so scared and I couldn't find you anywhere." Well I told him "You have found me now and there are no dead men outside and if there were it would not be your fault. You are just a little boy." You lie here close to me and go back to sleep. When you close your eyes I am always with you.

He wound his hand in my hair and I sung him a lullaby until I felt him drift off. I didn't go back to sleep right away. I remembered what the old Indian had said about Abraham when he was heavy in my belly. He would lead men but at a great cost. I prayed that this dream was not a premonition of that. I had to teach him that even though he would feel alone at times he never would be.

I prayed for God to watch over my sweet boy and give me the strength I needed to re-enter life with him. It has been a better day today. Abraham has dark circles under his eyes from not sleeping well last night but he appears otherwise ok. I did not drink as much of the pain draught today so I felt a bit clearer of thought.

Today is the day, I must exorcise this demon of my past if I want to move forward. I must allow myself to remember the details of that night in order to permanently forget them. Tom's drinking had gotten worse. He was unhappy with everything. Nothing I did or Abraham did was right. He had taken to staying away all night at times and would show back up in the morning. Things between the two of us grew quite strained. He was becoming more and more agitated that I had not received word from Mr. Abraham about sending more money. The night before everything happened he had come home drinking.

I had fixed supper for him and he said he did not like how it looked. He threw the plate out the door and said it was slop only fit for hogs. Abraham was sitting eating his and Tom snatched his plate also and threw it outside. He said he wasn't eating slop either as a matter of fact no one was going to eat slop under his roof. Abraham got away from the table and went and curled up in a ball on his cot.

Tom yelled at him and called him feeble brained that he would curl up and not say anything. I told Tom to quit picking on Abraham, he was just a little boy and he was scared. He reached over and grabbed Abraham and said "I'll show him scared." He picked him up and Abraham started screaming. Tom slapped him hard across the face and told him to shut up. I grabbed Tom's arm and begged him to let Abraham down. He dropped Abraham and I told him to run outside and hide. He ran out the door and that enraged Tom. He turned to me and slapped me hard across the face. "You will not tell that boy to run from me, I will not have it" he said, "Maybe you are the one who needs the beating, not Abe."

I was angry that he had hit Abraham and I foolishly said to Tom.

"His name is Abraham not Abe." He slapped me again and I fell to the floor. "You will not correct me in my own house woman. I will not stand for it. Maybe you need another arse whipping to learn your place." He undid his belt and started towards me. I tried to crawl to the door and he grabbed me by the hair. He pulled me up over the table and bent me double and raised my skirt. I begged him not to hit me. I said I would do whatever he asked if he wouldn't hit me.

He laughed in an evil way and said "I just don't know, you felt nice and warm last time I whipped you, maybe I would like to try that again." He hit me three times with the belt and then he dropped the belt and took me. He pounded me so hard that I scraped my chin on the table. When he finished he threw me down on the floor. He arraigned his pants and said "Maybe I just didn't beat you enough, it weren't near as warm as last time."

I just sat very still hoping he had exhausted himself. He sat down in the chair and looked at me. He said "You gonna just sit on that floor on your arse all night or you gonna get me something to eat?" I got up and fixed him something. He ate a bite and then took out a jug and started drinking from it. I just sat still in the chair trying not to anger him. After drinking a while he said he was going someplace where the women are friendly and had a little meat on their bones. "Damn Nancy" he said, "You feel like a twelve year old boy and you ain't even got no breasts no more. What kinda a man wants that in his bed."

He took his jug and went out the door. I heard him yelling to Abraham that he could come back in and hide under Mama's skirts cause he was done there for the night. Abraham waited until he was far down the road before he came back into the house. I checked his face where Tom had struck him. It was red and was going to leave a mark for sure. I put a cool cloth on it. He reached up to my face and said you need a cloth too Mama. I shushed him and he kissed my face. He said "I love you Mama." I told him I loved him too.

He asked me what was wrong with Tom, why was he so mean? I told him it was the drink that made him mean and that we needed to get on our knees and pray for Tom. We did just that we prayed out loud that God would enter Tom's heart and cure him of his affliction. We prayed that we would be better and not invoke his wrath.

Tom did not come home that night. I tossed and turned all night.

I did not know how I could endure this if it continued and I could not let him abuse Abraham. I prayed for God to send me a sign.

The next morning was a beautiful May day, there was a slight breeze, the sun was shining and the flowers looked beautiful in the fields. I decided to keep Abraham home from school as I was very tender when I tried to walk much. Around lunchtime Nancy Thompson came riding up with her slave on the wagon. I was so pleased to see her. I asked about John but she said he had to do some work in the upper fields so he couldn't come. She noticed the darkening bruise on my face right away and her eyes went up but when she hugged Abraham she saw the bruise on his face too and she couldn't hold her tongue. "Did Tom do this to you two?" she asked. Before I could answer Abraham said "Yes and he spanked Mama with the belt cause I heard him."

Nancy was mortified. She demanded that I gather up our things and come back with her. I told her I couldn't do that but it broke my heart when Abraham asked me if he could go. I told him to gather a few things and I would let him go for a few days. He put his arms around me and said "You need to come too Mama. Tom will just get mad and hurt you again." I told him it would be worse if Tom came home and we were both gone.

Nancy had brought me a letter from Abraham and some money. She told me that Mr. Abraham had heard rumors that Tom was drinking heavily and gambling and he told her to tell me to only give Tom a third of the money and to put the rest up so I could use it for me and Abraham. I separated the money and left a third in the pouch. The rest I put in Abraham's clothing pouch and told him to take it with him and he could bring it back when he came back home.

Nancy was trying to talk me into coming with them at least until Tom could dry out when Tom came bursting through the door much drunker than when he had left the night before. He screamed at Nancy that she couldn't be coming into his house and taking what was rightfully his, then he saw the money pouch. He picked it up and poured out the money on the table. He screamed "Is all the old man thinks it takes to keep up his harlot and his little bastard."

Nancy stood up and told him not to talk of me that way. He sneered at her and said "What do you know of your father's dallying. She spread her legs for him and God knows who else afore I ever bought her. I'm just the fool that got stuck with them both." He looked at Abraham clutching his clothes and said "Where do you think you're going boy?" Abraham just stood there mute and afraid.

Tom got mad because he didn't answer and he slapped Abraham hard across the head knocking him to the floor. "You gonna talk to me now you little bastard?" he said. Nancy jumped up and grabbed Abraham and said "You will not strike this child again." He looked at her and laughed and said "I have the right to strike anyone in my house and if you don't get out of my way I'll strike you too."

I begged him not to slap Nancy. He turned to me and said "Oh now you're begging again. You want me to give you what you got last night in front of your fine friend and the boy." I said "Tom just let them both go and I will do what ever you want." He grabbed me and said "You're damned right you'll do what ever I want and when ever I want it woman."

Nancy grabbed Abraham and then made for the door when Tom noticed the glint of the money in Abraham's clothing bundle. He pushed Nancy aside and grabbed Abraham's clothing bundle and ripped it open causing the money to fall out. He slapped Abraham again and said "You're stealing from me boy." Nancy got between him and Abraham and I grabbed him by the arm. He was like an enraged bull. He was screaming "I will not be duped by two women and a child. You will not make a fool out of me."

He struck at Nancy hitting her shoulder and knocking her down and he went after Abraham again. I threw myself between them and said "Take it out on me I was the one who told him to hide the money." He grabbed me in a blind fury and began to shake me. I screamed at Nancy to take Abraham and go. She grabbed him and ran for the wagon. Tom dropped me and started after them. I jumped on his back and started screaming at him to let them go. He turned back to me and punched me hard in the face, it blinded me for a moment but I did not let go.

I saw Nancy and Abraham riding off as hard as they could go. Tom grabbed me by the hair and drug me back in the cabin. He said "You wanted to take their punishment then so be it." I begged him to stop, to not hit me anymore. He just laughed and said "You steal from me and hide things and you don't expect to get hit. You're a Jezebel and a damned thief and I'll teach you that you will not hide things from me." He grabbed his razor strap and began to beat me. I tried to get away from him but there was no where to go. It infuriated him that I tried to get away. He grabbed me up and punched me in the face again. I remember falling down on the floor.

I came to naked with my hands tied over my head. Tom had thrown water on my face. He hung the straps on my hands on a nail on the wall and said "You need to be awake for your punishment. You took money from me and that's breaking a law and the sentence for that is to be whipped. I will teach you that you will not hide things from me. I am tired of being played the fool by you and old man Abraham."

I pleaded with him to let me down and he just laughed and took another drink out of his jug. When he saw me looking at the jug he said "Oh I got plenty to do me for all night here. I plan to teach you a lesson you won't forget." He grabbed the razor strap and said "I watched slaves get whipped before for lying and what you done is worse so I'm going to treat you like the lying thief you are, a lying thieving wife-slave."

He hit my bare bottom hard with the strap. I cried out in pain and he said "Good I want to know you are feeling it." He beat me and beat me with the strap all up and down my back, buttocks and legs. He finally got tired and stopped. I could feel blood running down my legs. I asked him if he would let me down. He said "No woman I won't, I ain't done with you yet. I just need to rest and drink a bit more to continue." I hung there a while.

He went outside to relieve himself and I had hoped he had forgotten me but it was not to be. He came back and turned me around. He ran his hands up and down over my nakedness. He grabbed my breasts and squeezed them hard. He said "I can't even get them to puff up when I squeeze them." Then he bit me on the breast and laughed and said maybe they would swell up and look like a woman's breast. He bit me all over my breasts like a dog. He broke the skin in several places and bit my nipples so hard they bled.

He grabbed my womanhood and squeezed me so hard it took my breath. He leaned forward stinking of alcohol and sour tobacco and said "Oh you like that do you?" He put his hands inside me spreading me far apart until I thought he would split me and he just laughed when I pleaded with him to stop before he killed me. He said "As many as been down there I don't think there is no danger of that." It seemed like that made him madder. He said "Ain't no man gonna ever touch you there again you hear me, no man." He then went to the fireplace and put in a metal rod.

"Remember what I told you woman last time, I told you I would brand you like the cow you are, well I'm gonna do that. Any man that gets near you there will know you belong to me." I started to struggle as I realized the madness that stared at me out of his eyes. This was not Tom, this was a devil. He saw me struggling and grabbed the strap and began to beat me on my front side with it. He beat my breast, my belly the front of my thighs. The more he hit me the madder he got. I cried and begged him to stop.

He finally stopped long enough to take a big drink out of the jug. I had never seen a man so crazed. He sat down in the chair and just looked at me. "Tell me how sorry you are" he said. "Tell me how you lied to me." I cried and told him I was sorry, that I would never lie to him again that I would never steal from him again if he would just let me down. He just sat there drinking watching my bloody beaten body hanging on the straps from the nail begging him to let me down.

I thought he might when he heard a hiss from the fireplace. He looked at me with pure evil in his eyes and said "Tell me about the schoolteacher." I said there was nothing to tell. He jumped up and slapped my face and said "You lie, tell me how you have laid with him. Tell me how he has taken you. Tell me, tell me now."

I shook my head and said "He never has. I would not let him." He screamed "You lie, I know you lie." He grabbed me and said "He will never take you again." I screamed "You are hurting me, please, please stop." He said "I'll stop when you tell me the truth. How many men have you been with? How big a fool am I? Do they all come and pleasure you when I am away? Do you let the boy watch." I just shook my head "No, no, no" I cried.

He walked over to the fireplace and got out the red hot iron rod he had placed in it. He walked over to my body and I could feel the heat of the rod. He said "They will never take you again without knowing you are mine." He pulled my legs apart and stuck the red hot iron on the side of my womanhood. I screamed and fainted. I came to as he threw water on my face. He said "I am not done with you yet. You got to be awake to feel this if you are to learn a lesson." He had reheated the iron and he pressed in on my breast. I smelt the sear of my flesh as it burned me. I did not faint this time but looked him straight in the eyes and said "If you are going to kill me then just do it."

He dropped the rod like it had burned him. He took me off the nail and unbound my wrists. I collapsed on the floor while he sat back down and drank some more. He said "You ever lie to me again and I will kill you." I couldn't get up so I just sat there. I asked for some water. He gave me some to drink. I thanked him and he got mad again. "You always trying to make me feel inferior to you ain't you." I said "No, I was just grateful for the water."

He jerked me up and bent me over the table. "I'll give you something to be grateful for" he said and he began to take me. The pain was almost unbearable from the burns but he kept on. The harder he thrusted the madder he got, he began to yell "Was this how the other men had taken you, has the old man done you this way?" Then he laughed and said "I'll take you like no other has I bet" and he violated me from behind like an animal.

I screamed in pain and rage. He laughed and said "I finally got to be first in you in something." When he finished he turned me over and said "My God you look disgusting." He dumped me in the floor. I just lay there moaning for a while. He continued to drink. I was praying that he would pass out soon.

He got quiet and I thought he had finally passed out. I began to inch towards the door. He jumped up when he realized I was trying to get away and he kicked me hard in the ribs. He then began to curse and kick me like a dog. He kicked my arms and legs and then he kicked me in the head. Everything went black for a bit and then I came to. He was grabbing me again and this time I tried to fight. I knew he was not going to stop until he killed me. He threw me into the wall and I felt my leg snap under me. I tried to roll away and he hit me with the chair and I felt my arm break. I tried to scoot under the table but he dragged me out and began to pound me with his fist. The last thing I remember is him repeatedly hitting my face. I guess I passed out when my head hit the fireplace.

Nancy said she had gone home with Abraham and tried to find John. He did not come in until late. She kept telling him that they had to go and get me. John was furious that Tom had shoved and tried to hit her. He told her she had to stay at home with Abraham. She refused and said somebody needed to be there for me.

They left Abraham there with the slaves and then rode down to the cabin. When they got there it was all over. John entered the cabin with his gun and found Tom passed out in the back room. He saw me unconscious, naked, broken and bleeding on the floor. He checked me and saw I was still alive. He ran out to Nancy and had her go and get the doctor and the sheriff. Nancy flew off in the wagon. John went back in the house and found a blanket to cover me.

When the doctor and sheriff got back with Nancy, John made her stay outside. He said he couldn't bear for her to see the horror inside the cabin. The sheriff woke Tom up and took him down to the jail. The doctor checked me out and told John that I was too injured to be moved anywhere and got him to help him put me onto the bed. Once they had me on the bed and covered John let Nancy come into the cabin. When she saw me she said she almost fainted. She had never seen anyone hurt that bad.

She and the doctor stayed with me for two days as he thought I might die from my injuries. After two days I had still not regained consciousness so the doctor said they could carefully move me to their house. He splinted my bones as best he could and had bandaged my wounds. Nancy said they carefully placed me on a mattress in the wagon and she, John, the doctor, and Abraham took me to their house.

I woke up about a week later. I didn't know where I was at first but was just glad to be alive. Abraham was the first face I saw. Nancy said he had been sitting in a chair by my bed all day since they brought me home. When I opened my eyes he yelled for Nancy. "She's awake" he yelled, "She's awake." Nancy came running and told him to quiet down. I tried to smile at him but could just barely move my mouth. He was the most beautiful thing I had ever seen.

I was broken and bruised all over. Abraham stayed by my side until Nancy would run him off. She said he had not left my side since I got there. He had even been sleeping on a blanket on the floor of my room. She spoon fed me and slowly brought me back. John came in and told me that Tom was in jail and wasn't getting out anytime soon and that they were taking care of Abraham for me not to worry about anything. He said "You can stay here forever if that's what you want." I couldn't talk but I tried to thank him with my eyes.

It has been a long recovery to get to where I am now. I have been here for eight weeks now and still cannot walk but I am getting stronger and I will recover. I have much more to show and teach Abraham. There journal, I have written down the evil that was done to me. I am innocent of all the charges that Tom laid upon me. Now that I have written it maybe I can purge it from my soul. I fear that my body must heal first but the mind may take longer. The scars you can see are one thing but the scars that both Abraham and I carry inside are not as visible yet just as ugly. Those I will have to work on just as diligently as the ones on my body.

This has exhausted me journal. Reliving all this pain and agony has worn me out completely. I may not write for a while. I think this just needs to settle in my head. I hope this will help me so I can help Abraham. He needs me so much right now. Good night journal.

--- Mr. Abraham came in today. I was sitting in my chair when he came in. He just stood in the door for the longest time looking at me with tears welling up in his eyes. When they spilled over onto his cheeks he came over to me and got on his knees and took my hands and said "Nancy, oh my sweet Nancy, will you ever forgive me for bringing this evil upon you." I looked at him and said "Mr. Abraham this was not your doing. No one could have known that drinking would let the devil in and take over Tom."

He touched my face which was almost healed except for the scar over my eye and said "John told me about how he found you. It is a miracle that you survived." I smiled at him and said "Your Nancy saved me and Abraham both." He stood up and paced around the room. He turned to me and said "Tom needs to pay for what he has done." I said he has been in jail for almost eight weeks, seems like that a lot of time for paying especially since he was not in his right mind when he did these things. "Nancy," Mr. Abraham said "surely you are not defending the animal that did this to you." "It was not him," I said, "I saw the devil in his eyes. It was the drink that did it, it allowed the devil to possess him. Tom would not do such an evil thing on his own. He has a good heart Mr. Abraham he is just not a strong man and the devil took advantage of that."

"He allowed the devil to take him over" said Mr. Abraham "and he must bear the responsibility of that action. No man drunk or sober should be allowed to treat someone like he did you." "Mr. Abraham", I said, "God has seen fit that I survived and God is the only true judge of us all." He said "There is God's law and there is man's law and he broke both of them. I am on my way to see him now. He at least deserves to be horsewhipped."

When he said that I shivered all over. "Please Mr. Abraham, don't do anything that would enrage him more against me. He already has difficulty dealing with me and you." "Don't you worry Nancy," he said, "he will never bother you again." I put my hand out and said "Please Mr. Abraham there has been enough pain." He again bent down on his knees and put his arms around me holding me gently against him and said "There will be no more pain for you. I will not allow it. You will live here until you recover and then I will make other arrangements. He will never hurt you again."

He stood up and said "I will take my leave from you now." As he was leaving Abraham came running into the room. Mr. Abraham looked at him and said "You stay close to your mother boy. She needs you now." He came running over to me and put his arms around my shoulders. He looked at Mr. Abraham and said fiercely "Nobody's going to hurt my Mama ever again." "That's right son," he said, "That's right."

Abraham stayed with me for a while. Matthew came in and said "John, Nancy and Mr. Abraham had gone into town." He told Abraham to go wash up for supper. After he left the room Matthew said "The boy looks like his father doesn't he?" I didn't say anything. Matthew said "I am not judging you Nancy but is this the reason Tom got so violent?" I looked at Matthew and said "It is a long and complicated story but Tom has always known who Abraham's father was. I never hid it from him. I was an indentured servant in Mr. Abraham's house when all this happened. Tom married me knowing the situation. He took us both and gave us a name and I will be forever grateful to him for that fact if nothing else."

Matthew looked at me and asked "Do you love him?" I asked him "Who?" He stopped for a minute and said "Either of them?" I told him "I will love Mr. Abraham for all my days. He was the first real family I ever had but it was not the kind of love between a man and a woman. I am not ashamed of our child. He was not a child conceived by sin but by Fate. As far as Tom goes, I did not love him, I had hoped that with time I could grow to love him. He came along not long after them man I loved died in an accident and I agreed to marry him. It solved a problem for me and for Mr. Abraham to have me married and away from Puzzle Creek where we lived."

He shook his head and said your life sounds like a Greek tragedy. I told him it was not a tragedy it was a triumph. "I am alive, Abraham is here and he will grow up to become a great leader of men. It was foretold to me and I know it to be true. That is why I work so hard for him to learn."

Abraham came back into the room so we stopped talking about this and we all had some dinner. After dinner I asked Matthew to help me stand for a bit. After a few minutes I felt steady on my feet and actually took a few steps. It felt wonderful. Abraham just clapped his hands in joy. I smiled at him as I sat down and said now you know how I felt the first time you walked.

It was a wonderful evening. Matthew and Abraham read the bible aloud to me until I got sleepy. They carried me to my room but I could not sleep. I decided to sit up and write for a bit. It has been a lovely evening. I have not felt this good in a long time. I hope everything went well with Mr. Abraham and Tom but I will not let it worry me tonight. I hope they will all be back tomorrow and we can put this behind us. Goodnight journal I think I will sleep now.

--- It is just the afternoon but I had retired to my room and thought I would write a bit. Mr. Abraham, Nancy and John returned late morning. It seems there was a horrible confrontation between Mr. Abraham and Tom. According to Nancy, Mr. Abraham had asked the Sheriff to let Tom out of his cell so he could talk to him. Nancy said that Mr. Abraham wanted to talk to Tom in private. She said she, John and the Sheriff waited outside.

They had been talking for a while when they heard a commotion. They ran into the room and Mr. Abraham and Tom were in a knock down drag out fight. Mr. Abraham seemed to be getting the better of Tom so the Sheriff let it go on for a bit but then Tom bit off a piece of Mr. Abraham's nose and the sheriff hit Tom over the head with the butt of his rifle knocking him out. Tom was put back in his cell and the doctor was called over to treat Mr. Abraham.

It seemed Tom did not bite it clear off but it was hanging by just a bit of skin. The doctor put the skin back on and put some medicine on it and bandaged it. He told Mr. Abraham that it might heal back but there would be a scar no doubt. Mr. Abraham had the doctor go check on Tom as he had gotten quite a few blows in himself and wanted to make sure he had not killed him.

They stayed in town for the night to make sure Tom woke up in the morning. The next morning the Sheriff came over and told them Tom was awake but a little worse for wear. He told them since I was not going to die he would just be sentenced to some hard labor for a while instead of hanging. Tom had asked if Mrs. Nancy would stop by the jail so he could apologize to her for his behavior. John said absolutely not but Nancy said she would go.

All three of them went to the jail. Tom's head was hanging low when they arrived. When Nancy spoke to him he looked up and softly said "Mrs. Nancy I am sorry I hit you, there was no call. You have never been anything but nice to me and you are a fine lady and I am sorry." He then asked her how me and Abraham was doing. She told him I was healing but could not walk yet and that the boy was fine. He told her he was sure enough sorry for what he did. He said he didn't remember most of it and when the Sheriff told him what he had done he was sickened by it. He said "The drink made me evil. I knew it was happening and I didn't stop it. I am so sorry and I know that Nancy and the boy will never forgive me. She is a good woman my Nancy and did not deserve any of this. I understand if she never wants to see me again but please send her my deepest apologies for what I done."

Nancy said Mr. Abraham looked at Tom and said "I told you yesterday you ain't never to see her or the boy again and if you try to I will kill you myself." He dropped his head and said "I will never lay a hand on her or the boy ever again as God is my witness." John said "Good, God is your witness and so are we." They left then and came home.

John said Tom will be in jail for a few more months of hard labor and then he will be released. He said for me not to worry he had given orders to shoot to kill if anyone saw him near the house. I just shook my head and said they'll be no need of that. I am sure Tom will see the evil of his ways. I pray for him every night, poor man. Mr. Abraham snorted and said poor man my arse under his breath but I heard him. I asked him if the nose hurt much and he said no it just throbbed a little. He laughed and said "I have been in worse fights."

It was time for a bite of lunch and I surprised everyone by standing up and walking to the table. It took all I could do but it was time for me to get better. I must put this behind me. Needless to say after the meal I asked for help to get to my room. I am not ready for stairs yet. Oh journal I wish Mr. Abraham had not fought with Tom and gotten injured. How many more people have to suffer because of this? Poor Tom, he sounds broken almost. I know he don't remember what happened, I saw the madness in his eyes. I pray for him to find peace and stop drinking heavily. At least being in jail will keep him from drinking. Maybe by the time he gets out he won't need it anymore.

I do not want to see him, maybe in time I can but not now. I must learn forgiveness in my heart for him and I have not yet. I will pray to learn forgiveness and maybe with time God will grant me that power. In the meantime I must concentrate on Abraham. Life is short and he has much to learn.

Funny thing about talking with Matthew yesterday, I did not feel ashamed or judged. It was I imagine like having a brother. I can talk to him, he understands. I am glad he is here. Again I think it is fate. He can teach Abraham so much being with him all the time and I need to learn more about our country if I am to teach Abraham to lead men someday. I am going to lie down and rest a bit before dinner. I pray that peace will come to us all soon. It is time.

--- Mr. Abraham left today to go back to Oconoluftee. He said he had been gone long enough and needed to return home. He has stayed for two weeks. He has helped me walk and get my strength back in my legs. He has carried me up the stairs many a night. He swears I am smaller than when I was a twelve year old child first come to Puzzle Creek. He has treated me like a loving father. He has made no advances or gestures that could be misconstrued.

Last night he came into my room after everyone was asleep. He had seen the candle in my window. He pulled up a chair and sat beside me stroking my hair. He said "Nancy you know that I love you and the boy and I would do anything for you that I can. This has broken my heart and made me realize the depth of my feelings for you. I will never come to you again unless you first ask me to but be advised if you indicate that I ever would be welcome in your bed I will come. You are in my blood like a sickness for which there is no cure. My life is not such that I could be with you like a husband. I have Sarah and the children to think of and I do love them. Sarah is a magnificent woman in her own right and she has done right by me even when I have done wrong by her, but I will take care of you in what ever way you need. You are without a man now but if you need me I will be there. Even lying there right now you stir my blood but I will not molest you Nancy. You are too good, too sweet and too kind. It will have to be enough to remember and know that we have a son together. A fine, smart, strapping lad who will grow up to make me proud I am sure."

I looked gently at him and said "I love you Mr. Abraham and I too am proud of our son. I will not ever ask you to share my bed because you belong to Mrs. Sarah and I love her too. I do not have a man but I think it is time for me to start to take care of myself. Not all women have a man and they do just fine in life." He said "But a young woman like you needs love." I told him I had plenty of love from my friends and Abraham and someday when it was time Joshua would come for me and I would have love again. I was in a good place and he need not worry.

He leaned over and gently kissed my lips and said "There will never be another woman like you Nancy Hanks, never again." I smiled and reminded him I was Nancy Lincoln now and intended to keep the name. He bid me goodnight and put out my candle and left.

I laid there for a while and thought about our conversation. This had changed our relationship, for the first time I did not feel that he had some kind of magical hold over me. I loved him but it was a pure and sweet love and I felt sure his would turn to that someday to for me. Abraham is my life now and that is how it should be.

It was a quiet afternoon after he left we had a nice dinner with Abraham, Matthew, John and Nancy. The evening ended with

Abraham reading from the bible with Matthew's help and Nancy and I doing some sewing. I managed to get up most of the stairs tonight but still needed help with the last few. I am getting stronger every day. It is time to start a new life. Goodnight journal.

--- I made it down the stairs alone today. I felt quite proud. I have a bit of a limp from the broken bones in my leg but it doesn't hurt much. The doctor thinks it may have healed a bit crooked but it holds me up and that's all that matters. I do have multiple scars. The ones on my back are the worse and of course where I was burned but they are all covered and no one sees them but me. The scar over my left eyebrow will fade some the doctor says. I do not care. I am more than my scars.

Matthew and I have been talking about Benjamin Franklin and what he has done for our country. He is a brilliant man and I love to talk about him. Little Abraham sits and listens to Matthew weave his tales about Ben Franklin, George Washington and Thomas Jefferson. He talks about the Revolution and makes it feel like it just happened. He talks of laws and the Constitution and what it means. He talks about governments and the states. He tells Abraham how he will grow up someday to a great country, the greatest country in the world where all men are free.

Abraham asked him if all men are free why are there slaves? Matthew thought about that for a while and then said "Well that's a fine question young Mr. Abraham. Slaves were brought here from a country called Africa to work. They did not know the language or how to care for themselves. We needed people to work our land and we bought them. A good man takes care of his slaves and treats them with dignity. They are a different people and not as smart as us but they are a good people just simple in their needs and wants."

"But if we are all free in America shouldn't they be free too?" Abraham asked. Matthew said that a lot of people felt that way but that if there were no slaves the South could not produce crops so before slaves could be free they had to figure out a way to tend crops and harvest without them. He said as long as a man treated his slaves with honor that slavery was not necessarily a bad thing. Abraham said he was glad he was not a slave because then he could never be a great leader and he was going to grow up to be a great leader.

Matthew laughed and said "Yes you are going to grow up to be a great leader. This is America you can grow up to be a doctor, lawyer, teacher or even president if you study and try hard enough. A learned man cannot be held down by his station in life."

Then we had to talk about England and the monarchy. I think I am learning more than Abraham but he is quick and listens to everything. Matthew will be moving back to the schoolhouse soon but he says he will come up often to work with Abraham. He laughed and said "When he becomes a great leader I do not want him to forget me."

I made it up the stairs all by myself tonight. I think tomorrow I will try to walk around the yard by myself a bit. I think of the hardships that George Washington had to endure for us to have this country and I am eternally grateful that he has made it possible for my son to rise to greatness. I must ask more about Thomas Jefferson, he sounds like a very opinionated person.

I am healing journal, I do not have as much pain when I think of Tom. I feel so deeply sorry for him. It cannot be easy for him being in jail and doing hard labor. I will say an extra prayer for him tonight. Maybe I will talk to Abraham about him tomorrow. It is time for him to begin to heal too. Goodnight journal.

September - Mathew has moved back to town. He has left me some books to study to help teach Abraham. I have learned that there are Federalists and Constitutionalists. They have different opinions about how a government should be run. I told Abraham that he did not have to be one or the other but that he could make up his own mind. In order to lead men you must first understand them and what they cared about. You did not necessarily have to agree with them. That is why watching and listening is so important. A doctor always watches and listens to figure out what is wrong with you and that works in all things.

I told him that one of his Changeling gifts was the ability to read people. When he could do that he would know how to give them what they wanted so he could get them to do what he wanted. He asked me if this was lying and I told him he didn't lie to them about how he felt he just learned to talk around it so they didn't realize that he did not feel the same. He looked confused but I told him that was why he had to study and read and learn all he could. I told him he always had to be true to himself and as long as he did that the other did not matter. He seems to be listening and taking all this in.

We talked about Tom today for the first time. I asked him how he felt about Tom and he said "I hate him and I wished he would die." I gently told him that it was not good to wish people dead. He said "Well I do, I do wish him dead." I asked him why and he said "Because he hurt you." I told him that Tom was not the person who hurt me but that it was the devil that took hold of Tom because of vile drink.

I reminded him of the good Tom, the one who made him toys and walked him to school. The one who let him ride the mule and saw wood. I asked him if he could remember the good Tom. He reluctantly shook his head yes. I said the good Tom is still there. He would not hurt us on purpose. That is why we pray for him. He asked me if I hated Tom. I told him no and I honestly meant that.

I did not hate Tom. The bible teaches that you can hate the sin but love the sinner. I told him that I did hate what Tom had done to us but I did not hate Tom. "Hate is an evil curse that eats away at your insides" I told him. "You don't want to carry something around inside that would eat you?" I asked. "No," he said, "I don't want to be eaten." "Good" I said, "so when you feel hate you must pray to have God take it away from you."

He looked at me so seriously and said "I will Mama, I will pray for God to take the hate away from me." I hugged him and told him he was a good boy. He then said "But will God take away the sadness I feel. Sometimes it is like it is crushing the breath out of me." I was concerned and asked him if he felt this often. He said "Just sometimes when I worry about you. I want you to be all better Mama. I want us to go look at clouds down by the river again." I hugged him tightly and said "When you feel that sadness come over you then just close your eyes and think about me and it will get better. I am always in your heart Abraham, always."

"Tomorrow" I said, "we will go to the river and have a picnic and we will watch clouds. I promise!" He jumped up all sadness forgotten and said "Hurray a picnic!" I smiled as he ran off to tell Nancy.

He is a good boy. I must teach him how to deal with the sadness. We will pray for Tom together tonight and for God to soften Abraham's young heart towards him. I do not like to see such a grown up expression of concern on such a little boy's face.

I wish I could send him back to school but it is just too far from here and I do not want to go back to the cabin even if Tom isn't there. I think I will see if we can get some applesauce to take for tomorrow. Abraham loves applesauce. I am going to finish up here now. It will be time for Abraham to read to me. My favorite time of the evening. Until later journal.

--- What a lovely time we had at the river today on our picnic. John helped us get down to the river bank and spread a blanket for us. He said he would come back in a few hours. I could not ask for a better man than John Thompson. He has taken us under his wing and just cannot seem to do enough.

I watched Abraham run and play with the old dog that lives here and then we sat down to have lunch. We had some chicken and ham with biscuits and then had some applesauce. It was food from heaven. Abraham took his shirt off and his little belly was so full I laughed at it. He just rubbed it and said it's all round now. "That's ok" I said, "It will be flat soon and you will be hungry again but for now lay back and rest with me and let's play clouds."

We both laid back on the blanket and started to find the shapes in the clouds. He has gotten so much better at this than me. Where has the time gone? It just seemed like yesterday he was a baby. It was a lovely warm day and listening to him lay beside me and find cloud shapes made me drift off to sleep.

I woke up to find him sitting beside me staring intently at my face. "What's wrong" I asked? He touched my scar over my eyebrow and said "Does it hurt?" "No" I answered. "I don't even feel it anymore." I asked him why he was staring at me like that. He said "You looked so peaceful and beautiful lying there Mama. I was watching you breathe and memorizing your face. I want to be able to close my eyes and see your face." "Silly boy" I said as I sat up, "You can see my face every day." "No," he said. "I have to remember it for when I can't see it. It is not good to have you in my heart if I can't see you Mama." I said "Then look all you want for I want you to know I am in your heart always."

He hugged me hard and said "I am always in your heart too Mama." I laughed and said "Yes, you are always in my heart, as a matter of fact I carried you right under it until you were born." He shook his head and said "You're too skinny to carry a big baby in your belly." I said "I was not as skinny then as I am now and yes I carried you in my belly sure enough. God makes it so Mamas can carry their babies no matter how skinny they are." He then gave me a piece of ham and said I needed to eat so I would not be so skinny. I ate the ham and said "Are you trying to get my belly as round as yours?" He laughed at that and then I tickled him on his round white little belly.

We were laughing and giggling when John came to fetch us home. He was smiling ear to ear and said "Now that's the sound I like to hear." As we were riding home Abraham asked me if I was ever going to sing again. I told him I had not really thought about singing much. He said "Well you won't be well till you start singing again." What a wise little man he is. I think he may be right. Singing may be what it takes to heal my spirit. I had not thought of it before.I told him "Well if singing will make me well then I will have to start doing it again won't I?" He smiled.

It was a great day. I think he and I are finding each other again. Some of the darkness is lifting. I am hopeful that we will get through this. I know it cannot help but scar us both but I am hoping the scars will make us stronger. There is so much more for him to learn, so much for me to teach. We have time though, we are in a good place now. His is a happy place. I was very tired after our trip out today so he came to my room to read to me. After he left I was so grateful for the wonderful day that I wanted to tell you about it journal. Thank the Lord that he is still a little boy and thank the Lord that he sent me Abraham to help me learn how to be a mother. Good night journal.

October - The days are passing and I am getting stronger and stronger. Abraham and I work on his lessons and take long walks and just talk. I could listen to him chatter nonstop but sometimes I have to make him be still and quiet so he can learn to listen. Matthew comes up on weekends and works with Abraham. I wish the school was closer so he could go every day. Matthew was talking about

President Jefferson this past weekend. He was telling us how he could speak several different languages and had traveled to the continent. I said he must be the smartest man in the world and Matthew laughed and said he is probably the smartest man in America. He is going to grow this country he said.

Matthew is still talking about going West. I hope he waits awhile. He is teaching Abraham so much. He brought Abraham a book. He said it is a primer written by Noah Webster. Abraham was so excited that he had his own book. Matthew told Abraham that as long as there were books to read a man could be anything he wanted to be.

The doctor rode out to check on me this week. Everything seems to be healing. I have a slight limp but he says that is to be expected after how badly the bones were broken in my leg. He said as long as it doesn't pain me it should be alright. After he left Abraham decided he was going to be a doctor when he grew up. He has been splinting the poor dog's legs all week with sticks and had been asking all of us to stick out our tongues. When we do he says "well I think you'll live." He had John laughing so hard I thought he was going to fall out of his chair.

I don't know what he will be when he is a grown man but he will be successful at it. Nancy and John are so good to us. I do hope that they have a child soon. She so yearns for a baby. I need to put this away now it is time to go help Abraham work on his book. Oh goodness, his book, just saying it thrills me too.

November - The Sheriff rode up today to talk to me. Tom will be getting out of jail soon and he wanted to let me know. He said that Tom had been no trouble and had been a hard worker. He said he had talked to Tom and he promised to not bother me or Abraham. He said that Tom had asked him to please tell me how terribly sorry he was about everything. He told me he thought Tom might be a good man if he would just leave the whiskey alone. I thanked him for riding up to tell me. He said he was sure glad to see me getting along so well. John came in and they went off to talk.

I came up to my room to think about this. I don't know how I feel about Tom. I don't hate him or wish him ill and I too, believe that without the whiskey he could be a good man, but Tom has to want to be a good man and nobody can do that for him but him. I have tried to put what happened out of my mind. He was crazed that night, I knew that better than anyone, I saw it in his eyes but I didn't want to bet my life on whether it could happen again and I sure won't put Abraham in that kind of danger.

I need to tell Abraham about Tom. He doesn't talk about him to me. I think he has tried to put it out of his mind too. I hope I can teach him not to hate Tom. Hate is such a destructive emotion, but he is so young I hope it has not had time to settle in. He must understand he has no room for hate, he must concentrate on what he is to become not what was. We cannot bring back yesterday, we cannot undo what has been done but we can put it behind us and move on. The future is what we make it.

My future is Abraham becoming the man he is meant to be. I am going to go find him. I do so hope he will not be afraid. He really has nothing to fear from Tom. He has no power to hurt us anymore. I will not let him.

--- The sun was shining brightly in the study this afternoon so I asked Abraham to sit with me. He came in and sat down beside me and asked what was wrong. I said nothing was wrong we just needed to talk. He said "Mama I know the Sheriff came today. Did he come about Tom?" I said "Yes he did. He came to tell me Tom will be getting out of jail soon and he wanted me to know." "He's not coming here is he Mama? If he is I am going to get John's gun and shoot him." "Abraham." I said, "That is no way to talk, we do not go around shooting people even if we don't like them."

"Well, I don't like him at all" he said. "Abraham" I said, "Remember how we prayed for Tom." "Yes," he said reluctantly. "Well, we need to continue to pray for Tom. He is not a bad man sweetheart, he just drank too much and let the devil in to take him." Abraham said "But he hurt you Mama, he hurt you bad." "No, dear he didn't hurt me, the devil in him hurt me. It is the devil we should blame not Tom." "Well he shouldn't let the devil in then" Abraham said. "No," Abraham, you are right he should not have let the devil in but he did. That's why we need to pray for him, he has to live with the fact that he let the devil in and acted like that."

"Are we going back there?" he asked. "No Abraham we are not, we are staying here" I said. "The Sheriff said Tom was not going to bother us and I believe him. We need to forgive Tom. The bible says we must forgive those who have sinned against us. The law has judged him and he has to answer to God at his reckoning for the things he did here. I want you to pray with me Abraham, we will pray that Tom will find forgiveness in himself and that we can forgive him for his transgressions against us." Abraham looked at me so solemnly and said "I will try to forgive him for you Mama but it will be powerful hard." I said "I know it is hard son but we must try. That is all I can ask is that you try."

We held hands and we prayed. When we finished he looked at me and said "It's not working yet Mama." I hugged him and said "Give it time son." He ran off to play and I thought to myself give it time. Words of wisdom for both of us.

December - Nancy had some wonderful news today! She is expecting a baby sometime this summer. She thinks near the end of July. Oh I am so excited, she will be such a good mother and John is so excited he could barely contain himself. We both started laughing when he asked if he needed to move the bed downstairs so she didn't have to climb the stairs. It is so sweet to see him so worried about her. She hugged me today and said she was so happy I was here to share this with her. I told her I could not be happier. Abraham told her she didn't look like she had a baby in her belly. She laughed and told him the baby had to grow before he could tell.

John grabbed him up and took him riding and left us to chat about "woman things". Matthew rode up since school was out for a while. He came in the door and we both told him about the baby at the same time. He was thrilled and complimented John. Nancy swatted him on the arm and told him "John nothing..." I loved watching them banter.

This was a good day. Nancy begged her leave of us to go and lie down for a bit. After she left Matthew said "Tom came by the school today before I left." I just looked at him and waited for him to go on. "He said he knew I came up here from time to time and he asked me to bring up a gift for Abraham." I said "A gift?" really surprised. He said "Tom said to tell you hello and he knows he can't make it up to you but he wanted to send the boy a toy." He showed me a wagon with a carved horse. He said Tom asked if Abraham was keeping up with his studies and seemed proud when Matthew told him how smart he was. Tom said "He is the smartest little fellow I ever seen, his Mama does real good by him. Nancy is a reader but I guess you know that already. I don't read myself but it is a good skill to know I guess." He put his hat back on and went out the door. As he was riding off he turned to Matthew and said "Tell Nancy how sorry I am and I'm glad she and the boy are happy."

I turned the horse over and over in my hand. It was a bit crude but Tom had worked on it. The wagon even had little wheels that rolled. Abraham would love it if it had come from anyone else. Matthew said "I am giving it to you. You decide if you give it to Abraham, it's not my place." I asked him how Tom looked. He said he was thinner but looked clean, he heard he was working on a farm some. He said "I see this is worrying you and I don't mean to worry you none so let's stop this talk of Tom and tell me how Abraham is coming along with his primer."

We talked about letters and history. Abraham came running in with John and I quickly hid the wagon. It was not the time in front of the men. I would give it to him later in private and leave him to decide to keep it or not. It was a nice gesture from Tom. He may have cared about us some after all.

We spent the evening reading and Abraham showing off his skills to Matthew. It was lovely. I will give him the wagon tomorrow and we'll see. Even as young as he is this is his decision to make. We pray for Tom every night but I don't think Abraham has found forgiveness for him yet. Have I? I wondered.

--- I gave Abraham the wagon and horse today. He was excited at first until I told him that Tom sent it. He put it back on the table in my room and just looked at it. I told him he could keep it or throw it away. It was his choice. He was so torn, I could see it in his face. He finally said "If I take it do I have to forgive Tom?" I said "No you do not but it would be nice if you did." He said "I will just leave it here for now." He looked so sad but he would not allow himself to touch it. I hugged him hard and said "You do not have to decide today. We will just leave it here for now. Go ahead and go play with Matthew."

He ran out and downstairs. I looked at the wagon for a long

time. I wonder if this was a sign for me? I too had put off thinking about Tom. It is almost Christmas and I am singing a solo at the church this year. It will be a healing thing for me to do. Abraham was right, I will not heal completely until I sing again.

I need to go downstairs. Matthew is going to talk to Abraham about George Washington. He never tires of hearing about the General who became President. Maybe he will play President this time instead of doctor. The poor dog would rather listen to speeches than be splinted again. Oh I love that child of mine.

--- I sang in the church today. I felt the Lord enter me as I sang. It was as if his healing light was shining right through me. I sang straight to God. When I finished I could have sworn I saw Tom standing by the door but by the time I sat down he was gone. Nancy was sitting there with tears running down her cheeks. John was giving her a handkerchief to dry her eyes. Abraham was smiling from ear to ear. He waved at me when he saw me look at him. After church the preacher said he had never heard anything like that before. Matthew told him he thought I could sing better than anyone he had ever heard. I blushed a bit over that one. I told the preacher I would be happy to sing in the church when ever he wanted me to.

Abraham was bouncing up and down holding my hand and said "I told you so Mama. I told you would get better when you sang." I swept him up in my arms and said "You were absolutely right my little man" and hugged him till he squirmed to get down. We came home and had a wonderful dinner and opened gifts.

I had made some things for Nancy and John. Abraham was so excited his gift was notes to us all that he had written with help from Matthew. I had made a scarf for Matthew and he gave me and Abraham a book he had telling about George Washington and Ben Franklin. Abraham was beside himself. "Another book", he shouted, "I have two books now, we are rich Mama, we have two books."

After he settled down some I noticed that he had brought the wagon down and was playing with it. When he saw me looking at him he said "I forgave Tom a little bit so it would be alright to play with the wagon." I smiled and told him what a good boy he was and yes it was ok to play with the wagon. When he said prayers tonight he was thankful for the wagon and asked God to help him learn to forgive Tom a little more tomorrow. I was glad his eyes were closed so he could not see my smile. It was truly nice of Tom to give him the wagon. I think when I say my prayers I will ask God to help me forgive Tom a little more tomorrow too. I wonder was he really at the back of the church today or did I just imagine him there. Good night journal.

In the year of our Lord 1809 …..

January - We have had quite a snow this past week. It is beautiful to look at. I woke up for some reason in the wee hours of this morning and just stood starring out at the full moon on the snowy ground. Far off in the distance I heard a wolf howl and thought of the old Indian who had cared for me on that long ago November trip to Puzzle Creek. I shivered with the cold, wrapped my shawl around me and went to check on Abraham. He was sleeping so peacefully. I leaned over to kiss his head lightly and marveled at how beautiful he looked lying there. So quiet and peaceful.

A fleeting dark shadow passed over his face for just a second but for some reason it frightened me terribly. I dropped to my knees and prayed for God to please keep my son safe. I begged him to never make me leave him and if my body had to die please let me stay near him so he would not feel alone. I laid down beside him and put my arms around him and fell back asleep. I woke back up to light kisses on my eyelids and him whispering "Mama, Mama is it still snowing?" We got up and looked and it had stopped and the sky was blue. He got very excited because he saw a bluebird outside and immediately wanted to get dressed and go out. I told him he had to eat first and we needed to do his letters and then we would see.

He was dressed and off like a flash. It took me a bit longer, the cold makes my leg ache some and I was slower going downstairs. He was sitting at the table reading his primer and I had a sudden impression of him as a much older man with a full beard sitting in the same position reading. Goodness I am prone to fancy today it seems. I do so wish he could go back to school every day. He must get all the learning he can. It is his path to greatness. I have put him off as long as possible so it is time to go outside. I am excited too, it is beautiful outside.

February - I think I saw Tom at church again Sunday. He was almost a shadow standing near the door but as I finished singing I was sure I saw his face. After the service I looked around but he was nowhere to be seen. He has not tried to contact me since he got out of jail and except for sending Abraham the toy wagon I had heard no word from him. I wonder what his coming to hear me sing means. Tom was not a church going man but people do change. I did not say anything to Abraham. I don't think he is any more ready to see Tom than I am yet. Even as I write this I wonder am I ready to see Tom? I do wonder how he is doing. Poor Tom has had to live with his demons. Abraham and I escaped to a beautiful happy place with Nancy and John.

My birthday was yesterday. It is not something I celebrate but it does make me aware that I am another year older and that my sweet boy will be five soon. Time seems to pass so quickly. I feel a bit sad today. It is something I try to conquer. Time to get busy and stop thinking so much.

--- Today was Abraham's birthday. Five years old and such a little man. Tom had sent him a wooden gun he had carved by Matthew. Abraham didn't even ask if he should keep it. He ran up to me and said "Did you see my gun that Tom made me?" He seemed thrilled with it. It was an awfully nice gesture by Tom. Time seems to have eased Abraham's mind some about Tom. We remember him in our prayers every night.

Matthew says Tom is working and is fixing up the cabin. He said no one has seen him drinking since I left. I asked him if he thought Tom has truly changed. He said "I do not know him Nancy so I cannot say. Only you can be the judge of that." I said "True, that is true no one knew him like me." He asked me if I was going to see him again. I told him I had been thinking about it but I did not know if I was ready. The more I think about this today the more I think I am ready to face him and see for myself if he had changed. I shall pray about this tonight.

--- John came up to me today and said Tom has been asking to see me. He saw him today and told him he would ask me if I would allow it. I told him yes it was time. John said he would tell him to come up to the house. He did not want me to meet him alone. After John left I prayed about it and yes it is time for Tom and I to lay this matter to rest with each other. Nancy is a bit nervous about me being ready but I assured her I would be fine. I think will ask her to keep

Abraham occupied however. This is something I need to do by myself.

March - It has been a few weeks since Tom came up. I needed to think about it before I wrote it down. He showed up with his hat in hand and asked if we could talk. We went into the study and shut the door. We sat down across from each other. He was having a hard time meeting my eyes. He finally said "I did not come here to bother you Nancy I just wanted to tell you myself how very sorry I was about what happened. I was drunk out of my mind and I don't remember much about what happened but I do know what they told me when I sobered up."

I asked him how he could ask for forgiveness if he didn't even know what he done? He said "They told me I almost killed you Nancy, that I almost beat you to death. There was no call for me to be that way, you ain't never been nothing but good to me and I knowed about your past when I married you. I ain't got no excuse for acting that way. The whiskey just got hold of me."

I looked at him and said "Tom if you want my forgiveness then you need to know what your asking for." I preceeded to tell him everything that happened that night, what he said and what he did. The more I talked the more upset he got. Finally as I was telling him the last he cried "Please no more, don't tell me no more." He buried his head in his hands and sobbed.

I just sat there and let him cry. Finally saying it all out loud had taken away it's power. I felt like I could truly let it go now. It was as if a huge weight had been taken off of me. Tom stopped crying and got hold of himself and got down on his knees and said "I will ask you again for forgiveness Nancy knowing now what I ask, if you can't find it in your heart I can't blame you."

I told him that I forgave him. It seems like it just came out of my mouth before I thought about it. If Jesus could forgive those that crucified him then I could forgive Tom. He thanked me and said he would be going. As he stood up he saw the wagon and horse he had made Abraham. He asked "Did the boy like his toys I made him?" I told him he liked them a lot. He asked if it was too soon to see the boy?

I called Abraham in, I knew he knew Tom was there. Abraham

came into the room and stood close to me. Tom said "I can't get over how much you growed boy." Abraham stood up tall and said "I am five now." Tom said "Yes you are." He got down on one knee and looked Abraham in the eyes and said "I come to ask your Mama for forgiveness boy but now I need to ask you. Can you think about forgiving me Abraham? I am powerful sorry about the way I acted. If you can't forgive me I understand boy and I don't hold it against you." Abraham looked at me and I said "This is your decision Abraham."

He looked hard at Tom and said "I done forgived you some but I guess I can think about forgiving you more." Tom stood up and said "That's more than enough for me boy. Thank you for even considering it." Then he did something that surprised me he stuck out his hand for Abraham to shake it. They solemnly shook hands and Tom said "Well I'll be going now. I just wanted to talk to you both in person." We told him good bye and watched him ride off.

Abraham looked at me and said "He looked sorry Mama didn't he." I said "Yes son he sure did." Abraham went back to play and I just sat deep in thought. I have been thinking about it for the last several days. I don't feel angry or even hurt anymore. If it wasn't for the scars and the limp I wouldn't even notice sometimes. Tom is a good man in his heart, maybe he is finally finding out who he is. I think it's time for me to figure out who I want to be. Good night journal.

April - Tom has come up several times in the past few weeks. He brought some things for Abraham and he took him fishing. Abraham says he don't talk much just shows him how to do things. He doesn't say much to me just asks if the boy can come with him and then thanks me when he brings him back. Abraham said Tom had built the extra room on the cabin and that he could come see it some day if he liked. I told him that we would do that someday soon.

I love living here and John and Nancy are so good to us but I miss the feeling of having my own house. I am still Tom's wife at least in name and I still remember how thankful I was to have a name for me and Abraham. We walk with no shame and he can go through his life belonging. It does make me think.

May - Today when Tom came by I decided to go down to the river with him and Abraham. I packed up some food and we went to the river for them to fish. Tom came and sat by me not saying anything. I asked him about the cabin and he told me he had fixed it up and built the extra room I always wanted. He said "It looks right nice if I do say so." He asked me if I would like to come and see it someday. I told him I thought that would be nice. He then looked at the ground and said "I sore do miss you and the boy Nancy. I ain't never really had a home until I married the two of you. I don't think I ever really knew how to act. Sometimes a man don't know what he's got till it's gone." Then he said "Do you have any good memories at all Nancy, I mean about us?" I patted his arm and said "Yes I have some good memories Tom."

Abraham got a fish about then so he left to help him land it. We didn't talk any more until we got back to the house. He said "I had a good time Nancy, thank you for coming down with the boy and me." I smiled and told him I had a good time too. He said "Just let me know when you want to see the cabin, you can come down any time." I said I would let him know and he left.

I sat on the porch smelling the flowers. He has changed. Nancy and John were going to have their own family before too long. I needed to think about mine. It would be nice to have another baby. Oh well, just having fancy thoughts. Time to get busy.

June - Poor Nancy, she is weighing heavy with the baby these days. I reminded her about John bringing the bed downstairs and she laughed and said it sounds like a better and better idea the bigger she gets. Matthew has moved back in and is helping John around the farm. He and Abraham have their nose in a book every night. He says Abraham is moving right along. Abraham says he wishes we lived closer to the school so he could go every day.

I have been thinking a lot about that. Abraham going back to school is the most important thing in the world to me. Tom is coming by regular these days. He even helped John and Matthew work on the barn the other day. Abraham and I went down to see the cabin. He has done a good job and the new room looks tight as a drum. I felt a little homesick when we left. That cabin was the first real house that was mine. Is it wrong that I miss it?

--- Nancy had a beautiful baby girl today. She had an easy labor thank goodness and she and the baby are doing fine. Abraham marveled at how tiny her fingers and toes were. I rocked her for a bit today. How I missed babies. I never thought much about it but Mrs. Sarah had a baby around about all the time. As I held her I thought about how nice it would be to have a little girl of my own. Tom had made mention the other day about me and Abraham moving back to the cabin. He said he would go stay some place else if we wanted to move back. I told him I would not make him move out of his home but he said it was the least he could do after all he had put us through. I told him I would think about it. It would be closer to school so Abraham could go every day.

I just don't know how I feel about making him move out and live somewhere else. Somehow it just don't seem right. I don't think Abraham would mind much if he got to go back to school every day even thought he would miss John. They have gotten to be great friends. Oh well it is something to think about. Right now I get to enjoy the new baby.

July - It's been hot for a spell now. The baby is doing well. Nancy named her Mary after John's grandmother. She is a beautiful little thing. Abraham is so funny when she cries he demands that someone go pick her up right then and there and then he hushes her and tells her it's ok. Nancy got a letter from Mrs. Sarah. It seems she and Mr. Abraham are coming for a visit to see the new baby. She doesn't know that Abraham and I have been living here. Mr. Abraham has sent a letter and some money to me saying that he would pay for me to stay somewhere else during their visit. I just don't feel right doing that.

I talked to Nancy and John about it and told them that Abraham and I would move back to the cabin. Tom had said it would be alright and he would stay somewhere else. I told Tom about my plan when he came by. He seemed really pleased and said he would get a wagon and help move our things down to the cabin. He said he could stay in the Johnson's barn as he was working on their farm right now. I sat Abraham down and told him we were moving back so he could go back to school. He said he would miss John and Nancy but he sure wanted to go to school again and now he had his own room.

Tom will be back in a few days with a wagon and we will move back. I guess it is time to start my own life now, mine and Abraham's. It has been a long day and I am quite tired. Goodnight journal.

August - I have been busy since we moved back in to the cabin. Tom moved to the Johnson's barn. Word had got out that we are back. Several ladies from the church brought food and I have several sewing jobs to do. I am looking forward to going to church this Sunday. Abraham has been playing with his friends. He seems happy to be back. It seems strange here without Tom. He stops by in the evenings to see if we need anything. We had a nice dinner last night before he went back to the Johnson's.

John and Mr. Abraham came by today. Mrs. Sarah is up at the house with Nancy and the baby. Mr. Abraham asked me if everything was alright. I told him that we were fine and that Tom was being good to us and not causing any problems. He gave me a goodly sum of money and told me to put it back so we would not do without this winter. He told me to send word to Felix if we needed anything more. I thanked him. He and John did not stay long. I sent my love to Nancy and the baby and John whispered that he would let me know when the Enloes were gone.

Abraham is playing lawyer tonight so I have to go listen to him argue the cat's case to the court. He is such a funny little man at times. Good night journal I hope the cat gets to go free.

September - Abraham started back to school this week. Tom asked if he could walk him there in the mornings. I said yes, if he would have some breakfast with us first. Tom gets up and walks here, eats with us then takes Abraham to school and goes back to the Johnson's to work. He is trying so hard to make it up to us.

I miss Abraham being here, I had gotten used to having him around and him being at school all day makes for a long day for me. He comes home full of what he learned that day. I often think if I had a baby I would not be so lonely. If I let Tom come back maybe we could have a child. I think a baby would be good for Tom. I think I would like him to move back in but I must talk it over with

Abraham. We are in this together he and I. I know he still has some feelings of mistrust with Tom. I guess it's just natural. Boys are protective of their mothers. He is my little champion.

I love that child so much. He is so smart and so good. I remind him that he is going to grow up to be a great man. As long as he goes to school and reads books he can be anything he wants. Matthew keeps telling him that too. I hope Matthew keeps teaching here for a while longer. He is so good for Abraham and teaches him so much but I know he is itching to go West and I am afraid he will not stay here much longer. He has become the brother I never had. Even Tom throws up his hand to him when he sees him.

Ah to be a man and just up and go when you feel like it. It must be wonderful to be able to do that but then again I wouldn't give up being a woman and having children for all the travel and adventures in the world. I will talk with Abraham before bed tonight about Tom and then I will decide.

--- I talked with Abraham about Tom moving back in and he said if I was ok with it he would be ok with it. He just said "If he don't behave can you make him move back out." I told him "If that happened Tom would move out or we would. We will not live like that again." I sat down and wrote a letter to Mr. Abraham explaining that I was Tom's wife and that we were going try to make it work. I told him how Tom had changed and that I felt like this was for the best. I asked him to wish us well and told him not to worry that if Tom ever started drinking again we would move out. I wished him and Mrs. Sarah well.

When Tom came by for dinner tonight I asked him to walk to the orchard with me. I asked him if he missed living in the cabin? He said yes but he missed living with us more. I took his hands in mine and asked him if he wanted to move back in with us. He just looked at me and said "Do you mean it?" "Yes" I told him, "but this time it is me and you making the decision. No money, no Mr. Abraham just us." He put his arms around me and swung me wide. "Oh Nancy, nothing would make me happier than to be back with you and Abraham" he said.

I closed my eyes for a moment and just enjoyed how it felt to be held by a man. It had been so long. He held me tight and then suddenly let me go. "I didn't hug you too tight did I Nancy?" he asked. I laughed and hugged him hard. "No" I said, "Don't worry if it is too hard I'll tell you I promise." He smiled and we walked arm and arm back to the cabin. When we got back Abraham looked at Tom and said "I guess you moving back in here?" Tom looked at Abraham and said "Are you alright with it?" Abraham looked at him long and hard and said "As long as my Mama's happy then I'm ok with it."

Tom went to get his clothes from the Johnson's barn and tell them he was moving back home. After he left Abraham looked at me and said "I'm going to watch him Mama just to be sure. He ain't going to hurt you ever again." I hugged Abraham and said "No son he won't hurt me ever again I promise." Abraham pulled away from me and looked so much older than his years as he sighed and said "I hope not." I am going to put you away journal. Tom will be back soon and I am as nervous as a new bride. Goodnight journal.

October - We are all getting used to our new life here. Abraham is excited about school and full of what he is learning but he is reserved around Tom. Tom is not a talkative man but he is trying. I had a scare the other day with the two of them. Abraham had been playing with some of Tom's tools and did not put them away. Tom was furious. He yelled at Abraham about it and went to raise his hand towards him. Abraham's eyes got wide and he shrunk down. Before I could say anything Tom dropped his hand and turned to me and said "I won't strike him, if it needs to be done then you'll be a doing it." He just told Abraham "Go put them tools up right boy and don't leave 'em out no more." Abraham didn't move he was so scared. Tom said "I ain't gonna hit you boy, just go put up the tools."

Abraham dashed out of the cabin to put away the tools and Tom sat down hard in the chair. I put my hand on his shoulder and he said "I'm sorry about the way I treated you both in the past. The boy ain't never gonna get over it is he?" "I don't know Tom" I said, "He is young." "I almost killed his Mama, I can't say I blame him" he said, "I wouldn't forgive me iffen I was him." I patted him on the back and said "Give it time Tom, you just got to give it time." He looked at me and said "What about you Nancy, you ready to forgive me and let me be your husband in full? I won't hurt you and I promise to be easy and if you want me to I'll stop anytime. I will never force you again."

Abraham came back in and said "I put them all back." Tom told him "Just make sure you put things back in their place when you're done with them boy." I leaned over to Tom and whispered in his ear that I would think about it. He smiled and said "That's good enough for me, you just tell me when you decide."

After I cleaned up from supper, Tom and Abraham went outside to look at our fence where part had fallen down. I don't know what to do journal. Part of me wants him to lay with me. I miss how that felt. I liked the way a man felt in me when it was right. I lay beside him at night and feel him next to me and I feel the warmth deep in me. I see his desire but he don't say anything. He told me when I let him move back in that he would never take me again until I said I was ready.

Am I ready? I want to lie with him, I want to have babies but I am afraid. No one has seen me naked since the beating. I have scars all over my backside and the burn scars left bad marks and I don't know if it will hurt or not. What if Tom sees me and don't want me. I just don't know how to feel. It don't seem right that I let him move back in if I ain't going to be a wife to him. He has been good to us but he is a man and a man has needs. I know that better than most. Do I want Tom to go be with another woman because I can't be with him. I think I am just going to have to pray on this before I decide. Goodnight journal, I need to get things ready for tomorrow.

--- Tom took Abraham to school this morning. I had prayed hard about this last night and decided that the first time did not need to be when Abraham was home. I asked Tom to come back by the house before he went to the Johnson's. He looked puzzled but said he would. I paced around the cabin like a caged animal waiting for him to come back. I was so nervous. When he came back in I told him I was ready to try if he wanted to but he needed to see me first to see if he still wanted to. He laughed and said "Nancy I know what you look like" and put his arms around me. I pulled away and said "No, Tom you don't know what I look like now. I'm different."

He sat down in the chair and I nervously pulled my nightgown off and stood before him in the light of day. I slowly turned and let him see my scars. I had tears in my eyes when I turned back around. I think this was the hardest thing I ever done. Tom looked at me and his eyes filled up with tears, he said "Oh Nancy, how can you even look at me after I done such terrible things to you. I am sorry. It ain't right that I ever ask you to let me lay with you again." He buried his face in his hands and just shook. I walked over to him, my nakedness forgotten. He was clearly in so much pain. I put my arms around his shoulders and said "Tom, it weren't you, it was the drink. I know that." He looked at me incredulous and said "You can forgive me after all this?" I said "Yes Tom, I can forgive you but can you forgive yourself." He said "I don't know if I ever can." I sat down in his lap and put my arms around him. "The Lord preaches forgiveness Tom."

He put his arms around me and said "I didn't know how good you really were till I heard you singing at church. You were standing there singing and the light was shining on you and I never seen or heard so much goodness in one person in my whole life. I didn't think you would ever speak to me again much less forgive me. God let me have an angel and I almost killed her." He buried his head in my chest and in a shaking voice said "I am so sorry Nancy, so sorry."

I raised his head up with my hand and said "Do you still want me Tom, I mean like a man wants a woman?" He looked at me and I felt him rise. He said "I never have not wanted you like a woman Nancy." He started rubbing my back being very gentle on my scars, then he started kissing my breasts. He tenderly kissed the burn scar and all around as he began to stroke my thighs. I began to feel warm all over like I did when I was younger. I felt my back arching and I told him that I was ready.

He picked me up and carried me into the room to our bed. He took me there, slow and easy. It was it think one of the more beautiful experiences I have ever had. He was trying to be so careful to not hurt me I finally had to tell him that I wanted a little more. Afterwards we lay in each other's arms as the sunlight shone down on our bodies. He looked at me and said "Can we do this again tonight?" I laughed "Well not quite like this, I can't sit on your lap naked with Abraham home." He playfully rubbed my bottom and said "Well I'll just have to come home more while he is in school."

He got up and dressed to go to the Johnson's and I just laid there a bit. It felt good to feel like a woman again. Maybe I could have a baby before too long. We could be a family, a real family. I got up and cleaned the house and did some sewing. I walked to school to get Abraham and on the way home we sung silly songs. Abraham was doing his reading when he looked up at me and said "Mama you ain't looked this happy in a long time." I hugged him and said "I am happy son and if you keep on getting better at your lessons I'm just gonna get happier!" He smiled and said "Then you can get happier Mama cause I'm just gonna get smarter and smarter."

I got supper ready and sat down to write in you journal. Today, my cup floweth over. Tom will be in soon and after I put Abraham to bed. I think I am going to be ready to work on that baby again. Goodnight journal, I do think it's definitely going to be a good night here at the Lincoln house!

November - I have been going to the school in the afternoons to help the younger children with their letters. Matthew thought it would be good for me as I miss Abraham so much during the day. Today we had a special visitor. One of Matthew's friends from his old college came by the school. He is traveling through to the new territory. Matthew had him talk to the students. He is a lawyer from New York and is going out to the Orleans Territory. The children were all excited and asked questions about Indians and wild animals, but they all quieted down when he started talking about New York and living near the ocean.

He talked about swimming in the ocean and fishing and riding in big boats with sails. I was as fascinated as the children. He then told them about going to college. He talked about a big building with more books than you could ever imagine and all the things they taught there. Abraham raised his hand and asked him that if you read all the books did you have to go away to a college to learn? He looked earnestly at Abraham and said if you read all the books then you can become an expert on things and you will know more than the people in college. The secret is to read and know the books. He said that was one reason he liked studying law was that he could learn it by reading books no matter where he was. He talked about knowing the law of the land being the most powerful tool a man could have.

Abraham was hanging on his every word. After school we

stayed and listened to him talk about former president Thomas Jefferson and how he wanted everybody in the country to go to school. He told Matthew how noble he was to be teaching children. I don't think Matthew felt noble, he just kept asking questions about the new Louisiana Territory. I could hear the yearning in his voice.

I am afraid he will not stay much longer. Abraham talked about the visitor all the way home. He kept saying "I am going to read all the books in the world Mama." I told him that was a worthy goal. Tom was already home when we got there so I quickly got supper. Abraham was so excited that he told Tom about the man from the ocean. Tom even enjoyed hearing about the ocean and the ship with sails. He told Abraham that it took a brave man to go out to sea.

After supper they went outside to gather up some wood and I took the chance to write a bit. There is nothing quite as wonderful as seeing your child's eyes light up about learning new things. Matthew said he had a surprise for Abraham for Christmas this year. I secretly hope it is another book. There is nothing that boy loves more than books. Maybe he will get a book for Christmas and I will get a baby.

I am so hoping Tom and I can have a child. At least I know it won't be for lack of effort on Tom's part or mine these days. Goodness I am making myself blush. Maybe tonight will be the night it happens. There is a full moon and magic happens during a full moon. I will keep my fingers crossed tonight just in case. Goodnight journal, time to put you up for the night.

December - John and Nancy came down last week to look at some property. John speculates some and buys a few pieces of land and then rents it out. He, Tom, and Abraham went to look at some land while Nancy and the baby visited. Mary is just the sweetest baby. Her little cheeks were so round I just wanted to kiss them all over. My arms just ached for her when I handed her back to Nancy.

Nancy asked me how things were going she said I looked like I had finally put on a little weight. I laughed and told her I thought I might be with child but wanted to make sure before I told Tom. She hugged me tight and said that was wonderful. She knew I had been wanting a baby with Abraham being so big and all. We had a nice visit and after they left Tom was talking about the property. He said it was a shame we didn't have some extra money to go in with John.

Owning some land for the rent was a good way to make some money.

I asked him how much money was he talking about. When he told me I smiled and said "Tom, before you moved back in Mr. Abraham gave me some money to get through the winter but since you're back we might as well use it to get ahead." I went and got the money. "I think it will be enough with a little bit left over" I said. He jumped up and said "Do you mean it Nancy, you will give me the money to buy some land?" I looked up at him and said it was for us, all of us. He rode up to John's the next day and they went down and signed the papers.

I think this might just be a whole new start for us. He and Abraham went by to look at it today, Tom sure is proud. I know now that we have a baby coming but I'm going to wait to Christmas to tell Tom. Landowners and a new baby coming. It's gonna be a fine Christmas at the Lincoln house for sure.

--- Today was Christmas. Me and Abraham went to the church for services. Tom still don't cotton to church so he stays home. We had a fine dinner and Matthew came by. He wanted to give Abraham his present. It was wrapped up in brown paper and Matthew told Abraham to be careful opening it. When he opened it he just stared at the papers in wonder. Matthew laughed and said "Read the top to your Mama." Abraham read "Copy of The Declaration of Independence." Abraham asked him if it was the real one. Matthew laughed and said it was a copy that his friend brought him and he wanted Abraham to have it. "If you want to grow up to be a lawyer you need to know this first. It's the most important piece of paper in this country." Even Tom was impressed.

After Matthew left we gave Abraham our gifts. Tom had made me some shelves I had been wanting and after he and Abraham put them up I told him I wanted to give him my gift. I just stood there and he finally said I don't see nothing. I patted my belly and said not yet but you will soon. We are going to have a baby. He jumped up like he had been shot and then picked me up and swung me around the room. I have never seen a man happier than Tom today. Abraham came up to me and put his hand on my belly and smiled at me and said "Hello little baby I'm gonna be your big brother." It was a lovely, lovely day. Tom had to go out to the barn and feed the cow so I thought I'd write in you journal. What a merry merry Christmas at the Lincoln house. Goodnight journal.

In the year of our Lord 1810 .....

February - I can't believe Abraham is six years old now. Time is passing so quickly. The baby should be here sometime in July I think. I wrote Mr. Abraham a letter telling him about the baby and what we did with the money he gave us. I felt like he should know since he gave it to me. He sent a letter back approving of the land purchase and sent us some more money to buy some more land. He said it would be a good start for the boy's future. Tom couldn't believe his good fortune. He said it would be enough to buy two or three good pieces.

He rode up to talk to John about it. I stayed home as I seem to get very tired these days. I guess it's the baby but I didn't remember being this tired last time. My waist is getting thicker but I don't think I'm putting on much weight elsewhere. Tom is a little worried he says my face looks thinner and he tries to get me to eat more. He is going to be a true worry wart if this keeps up. I am sure as it gets closer to Spring I'll thicken up. I think I'll go lie down and rest while the men folk are gone. Better do it before the baby comes, I remember how they can stay up at night.

April - I am sorry I have not written in a while. I have been just plumb tuckered out with this baby and I have had this bout with a cold. Tom was scared to death it was pneumonia. It took all I could do for him to leave the doctor alone. Lots of women have colds in the winter. He is right about one worry, I can't seem to put on any weight. My belly sticks out like I swallowed a watermelon but my arms and legs look like sticks. I talked with Nancy about it the other day. She thinks I need to eat more beef broth to make my blood strong.

Matthew has been walking Abraham home from school they talk about the Constitution and law and history. Abraham sets quite a store in Matthew. He had read the Declaration so much that he about has it memorized. Matthew thinks he is quite amazing and so do I. He is destined for great things that boy of mine. I remind him of it every night when we say prayers. We have rent coming in from our properties now. Tom has talked about moving into a bigger house and renting the cabin since we have a baby coming. I want to wait a bit so we can gather a bit more money. Tom has a lot of pride these days. It is good for him. He even encourages Abraham in his reading. He says he is going to need to be a learned man when he grows up so he can manage the properties.

The baby is weighing heavy on me today and my back aches something fierce so I think I may go lie down. Tom don't seem to mind me resting so much with the baby coming and all. I'll just go out and get some wood for the fire for supper and then I'll take a little nap. I'll try to write a little more often journal.

June - I have been too heavy of heart to write. My beautiful sweet precious baby girl came early. I had brought the wood in and laid down for a nap. I woke up in a great deal of pain and got up to walk around when I started bleeding. I grabbed some towels and tried to stop it as best I could. Tom and Abraham came home and found me lying in the floor. I was too weak to stand. Tom sent Abraham to get the doctor. While he was gone my sweet angel was born. She never even cried just took a deep breath of air and looked at Tom and closed her little eyes. When the doctor and Abraham got back she was gone.

The doctor said it was just too early. Tom wrapped her in a little blanket and handed her to me. I rocked her and cried. The doctor said I was bleeding awfully bad and had to lie down. He packed me and said he would be back in a few hours to check on me. He told Tom to keep me as still as possible. I asked Tom if I could just hold her for a while. He let me keep her for a couple hours before he came in and said he had dug her a grave and needed to take her. He had tears in his eyes when he took her from me. He kissed her little head and said "I'm sorry Nancy, I'm so sorry." I turned my head to the wall. I could not watch him leave with her. He had Abraham to stay with me so I wouldn't be alone.

When Tom left Abraham sat beside my bed and held my hand. He didn't say anything, just held my hand while I cried. The doctor came back and changed my packing and said it looked like the bleeding has slowed some but I had to stay in the bed. He said he would come back the next day. Tom slept in the chair by my bed all that night. It was weeks before the doctor said I was strong enough to get up and about some. I had lost so much weight I looked like I had never even had a baby. Even poor Abraham tried to get me to eat more. It has been a terrible time, I didn't even take any pleasure at listening to Abraham read at night.

I don't know why God felt like he had to take my baby. I go to church, I pray, I try to be kind. It just don't seem fair. Tom seems to think it was his fault for some reason. He don't like to talk about it. I finally took some flowers up to her grave. We never even named her. I been grieving something terrible. I realized it today when Abraham asked if he could go stay at John and Nancy's for a while. When I asked him why he said "I just can't do nothing to make you feel better Mama and I just can't stand it no more." I leaned down and hugged him and said "Son just having you around makes me feel better." He just looked sad and said "It ain't making you feel better enough."

I told him he could go for a few days if he wanted but it made me realize how selfish I had been to him and to Tom. I had been grieving for how I felt and not taken into account how sad they were. I had Tom take him up to Nancy and John's for a few days. I sat down and finally wrote out the baby's name and birth date in the bible that Widow Byrd gave me. I called her Mandy after my sister.

While Tom was gone a trader stopped by and told me he had a message for me. He said he had run into Mike Tanner and he was coming up this way to see me in a week or two. It will be good to see my father again. He will be amazed at how much Abraham has grown. It is time for me to make it up to Tom too. It has been far too long since we had been together like a proper man and wife. Most folks are as happy as they make up their minds to be. It's time for me to make up my mind.

July - Things have gotten much better around the Lincoln house. My father came and as I predicted was amazed at how much Abraham had grown. What he just couldn't get over was how smart he was. When Abraham recited the Declaration of Independence to him he almost burst with pride. He said that boy is a Tanner through and through. He said he wasn't as smart as Abraham cause he just didn't apply himself to books but he had a brother who was like him, smart as a whip. He did a surprising thing. He gave me and Tom quite a bit of money. He said he had been thinking about how he never did nothing to find me when I was little and felt bad about me having to indenture myself to the Enloes and everything that happened. He wanted me and Tom to buy some property and build us a nice home. I told him it was too much and I thought Tom's eyes were gonna pop out of his head looking at me but my father said it weren't near enough for what all I had been through. He told Tom to go buy us some cattle so I could put some weight on.

I told him about the baby and he said it was a sad thing but such things happened and the best thing was to just have another one. He patted Tom on the back and said "You gotta get to it man" and they both laughed at me blushing so hard. I didn't tell him that Tom was keeping up his end every night. Tom was not lacking in that department, he was never too tired to do that. I think if I can just put on some more weight maybe we could have another one. The cows might not be a bad idea. It looks like we are going to have better times ahead for sure.

My father took his leave and as Tom walked by me to go with him to the Inn he get patted my bottom and whispered in my ear "I think maybe we need to try two or three times tonight." I giggled and told him to get on with himself.

Abraham was reading and practicing his letters. He looked up and said "It's good to see you smile Mama." I ruffled his hair and said "Well I was thinking of you young man. It's good to see him reading." He has been quiet around Tom since the baby passed. He hasn't talked to me about it much but I think somehow he blames Tom. I need to sit him down and talk about it one day. It is just still so hard to talk about the baby. I have put Abraham down for the night and Tom will be back soon. I just may see how much of a man he is and hold him to that two or three times business tonight. Goodnight journal.

August - We got some sad news today. Matthew is leaving. He is going down to New Orleans to see his friend from New York and then plans to go up and explore the territory. Abraham is beside himself. He ran to his room and just cried and cried when Matthew told us. I wanted to go and comfort him but Matthew asked if he could do it. I left them alone and went out to do some chores. I cannot let Abraham see how devastated I feel about this. Matthew and I have become fast friends over the years. He is the only one I can really talk to about history and books. Matthew said a new teacher would be coming and he was sure we would like him. I feel like I am losing part of my world too. When I came back Abraham was better, he and Matthew were deep in discussion about the Constitution. He promised to get Abraham a copy of the Constitution and said he was going to send him some copies of Thomas Jefferson's writings. He has promised to write us both as much as possible.

When he left he hugged me tightly and said "Nancy if you had not been a married woman you could have made me stay." I hugged him back and said "Matthew if I was not a married woman I would go with you." He kissed me lightly on the mouth and left. I was stunned as I had never thought he felt that way about me. It didn't matter however I am a married woman and he is leaving in a few days. It will be a great loss for both of us. I promised Abraham we would write him regularly but since he was going adventuring he might not get the letters. Abraham told me it was all right that Matthew had told him that as long as he kept learning it would be like he wasn't gone.

Tom came home and Abraham went out to play. He does not stay around much when Tom is home anymore. I really need to have that talk with him. I told Tom about Matthew leaving and he said it would be good for him and besides Abraham was getting way too close to him. I told him that Abraham loved Matthew and he said "I know but you seem to love everything the boy does so it's probably for the best that he will be moving on." I looked very sternly at Tom and he said "I ain't saying nothings going on with you two now so don't get your hackles up. I know you ain't that kinda woman but it don't hurt to have any temptation moved away."

He put his arms around me and said "You don't know how tempting a woman you can be Miz Nancy, do you?" I laughed and told him to not be trying to sweet talk me. He said "Bet I can sweet talk my way here" and he put his hand up my skirt. I grabbed at the crotch of his pants and said "Let's see if you can do more than just talk sweet." He hustled me in the bedroom and we quickly got down to business. I didn't even take time to pull off my dress, he just flipped my skirt up and we went at it. After we finished we were giggling like two school children who had been bad. He said "I gotta sweet talk you more often woman." I told him to get on with hisself and let me go and call Abraham for supper. He held me close and said "Nancy I am sure glad that nobody else knows how good you are at this business in the bedroom, why I could never leave the house if they knew." I laughed and told him to go call Abraham in. He swatted my bottom and said "I'll call the boy and maybe when can do this again tonight but naked and slow." I giggled and said it sounded like a good idea to me.

I fixed supper while humming a song. Abraham seemed a little surprised that I was so happy after Matthew's news but as I told him most folks are as happy as they make up their minds to be so it is just for the best for us to be happy. He thought on it for a minute and said "I guess you are right Mama." "Of course I'm right," I told him, "I'm the Mama."

Tom is working on the fence. I think we may be moving soon and this place needs to be right to rent out. I'm going to get Abraham ready for bed and then if Tom's not back yet I may just slip into bed naked and wait on him. I think that might make both of us happy. Good night journal.

October - We have moved into our new house. It has three bedrooms and a kitchen and a study with a big front porch. I love it. I told Tom we had a palace fit for kings. He laughed and said he was glad I liked it. He has bought some more land and we are getting rents regularly. He even has hired a woman to help me around the house some and do some cooking. I feel rich indeed. Abraham likes the study, he has a desk for just his books and papers. Tom bought it for him. Abraham loved the desk but he was a bit lukewarm thanking Tom for it. I had put off this talk long enough, it was time for me and Abraham to air out some things.

I took Abraham on a walk to the orchard. We even got our own orchard now. We sat down on a stump and I asked him what was wrong with him and Tom. He just hung his head and said "Nothing." I tilted his chin up with my hands and said "Don't tell me nothing Abraham you ain't been right with Tom in a good while." He said Mama "Tom done put that baby in you and then he made you lose it." I said "Abraham, Tom did not make me lose the baby. The baby came early was all it wasn't Tom's fault." He looked at me and said "I heard the doctor talking to Tom afterwards and he said that you might just not have been strong enough after the beating to carry a child. That makes it Tom's fault Mama. He made you so you couldn't carry the baby like you should." He put his arms around me and just cried. "She was so little Mama, I saw her. She was just too little and her coming early was Tom's fault. He hurt you all over again after I promised you I wouldn't let him." "Child," I said "he did not hurt me and the baby dying was not his fault." "It was too" he said, "and I hear him trying to make another baby with you at night. I'm not a baby I know what he is doing to you Mama. He's hurting you and I can't stop him. I am so sorry Mama I just ain't big enough to stop him from putting another baby in you." "Oh Abraham, son you got it all wrong."

How could I have let this get this far I thought. "Abraham, the baby just came too early, that was God's doing not Tom's or mine and he is not hurting me at night. We are husband and wife and as such we do try to make babies. He is not doing anything against my will son. I let him because I want to have another baby. It is alright." He looked at me and said "He ain't hurting you when he does that to you at night?" "No Abraham," I said, "he ain't hurting me. You cannot go on blaming Tom for everything. We forgave him for what he did in the past and we need to forget it. He is a good man and he cares for us. Can you not see that he cares for us?"

Abraham was quiet for a good while and then he said "Well, he don't hit us no more and he don't yell as much but I still don't trust him Mama. What if he drinks tomorrow then we would be right back with the evil Tom?" "He won't son, he won't" I said, "Abraham please try to understand Tom. I know he is different from you and me but he is trying so hard and we owe him so much. He gave us a name so nobody would make fun of you and me. He gave us a house and now he is making money to give us nice things. He bought you that desk you like so much didn't he." Abraham shook his head yes. "So Abraham do you think you could try to not be so mad at Tom and talk to him a bit more." He said "I guess I can try Mama. You swear to me that Tom ain't hurting you at night, you swear?"

Normally I would have washed his mouth out for swearing

anything but this time I decided to let it go. I said "I swear it and cross my heart hope to die if you catch me in a lie." He jumped off the stump and hugged me really tight and said "I believe you Mama and I hope you never die." I got a chill that shook me to the bone when he said that. He said "Did I hug you too tight?" and I laughed and said it was cold and he was getting to be a strong boy.

He laughed and we walked back to the house. He seemed to have a lighter step on the way back. I felt bad I had put that talk off way too long and he suffered for it. I broke my own rule. One cannot escape the responsibility of tomorrow by evading it today. I remember reading that in one of Mr. Abraham's books back in Puzzle Creek.

I am glad that we have a bigger house now so Abraham can't hear us at night. I guess I do sound like he is hurting me sometimes but it is a hurt so good and my favorite part of being married. Poor Abraham he has a lot to learn about men and women. I'll have to figure when to talk to him about such things. I think it would be better coming from me than Tom.

Abraham went back in to work on his papers and I did my few night time chores. Tom should be home soon and we might just have to practice being a little more quiet tonight, maybe until we get it right. I can't rightly say that I love Tom, I don't think I'll ever feel that way about anybody like I did Joshua, but I sure do like that part of our life. Good night journal. I'm going to get ready to do some practicing.

December - I am really looking forward to the Christmas service this year. I am singing songs and the children are doing a play about the baby Jesus. It has been a prosperous year for the Lincolns. Tom and I are working hard to make another baby but no luck yet. I did go and talk to the doctor and he said I needed to try to gain some more weight. He felt like that would help. He gave me a foul bottle of medicine to drink said it would be a blood tonic. If it will help I will drink it I guess.

We have made enough money to buy a few more pieces of land. Tom says he plans to be the richest man in Kentucky. I told him I thought we were fine just like we were. I hope I can talk him into coming to church this year. Abraham is narrating the Christmas story for the children's play. He is so proud they chose him to read it. I told him it was because he was the best reader in church. The new teacher is here and he seems like a nice man but he is a lot older than Matthew was and I'm afraid not as smart. He seems dumbfounded at what all Abraham can do in school but he is letting him learn at his own pace and not making him do what all the other children his age are doing. Matthew had left him a letter about Abraham's reading ability so he is encouraging it too. I don't think Abraham will be as close to this teacher as he was Matthew. I know I won't.

I have been sewing for the church play and one of the ladies at church wants me to sew her daughter's wedding dress. She has fabrics coming from France. It will be a beautiful dress to work on. She is paying me well to make the dress and said I could have the left over material. I love getting the left over material. I have made two quilts out of that so far.

I have ordered a copy of The Federalist papers for Abraham for Christmas. I think he will love them and I am anxious to read them myself. You give that boy something to read and he is occupied for hours. Tom wants to give him his first gun this year. He seems young to me but Tom assures me all boys his age know how to shoot. Tom promised to teach him how to be safe with it.

I never have told Tom that I know how to shoot. Mr. Abraham made us all learn when we was going to Oconoluftee because of the Indians and robbers in the mountains. Why, Mrs. Sarah could out shoot Mr. Abraham any day. I could hit my targets but I didn't like the idea of killing things with a gun. I can skin and clean an animal all day long but I don't like to kill them. He should be all right with it. He seems to be good at anything he puts his mind to. I'll just have to stop worrying. I have lots to do between now and Christmas journal so I need to get busy. Goodnight journal.

--- The play at church today was wonderful. Everybody said it was the best service ever. Abraham read the story while the children came in and played their part. We had a real sheep, a cow, a donkey and a pig in the church! Nancy's little Mary played the baby Jesus and she was wonderful. Tom came and watched from the door. He said later he was glad he didn't have to clean up after the animals but I think he enjoyed it too. We had a big dinner and opened gifts. I was a little sad remembering last Christmas but I put it out of my mind and just enjoyed the evening. I think Tom was thinking the same thing. He didn't have much to say and looked sad.

When I finished cleaning everything up he said he thought he might just go on a walk for a while. I knew how he felt. I am remembering you my sweet baby on this day especially. I think I will remember you every Christmas from now on sweet girl. Maybe tonight will be the night it happens. I am gaining a bit of weight and feel much stronger these days. I hope Tom isn't too sad. I will just have to wait and see. Goodnight journal.

In the year of our Lord 1811 …..

February - Seven years old, goodness seven years since my precious Abraham was born. I fixed him a pound cake this year like the ones that Bessie used to make me. He loved it. I told him how Bessie used to bake them and always save me a slice or two. I love them too. He was so proud that we ate the squirrels that he shot. He has gotten quite good with that rifle. He brought us a rabbit the other day for supper. His teacher says he is moving right along. He says he is much farther along than some of the other children even the older ones. Abraham has gotten so good at his numbers that he is helping the other children. I am so proud of him.

I reminded him today of the story of the old Indian who traveled with me from Oconoluftee to Puzzle Creek and how he foretold of his greatness someday. Abraham never tires of hearing that story. He smiled and said "I am your Changeling ain't I Mama?" I hugged him and said "Yes my son you are my very special Changeling."

Mr. Abraham sent some more money so Tom bought some more properties. He is buying for Abraham's future. It all looks so bright. I would not have believed you if you had told me Tom would be a prosperous landowner someday. He encourages Abraham to read but tries to teach him some practical skills. Abraham just is not as interested in learning to fix fences and build things as he is in reading. I know it is frustrating to Tom but he tries.

We are doing well but no sign of a baby yet. The doctor tells me not to rush it that my body had lived through quite a shock and it takes time. I am starting to feel quite old these days. I even noticed some lines around my eyes that weren't there last year. We have this nice big house and I would like to fill it with children someday. Maybe this will be the year for us. Goodnight journal.

May - It just seems like I am too busy to write these days. I have started helping at the school again. Abraham is going by the doctor's house two days a week. He is letting him read his books in exchange for doing a few chores around his house for him. The doctor tells me Abraham has quite a remarkable talent for reading. I do have a sinful amount of pride in that boy. I wish he and Tom got along better. He goes with Tom to learn how to do things but his heart is not in it. Tom usually gets cross with him and sends him back home.

Tom is doing well with managing our properties. John even has him looking after his too. We don't have a baby yet but I keep hoping. The doctor just tells me to give it time. Goodness I get so tired of hearing that. He says it is good for me to stay busy. Busy seems to be my middle name these days. Abraham and Tom will be in soon and I need to make sure that everything is ready for supper. I'll be putting you up for now journal.

July - Things are going good. Abraham got a letter from Matthew this week with a book that had the copy of the Constitution in it along with some of Thomas Jefferson's writings. Abraham was thrilled that Matthew had not forgotten him. It was a good letter and it sounds like he is having an exciting time in New Orleans.

Tom has been taking Abraham with him to help build a neighbor's barn. He complains that the boy spends more time daydreaming than working. He says the boy better be able to do something with reading cause he sure ain't gonna make a living with his hands. Abraham don't pay him no mind he just goes and takes his book outside to read. I asked him the other day if he was still mad at Tom. He said no but he still watched him to make sure he was behaving. I just shook my head and told him he didn't need to be worrying about Tom and maybe he could just try a little harder to learn the things Tom was trying to teach him. He just shook his head and said "I ain't going to be no carpenter Mama." I told him it didn't matter if he was going to be one or not that every man needed to know how to build things to make sure it was done right.

Oh that boy of mine has so much to learn. He is so book smart but a man has to learn how to live life too not just read about it. I have to go and do the books for Tom. I am keeping the accounts for the properties for him and John. Time to put you away journal.

October - Goodness how time has flown by this year. I did not realize I have not written in here for so long. Abraham is back in school. The teacher asked me if I had ever thought about teaching school. I told him I was not qualified to teach school. He laughed and said I was as qualified as some that were teaching. Sometimes I feel like I am teaching school. I am there helping almost every day. I do love helping the little ones. They are so sweet.

Tom talked about buying some slaves to help him around the properties to keep them up. I just did not approve of the added expense. I told him by the time we provided housing and clothes and food we could hire some locals to work for him cheaper. I think he just wants them because John has some but I can't warm up to the idea. I told him that being an indentured servant was bad enough for me and I just can't see myself as a slave owner. We are doing well but we are not rich and John wouldn't have slaves if his family didn't give him some. It made me think however about slavery as a whole. I can't say I agree with it completely but some people like Mr. Abraham was good to his slaves. We are lucky here that we can hire people to do the work but if we had hundreds of acres to farm I don't think we could do it without slaves. People just need to treat each other with respect slave or not.

I must run now, I have several things to do before Tom gets home and having him find me writing in this is not something I am ready to share with him.

November - Tom told me today that the farm at Knobby Creek will be up for sale after the first of the year. He said we could buy if I liked it. It is one of the finest houses in town. I told him I thought it would be a fine idea. It would be nice to live so close to the school. Maybe it will be the start we need for a baby. I'm not giving up on that. Tom has slowed down a bit with the added responsibilities of managing the properties and I have to admit I go to bed tired a lot too.

I think I may ride up to see Nancy tomorrow. She is expecting again and it has been too long since we have had a good visit. I am sure that Abraham will enjoy seeing John again. It has been a long day for me and Tom went to bed a while ago. I think I will turn in too. Goodnight journal.

December — Christmas will be here soon. I always look forward to the special programs we do at church. Abraham is preparing a special reading and I am doing a special song. I asked Tom if he would like to go with us. He said "I ain't wasting no time going to no church." I didn't press him on it. Tom just ain't a church going man and never will be. He has been mopping around lately. I really think Christmas reminds him of losing Mandy. I do so hope I can have another baby soon. I think it would take the darkness out of Tom. Funny, this will be one of the most prosperous Christmas' we ever had yet it feels kinda sad. I will say a special prayer for Tom this year I think. Goodnight journal.

In the year of our Lord 1812 .....

February - A birthday again. It is hard to believe that my boy is eight years old. Mr. Abraham sent him a book by Nancy and John. It is so nice that he remembers him. Abraham knows he has Enloe blood but we don't talk about it much. His name is Lincoln now and that is all that matters. Abraham was fussing today because he is not as tall as his friend. I told him not to worry he would grow soon enough. He is a wiry boy but I think he will grow to be tall since he takes after Mr. Abraham so much. He just says he wants to be taller than Tom. I promised him that he would be, for Tom is not much taller than me. Why Mr. Abraham is well over six feet and then some so Abraham should be a tall man when he hits his growth spurt.

I have had a beef roast fixed for his dinner. It is nice to have cows for beef. Tom said today we will be moving in the Spring to Knobb Creek. I am looking forward to it but we have so much more to move this time. My how life has changed for us. It was not that long ago we didn't have enough food to eat now look at us. Even I am beginning to put on some weight.

Maybe this will be the year for a baby. My arms do so ache for one. It is hard to believe it has been so long since I rocked Abraham to sleep as a baby. I am not going to dwell on that now. I am making some garments for Nancy's baby. I had some beautiful satin left over from a wedding gown I made so I am sewing a Christening gown for her. I think she will like it. Time to get busy and stop letting my mind wander. Writing can do that to me sometimes. I need to go see what Abraham is getting into anyways.

April - We are all moved in to Knobb Creek. It truly is a fine house. It seems a bit large for just the three of us but Tom is so proud of it. I was in town buying some things today and heard some women talking about the Lincoln's taking on airs since they bought Knobb Creek. I just walked by them with my head held high. Taking on airs indeed. I have lived with whispers before and have found that they best way is to pay them no mind.

We live right near the school. I can almost see it from my backyard and Abraham loves it. We have room for a library and I am trying to get some new books for Abraham. He and I have been spending more time together in the evenings. Tom has been so busy that he comes home late most days. I often tell Abraham the story of the old Indian. He never tires of hearing it. I remind him of how he will grow to be tall and be able to see into men's souls. I warn him against become too sad over other people. You cannot be responsible for decisions other men make I told him but you have to learn to live with your own. Make a decision and then stand by it. Always be true to yourself for you are the only one that faces you in the mirror.

We enjoy these evenings without Tom. It just seems the older he gets the less he and Tom have in common. It is our time together. We have a special bond, he and I. My sweet Changeling child I do love him so. He has gone to bed and I think I will too. Tom should be in soon. Goodnight journal.

June - John came down today and asked me if I could come up and stay with Nancy. She is having a difficult time with this baby and needs some help with Mary. I told him I would straighten up some things and be up in a few days. I told Tom and he said it would be fine. We only had words when I told him that Abraham was going with me. He said there was no reason why the boy could not stay home with him. I told him that he was not home very much and Abraham did not need to stay home alone. He was just too young. Tom stomped his foot but I had my way. Abraham would go with me. Tom went outside to cool off a bit and I went to tell Abraham. He was thrilled.

I have so much to do to get ready to go. The baby is not supposed to come until August and I know how important it is to rest that last few months so the baby can get here all right and it will be nice to take care of Mary for a while. Tom has already gone up to bed and I think I need to make it up to him for giving in on letting me take Abraham besides I may be gone for a while. Goodnight journal.

September - I am finally back home. I realized I had left you after a few days at Nancy and John's. I know I do not write in you as often as I should but I am trying. I have missed being home but getting to care for Mary and be there when the new baby came was worth being gone. Oh how my heart ached when I held Nancy's baby for the first time. He was so beautiful. I remembered my Mandy, she was so small compared to little John Jr. I stayed until Nancy was getting back on her feet and Abraham had to come back to go to school. Tom had come up to see me several times while I was at Nancy's and he was sure enough happy that I was coming home. It is so nice to be back and I am looking forward to sleeping in my own bed especially with Tom. I have so much to do but I wanted to write just a bit in you journal. You are my secret friend. Good night.

November - I thought for a while that I might be with child but it was not meant to be. I did not tell Tom as I did not want to get his hopes up. I talked with the doctor about it and he told me that sometimes a body is not meant to have babies. He was honest with me about the fact that the beating could have caused me some problems that he couldn't see. He said that sometimes we had to just leave these things up to God. I am trying not to be heartbroken about it but I have been good and I pray every night. I just don't know why God doesn't want me to have another baby. Maybe I am just being selfish. I do have Abraham and a mother could not be prouder of a child than I am of him but I long to hold a baby in my arms and I know Tom wants one. It is getting hard on him that we have not had a child yet.

It is not easy between him and Abraham. They are just so different and the older Abraham gets the more evident it is. Tom works hard and he is a good man he just don't know how to talk to Abraham and I am afraid that Abraham will never open his heart to Tom. There are some wounds in children that just don't heal. I must not let myself become melancholy over this. I feel the darkness around me and I just will not let it take me. It is up to me to stay in the light. I must pray and let God know I am sorry for questioning him. If he means me to have a baby I will. I just wish he could reach Tom's heart for I know this bothers him too.

I have taken to staying up after everyone has gone to bed. I like the quiet of the house but I need to go up and be with Tom. He doesn't know why I am sad but he knows something's wrong. I think I just need to go upstairs and put my arms around him and hold him close. Goodnight journal.

December - We made it through Christmas this year. Tom and I both seem to feel the cloud of heaviness hanging over us. We both remember the Christmas I told him that Mandy was coming. It is hard to think that it has been two years ago. I didn't sing at church this year. I just didn't have my heart in it. Abraham feels the sadness. He asked me what was wrong the other night when we were reading. I told him we were just remembering little Mandy and it made us sad. He said "Well Tom should be sad, it was his fault." I am afraid I was sharp with him when I told him to stop blaming God's will on Tom. He just snorted and walked away. I don't think he will ever get over what happened between me and Tom long ago and I can somewhat understand it. Just as he means everything to me I know how much I mean to him. He thought he was going to lose me on account of Tom. That's the kind of thing a child could never get over.

I don't like the idea that he holds bitterness in his heart. It will just weigh him down with time but I am afraid I cannot take it from him. I pray that God will lighten his heart towards Tom not just for Tom but for him. He is too young to understand how that bitterness can poison your soul if left unchecked. I hope that the coming year will be one that lightens all our hearts.

Tom is pulling away from me. I can feel it. We never talk about losing Mandy and we never talk about having another baby anymore. I am afraid he thinks I am barren and he feels responsible for it. That is just too much guilt for him to carry. I wish he would talk to me about it but he won't. Tom don't like to talk about feelings. He just pretends they are not there.

It is late and the house is cold so I think I will go up to bed. Tom always pretends he is sleeping these days when I come to bed. I wish he would just roll over one night and be with me. I have tried but when I touch him even though he responds and gets firm he still pretends he is asleep. We are going to have to talk about this soon even if he don't want to. I miss being with my husband. I will put you away now journal. Goodnight.

In the year of our Lord 1813 …..

January - I am going to start this year off on a positive note. I am going to talk to Tom. A house divided against itself can't stand and I feel we are divided. He and I are going to have to get this cloud out from between us. I am tired of his short answers when I ask him a question and I am tired of Abraham and him not talking and I am really tired of not being with him like a wife. It just ain't natural for a man to never want to be with his wife especially when I darn well know that his body wants to. This is going to end if I have to just jump on him and pester him until he takes me. I miss my husband in my bed.

While I am on a tear, Abraham is going to start doing more things with Tom. They are not going to get along if they don't do things together. It is a new year and we are going to all have a new start here at the Lincoln house. I will not stand for it to keep being the way is has been. If God don't mean for me to have a baby that don't mean that God don't mean for me and Tom to be together like a man and a wife should. We get pleasure out of it without making a baby and I want that back. I am determined this year. I am putting my feet in the right place and standing firm on this with both of them. I am sweeping the cobwebs out of my marriage bed tonight and Abraham will go help Tom some at work starting tomorrow. We are gonna make this house a home again.

I feel better just writing it down. Journal you have been such a comfort to me, my guilty pleasure. I have never shared your existence with Tom, I know he couldn't read you but he I think would be jealous that I put my thoughts down in you. I am so careful about hiding you away from him and Abraham. Abraham knows I keep a journal but I am not ready to let him read it until he is much, much older. He needs to understand much more of life before he can read about mine if I let him then.

You are the writings of my soul, journal. No one knows my thoughts and feelings but you. This journal and Widow Byrd's bible are the two books I hold most dear. One has me written in it and the other has my babies birth's written in it. That bible was what Abraham leaned to read in and he still reads it every night. I tell him every man needs to know his scriptures no matter what his profession. I have talked to Abraham about writing in a journal and why it is important to record his thoughts. He doesn't know that I am giving him one on his birthday next month. I hate to think I am another year older too but time waits for no man or woman. Goodnight journal tomorrow is a new day at this house.

February - Nine years old. My baby is nine years old today. We actually had a little party at school for him today. This is a special birthday. Nine years, oh my goodness. I was just a girl when I had him. We opened the bible and I traced his name that the doctor had written long ago beside it I had written in Lincoln. He asked me should he call himself Abraham Hanks Lincoln. I told him no, he was Abraham Lincoln now and that was who he stayed. I patted Tom's arm and said "Ain't that right." Tom smiled and said, "Yes boy that's right."

It has been a good day. Tom and I finally said our piece to each other about the baby. He told me that he just felt responsible for everything and didn't feel like he had a right to bed me any more. I sat him straight on that matter. I let him know that I didn't let him pleasure me to just to try to make a baby. I liked it and missed it and wanted him back in my bed one hundred percent. It didn't matter if we made a baby or not I wanted him. He has kept up his end of the bargain. He has been like a young man here lately at night. I been singing around the house a lot lately too.

I set young Abraham straight too about his attitude and that he was going to spend more time with Tom and just learn to like it or at least tolerate it. I will not have any more unhappiness in this house. Times are good for us these days and we all need to be a little more grateful.

I gave Abraham his journal and he sat right down to write in it. He did not need as much instruction with his as I did when I got mine. He wrote two pages full and then put it up and gave me a big bear hug. He said "I got one like yours Mama." I told him yes he did and for him to keep it safe like I do mine for our thoughts are not for others to read just us. He said "I would never hide it from you Mama, you can read it anytime you want to." I smiled and thanked him but said "It is for your eyes only son and I respect that so you keep it put up." All in all it was a good day. I have put him to bed and Tom is waiting for me. I think I need to remind him tonight how much he likes it when I come to bed naked. Goodnight journal, I know it will be for me and Tom.

April - The weather has gotten warmer and the trees are budding. Abraham and Tom seem to be getting along better and I know that Tom and I are. I am opening windows and sweeping cobwebs out of this house. We have had a lawyer move into town, a Mr. Dunlap. Abraham has haunted his office since the day he moved in. He has been over to dinner a few times and is amazed at Abraham's knowledge and skill at reading and writing. He can't get over the fact that he is only nine. He talks the Constitution like an old man he says. He has Abraham coming over almost every day to read his law books. He said any boy that had memorized the Declaration Of Independence could read his books any day.

I told Abraham he had to sweep up the office every day if he wanted to read his books. The boy has to learn the importance of paying your way. I don't want him to expect people to give him things for nothing. That is not the way the world works. He says he going to grow up to be a lawyer some day. Mr. Dunlap says that is a worthy goal.

I have started to gain some weight finally. One of my old dresses fit well today. Tom said he was glad to see me filling out again some. It had been a while since he has seen my cheeks this full and he laughed and said my face was filling out some too. Oh that man can be so silly sometimes. We get along good when things are happy in the bedroom. Now that we ain't worrying about making a baby we both seem to enjoy it more.

I am singing at church again and trying to teach Abraham to sing. I hope the boy is a good lawyer cause he ain't got my singing skills but we try. He needs to learn how to sing at church without scaring somebody. I been trying again to get Tom to come to church but he just says what he always says about church. "When I do good, I feel good. When I do bad, I feel bad. That's my religion." I don't think I'll ever get that man to church.

I think I'll make some clothes for John, Jr. Last time I talked to Nancy she said he was growing like a weed. They shore do that those first few years. Abraham seems to have slowed down for a bit.

It worries him but Mr. Dunlap who is almost as tall as Mr. Abraham told him not to worry he didn't grow hardly none at all until he was about seventeen and then he shot up like a tree. I am sure he will grow soon enough, right now I am just glad that his shoes fit. It's a good spring we hardly got any shadows between us in the house right now. I have everybody down so I think it's about time to go ask Tom how round those cheeks have really got. Oh, I made myself giggle, somebody would think I was talking to spirits. Good night journal.

July - Abraham is out of school now and he wants to stay at Mr. Dunlap's all the time. I finally made a deal with him. If he would learn to split and build fence two days a week then he could spend the rest of his time with Mr. Dunlap. He agreed reluctantly but even Mr. Dunlap said that it is good for a man to have a skill to fall back on and fence building is always needed by somebody. Tom is happy that he is working at some sort of trade.

It looks like it's going to be a hot summer. I thank goodness we have a shaded porch that is cool in the evenings. Some days I think about going back on my promise to not ever swim naked again. It would be so nice when it's this hot. Abraham does it enough for all of us I guess. He is a good swimmer they say. He and his friends go down to the river and fish and swim in the evenings. I can't complain, we have had some good eating from it. It is nice to finally feel rounded out like a grown woman. I guess it is just part of getting older but this part I like. I think I am going to put you up journal and have something cool to drink and go sit on the porch.

August - Yesterday was one of those hot, hot, dog days of summer. No matter what I did I felt my clothes sticking to me. Tom came in to sit on the porch during the worst heat of the day. Abraham had gone up to John and Nancy's for a few days so we had the house to ourselves. We had sat there for a while and I asked him if he was hungry. He said it was almost too plumb hot to eat. The sun was hanging low in the sky when I said I know somewhere that might be cooler and we could have a late picnic. Tom said he was game for anything that might be cooler.

I packed us some fruit and chicken and biscuits and a little bit of elderberry wine in a basket. I told him to grab a blanket and we headed to the riverbank. We laid the blanket down on the ground under the big oak tree. It was much cooler down by the river. Tom and I had a feast. We ate the chicken and biscuits, finished the fruit and drank almost the whole bottle of wine. Tom had taken off his shirt and I had unbuttoned my bodice some and uncovered my lower legs to get cooler.

The sun was almost down and a beautiful full moon filled the sky. The river looked so inviting. I told Tom how when I was young I used to sneak down to the river and swim naked. He laughed and said he did it all the time when he was a boy. Then he stood up and dropped his pants and walked stark naked into the water. He went under a few times and said "Nancy you ought to come in, there ain't nobody around." I told him I thought I better not. He laughed and said "You're just scared, go ahead and stay hot up there on the bank."

I watched him swim for a few minutes and he was having such a good time. I guess the wine had gone to my head cause the next thing I knew I was standing up on the blanket and slowly taking off my dress. Tom stopped swimming and just watched me. I stripped naked and just stood there a minute in the moonlight with my hands raised over my head feeling how good the cooler night air felt on my hot skin. Tom said "You going to stand there all night or come swimming with me?" I walked down into the water and dunked my head under. It felt wonderful.

Tom and I swam and played like children for a while then it turned much more adult. Tom had me in his arms and our bodies were both wet and slippery in the water. I had never in my life felt anything so good as Tom taking me in the water. As he held me close afterwards I felt the wood spirit entering me or maybe the wine spirit but I left him and walked out of the water and stood on the riverbank in the moonlight with my arms held high and bid him come to me.

He walked out of the water watching me the whole time with his manhood erect and firm. I told him to lie with me in the moonlight and he took me again. We lay on that blanket entwined together under the moonlight for several hours. When we got up I gathered up my clothes and he got the blanket and basket and we both walked back to the house naked as the day we were born. We dropped our things on the floor and went to our marriage bed where we came together again. We drifted off as the sun was peaking over the horizon. When we awoke the next morning we looked at our clothes and the basket on the floor and both laughed. He said "I never saw you like that before Nancy, you were like a vision in the moonlight" and I told him he acted like a young man of twenty.

We got dressed and started our day and went our separate ways. It was a night of magic journal. The wood spirit was still inside me. I was so happy today I almost danced even with my limp. Today I feel like I am all woman. I love my house and maybe if life stays like this I may grow to love Tom. Abraham will be coming in soon. I always miss him when he is gone but maybe not quite so much this time. I will put you up journal. I just wanted to share the magic.

October - I have such news journal and you are the only one I am telling for now. I am with child. I'm not telling Tom yet because I want to make sure everything is alright. I went to see the doctor today and he agrees that I am indeed with increase. Oh my goodness I am excited and scared. I really believed that I was not to have any more children. My Abraham will be ten years old when this baby comes. God has answered my prayers.

The doctor said for me to take it very easy with this one. No lifting or excessive walking. I am a better weight now than I was when I was carrying Mandy. I don't know how long I can keep this wonderful, wonderful secret. The only cloud on the horizon will be Abraham. I have to make him understand that this baby is a good thing. He seems to think that Tom hurt me with the last baby. I just need to get him to understand how very much I want this child. It is truly an act of God. He is rewarding me and Tom with a child. It had to be that night we spent on the river. It was the magic of the wood spirit. She made me fertile again. I am a blessed woman to have two Changeling children.

The doctor says not to let Tom bed me while I am with child. He said it could be dangerous to the baby. I will have to figure out something for the next few weeks until I am sure that this baby has set proper. I think I may try to knit a blanket to calm my nerves. A baby, oh journal how very blessed I am. I shall put you up now that we have shared my secret. We are having a baby.

November - I was going to tell Tom today about the baby. The doctor thinks it will be alright now. Tom came in behind me while I was getting dressed and cupped both my breasts in his hands. He started nuzzling me on my neck and said "It has been a long time Nancy. Your breasts feel so firm and full and you have gotten so rounded and soft." I could feel him hard up against me and I knew I couldn't wait any longer. I turned around to him and dropped my nightgown to the floor. He started taking off his breeches and I said "Stop, we can't do that now." He looked surprised and said "Well why did you get naked for me?" I smiled and said "Tom feel how full my breasts are." He said "I done told you I felt that." I moved his hand down to my belly and said "Feel how round my belly is." He said "I know that too and so does my other parts" and he sat me down on his lap on the bed. "Tom," I said, "Why do you think my breasts are so full and my belly round?" He laughed and said "Cause you are finally eating better." I said "No, cause we are going to have a baby."

He jumped up so fast he about spilled me in the floor. "A baby," he said. "Are you sure?" "Yes, I'm sure" I said. "Remember that night down by the river, well I'm sure that's when it happened. The doctor says we should have a fine baby by May sometime. That's why we can't be bedding each other no more till then." "So that's why you been not letting me bed you at night?" "Yes," I smiled big at him. "We done good didn't we Tom?"

He picked me up in his arms and swung me around the room. "A baby, we're finally gonna have a baby." Then he sat me gently down on the bed and said "We got to be careful of you this time. No working, no doing nothing till this baby comes." "Don't you worry," I said. "I'm gonna take good care of myself." Then before I could stop him he went running downstairs telling everybody in the house we were having a baby. I went down and told him to let me tell Abraham went he came home from school. He agreed and went out to look after the properties.

I walked around nervously when it was time for Abraham to come home. He ran in and said he was going to Mr. Dunlap's and I asked him if he could spare me a minute. He came in and sat down and said "What's wrong?" "Nothing is wrong," I said, "This is really,

really right. I am going to have a baby sometime in May." He looked alarmed and I said "The doctor says everything is fine." He said "This is Tom's doing, and it don't feel fine to me." "Abraham please try to be happy for me, you know how badly I have wanted a baby" I said. He said "I want you to be happy Mama as long as you stay healthy." I told him the doctor would be watching me closely and I would be fine.

He then said "Can I go now?" I wanted to talk to him longer but I let him go. I know he will accept this when the baby comes. What a wonderful, wonderful day. I plan to sit around from now until May knitting and getting fat. My prayers have been answered journal. I will write soon.

***December* -** We are preparing for Christmas or I should say Tom and Abraham are. They make me sit and tell them what to do. I enjoy sitting and feeling the baby move. This one is already a kicker. Even Tom has felt him or her kick. Tom is a delight. He just cannot seem to do enough for me. Even Abraham has lightened up some around him. He and Tom are working in the barn building a cradle for the baby. They work on it in the evenings.

Abraham is excited because Mr. Dunlap is teaching him to write something he calls briefs about law cases. Mr. Dunlap says Abraham beats anything he has ever seen. I am glad he likes the boy. I plan to go to church and sing at the service this year. The doctor says it should be fine. Even Tom has agreed to go. A real miracle for sure. I need to put you away journal Tom will be back in soon and will insist that I retire for the evening. Goodnight journal.

--- Christmas has come and gone. Watching Tom sit in church with Abraham made my heart swell with pride. He said he would come this one time for the baby. We are finally a family. I am so filled with happiness journal that I feel like I am going to bust. Sometimes I wonder if it is a sin to feel this happy. Oh well, I am not going to let that bother me. I am so looking forward to the new year and the new baby. My dreams are coming true. Goodnight journal.

In the year of our Lord 1814 .....

February - Another birthday for Abraham. This one makes ten. Mr. Dunlap has been talking about another school for Abraham to go to. He says it is not far and it teaches more than this one can. He thinks I ought to look at sending him there in a year or two. I told him I would think about it. He got a letter from Matthew this week telling him about New Orleans. It seems that Matthew really likes it there. He is working with his friend the lawyer and thinks he might take it up himself. He told Abraham to keep studying and may be could join him someday. I told Abraham that was a long way off. He sent him a book about Thomas Jefferson that had been translated from French. Abraham was very excited over that.

We are doing well with our rents so Tom got Abraham his own horse. He told him he would have to care for it and feed it every day or he would take it back. Abraham was excited to the point I think he almost liked Tom right at that minute. The baby is getting large. It kicks Tom in his back at night. I think it's funny when Tom grunts at the baby kicking him.

I am having a little trouble with my weight again. The doctor says some babies just take a lot out of the mother. Tom is worried, he worries over everything about this baby. I get tired really easily but I rest a lot. I am trying to eat but I just don't have an appetite. I don't think Abraham has noticed much. I surely do not want him worried. I want to go look at Abraham's horse but maybe tomorrow. I am very tired tonight. Goodnight journal.

March - My back started hurting really badly today. I remembered last time and had Tom go for the doctor right away. He came quickly and told me everything looked alright except the fact that my weight was falling off so much. He gave me a draft to drink to strengthen my blood and told me I had to stay in the bed until my back stopped hurting. It felt better just laying down so I told him I would not get up if I have to lay here until May.

Abraham came in and sat with me when he got home from school. I asked him to go and get the bible and read it to me as it gave me such comfort. He went and got the bible and read to me for about an hour. He laid the bible down and took my hand and said "Mama did the doctor really say you are alright?" "Yes," I told him, "he just said I needed to stay in bed. The baby is just really big and I am really small." Abraham looked at me and patted the baby through my belly and said "We will look after you little baby don't you worry." I told him we both felt better knowing he was watching out for us. I got Abraham to bring me my journal so I could write in it. He is ready to put it back before Tom comes is so I will say goodnight. I am praying for my baby and me.

April - I have been lying here like the doctor told me. I try to get up and do anything and the back pains start. The doctor said today that if I could just make it a few more weeks we will be there. I have gotten so weak just lying around. My legs look like sticks under my big swollen belly. Poor Tom walks the floors. He worries so. Abraham comes in and reads to me and tells me stories. He has become quite the story teller. It is not bad lying here and if it will help keep the baby in me longer then I will gladly do it.

Nancy is coming down tomorrow. She has been worried about me. I need to get up and stretch as I feel my legs cramping. I got up and walked around the room and it made my legs feel better but the minute I stand up those back pains start again. I am back in the bed and it is getting better. Oh journal I am afraid. I dare not tell Tom as he is so frightened himself and Abraham, dear Abraham what would he do? I will talk to Nancy tomorrow, I can tell her these things. Mary and little John will be a good distraction for both Abraham and Tom. I am glad John is bringing them. I think I will try to sleep a while journal. Abraham will be in to put you back in a minute. Good night journal.

--- Nancy came today. I feel so much better just talking to her. She could not hide her alarm at how much weight I had lost but said me staying in the bed is a good idea. We chatted and she brought me some baby things from little John. It was a nice visit. Abraham told me he had fun playing with the children. Sounds like we all had a good day. Tom came in to bid me goodnight. He sleeps in the other room to not bother me. Abraham just popped his head in to see if I was ready for him to put you up. I guess I should say goodnight so he can put you away and go to bed himself. Goodnight journal.

--- Journal I am scared, really scared my back is hurting even though I am laying down. Tom is working out by the barn so I had Abraham run to get the doctor. I had a dream last night. The old Indian just stood by me starring with such sadness. He placed his hands on my swollen belly and said be brave and then he was gone. I don't know what he meant. Was he telling me to be brave or the baby. It is still too early to have the baby. He is not due to come for at least a fortnight according to the doctor.

I am trying to be calm journal and wait for the doctor but these pains just are getting worse. I will pray. Surely God will not let this happen again. I must be calm it will not help the baby if I am not calm. I am going to put you away journal. Abraham will collect you when he gets here. If you were a person journal I would ask you to pray for me and my baby too.

--- I am so very tired but I wanted to write down my son's name and birthday Thomas Lincoln, Jr. April 14, 1814. He is very, very small but holding his own so far. I asked Abraham to bring me my journal so I could record his name. I am still bleeding and very weak so I must go now. He is beautiful journal, just beautiful.

--- Tom, Jr. is one week old today. He is so very, very small and does not want to nurse. The doctor is having me express milk out and we drip it into his little mouth. I am too weak to get up and go to him. I made Tom bring me the bible so I could write his name and birth date in it. I put his name right under Mandy's.

I am still bleeding heavily and the doctor is very worried. He has been staying here most all day since Tom, Jr. was born. He looks worried. Tom just looks frantic. I told him to rock the baby and it would help calm his nerves. He wrapped him up in a blanket and rocked him for me. I could see his face relax some. He was holding his little fingers amazed at how small they were.

Abraham rocks the baby too. He is worried as well. Little Tom is so, so small. He almost fits in Tom's hand. I am praying harder than I ever have and I am trying to be brave. Nancy is coming tomorrow to stay with me and the baby. I know it will be better tomorrow, I just know it. Bless my sweet baby Lord, bless him and me. Good night journal.

May - My beautiful tiny son passed away yesterday. He just couldn't eat. Nancy is with Abraham and Tom. I just want to be alone. I wish you could talk journal. Why has my God deserted me? Why. Why, why?

September - I decided to write today. My grief has known no bounds these past months. Tom and I do not speak except out of necessity. Abraham has withdrawn into himself and rarely says anything. I think I may have gone on forever in this black fog of pain had Mr. Dunlap not come by today. He came in the house and asked to speak with me privately.

I showed him into the study and sat down. I really did not care what he had to say but I am as always polite to a guest. He did not mince words but came right out and asked me if I loved Abraham. I was slightly offended at his tone but I told him of course I loved Abraham, how dare he even question such a thing. He said "Well if you love him why have you abandoned him?" I told him I thought he was speaking out of turn. He said "I have watched the change in Abraham since the loss of your son. He has gone from a happy talkative boy to one who sits and reads in silence. He wears his sadness like a heavy cloak that is weighing him down. I respect your grief at the loss of your newborn son but do you want to lose Abraham too?"

I stood up agitated and said "I am not losing Abraham." He said "My dear lady you most assuredly are losing Abraham and if you can't see it those of us that care for him can." I turned away from him and thought about this. In my grief I had turned away from everyone including God. I spent the first month after little Tom's passing just lying in bed without the strength to get up. I did not want to see or talk to Tom. My pain was so great I could not bear his. Abraham would come in and read to me at night and try to comfort me but he could not reach me either. I finally told him as I did Nancy I just wanted to be alone. He did just that. He and Tom both left me alone.

Our house has been a house of silence. I never stopped to

consider what was happening with Abraham. Mr. Dunlap was right I had abandoned my son. The only child I had or was ever likely to have. Oh my God what have I done?

I turned to Mr. Dunlap with tears streaming down my cheeks and asked him if he thought this could be rectified. He took my hands in his and said "You are his mother, he needs you in his life. You have to let him in yours." I thanked him profusely and told him I would talk to Abraham when he came home from school.

After he left I looked around the house. It was dark and dreary and not a place for a young man of Abraham's age. I had kept the shades pulled on the windows keeping the light out. It was September, school had started back for Abraham and he had had no one to talk to for months. I know he and Tom never talk anymore. How could I have done this to my son that I loved more than life itself. How could I have been so, so selfish?

I dropped to my knees for the first time in months and I cried and prayed to God to forgive me for turning away from him and from Abraham. I begged him to help me make it right. I got up and took a good look at myself. I was way too thin and dressed all in black. Did I look like I could ever be a comfort to anyone? I opened the shades and went upstairs and found a blue dress. It was too big but I tied an apron around my waist to make it fit more. I brushed my hair and tried to smile. It almost hurt my face it had been so long. I had to show Abraham his mother was back. I pray it is not too late. I pray that he has not turned against me. Please God let me reach his heart. Let him know that he is loved. I promised him I would never leave him and that is exactly what I did. He will be home soon. I must have courage. I must be brave.

Suddenly I thought of the dream of the old Indian from months ago. He was telling me to be brave, I needed to be brave for Abraham. He will be here soon journal. I must try. I must bring my boy back to me. He and I are joined. We have the same spirit. How lonely he must have been. I will be brave. I will bring him back to me.

--- Oh journal this has been the hardest day. Abraham came home and I saw the mantle of sadness over him. His shoulders were stooped and his eyes looked so old. I called for him to come in the study. He walked in and saw the shades up and noticed I was in the blue dress. I stood by the window with tears on my face and held out my arms and said "I love you my son and I am so sorry, please find it in your heart to forgive me."

He rushed into my arms and I held him tight. He buried his face in my chest and with sobbing breaths he said "I thought I had lost you forever Mama." I stroked his head and said "You have not lost me Abraham I have just been gone for a while but now I am back and I swear as God is my witness I will never, ever leave you again if you can just find it in your heart to forgive me." He pulled away and said "But Mama I am the one who needs forgiveness. I could not protect you from Tom hurting you again. He took you away from me again." "Oh Abraham," I said, "This was not Tom, this was me. I went away from you both."

We sat down and I took his hands and said "Tell me what you feel about everything even if you think it will make me feel sad. I want to know. I need to be part of you as you are me." As he talked and talked I felt each word pierce my heart like a sword. He told me of Tom's grief at the baby's passing and how he asked the doctor what caused it to happen. He said when the doctor said that something was not just right inside of you Tom grabbed him by the arms and said "Is this my fault? Did I do this to her?" The doctor looked at Tom and said "I can't say you didn't. She was hurt so badly when you beat her that only God knows what happened inside her." He said Tom howled like an animal that had been shot and told the doctor that God was punishing him.

The doctor did not help matters by telling Tom that the Lord merits punishment when he thinks it is due. Abraham said Tom looked at him and said "Get away from me boy I can't bear your face right now." Abraham choked back tears when he said "I tried to help you Mama. I came and read to you and tried to talk to you but you just turned away. When you told me to leave you alone it broke my heart Mama. I watched you every day, you just didn't want to eat and the doctor told Tom he was worried that you would grieve yourself to death. He told Tom you were not a strong woman and women had passed over much less, that's when he sent a woman in to care for you. I watched Tom too Mama, I was not going to let him hurt you any more but he has stayed away. I have tried to stay away from him. I can tell when he looks at me he don't want me here. Oh Mama," he cried, "Please don't leave me again. I have been so lost I thought about just throwing myself in the river and drowning."

"Oh my sweet and precious boy," I said, "You can never let yourself feel that sad again. That is never the answer to sadness. This is all my fault, I should have never left you, even in my grief I should not have lost sight of what I have." He hugged me and said "Mama I know you are sad that little Tom died. I remembered what you told me about flesh of your flesh and blood of your blood." "Oh Abraham," I said, "The bond between a mother and child is the most powerful God ever created. It takes time to overcome such a great loss but I am so grateful to have you. I love you Abraham, I love you with my whole heart."

We had talked for hours and then he said "Mama can I read to you?" He pulled out the old bible with its well worn pages and he read to me. I watched his face as he read and I knew that I could never leave him again. That no matter what happens in this world or this life my spirit will never leave him. He is my Changeling and I must teach him to overcome this sadness that lives within us. Somehow I must make him strong.

We got ready for bed and I realized Tom had not come in. Abraham said "He doesn't come in a lot Mama don't worry about him." I felt a momentary sense of guilt because I was not worried about him. I was finding my way back from grief for me and Abraham, Tom had to find his own way. I could not help him with this. Goodnight journal. My boy and I are on our way back to each other. That is all that matters.

October - Abraham and I are back on track. He is doing his studies and working with Mr. Dunlap. I owe that man such a debt of gratitude. God had not forgotten me even though I had turned on him. Our God is merciful. Tom has noticed that I am back but he has not approached me to talk about the baby. I honestly do not know if I can talk to him about it. I am trying not to place blame on Tom but it is hard not to. I am trying to forgive his past sins but I feel my heart harden when I think that God's punishment of him has caused me so much pain.

Abraham received a letter from Matthew today. He has still not left New Orleans. He seems to really like it there. He is working as a lawyer now with his friend. He asked about me, which was nice and sent his best to both of us.

Abraham looked up at me and said "You know he liked you a lot Mama." I said "Yes I know." "Why didn't you marry him after Tom beat you so bad?" he asked. I said "Well for one thing I was still married to Tom and you just can't up and marry someone else when you are still married and besides he never asked me." He looked at me and said "Do you love Tom?" I answered him as best I knew how. It was not the time to lie. I said "I care about Tom he is my husband and married people care about each other."

Abraham said "Have you ever loved Tom?" "No," I answered him, "I never have loved Tom. The man I loved died when you were a baby and I don't think I will ever feel that way about anybody else married or not." He gave me a hug and said "I don't want you to be sad Mama. You just have lost so many." He had no idea what that statement triggered in me. I had lost so many, my Mama, my sister, Bessie, Joshua, Matthew, little Mandy, and now little Tom.

I hugged him tight and said "It don't matter none how many I lost as long as I get to keep you, son. That's all that matters. You are going to grow up and make me so proud almost as proud of you as I am now." He laughed and went out to play. His laughter is like music to my ears. Thank you God for making him laugh again.

He did make me reflect on Tom. I did care about Tom and he was hurting. Maybe I can reach out to him. Maybe if I reach out he will meet me half way. Maybe we could be a family again. Journal I do not know if I can however. I am afraid Tom and I are as broken as the insides of my body.

November - Things are so strained between me and Tom. He does not share my bed and I have not offered it to him. Abraham is right he does look at him with anger. Abraham just stays out of his way as much as possible. The better Abraham and I get the worse Tom seems to get.

He is managing the properties with John and the rents are coming in steady. We have plenty of money now but it does not make him happy. Abraham spends most afternoons with Mr. Dunlap reading and studying. Tom doesn't even ask him to do chores anymore. He is generally in a bad mood and just comes in and eats in silence and goes to his room.

Abraham wanted to go ride his horse to a friend's house the other day. Tom started to say something to him then he looked at me and dropped his eyes and waved him off to the barn. Tom still cannot meet my eyes. He carries his guilt around him like a dark cloud. I have just come back into the light. I will not go back to that darkness on account of him. Abraham is getting ready to read before bed so I will go to him now. Good night journal.

December - Abraham and I went to church for Christmas service. We came home and had a nice meal and exchanged a few gifts. I had him a book and he had written me a story that Mr. Dunlap had helped him with. Tom stayed for dinner then he just up and left. I didn't ask him to stay. It was Christmas and I was going to enjoy it with Abraham. I have had enough sadness to do me. I am ready for bed and Tom has not returned so I am going to say good night journal. He can find his way to his own room.

In the year of our Lord 1815 …..

February - Goodness my little man is eleven. Eleven years old. I remember the story of Jesus in the temple as a young boy. I often wonder if he had that same sad look in his eyes that Abraham has at times. He is so concerned that he has not grown much yet. I keep telling him to be patient it will come. There is a little girl at church that he is sweet on. I see him talking to her after services. It makes me smile to see him look at her so shyly. I am making a special dinner tonight. I wonder if Tom will come home for it or not. I am not going to worry, come or not it is his choice.

March - Tom and I had words this week for the first time since little Tom died. He has been staying out several nights during the week and not coming home. When I was in town I heard one of the ladies gossiping about Tom and one of the girls down at the tavern. It seems they had been seen by several of the ladies in a somewhat intimate situation.

When they saw me around the corner they all blushed and left except for Mrs. Jones, the storekeeper's wife. She just looked at me and said "Did you hear us?" I held my head high and said "Yes." She said "It ain't none of my business or anybody else's but Tom has said you ain't let him in your bed since the baby died." I told her she was right, it was none of her business. She said "Well you can't blame a man for seeking comfort when there ain't none at home." I paid for my purchases and left.

How dare he shame me so? I was more angry about him telling people we did not sleep together than the fact that he seemed to be bedding the tavern wench. I waited up for him that night. He came in smelling of tobacco and cheap whiskey. I met him downstairs and was furious that he would come in my house drinking. I confronted him about the tavern girl. He didn't deny it. He said "I got to get some comfort from somewhere, I am still a man even if you don't know it." I said "Yes and you are acting like one drinking and bedding strange women ain't you?"

He grabbed me by the arms and said "You don't know woman, you just don't know." I pulled away from him and said "You come here to me with whiskey on your breath and you grab me. You got no right to grab me." He held me closer and laughed and said "I got no right, no right! Well I got right sure enough. I got the right to take you right here Miss High and Mighty. You think cause you live in a fine house with fine clothes I bought you I can't take you right here. It's my house and you're my woman."

He grabbed at my breast and I said "Go ahead Tom, take me with your drunk courage. We both know how that works out don't we. Are you going to beat me too?" He pushed me away from him like I had burned him. He said "Oh God, Nancy I don't mean to hurt you. I just can't stand it no more.

It's my fault. All of it. My fault that you are broken inside and God is punishing me for my sins by taking my children from me. I live in hell Nancy, can't you see that. I am a man that lives in eternal torment. I drink cause it eases it up a bit but it won't never go away. I can't bear to look at you seeing the pain and blame in your eyes for taking your babies. Don't you think I know? I ain't educated like you and the boy but I know. I see how the two of you look at me and damn it to hell every time I look at Abraham I see what I lost. He carries my name but he ain't mine Nancy. I got no child to really carry my name. I told you once all I had was my name and I sold it to the devil and God has made me pay for it ever since."

He sunk to his knees and quietly said "I am a soul in hell. There is no hope for me." I wanted to go and comfort him journal. It is my nature but I could not move. I just stood there and looked at him. I felt so sorry for him, for me, for my lost babies and for Abraham. I told him to go up and get his self to bed. I was not going to sit up all night arguing with a drunk man.

He slowly got to his feet and went to his room not saying anything. I went up to my room and got down on my knees and prayed for guidance. I was so afraid when he grabbed me at first and then I realized he can't hurt me ever again. I control what hurts me and what don't. I slept uneasy that night. I decided the next day that I would talk to him, I mean really talk to him when he was sober. Neither of us could go on living like this.

After Abraham went to school I waited on him to come downstairs. He came down and I handed him a cup of coffee and told him we needed to talk. He would not look at me and I told him I was not going to talk to the top of his head anymore. "If you can't even look at me," I said, "then you just need to pack your bags and leave cause we ain't got nothing to gain by living together." He raised his head up and said "Do you want me to go away Nancy? I will if that's what you want. I just don't know how to make it up to you. I don't even know where to start."

"Well I do" I said. "First you will stop going to the tavern at night, stop drinking and stop bedding other woman. Then you are going to start having meals with us, talk to us and move back into our room." He said "Do you mean it Nancy, you want me back after everything I done to you?" "Tom," I said, "you are my husband in the eyes of the law and of God and of me. We will just have to try to work through this. It will not be easy but if we both try we just might make it happen." He promised to try. He left to go work and I moved his things back in my room. Tonight we will have dinner and we will see. That's all I can promise.

April - Things are better, at least between me and Tom. I think there is just too much damage for him and Abraham. They just kinda stay out of each other's way. Tom and I are back together. The first time he bedded me was uncomfortable but it got better. I don't know if I ever will feel the joy of it that I used to but then again I am not who I used to be and neither is he.

Abraham and I talk a lot about him growing up and responsibilities. Since him and Tom don't get along I am trying to teach him things as both mother and father would. We talk a lot about life and people and how to talk to people. Sometimes he gets a bit carried away talking and I told him that it is better to be silent and thought a fool than to speak and remove all doubt. He just laughed.

We go on long walks, me limping along and him just chatting away. It is our time. He loves school and I worry that he has to stop when he is fifteen. I told him we would figure it out when the time comes. He can read forever and the way he loves it I think he will.

Life does go on journal even when we think it won't. I think I may just really work hard on being a good mother to Abraham and a good wife to Tom. That's what is important to me now.

July - Hot, hot, hot. It is a hot July this year. Just thought I would write a minute. I have been so busy that I have neglected you journal. It has been a good busy. Abraham and I are going up to John and Nancy's for a month to help her with the children. She is expecting again and it is early so she is not feeling well in the mornings. I am happy to do it. I love her two little ones and Abraham never minds going there. Well I need to go pack. Time is a wastin'.

September - Back home and Abraham is back in school again. He is finally starting to grow a little. Tom seems glad we are back. I do think he missed us. Life is going on. Back to our routines. I hear Tom calling so I must go. Goodnight journal.

December - It is nearing Christmas. Tom is moping around. I think Christmas will always be hard for him. Abraham and I have been practicing for our Christmas service. I am singing and he is doing a reading again this year. It will be lovely. I would ask Tom to come but it would be a waste of breath. I have to accept Tom for who he is. It is hard to believe that another year has passed this quickly. I am getting older and more settled in life I think.

--- Well we have finished another year. Sometimes I think about looking back but I think it is better to look forward. The future belongs to Abraham and I am going to see to it that he is ready. Goodnight journal.

In the year of our Lord 1816 .....

February - We celebrated Abraham's twelfth birthday today. It just does not seem possible that this sweet young man is my precious baby. He is so smart and so good to me. Why I don't know what I would do without him. He comes home and we talk about what he learned at Mr. Dunlap's or what he has read. He is so far ahead of the other students at school that the teacher has trouble finding things for him to work on. That does concern me. Three more years and he will be finished with school here. I wish we could find somewhere that he could continue his education more.

We measured him on the door frame today. He was complaining that he wasn't growing fast enough but I told him steady and slow. He will grow soon enough. I remember being twelve. It was the age when I came to the Enloes. It was a lifetime ago for me. I wanted to take a minute to write but he is calling for me so I need to put you away.

April - Mr. Dunlap came by today and told me he was getting some information about a school for Abraham. There is one not far from here that a friend of his is teaching at. He says they are further along than the school here. It would mean a horse ride every day but it would be worth it. I mentioned it to Tom but he just said do whatever I wanted to do.

Tom doesn't pay much mind to what Abraham does anymore. Tom and I seem to get along as long as we don't talk about Abraham. He stays busy and leaves me and Abraham alone most of the time. I have been sewing some more to earn a little extra money to use for any school expenses Abraham might have. The less I have to ask Tom for the better. He wouldn't deny me the funds but given how he and Abraham feel about each other it is for the best. I have taken to sitting up later at night again. I do like the solitude of the quiet house. Good night journal.

May - Mr. Dunlap has gotten the information about the school. He feels like it would be a good idea to say Abraham is younger so he can stay longer. He is writing a letter to the headmaster to tell him how advanced Abraham is. I talked with Abraham and we decided we would say he was only ten so he could go to this school for five more years. That way they wouldn't make him leave in three years.

As much as he hates saying he is younger he so wants to go to school for as long as possible so he agreed to it. It is far enough away that they will not know how old he really is. Mr. Dunlap said for us to just to say he is big for his age. I am going to ride down to the county courthouse and have his birth date recorded just as Mr. Dunlap suggested saying he was born in 1807. Mr. Dunlap is writing me a letter telling the clerk what date to record.

I don't know what we would do without Mr. Dunlap. He is one smart lawyer. He said I need to record the new date in case there is ever a question from the school. I will ride down to Hodgeville to get it put on the record. He told me to be sure and give the clerk a little money for recording it. I know it is telling an untruth but this is to help Abraham. Sometimes a small untruth must be told for the greater good. Abraham going to school longer is for the greater good. I am sure the Lord will let me by with this one.

--- I rode down to Hodgeville to give the clerk the letter from Mr. Dunlap. He was a harried little man that seemed almost too busy to talk to me. I offered him some money and he gave me his full attention. I handed him the letter and he read it and picked up a big book that he said was the record. I had to swear that I was Abraham's mother and then he wrote the date down in the book.

I was looking over his shoulder and he wrote down the year as 1809. I mentioned to him that it was 1807 and he said the letter said 09 and if I did not agree with that then I would have to bring him another letter. I decided it was not worth arguing with him over and besides it was a long way to ride. If Mr. Dunlap thought changing his birth date to the year 1807 was good then 1809 would be even better.

I brought the letter back to Mr. Dunlap and told him what occurred. He looked a the letter for a minute and then laughed and showed me where he had written down the number seven with a dash through it and he bet the old man read it for a nine. I asked him if there would be a problem and he said no just if the school asked to tell them the birth date was recorded in the clerk's office if they needed it. He said they never really check those but it was good to have done it. He picked on Abraham a little for now being awfully big for a seven year old. I think Abraham would have agreed to being five if it meant going to school longer.

We walked home together and I told him how proud I was of him for agreeing to this farce for a while. It would be worth it in the long run and he didn't know anyone at this school so it would not matter.

He did some chores for me and did his reading and went on up to bed. Tom had gone up a while ago. I sat here and opened the bible that the doctor had recorded Abraham's birth date in so long ago. I traced over his name the way I used to do when he was a baby and said "Abraham." So many memories. I looked at my three babies names and wished them all peace. I am becoming weary. It has been a long day. Good night journal.

July - Abraham has been up at Nancy and John's for a while helping out. He is getting quite good at fence building John says. I miss him terribly but it has been peaceful around here for me and Tom. He even joked the other night about me sitting naked on his lap. I told him those days were long since past but I did smile at the memory.

I have been dreaming of the old Indian again. He does not say anything just stands and watches me with the saddest eyes. I feel like there is something he wants to tell me but it just is not the time. I have seen him in my dreams several times now. Tom has been having trouble with some of the leased lands. There has been some talk of him not owning them. He has talked to John about it and they seem to have it in hand. Somebody somewhere is always unhappy it seems. I guess that is just the nature of men.

I think I may just have to think twice about the sitting naked with Tom. It gives me a warm flush just thinking about it. Maybe not in the dining room but we do have a chair in our room. Maybe I am not the old woman I pretend to be yet. I think I just might go up early tonight. Good night journal.

September - Abraham started his new school this week. Mr. Dunlap was so excited about it he decided to take him that first day. Abraham thinks he is going to like it. He says this school has many more books than his old one. He laughed because all the children think he is so tall for his age and all excited because he gets to ride a horse to school. I think this is going to work out.

I am so grateful to Mr. Dunlap that I am helping him out in his office a few days a week now. It is a nice change to be around a learned man all day. He talks of politics and history like Matthew did. He talks of President Madison and the upcoming elections. Abraham loves to talk about politics and law. He and Mr. Dunlap talk about how important the elections are and how the states go about electing a president. Mr. Dunlap told him that America was such a great land of opportunity that even he could become President someday if he wanted to. We both laughed about that but I do remember what the old Indian said about him being a leader of men. I told him to never stop dreaming of what he could become. A man is only limited by his own expectations.

Tom actually came in to talk to Mr. Dunlap today about his land holdings. He has a few who are not wanting to pay rent saying he don't own the land. Tom says they are no better than squatters. I hope we get this straightened out soon as it sure has put Tom in a sour mood. I am going to put you up early tonight journal as I want to do some reading with Abraham. Good night journal.

November - Mr. Dunlap gave Tom some bad news today. It seems that there is a legitimate question as to the legal ownership of a few of the parcels that Tom bought. He said he would keep looking into it but Tom can't make the renters pay until he gets clear title. Tom rode up to John's to discuss it with him. He said he was going to stay the night so it's just Abraham and me here at home.

I can't seem to shake this feeling of foreboding that I have. It just feels like a heaviness in my chest. Even Abraham picked up on it tonight. He kept asking me if I felt alright. I am sure everything will be fine I am just worrying over nothing. I will say an extra prayer tonight. Goodnight journal.

December - It is not looking good for John and Tom on the land. It seems that some of the titles were not transferred correctly. Mr. Dunlap is worried. He wants to see all the papers that Tom and John have on their land purchases. This just does not feel good to me at all. John has his farm to fall back on but me and Tom only have our rents to make our living. It is putting a damper on Christmas. Poor Tom don't do well this time of year no how. This worry is not helping. The old Indian is getting closer to me in my dreams. I wish he would talk to me. He just looks so sad it makes my heart hurt.

I have come down with a cold this winter. I just keep having this cough. I don't have any fever to speak of but I am weary of this coughing. I guess my lungs will always be weaker cause of the pneumonia I had so bad that one year. I'm going to have to tell the preacher than I can't sing this Christmas. I think I'll miss it more than him. I am going to go put some salve on my chest and go to bed. I am tired. Good night journal.

--- Christmas has come and gone. Abraham did his reading and some of the other ladies sang. It was a nice service. We had our meal and then as usual Tom left to go walk around. I am just bone weary tonight journal. I will write again later. Good night journal.

In the year of our Lord 1817 .....

February - A birthday again. Thirteen years old. He is starting to get a little height on him but not terrible. No one at his school has said anything about him being so tall for his age. Mr. Dunlap just told them he is a prodigy and tall for his age. He laughed and said if he was really just ten he would grow up to be seven feet tall. We had a good laugh over that. Thank goodness, we have precious little laughter in this house these days.

Now that the word has gotten out that some of Tom's property was not rightfully his it seems that everybody wants to check the title of their lease. He is worried. I told him can we just go back to farming and building. He will have none of it. He declares that he bought the land proper and legal and that they are wrong. He asked me today to write a letter to Mr. Abraham and ask him for his help on this matter. He says Mr. Abraham and Mr. Felix know more about land purchases than any lawyer. His patience is wearing thin with Mr. Dunlap. I sat down and wrote the letter. It has been a long time since I sent Mr. Abraham a letter. I told him about the situation but I also told him about how smart Abraham had gotten and that he wanted to be a lawyer some day. I wished him and Mrs. Sarah well.

I wish I could wish me well. This cold has just drug on this winter. I have started falling off again and all my clothes are just way too big. Tom ain't paid much attention as he has been consumed with this land business. Abraham has been worried though. He tries to get me to eat more but I just don't have any appetite. He told me today I looked like a willow branch. I just laughed and told him that willow braches bend but they don't break and that I would be fine.

I sure hope Mr. Abraham can help us out with this. I just don't have a good feeling about it. Fine houses and nice things don't make for happiness but I don't know if Tom could stand it to go back to where we started and I don't know what Abraham would do. I cannot worry on this all night so I am putting it and you away. Good night journal.

March - We got a letter from Mr. Abraham. He is talking to Mr. Felix and they are coming up in April. Tom and John are both relieved that they are coming. Tempers are getting ugly in town with all the speculation. Some of the renters have talked to Mr. Dunlap about representing them in court. Tom says if Mr. Dunlap takes their cases he will not be welcome here. Needless to say this has put some distance between he and Abraham. Mr. Dunlap can do no wrong as far as Abraham is concerned.

I am just trying to get a little more strength in my bones. I just am so cold all the time. I went to see the doctor but he says he thinks my blood is just too thin. He has me drinking a terrible tasting drought every day but if it works then I will drink it. As I tell Abraham sometimes you got to do things you don't like in order to get what you do like done. He is worried about this land dispute. He keeps asking me what we are going to do? I tell him over and over to not worry his head about this just concentrate on his studies. He does tend to worry a lot. It pains me sometimes to see his brow so furrowed so young. I am going to bed journal. Rest is my best medicine and Spring will be even better. Good night journal.

April - Mr. Abraham and Mr. Felix are here. They are going over the land transactions and talking with Mr. Dunlap. Mr. Abraham could not get over how much Abraham has grown and Mr. Felix cannot get over how smart he is. He pulled me aside to tell me that Abraham was the spitting image of his father as a young man. I asked about Mrs. Sarah and he laughed and said she was still going strong. "Does she ever talk of me?" I asked. He said "She and Abraham still have words over you occasionally but it seems to have lost some of its bite." "Good," I said, "I hope she can find it in her heart to forgive me someday." He patted me on the shoulder and said "Don't be holding your breath on that one."

I was walking out in the orchard when Mr. Abraham came upon me. We walked a bit in silence and he asked me if my limp hurt much when I walked. I told him it bothered me a little when it was cold but otherwise it was fine. He said "You don't look well Nancy, is anything wrong with you?" I told him "Nothing that getting this land dispute settled wouldn't fix."

We passed a downed log and he said let's sit for a spell and rest. He looked at me and took my hand in his and said "I am sorry for the trouble you have had in your life Nancy. I never meant you to come to any harm. If I could do it all over it would be different." I put my hand to his lips and said "I have no regrets. I was not forced into anything that I didn't agree to and besides I wouldn't trade Abraham for anything in the whole world."

He put his arms around me and said "Nancy you are the sweetest soul God ever put on earth." He smelled my hair and held me close and said "You still smell like sunshine." I just leaned against his broad chest and smiled. He held me a little tighter and said "You still can stir my blood Nancy even after this long." I pulled away from him and said "That may be so but it doesn't matter no more. I am past the age of such foolishness and so are you Mr. Abraham. I think it's time we head back to the house."

As we walked back he said "What are you going to do if this land business does not go your way." I said "Well we will go back to the beginning I guess. The only thing I am worried about is Abraham." He said "Nancy I swear to you I will not let Abraham suffer if it is ever in my power." I told him I knew that but it made me feel better to hear it. When we got back to the house Abraham was waiting on me. He had an odd look on his face. I told him we would talk later.

Mr. Abraham and Mr. Felix left to go meet John and Tom at Mr. Dunlap's. Abraham and I sat down on the porch and he said "I guess I always knew Mr. Abraham was my father but I never really thought much about it till today. I look a lot like him don't I?" "Yes," I said, "You do look like him and that is a thing to be proud of just as I am proud of you every minute of every day." I waited on him to judge me and instead he put his arm around my shoulder and kissed my head. "I love you Mama more than words could say." I told him I loved him too.

We went in to wait on the men folk to come back. I felt a cold chill settle over me as I walked back into the house. Things were shifting I could feel it. I hugged Abraham a little harder and a shudder came over me. He asked if I was ok and I said "Yes son, just a chill" but inside I wondered.

Mr. Abraham, Mr. Felix and John did not come in when they returned. Tom said they rode on to John's for the night. Tom just looked beaten. I asked him how it went and he said "It don't look good Nancy." He said he was tired and just wanted to go to bed. I sat down to write in you journal. You have been my witness to many things in my life. I guess in a way you tell the story of my life good and bad. I will be forever grateful that Mr. Abraham started me writing in you so long ago. You have been my only friend at times. Good night journal, I am afraid it will be a long day tomorrow.

May - Mr. Abraham and Mr. Felix did all they could but it was to no avail. Tom and John had not gotten the right signatures on the sale of the properties. It didn't seem to matter that they had receipts for the sale. Mr. Dunlap said they could sue to try to get their money back but he said it wasn't likely to happen. John said he and Nancy would be alright.

Tom was so bitter he said "Yes they'll be alright the old man will see to it. We ain't got nobody to bail us out." I told him that Mr. Abraham would help us. He spat on the ground and said "I done took all I'm going to from that old man. He has caused me nothing but grief since I met him." I didn't want to make it worse so I stayed quiet. He told me "They're gonna auction off our house and possessions in July. It seems like I don't own this land neither."

He was so despondent I went to him and said "It's alright Tom we can move back to the cabin." He shook off my arms and said "I ain't going back to that shack either. I don't want nothing that the old man has had a hand in." I asked him what we were gonna do and he said "What I should've done in the first place. We are gonna strike out on our own. I ain't gonna owe no man no more. It has brought me nothing but grief all my life. I can still work and homestead and we will be done with this place and this cursed Kentucky."

He walked on out to the barn and left me sitting there. I didn't know how I was going to break this to Abraham but I didn't have to, Mr. Dunlap already told him. He looked so weary when he climbed the steps to the house. I just put out my arms to him and said "We will be alright as long as we are together." He stopped and said "Mama, Mr. Dunlap told me I could stay with him and keep going to school if I wanted to."

I dropped my arms and the look on my face must have frightened him for he grabbed me and said "Mama please don't faint." My knees had gone soft and I sunk down on the porch. I just never ever imagined that we would not be together. He cried "I won't leave you Mama please I won't leave you." I laid my head on his shoulder and said "Let's not talk of it tonight just help me in the house." He helped me to a chair and said "Mama you don't weigh no more than a youngin' are you sick?" I told him no just worried and he knew that I fell off when I was worried. He again said "I won't leave you Mama." I said "Abraham we will talk on this tomorrow." There just has been too much said today for me to take in.

We ate some supper and he went off to bed. Tom has not come back in so I took the chance to write. My heart is heavy. It is one thing to lose your belongings but another thing to lose your son. I can't imagine life without Abraham but I also can't imagine taking him away from his books he so loves. Is it selfish of me to want him near? I know that one day he will grow up and leave me but I did not expect it to be this soon. I would say good night but it is not, it is not a good night at all.

June - Abraham and I have not talked of him staying with Mr. Dunlap since that day on the porch. I have tried to bring it up several times but he avoids talking about it. I have been going through our things with Mr. Dunlap to see what we can keep. It seems we can keep our clothes and a few household items but it will not be much. John and Nancy said they will give us a wagon and a horse.

Tom has decided we are going to Indiana. They allow homesteading and he feels we can make a fresh start there and not be beholden to anybody. He almost didn't take the wagon and horse offer from John but I made him see it was a necessity for us to travel. There is a heavy cloud of sadness over our house. Tom and I do not talk much. He is like a thundercloud. Everything he says comes out as a roar.

I am so very tired these days. I just cannot seem to get my blood strong no matter how much of the doctor's medicine I drink. I think maybe some of it is the weight of my heart these days. I have decided that Abraham must stay with Mr. Dunlap but the thought of not being with him weighs me down like rocks in my shoes. I truly do not know what I will do not seeing him every day. He has been my reason for living. I live in his heart and his eyes but I am his mother and I must do what is best for him even if it kills me inside.

I have prayed and prayed about this but the Lord has not

answered me. This is a decision I must live with alone. I remember the words of the old Indian that my son would be a great man. He still visits me in my dreams but he has not spoken. I do not know what his purpose is but I am comforted by his presence. God knows I need some comfort in these dark days.

I must go down and talk to Mr. Dunlap about Abraham staying with him. I have not said anything to Tom yet about leaving Abraham here but I honestly do not think he will mind much. I feel as tired as an old woman these days. I think I shall go rest for a while journal.

--- Today I made the seemingly long walk to Mr. Dunlap's office. I went to give him my son. We talked at great length about Abraham and his future. He promised me he would care for Abraham as if he was his own son.

As I walked back to the house my heart was so heavy. Part of me was happy that Abraham would live in a fine house and go to school but part of me knew that the light in my life would go out when I left him there. It did not seem fair to me that I must lose all my children but how often was life fair? It is my duty to rip my heart from my bosom if it will help my son become the man he is to be.

I am trying to remember the old Indian's words to me when I was carrying little Tom, be brave. I know now he was talking to me and I must at all costs be brave not only for Abraham's sake but for myself. I must not let him see my pain for I am afraid he could not bear it. I must go in and fix the evening meal. We have no one to help in the house anymore. I am so tired journal, so very tired.

July - I have gathered out things that Mr. Dunlap said we could keep and packed them in the wagon that John sent down. Tomorrow they auction the property and all our belongings to pay our debts. Mr. Dunlap thinks it will be best if we all go to John's before the auction. He says such a thing is painful to watch and serves no purpose.

Tom has retired and Abraham is in his room for the night. I don't think any of us will sleep much tonight. I spent the evening walking through the house remembering the good times. As I sit at this table I suddenly realize this will be the last time I write in you here. So many memories. I do not know what life will bring but I grateful for what I have had so far.

Mr. Dunlap says we will need to stay for a few weeks to make sure all the details are worked out. Nancy and John have been kind enough to let us stay with them until everything is settled. I have not told Tom yet that Abraham is staying. I just can't seem to bring myself to say it yet. Mr. Dunlap offered to tell him for me but it is my place. I have kept up a positive manner when I talked to Abraham about it but inside I feel I am dying. I am going up to bed to spend my last night in this house with Tom. I wish he would just hold me but it no use, we are of no comfort to each other these days. Good night journal we will see what tomorrow brings.

August - It has been a week and I could wait no longer. Today I went to the barn and told Tom that Abraham is staying here. I expected him to be glad to rid of the boy but his reaction was quite the opposite. He was furious, said we needed strong backs to build a homestead. He said "We have come to a place in our lives where he can be useful and you are leaving him here?"

I told him it was so he could go to school. He said there are schools in Indiana. I said but he can learn so much more here from Mr. Dunlap. Tom then turned and viciously said "I took you both in and gave you a name, I put up with the old man coming around always making eyes at you, I have raised him as my own son even though you have not given me one of my own. The least he can do to pay me back is to help me get a homestead up and going before he leaves us for good."

I turned away as I did not let Tom see my tears ever. "Do you think this is easy for me?" I said. "I am dying inside over leaving him here but it is for his own good." "What about our good?" he said. "He is more important" I told him. Tom grabbed me by the arm and spun me to face him. "That's it isn't it", he said, "The boy is always more important! More important than me, more important than you, more important than anything to you."

"Tom you must understand," I pleaded, "He is destined to do great things, to be a great leader of men." "Then he can go do it after he is grown like everyone else" Tom said. I looked at him and said "He is my son and I say he stays here." Tom said "Well Miss Know

It All he is legally my son and I say he goes with us."

We both just stood there angrily looking at each other. Tom dropped his eyes first and said "Nancy are you staying too? I don't blame you if you do. I know I have not been a good husband to you and now I have lost everything we owned. Are you telling me you want to stay too?" "Tom," I said, "Of course I am going with you. I am your wife, it is my place to go with you just please, I beg of you, let the boy stay for my sake." He turned away from me and said "Fine he can stay. I'll say no more on the subject" and he left.

After he walked out I collapsed into a heap on the hay. I cried and cried and begged God out loud to help me be brave, help me to be strong without my Abraham. As I buried my face in my hands I felt a hand on my shoulder I looked up and there stood Abraham. He had been in the barn the whole time and had heard every word.

He put both arms around me and raised me to my feet. He said "Dry your tears Mother I will not leave you. I will not have you in this much pain because of me and besides Tom is right. I do owe him my time for both of us." I just shook my head and said "No, no you must stay." He held me close and said "No Mama I cannot leave you either. I will find a school in Indiana and everything will be all right. Do you not think I would do this for you after all you have done for me? Wipe you tears Mama so Tom doesn't see them and go tell him I am going with you after all. I will ride down and tell Mr. Dunlap. He will understand."

I did as he asked and went and told Tom. Tom looked relieved. I am waiting on Abraham to return as I write this. Oh journal what have I done? Have I caused him to lose his dream by coming with me? Has Abraham chosen me over his destiny? I pray that is not so. I could not bear it if I have cost him his legacy. Goodnight journal I must put you away.

--- We are leaving tomorrow. It is my last night in Kentucky. Tom has our things in the wagon and we will leave at first light. Abraham has his books and more importantly a letter of introduction from Mr. Dunlap. He told Abraham to find a lawyer in Indiana and give it to him and he would help Abraham. I am more at peace with the decision Abraham has made to go with us.

The old Indian finally spoke to me the other night in my dream.

He told me not to worry, that Abraham's legacy was secure. He will go on to do great things he said. Then he put his arms around me and said I will be with you on your journey, be brave in all things.

I wanted to walk outside for a bit tonight but after a few steps I was out of breath. I returned to the porch and just sat watching the moon. The shortness of breath is getting worse. I have not spoken of it to Tom or Abraham. This is not the time to be worrying them over me. I am sure once we are settled in Indiana I will be better.

I am writing in you by the light of the moon. It is so full tonight, it reminds me of the night so long ago by the river on the way to Oconoluftee. So much has happened since then. I have gone from North Carolina to South Carolina and back, then to Kentucky and now to Indiana. Some people stay in the same place their whole life. Maybe Indiana will be my settling place. I am tired, so very tired and would like to grow old in one place. It is time to put you up journal. I am glad you have been with me. Good night journal.

November - The wind is roaring outside the cabin. Tom and Abraham have been working on a neighbor's farm building fence. I am so grateful that we were able to get our cabin up before the cold started. It is only one room but it is tight from the wind and the fireplace keeps us warm.

It has been a busy time for us all. I am afraid I have not been much help as I just don't have the breath to do much but Tom and Abraham have just worked that much harder. It has been good to see them working together. Abraham has gotten much better at building even Tom says so.

Abraham has found a school and will start soon. We are still telling people he is only eleven so he can go longer. Tom is alright with it, he says that will keep Abraham around longer to help on the farm. The term farm is a bit presumptuous at this stage but Tom is hoping to make a go of it here. It is our land all nice and legal. Tom made sure of that before he started building the cabin. He says ain't nothing taking away his hard work ever again.

Abraham has not said or done anything to make me feel that he is sorry for his lot in life. He works hard and tries to have a good disposition at least around me. He comes in and reads at night by the fire and before bed he always reads in the bible aloud to me. Even

Tom has taken to listening at night when he reads. What a comfort my son is to me. God in his everlasting mercy has seen fit for me to have such a prize. I don't have much time to write as they will be back soon. Finding a place to hide you in this small cabin is difficult but possible. Good night journal.

December - Christmas will be coming soon. Abraham has been at a neighbor's for a few days helping repair a barn. It is the first time Tom and I have been alone since we moved here. Tom came in last night and we had supper and he built a roaring fire. It was warm enough in the cabin that I took off my shawl. Tom was sitting in the chair and I was by the fire. He told me that I looked like a young girl sitting by the fire like that. It made me laugh. He has not said anything like that in a long time. He said "It's nice to hear your laugh Nancy I have missed it."

He put out his arms and said "Come sit with me Nancy." I rose and went and sat on his lap. He put his arms around me and buried his face in my neck and said "Remember that time you sat naked on my lap." I said "Yes I remember." He said "Think we are too old to do that again?" I giggled feeling a familiar warmth flowing through me and I felt him rise underneath me. I said "I don't know if we are too old but I do think it is too cold to sit naked in a chair but now under a blanket is a whole other thing."

He jumped up out of the chair laughing like a young man and began to strip off his clothes. He stood naked in front of the fire and said "Do I look like it's too cold?" He had a point he was as ready as a randy boy of twenty. I smiled and started unbuttoning my dress. He said "Come over by the fire so you'll stay warm and let me do that." He slowly unbuttoned my dress and let it fall to the floor. He grabbed the blanket off the bed and held it near the fire to get it warm. He put it over my back and he began to rub my body all over. He said "I remember how warm you can get Nancy." I grabbed his manhood and said "I will show you how warm when you get in that bed with me."

It had been so very long for both of us I hate to say it was over fairly quickly but it was the first time we had been gentle with each other in a long, long time. He held me close afterwards and stroked my back with his hand. He whispered "Nancy you are as thin as a spring twig. I promise things will get easier and then maybe I can fatten you up." I laughed and said "Now Tom you know you don't want no fat and sassy wife." He laughed and said "Fat would not be bad but sassy no."

We slept close that night. I had not felt that content in many a year. We arose the next day and gathered out clothes and back to our routine we went. Abraham will be home soon so there will be no more nights like that for us for a while. I wore myself out cleaning the cabin today and have started with a slight cough again. I hope I am not getting a cold from last night. Tom will be home soon and maybe we can do it again but under the covers completely this time. Maybe we can find some happiness finally here in Indiana. Time to put you away journal.

---Christmas was spent with just us by the fire. I sang a bit but had trouble holding the notes. I just don't have as much wind as I used to and singing too long seems to make my coughing spells worse. Abraham read some bible passages. Even Tom seemed content this year. I think coming to Indiana may have been the best thing for us all. Goodnight journal.

In the year of our Lord 1818 …..

February - Abraham's birthday came and went. He said he didn't want any fanfare this year. He is fourteen now according to me and the bible but all his friends think he is eleven. He is growing so fast these days. He laughed and says he is finally able to say he is tall for his age. It is our joke. I said "At least you are not nine here."

I have not told him or Tom my news yet. I want to be absolutely sure before I say anything. They have both been concerned over my cough so I don't think it is time to tell them of the baby yet. I have tried to hide the fatigue that has plagued me the past few months. It is concerning but I am so much older with this baby and that must be what it is. I have assured them that I will be better once Spring arrives.

Abraham likes his school, he says the teacher has him doing lessons with the younger children but he enjoys helping them learn to read. The teacher has told him of a lawyer not too far from town. He plans to go see him about apprenticing some this summer. The teacher says Little Pigeon Creek is growing fast and he may can use the help. He says the letter from Mr. Dunlap will help. Tom told him he could apprentice himself out as long as he helped around the farm.

That would make me happy to see Abraham working with a lawyer again. He will be a great lawyer himself someday. I remember him playing lawyer when he was little. It seems a lifetime ago. I have wearied myself out today so I will close now. Tom and Abraham will be in for supper soon. Time to put you back under your board journal. Good night to you.

March - I had a bad coughing spell today. It left me weak and I noticed a little blood. There is a doctor in the next settlement but I just can't see burdening Tom with that expense right now. I am sure that spring will find me better. I have to tell Tom and Abraham about the baby tonight. It is becoming so visible that I am afraid I cannot hide it any more. I have not had the sickness in the mornings with this one so I guess that is a good thing. I pray that this child is strong and lives. Surely God would not send me another child this late in my life to just snatch it from me too soon. I am trying to be realistic about this baby, if it should not make it I will not go back to that place of darkness that I visited after losing little Tom.

I must lie down and rest before supper. I do not want them to see me as weak when I tell them of this child. I really am not sure how either of them will take it but I know it is an act of God and one must be grateful for acts of God. Time to be put away journal.

April - It is finally Spring! The flowers will be blooming soon and I can smell spring in the air. I cannot wait to sit outside in the warm sunshine. My body is getting weaker as this baby grows within me. I feel it more each day. I remember the doctor saying with little Tom that some babies just take more out of some women. I guess all my babies have been takers.

I am trying not to let Tom and Abraham see how I feel. They did not take the news of the baby well. I think Tom just has been hurt so much by losing Mandy and little Tom that he does not want to get excited. Abraham is just worried. I can see it in his eyes. He is very angry at Tom over the baby. They did not think I heard their exchange the other day. Abraham told Tom that if anything ever happened to me it would be on his head. Tom told him not to think that he did not worry about it every day. Abraham told him he should have left me alone that I was not strong enough to be having babies. Tom got angry at him and said "She is my wife and what we do in our bed is none of your concern boy." They both left going in different directions.

I don't know if I can ever get Abraham to stop blaming Tom for God's will. Lord knows I have tried in the past and they must stop worrying over me so. It is spring and I will be better now. The cough will go away with the sunshine I just know it. I talked to Abraham again about this baby being a blessing. He just paced the floor and said "It ain't no blessing if it just makes you sick and Tom don't need to be hurting you no more." I said "Abraham you are old enough to know that Tom is not hurting me and it takes two people to make a baby and I was just as much a part of it as he was. I will not have you blaming Tom for this."

I starting coughing after this and Abraham saw that there was blood on my handkerchief. He demanded to know how long this had been going on. I assured him it was nothing that spring would not cure. That night when Tom came in he told him that he needed to go to the next settlement and fetch the doctor. Tom looked worried as we both knew that was an expense we just could not afford. Tom looked at me and asked me if I really felt like I needed the doctor. I told him and Abraham both that all I needed was some good sunshine and I would be fine. There would be no sense in paying for a doctor to tell me that.

Tom seemed satisfied but Abraham said "If you ain't better when it gets warmer I'm gonna go get the doctor myself I don't care what Tom says." I hugged him and said "Don't worry so much son it will make you old before your time." He hugged me back hard and said "I love you Mama and I'll do anything I can to protect you. I just want you to get better." I told him I loved him too, more than anything else in this world.

Lord help me I was speaking the truth for I did care more for him than Tom or this baby. He is the light of my world. I must go rest now. At least with the baby coming they don't question me when I tell them I must lie down. I think I may let Tom fix supper tonight I don't feel much like eating. Good night journal I am afraid there are hard days ahead.

May - Tom moved my rocker out in the sunshine today. It felt wonderful on my face. I think the baby liked it too. I could feel it kicking as I rocked. I think my cough is better but my arms and legs just keep falling off and it makes my belly just look that much bigger. I get really tired most days now. Tom and Abraham have taken to cooking meals. They are quite good at it. Abraham keeps a worried expression on his face almost all the time now when he looks at me. He sits and has me eat at night. I think he counts every bite I take.

Tom has worked out a deal with a neighbor to get us a cow for milk. I feel blessed indeed today. Fresh milk, plenty of sunshine. It will be no time until I am up and about again. I don't see the blood when I cough unless it is just a really hard spell. I feel hopeful today. Maybe I can get Abraham to read to me a while tonight. It is time to put you back in my apron now journal. I will hide you when I go back in. Right now I am just going to close my eyes and enjoy the sunshine.

June - My back started hurting today. It scared me. I went and laid down as soon as I felt it. The only problem with that is that I cough worse when I lay down. Tom came in as I was having a bad coughing spell. When it was over he leaned down and said "Nancy I am gonna ride over and get the doctor to come see you. I don't care what it costs I think he needs to come." I was so tired I didn't argue.

He went and got Abraham to stay with me. The back pain stopped but I was so tired from coughing I couldn't get up for a while. Abraham got me a cool cloth for my head and he just sat on the floor and held my hand. I think I slept for a while. I was feeling better so I got him to help me up. He helped me over to the table. We sat down across from each other and just held hands. He got tears in his eyes and said "Mama you got to get better. Remember how you told me you would never leave me." I said "Yes" and he said "Promise me, promise me you will never leave me. I just can't bear the thought of living without you."

"Abraham," I said, "I will always be in your heart, you will never be alone on this earth. Even when I am not with you physically I am always with you." He said "Mama you just got to get better, you just got to." "Abraham," I said, "You asked me for a promise so now I'm going to ask you for one. Promise me you will always keep me in your heart no matter how old you get or where you travel to." He cried and said "I will never leave you Mama, never."

I patted his hands and said "All children grow up and leave their parents. It's the way God intended it to be. You will become a grown man and someday take a wife and have children of your own. You don't need your Mama around taking your time away from them." He dried his tears and said "I will always need you around Mama." I told him that was enough talk of that for now and that if he felt like fixing me something to eat I thought I could eat it. He jumped up and proceeded to fix me a meal and I ate every bite for him. It did make me feel better.

I told him to go outside and get some air and I would sit and write a bit in my journal. It will be tomorrow before Tom and the doctor get here but I do think I feel a bit better. I am going to put you up and go lie down now. I will say extra prayers for Abraham. I wish

I could get him to not be so distressed over me. Good night journal.

--- It has been a few days since the doctor was here. He seemed very concerned, more about my cough than the baby. My back still gets achy but he thinks it is because I am so thin and the baby is getting big. He says everything seems to be in order with the baby and he suggested I go lie down if I feel the ache. He is coming back next week to see a neighbor and says he will bring me some medicine that he thinks will help me sleep at night so the cough doesn't keep me awake. He told me to stay quiet as much as possible and said sitting in the sunshine would be good for me and the baby.

Tom offered to pay him for his time but he said they could just settle up when he came back. He said he needed to check on some patients in the area anyway. He was such a sweet man.

Tom has been leaving Abraham home with me during the day. I told them both that they were being foolish but they insisted and told me when I got strong enough to chase them off they would go. This baby sure does love the sunshine. It carries on something fierce when I sit and rock in the sun. Having Abraham around is the best medicine ever. He has been reading me the writings of Thomas Jefferson. He is a brilliant man. I think Abraham can learn a lot from his writings.

We watched clouds today and played the 'what is it' game with them like we did when he was little. It would be a happy time if I could just stop this cough. Even when he smiles at me I still see the worry in his eyes. He is doing his best to get on with Tom for my sake. No mother could ever be prouder of a son than I am.

He said he loves to see me write in my journal and asked me what all I write about. I laugh and told him I just write about my day or thoughts that I have or things that I have experienced. It is my friend I said. It is a record of me. I am tired and must go lie down so it is time to put you back in your secret place journal. Goodnight.

July - The medicine the doctor gave me does seem to help ease the coughing. The doctor talked with me for a long time during his visit. He is very worried. He says my chest does not sound good and he recommends that I sleep sitting in the chair with my feet up as much as possible to help me breathe better. He says the baby seems to be growing well and told me not to worry too much about it, he says nature takes care of them. He told Tom and Abraham not to hesitate to call him if I suddenly got worse. He seemed sorry that he lived so far away.

Abraham never leaves my side these days. I talk to him about everything except my fear of getting weaker and weaker. He carries so much fear in his eyes I am afraid to voice it. I have told him the story of his birth and how he got here. I have told him of the old Indian who prophesized that he would be a great man someday. We talk about the sadness that we both carry inside of us. I tell him not to give in to it. It is strong but he is stronger. We talk of Tom and I explained to him about Joshua and why I married Tom.

He is young but he has understanding beyond his years. I tell him why it is so important to pay your moral debts and that we both owe Tom a great moral debt. He doesn't want to hear that but I tell him that someday when he is older knowing that he paid his moral debts makes him beholden to no one.

I have not told him of the old Indian that comes to me in my dreams almost every night. That I keep to myself. He sits close to me in my dreams. He is very saddened in these dreams. He has showed me Abraham as a man, tall with a full beard in fine dress. Some nights he and I walk with the older Abraham down long dark halls. He has shown me my child. She is a beautiful little girl with bright eyes. I am comforted by this. I know she will live. I am tired now journal. I will put you up and go lie down. Abraham sits with me in the cabin. I don't ask him to leave. His presence comforts me. Good night journal.

August - This baby is getting so big. I like to put my hands on my swollen belly and feel her move. This is the biggest I have been with a baby I think. The cough is better but I take a lot of the medicine.

The time I have spent with Abraham has been magic. It is as if our souls have melted together. I think God has blessed me with this time. I have never been closer to my son nor he to me. There is so much to tell him, so much for him to know about life and about love. I want him to know love someday but not to be a fool for it like I was. I have told him how important it is to marry a woman with position in this world. One can love a rich woman as well as a poor one.

Tom comes home late in the evenings these days. He sits with me at night and we talk about the baby and we talk about Abraham when he is not there. I asked Tom to please be mindful of Abraham, that he is a good boy and he will do his name proud. Tom said "I don't regret giving the boy my name. He will surely do better with it than I have."

I get tired so easily that we don't talk long. Tom keeps asking me if I think I will be better when the baby gets here. I reassure him but I don't know the answer to that myself. The doctor is coming back by next week. Tom has promised to build him a fence after the baby comes for seeing to me.

He and Abraham talked during his last visit. He is as amazed by Abraham's intellect as have been countless others. Abraham has told him how he wants to be a lawyer and that he was going to apprentice this summer but he decided to stay with me. The doctor told him to come and see him after I had the baby and he would get him introduced to the lawyer. It is time for me to stop writing now journal. Good night.

September - The doctor came by today and saw me. I am so big with the baby I feel as if I must burst. He is very worried and told Tom he would make arrangements to find a wet nurse for the baby as he did not feel that I would be strong enough to nurse the baby myself. I did not disagree with him. I cannot get to the chair without help.

Abraham has decided he is not returning to school until after the baby comes. He is getting so strong. He lifts me from the chair to the bed with very little effort. I tell him how strong he is and he says he is not that strong I am just that light. The worried look never leaves his eyes any more. It makes him look so much older. I told him today that he must take good care of his baby sister. He asked me how I know it is a girl. I just smiled and said I just knew.

We cannot talk as much these days as the coughing gets much worse if I talk a lot. Abraham reads the bible to me. I close my eyes listening to his voice. It took me a minute to hear him calling my name today. I had dozed off and was dreaming of walking through a warm sunlit field. The old Indian stood by a tree and motioned me towards the light. I shook my head as I knew it was not time as I had to go and see why Abraham was calling my name. He was getting a little frantic when I finally opened my eyes. He held my hands and said "I thought you had left me Mama." I smiled at him and said "I will never leave you my son."

It is almost time for Tom to come in so I will finish and let Abraham put you away. Good night journal.

---Yesterday, I gave birth to my beautiful baby girl. She is a healthy looking pink bundle. I did not think I would have the strength to bear her but the old Indian came to me and gave me the strength to push her out. He held me as I birthed her and I saw tears in his eyes. I asked him if the tears were for the baby and he shook his head no, suddenly I felt afraid for I knew his tears were for me.

I had Abraham write her name and birth date down in the bible under little Tom's. Nancy Lincoln, born September 22, 1818. I named her after me. I had him bring me my journal because I wanted to write her name here. I must rest journal, the midwife says I have lost a lot of blood and must sleep. Good night journal.

October - The wet nurse has come by and brought the baby to see me. I held her in my arms and marveled at how healthy she looked. I could not hold her long as the coughing comes over me quite violently now.

I have not stopped bleeding since the baby came. I fear my time is not long for this world. I feel it harder and harder to come back to Abraham when he calls for me. He wants Tom to ride to get the doctor but I feel that it is a waste of time at this point. I do not feel that there is anything the doctor can do for me.

I have prayed to the Lord that if he must take my body, to please let my soul remain with Abraham. I bargained with him that since I had given him my other two children he should grant me the right to stay close to Abraham until his time to come home to heaven with me. He answered my prayers.

I did get enough strength to talk to Abraham today and tell him not to despair, that I had asked the Lord to let my spirit stay with him and he agreed to let me stay until such time as Abraham himself should be called home. Abraham cried and asked me to please try to stay with him. I told him my body was just give out and it would soon be time for me to go.

I told him to take my journals after I passed and read them so he would know me. All of me, even the parts I have never shared with anyone. "They are for you" I said, "Only for you. Keep them safe and secret and whenever you are missing me read them and know I am with you. Go be by yourself, close your eyes and I will come to you. Never fear my sweet son, I will not leave you. Please look after your sister, stay with Tom until our debt to him is paid. You know why it is important. I leave you my journal and our bible. There is a letter for you inside the cover. It is my legacy to you. Know for all your days how proud I am of you."

I asked him to bring you to me journal so I could make this last entry. I am saying good night to you my journal, my friend, for the final time. I leave this world with no regrets and know that I have made it a better place by giving it my son. I will give this to Abraham now, it is his for safe keeping. God bless him. Good night.

Good Bye

(Letter to Nancy from Abraham)

April 13, 1865

My Dearest Sweet Mother,

It may seem foolish to some that I write you a letter after your long ago passing but I feel particularly close to you tonight and I remember what great store you placed on writing and receiving letters. I have accomplished the things you wished for me. I have fulfilled the old Indian's prophecy. I am a great leader of men but it has not come without great cost to me and this country. I am weary Mother, the burden of this office and the weight of this responsibility has often brought me to my knees. So much has happened, so many lives lost. Brothers fought against brothers and families have been torn apart, I am afraid, forever. The glorious days of the South are over . The plantations and the families of wealth will never be the same. Some things did need to be changed I agree, but at such a high cost I often wonder if in the end it would be justifiable. There are a great many in this country who will rejoice when I leave this world, in the South and in my own camp. I wonder at times if I am the worst of them. My greatest task will be to pull this weakened and beleaguered country together trying to maintain some dignity for the South. I know my roots come from the South. My Grandfather from Virginia, my Father from North Carolina. I do not wish to see them scorned and belittled. There are those who would subjugate them but in order to survive as a nation we must accept them back as the family that they are.

This will be my greatest test I fear. Not the war that has preceded but the healing that must take place. There are many that wish me failure in this. Plots and threats surround me. I read your words often. They help me get through the ever increasing darkness that threatens my very soul. My man servant is Bessie's nephew, every time I see him I am reminded of you as a young girl sitting in the kitchen with Bessie laughing and talking about life. I miss your smile Mother, your ready laugh, and the way you would tug my ear to remind me of the goodbye kiss on your cheek when I would leave for the day. You left me so soon but you have always been here in my heart. I know you walk these halls with me late at night. I feel you here.

I feel that I do not have long for this earth. It would be scandalous for others to hear but I think I will welcome that time when it comes. There are dark clouds on the horizons and I feel a long and powerful storm is brewing for this country. I pray that we all survive it. You told me you would always be with me. I feel you closer tonight than I ever have. Walk with me dear Mother, help me on this path that I must tread. Fate will be served, it changes for no mere mortal and as special as you always told me I was I still am a mere mortal.

I feel I will see you soon. We will walk in the golden fields of wheat with the sun on our face and the breeze in our hair. All will be at peace and we will both finally be truly happy. Goodnight dear Mother. I shall place this in your journal for I know that is where you reside. My manservant has been instructed to forever care for and keep these journals safe in the event of my demise. He is from Bessie's family. I know I can trust him.

My greatest thanks to you for caring for me and teaching me to become the man that I am today and my deepest love to you for never leaving my heart and giving me the strength to face what trials life does bring.

Your ever devoted son,
Abraham

For Further Reading About Nancy Hanks Lincoln:

Caroline Hanks Hitchcock, *"Nancy Hanks, the story of Abraham Lincoln's mother"* (1863)

Charles Ludwig, *"Nancy Hanks: Mother of Lincoln"* (1965).

Alden Franklin Young, *"Nancy Hanks, Single Mother of Abraham Lincoln"* (2004)

Annis Ward Jackson, *"Into The Twilight"* (1979)

James Caswell Coggins, *"The Eugenics of Lincoln"* (1940)

James Harrison Cathey, *"The Genesis of Lincoln"* (1899)

John McKinsey, *"The Lincoln Secret"* (2008)

Jerry Goodnight & Richard Eller, *"The Tarheel Lincoln"* (2003)

Jerry Goodnight, *"Searching for Lincoln"* (2008)

Don Norris, *"Abraham Enloe of Western North Carolina: The Natural Father of Abraham Lincoln"* (2008)

Elbert Hubbard, *"Abe Lincoln and Nancy Hanks"* (1920)

Meridel Le Sueur, *"Nancy Hanks of Wilderness Road A Story of Abraham Lincoln's Mother"* (1949)

Aiden Baber, *"Nancy Hanks of undistinguished families; a genealogical, biographical, and historical study of the ancestry of the mother of Abraham Lincoln"* (1952)

William Macon Coleman, *"The evidence that Abraham Lincoln was not born in lawful wedlock: or, The sad story of Nancy Hanks ..."* (1899)

Harold Edward Briggs, Ernestine Bennett Briggs, *"Nancy Hanks Lincoln: A Frontier Portrait"* (1953)

William Eleazar Barton, *"The Lineage of Lincoln"* (1929)

Lucinda Boyd, *"The Sorrows of Nancy"* (1899)

Louis Austin Warren, *"Lincoln's parentage & childhood: a history of the Kentucky Lincolns supported by documentary evidence"* (1929)

Ludy Wilkie, *"The Ballad of Nancy Hanks"*...(musical) (2005)

Janie Malloy Britt, *"Nancy Hanks, Bondwoman,"* UNC-CH Theater Dept. (1930's)

To order some of these books and for more information about Nancy Hanks Lincoln and Abraham Lincoln contact:

The Bostic Lincoln Center, Inc.
P.O. Box 153
Bostic, NC 28018
(828) 245-9800

www.bosticlincolncenter.com

"Like" *us on our facebook page "My Name Is Nancy" for publishing updates, appearances, book signings, and special announcements. Thank you for reading the book and we sincerely appreciate your feedback.*
-Deborah